CW01468057

A STAR UNBORN

Can love alone heal the wounds of the past?

ISABELLA WILES

Moria,
And the final book in the
series... but how will it all
end? Read on to find out.
Love.
Bzy

Aurora Independent Publishing

The Three Great Loves of Victoria Turnbull

BOOK THREE

A STAR UNBORN
The Celt

A gut-wrenching story of love, loss, and the healing power of forgiveness

ISABELLA WILES

Other books by Isabella Wiles

To Kevin,

For never sharing Gav's opinion on the things that matter most.

You are my absolute world.
I love you,
Today, tomorrow, always.

x

Contents

Author's Note   xiii
Get a FREE Victoria Turnbull Novel   xv

Part I

Chapter 1   3
Chapter 2   9
Chapter 3   19
Chapter 4   25
Chapter 5   33
Chapter 6   45
Chapter 7   55

Part II

Chapter 8   67
Chapter 9   74
Chapter 10   86
Chapter 11   91
Chapter 12   99
Chapter 13   104
Chapter 14   113
Chapter 15   118

Part III

Chapter 16   131
Chapter 17   138
Chapter 18   143
Chapter 19   153
Chapter 20   159
Chapter 21   168
Chapter 22   174
Chapter 23   181
Chapter 24   187
Chapter 25   194
Chapter 26   201
Chapter 27   210
Chapter 28   219

Chapter 29   227
Chapter 30   234
Chapter 31   245

Part IV

Chapter 32   257
Chapter 33   267
Chapter 34   277
Chapter 35   285
Chapter 36   293
Chapter 37   301
Chapter 38   307
Chapter 39   317
Chapter 40   327
Chapter 41   336
Chapter 42   345

Part V

Chapter 43   353
Chapter 44   358
Chapter 45   367
Chapter 46   373
Chapter 47   379
Chapter 48   390
Chapter 49   403
Chapter 50   410
Chapter 51   414
Chapter 52   420
Chapter 53   434
Chapter 54   441
Chapter 55   450
Chapter 56   457
Chapter 57   466
Chapter 58   469
Chapter 59   478

Bonus Epilogue   495

A word from the Author   499
Book Club Questions   503
About Isabella Wiles   505
Acknowledgments   507
Resources   511

Author's Note

My stories include many themes, some beautiful, some painful and ugly. My intention is never to sensationalise trauma—many of us have wounds—but rather, through the safe medium of storytelling, to give them air, so that our collective societal stitches may heal.

This particular story includes themes around infertility, abortion, premature birth and miscarriage, with some graphic scenes. At the back of the book you'll find contact details for organisations that can offer support, if you're at all worried your own stitches may tear open.

Also, international readers may notice some spellings or meanings of words may differ from their own everyday use of the English language; this novel is written using British English (interspersed with some Kiwi and Geordie slang) which befits both the setting and the characters of this story.

Please do share your comments and feedback on my Facebook Page, follow me on Instagram and TikTok, and ensure you sign up to my newsletter to be the first to hear about new releases. Your encouragement inspires me to keep writing. I have lots more stories in me which I can't wait to share.

Much love,

Izzy x

Get a FREE Victoria Turnbull Novel

For a limited time, to celebrate the launch of *The Three Great Loves of Victoria Turnbull* series, you can get an exclusive free copy of the series prequel novella *A Life Unstarted*.

Claim your free copy at www.isabellawiles.com

A chance at a new life, a past that refuses to stay buried, and a dangerous encounter that threatens it all.

Victoria is excited to get her new life started, but paradise quickly turns to hell during a weekend trip to Istanbul. Forced to confront her inner demons, she must find a way to save her friend and herself before it's too late, in this fast-paced origin story.

Claim your free copy at www.isabellawiles.com

Part I

Chapter 1

VICTORIA

Tuesday 30th December 2003

*E*very muscle in my body shakes but sucking in a lung-filling breath, and rather than giving into the weaknesses of my frame, I deepen my Goddess pose.

"That's it ladies. Breathe in your power," the yoga teacher encourages before dragging in an audible breath through flared nostrils. She changes position and we all follow her lead, straightening our outstretched legs and reaching our hands up to the corners of the ceiling. "Now feel your Stars twinkling bright, and on your next out breath, return to your Goddesses. *Feel* your inner power."

I straighten my arms and legs into a four-point Star pose, lengthening my muscles before—on my next breath—returning to my Goddess stance, bending my knees into a deep plié once again, and opening my arms from my chest, my fingers splayed. A mix of tension and power rushes through my thighs. My muscles still shaking, I remind myself: *It's only fear and weakness leaving my body. I'm in control and I am strong.*

Out of my peripheral vision I spy Vanessa, who's given up on the pose and is shaking out her arms and legs. With a free hand she sweeps away a tendril of red hair which has broken free from her ponytail, before she sinks down to her mat and curls up in Child's pose.

We catch each other's eye and smile, before I close my eyes, returning my focus inwards as I blow out another long breath through pursed lips.

I will not lose focus. I am strong. I am my own Goddess, I say to myself over and over.

"See you tomorrow," Nessa says as we roll up our mats at the end of class.

"Tomorrow?" I ask, faking innocence.

"*Durr.* Don't pretend you don't know. New Year's Eve, round mine. You're the only one who hasn't confirmed. But you have to be there."

"Why? What difference would it make if I skipped this one?"

"Are you friggin' kidding me? You're becoming a recluse, Tor. Working far too hard. Let your hair down for once. What is it the proverb says? *All work and no play makes Jack a dull boy?*"

"Maybe I enjoy being dull," I fire back at her.

"Don't be ridiculous, Tor, you're normally the life and soul of every party. You've missed so many this past year; make an exception for this one."

Seven years ago, when I moved back to the town I was born and raised, I used to go swimming with Nessa and my other girlfriends twice a week, and every other spare minute was spent hanging out in The Red Lion, or drinking down on Newcastle's vibrant quayside, our partners in tow. Most weekends, and sometimes more nights in the week than not, we'd be there, drinking, watching whatever match was playing, and taking the mickey out of each other. It was our religion, but these days everyone's lives have moved on. My high-powered job, Nessa's energy zapping but cute-as eleven-month-old twins consume all of her spare time, and all the other girls' lives are equally busy. So when everyone does come together now, it's usually for an event. A birthday, a christening, a formal dinner party, and there are only so many do's I want to attend on my own.

I'm not ashamed or unhappy at the way my life has turned out—far from it—but it's exhausting having to muster the extra energy to confidently walk into a room alone, before having to explain to someone new, the reasons why.

Nessa places an arm around my shoulder as we make our way outside. "It wouldn't be a New Year's Eve party if you weren't there. You started the tradition, remember? You and Craig. Your New Year's Eve parties were legendary."

"Different times." I shrug. My breath forming clouds of condensation in the freezing air outside.

"I'm not taking no for an answer, Tor." She glances sideways at me.

"Alright then. Let's say I do come. What am I meant to do when you lot all lock lips with your better halves at midnight? Stare at the ceiling? Err, *no thank you.* I plan to snuggle up with a nice cup of hot chocolate and see the New Year in with Jools Holland's *Hootenanny* on BBC2."

She shakes her head, smiling. "Have you heard yourself? BBC2?!" Her eyes dance with laughter. "Do you know how hard it was to find a babysitter? And Anth's spent hours putting together a playlist. When was the last time we had a proper lairy bash?"

I was over the moon when, this past summer, Nessa and her husband Anth asked if I would be godmother to their *two loveable monsters,* as she likes to call them; the arrival of her instant family, though, has made even our weekly trips to yoga a logistical nightmare.

"I'm not planning to ship the kids off and go to all this hassle to *not* have the whole gang there... including you. Now everyone's settled down—" She catches her words and winces.

It's not often anyone drops the faux pas these days, my single status of two years having been firmly established in our social

5

group. While everyone else's lives have gracefully transitioned into marriage, kids, bigger mortgages—including my own ex-husband, who I've heard on the grapevine has re-married and started his own family on the other side of the world, in Asia—I have made peace with my singledom. I have everything I want: a fulfilling career, money in the bank, a nice house, a great group of friends, and I'm happy being Aunty Tor to all of their babies.

"Sorry." Nessa tries to recover the situation. "You know what I mean. It's just much harder for some of us to have a night off these days. I mean, when was the last time we were all in the same room —kid free? Everyone's planning to let their hair down and it won't be the same if you're not there."

Vanessa is one of my oldest friends. We've been mates since secondary school. I may not want to go to her party, but I would do anything for her.

"Okay. You win." I exhale.

She claps her hands like a seal, and squeaks.

"Do you need me to help set up, or cook anything?" I ask.

"Nope. Just bring yourself and whatever you want to drink. Anth's roped in a guy from his work to help set up the fireworks, and Becca and I are on food. Just rock up anytime between seven-thirty and eight o'clock."

Rebecca is another close friend of ours, and for the past seven years, since I moved back to the UK from New Zealand, the four of us: Nessa, Becca, my cousin Julie, and I have supported each other through marriage, pregnancies, births and, in my case— divorce. I'm not sure how I would have survived *The Divorce Years* without the support of my girls and a permanently stocked wine fridge.

"You never know," Nessa winks, "this could be the night you finally meet your Mister Right."

"Not likely. Not if it's just our crowd." I sigh, then catch a glimpse of her impish grin out of the corner of my eye. "How big is this party, Ness?"

She shrugs, her lips pressed together into two thin lines.

"Whatever." I shake my head. "But you know I'm never giving up my hard-won independence again."

Having spent the entirety of my twenties rolling unintentionally from one committed relationship to the next, finding myself suddenly single in my thirties was not part of my original life plan. But being on my own does have its advantages. My telly isn't tuned to any sporting channels. I never have to rinse the washbasin of crusty shaving foam and stubble before I clean my teeth. Never once have I had to put the toilet seat down, and, best of all… I only shave my legs on special occasions.

I may be considered unlucky in love, but I'm grateful that I have known love—twice. Even if neither were destined to be forever.

My first serious relationship was with Chris, and that relationship took me all around the world, fuelled by our insatiable passion. Eventually after two years together, I left him in his native New Zealand and came back to the North-East, when I realised that our relationship could not survive on passion alone.

I met Craig shortly after, and thought he was *the one*. We married four years later, but no one could have predicted him walking out of our marriage less than nine months later, ironically, chasing a different life on the other side of the world.

I've not been completely celibate since my divorce, but my dating disasters have only confirmed my desire to remain permanently unattached. There was the *'have your cake and eat it smug-married'*, who lied about his marital status until his angry wife confronted me in the middle of Tesco. After *that* showdown, I now do my weekly shop in a different supermarket.

Then there was the *'slightly past-it singer-songwriter'*. No doubt talented, I initially found his creativity alluring, but soon realised our fling, along with his refusal to accept his failed chart success and advancing age, were symptoms of his own mid-life crisis.

There have been plenty of *'city boys'*. Stunningly handsome men with jawlines as sharp as their pin-striped suits. Their lives filled with the trinkets of material success: fancy apartments, flashy cars, and wallets overflowing with plenty of cash to flash. But, as befits their one-dimensional image, I was using them as much as they were using me. Once I'd had my fill I always lost interest in continuing as their *trophy girlfriend* who looked good on their arm at their swanky corporate do's or polo-club balls.

Nope, I may not have kept my legs crossed these past two years, but my heart has—and will remain—most definitely closed.

Nessa and I say our goodbyes and fifteen minutes later I pull up outside my five-bed Victorian villa in the centre of town.

At least I got to keep the house in the divorce, and I've thrown everything I have into remodelling it to my own taste.

Slamming the car door, I spot my trusty companion sitting in the lounge window, patiently waiting for my return. I'm only two steps inside the house when Leo wraps himself around my legs and purrs loudly.

"Aww, I'm so sorry to have left you for all of…" I check my watch, "… an hour and a half." I pick him up and tickle him under his jet-black chin as he rubs and strokes his head against my palm. "At least I can always rely on you for cuddles, ya big old softy. Although I'm sure if I stopped feeding you, you'd soon scarper. Just like every penis-possessing male-member of the human race before you."

Jesus, listen to me. Talking to my cat.

I set Leo back down, head to the kitchen and flick on the kettle. Looking around my beautiful home, all remnants of my life before erased: the walls, now repainted in soft hues by Farrow and Ball, are filled with pictures of me with my friends and their children. This may not be the life I'd envisioned for myself when I was in my twenties, a full unchartered life story laid out in front of me, but now I'm more pragmatic. I have everything I want—and I'm happy.

"Well Leo," I say to the cat. "If I'm going out-out tomorrow, that only means one thing… I'd best shave my legs."

Chapter 2

The following day I follow my usual routine. A green juice for breakfast, followed by twenty minutes stretching on my yoga mat.

Although as an ex-dancer I've tried yoga in the past, it's only since my divorce that I've really gotten into it. I used to prefer swimming to stay in shape, and still do go to the pool every now and then, but I've found the meditative part of yoga so beneficial these past few years. Plus, even if I'm too busy to get to a class, I can always make time for half an hour on my mat at home.

Once I've finished and my body feels supple and strong, I take a shower. Even though I'm technically on leave until next week, as I've got a whole day ahead of me before Nessa's party tonight I decide to nip into the office for a few hours. There'll be nobody else in and it means I can get ahead on the large tender that needs to be submitted immediately after the holidays.

Five hours after I left for the office I arrive home, and after feeding myself and the cat I realise I can't put this damn party off any longer. Opening the wine fridge, I pull out a nice bottle of Chardonnay that I'd been saving for a special occasion.

"Don't judge me." Leo's bright yellow beady eyes stare back at me. "If I have to go, I intend to rock up the right side of merry."

Turning my back on the cat, I pop the cork and take a swig directly from the bottle.

✫

As predicted, a few hours later I'm the awkward singleton in a house full of couples. Worse still, their house is rammed to the rafters with strangers. Lots of people—I assume—from Anth's work, old uni friends, or couples they've met since having their kids. I loiter on the outside of conversation after conversation. Forcing myself to laugh as I try to fit in. I float between the various rooms where couples stand, their arms around each other's backs. Eventually I make my way through to the lounge, which has been converted into a makeshift nightclub. The room is completely dark except for the retro eighties disco lights that whir and pierce the space with flashes of strobe colours.

Someone's raided their attic, I think to myself.

Glancing around, every surface is covered with indeterminate human shapes. Intertwined couples, making out as if their lives depended on it, their arms and legs illuminated every so often by the whirring red, white, and green lights that spin around the room.

God, this feels like a bad college party. I groan internally, scooching my arse onto the sofa next to an amorous couple, their faces glued to each other like something out of the film *Alien*.

Sitting on my lonesome, I steadily drink my way through my second bottle of wine of the evening. Couples come and go, and in front of me a few brave females attempt to draw their partners onto the makeshift dance floor, a glitter ball having been hung from the ceiling light. When their partners ignore them, they tumble back laughing and giggling to the edges of the room.

I check my watch. Only ten-thirty.

Bloody hell, I've got at least another hour and a half of this torture before I can make a polite exit.

I close my eyes and allow the music to vibrate through my solar plexus. Instinctively my body begins to move. My chin bobbing in time to the beat, my arms lifting off my lap, my hands circling along with the accents in the melody.

The previous track finishes and The Darkness's "I Believe in a Thing Called Love" comes on. Without thinking, I down the last of my wine and stand up.

I don't give a shit who might be watching me as I dance and twirl in the middle of Nessa's lounge. The music is my unconscious guide as I move my hips in time to the beat. Wrapping my arms around my torso, I hug myself, throwing my head back, my fingers at my throat, before I thread them through my hair.

For the first time this evening I begin to relax into my own skin.

The beat changes and so do my steps. My feet stepping forwards and backwards in time to the Latin rhythms. My left hand on my stomach, my other raised in the air as if I'm being partnered. I tap out a staccato rhythm before mimicking a *kiss kiss*, as instructed by Holly Valance's lyrics.

Spinning in a full three-sixty, I open my eyes to 'spot' against a fixed point on the wall opposite—the ballet training of my youth embedded in my muscle memory. I whip my head around, returning my gaze to the same focus point on the wall which is meant to stop me getting dizzy; however, no amount of dance training can compensate for the two bottles of wine I've consumed, and I lose my balance. Stumbling in the direction of the sofa, my arms flailing, I topple over.

Expecting to fall into an undignified heap on the floor, or worse still, land on top of a smooching couple, instead I feel two strong arms reach out from the sofa and catch me.

Cradling me like a baby in his lap, I look up, wanting to know whose brawny muscles have saved my dignity.

My gaze is returned by two amused hazel brown eyes flecked with speckles of grey, and a wide smile pulled taut by the cutest dimples.

"Well, hello," the beaming stranger says.

"Err hi," I say, planting my feet back on the floor and making to stand up.

"No don't go," he urges. "You were just getting comfortable."

"Trust me, my intention was not to land in someone's boyfriend's lap."

"It's a good job my lap only belongs to me then, isn't it?"

"What?" I turn back and look at him. "You're single? Came on your own?"

Only saddos or winos come to a house party alone, I think to myself, before wondering which category I fall into. Probably a wino.

"Yup. All on my Jack Jones. The saddo in the corner, trying to stay out of everyone's way."

So he's already labelled himself a saddo.

"That was until a beautiful girl landed in my lap," he adds.

Even though he's having to shout over the blare of the stereo, I feel the warm tentacles of a flush creep up my neck. There's something about his unpretentious honesty that dissipates my need to clamber off his knees. Instead, I hold out my hand for a handshake. "Victoria, but most of my friends call me Vicky, or Tor."

He wraps my slender fingers in his man paw. "Gavin, but most of my friends call me Gav."

"Nice to meet you Gav. How come I've never seen you before?"

"It's a bit of a long story."

"Well we've got all night," I exclaim, playfully slapping his upper arm. "Where are you from?"

"North Wales. Bangor, to be precise."

"Really? You don't have an accent."

"Chi yw'r fenyw harddaf a welais erioed," he replies in Welsh, making me laugh. I have absolutely no idea what it means.

"It's South Walians who have the distinctive accent you mainly hear on the telly," he continues. "Most North Walians tend to sound we come from Cheshire or middle England when we're not speaking our mother tongue."

"So how does a lad from North Wales end up at a New Year's

Eve party in the North East? Hmmm…" I drum my fingers against my chin. "Did you move for love, or money, I wonder?"

"Neither." He narrows his eyes, their pupils twinkling.

"Oh?"

I watch as he sucks in a breath, his broad chest expanding underneath his light blue Tommy Hilfiger T-shirt. "Like I said, it's a bit of a long story," he says, turning his gaze away from me and reaching down to pick up a half-drunk bottle of Bud.

"Well, like I said, we've got all night!" I slap him exaggeratedly for a second time.

Coughing and spluttering, my mistimed slap causing him to choke, he squeezes my knee. "And if I say I don't divulge my secrets to perfect strangers, no matter how beautiful they are, I suppose you're just gonna keep on slapping me until I give in."

"You know me too well already," I tease.

"I've just started working with Anth," he offers as a conversation starter.

"Ahh, so it was the job that brought you north."

"Not quite. I was looking for a fresh start." He rolls his bottle between his palms. "I'm not long divorced."

"Me too!" I slap him a third time and this time he turns and looks at me.

For a moment we hold each other's gaze in a way I've not done with a man in a very long while, at least not since before things went sour with my Craig. A tiny flutter of long-forgotten butterflies dances in the pit of my stomach.

"Who the hell let you go?" he says, suddenly serious.

"That's also a very long story," I say, dipping my head, my mouth suddenly dry.

"Well I think we've got all night." He gently punches my upper arm, the corners of his mouth turning into a shy smile. "You want another drink?" he asks.

I nod, and he disappears back into the kitchen for more booze.

Flopping back onto the sofa, I cover my smiling mouth with my hands just as Nessa walks past and gives me an exaggerated wink.

. . .

Over the next hour, Gav tells me about his first few weeks in his new role as Head of Digital and Content at the same software firm where Anth works.

"What specifically does a Head of Digital and Content do?" I ask, intrigued.

"Lots of things, but mainly make sure our end-to-end customer journey is available as a digital experience as well as offline." When I look at him, my eyebrows drawn together, he laughs then continues. "Trust me, over the next decade, digital content is going to become a game changer in all forms of marketing. Right now I'm rebuilding the company's website."

"Interesting," I reply, before telling him about my role as a Director in an outsourced Marketing Agency.

We share notes about our respective roles, which although different are both in marketing, and other than acknowledging that we've both been married previously, we avoid asking any detailed questions about each other's relationship history.

"What's North Wales like?" I ask. "I've never been."

"Very much like that…" Gav gestures to the snow that continues to fall softly outside.

It's been snowing all day, the outside world covered in a heavy blanket of white.

"I'm used to harsh winters, and love the mountains, which is partly why when I accepted the job in Newcastle I chose to buy a flat in the Derwent Valley. I'm much more a country boy than a city slicker."

"Me too. I don't mind working in town, but I much prefer to live where there's room to breathe."

"Another thing we have in common," he says, clinking his bottle against the side of my wine glass.

. . .

At a quarter to midnight, Nessa glides into the room balancing a platter of vol-au-vents above her head, and points at the stereo. "Can someone turn that off, please?"

Someone dutifully complies, and Nessa reaches down and switches on the telly, tuning it to BBC1. A picture of Big Ben fills the screen.

"Anyone need a top-up?" Anth bowls into the room carrying a six-pack of Fosters under one arm and a bottle of wine in the other.

Those who need to, top up their drinks, as everyone crowds into the lounge to watch the clock tick closer to midnight. Gav stands next to me. He's a good few inches taller than my five foot nine inches. We disguise our awkwardness by gripping our drinks with both hands, our heads bowed as if waiting for a priest to bless us.

Fuck, what's going to happen when the clock strikes twelve? Will he feel obliged to kiss me just because we've chatted for the last hour? Do I want him to kiss me? Do I want to kiss him?

I don't have much time to dwell on my insecurities as the crowd begins to count down: "Ten. Nine. Eight. Seven. Six."

Without looking at me, Gav slides his arm around my back and pulls me into him, and I allow myself to be held. His fingers move in tentative strokes back and forth over my hip bone, and unexpectedly my skin tingles at his touch.

"Five. Four. Three. Two. One. Happy New Year!" the crowd around us cheer.

Glasses are raised. Toasts are made, and instinctively Gav and I turn and look at each other as somewhere behind us, people release party poppers. Their loud bangs sending colourful paper ribbons shooting across the room like happy rainbows.

"Happy New Year, Vicky," he says softly before bending his face towards me. His lips landing a soft flutter of a kiss against mine.

We remain nose to nose for a long moment. Our eyes closed, I hear him breathe me in, and instinctively I initiate another kiss. This time his lips are firmer and we turn our torsos towards each other as we kiss properly. It feels nice. Strong but tender.

"Happy New Year, Gav," I whisper when we eventually pull back.

★

After everyone has clasped hands and muddled their way through the lyrics of "Auld Lang Syne", Nessa and Anth usher everyone outside—no mean feat in the now full-on snowstorm—to watch the fireworks that Anth and Gav set up earlier. The frost and thaw of the past few weeks, on top of the large amount of alcohol I've consumed, makes my balance as useless as Bambi's, skating on ice. I'm sliding all over the place, but Gav holds me up by my waist.

After watching a pretty impressive display of colour and explosions, Gav sees us both safely back inside again, where we reclaim our space on the sofa.

For the next few hours, time stands still as we chat some more. The party continuing on around us while we disappear into our own little bubble.

He tells me he grew up in a quiet household, his parents having met later in life, he, their only child. He returns home to Wales every three months or so, to lay flowers on their graves.

"Roses were my mother's favourite. '*I don't care what colour you get as long as it's roses*', Mam would always say to Tad." He uses the Welsh word for dad. "And he never let her down. Remembered every birthday and anniversary, and before the flowers were past their best she would clip the head off one and add it to the bowl of pot pourri made from all the roses he'd ever given her."

"That's lovely."

"It was. I still have their Villeroy and Boch crystal bowl of dried petals."

"Well maybe one day you'll find someone special to add to the collection."

He raises an eyebrow. "Perhaps. Life is full of surprises, don't you think?" He holds my eye contact and my insides feel like

16

marshmallow melting over a hot fire. The intensity of his stare unnerves me, so to break the tension I lean in and kiss him again.

This time he responds more fervently, his tongue parting my lips and demanding we deepen our kiss; I willingly oblige.

I have no idea how long we remain chatting and making out on the sofa, but at some point Nessa stops topping up everyone's glasses and instead offers tea and coffee to the remaining partygoers; the crowd having thinned out a good few hours ago.

"I think it's time I made tracks," I say after we've both accepted a tea from Nessa.

"I'll walk you home," Gav volunteers.

"You don't have to."

"It's no trouble. And," he glances outside, "the storm isn't showing any signs of letting up. I'd feel happier if I know you've got home safe."

After finishing our hot drinks, we say our goodbyes and leave together; ignoring Nessa's raised eyebrows.

Arm in arm, we slip and slide our way through the silent streets, the taxis long having been pulled off the roads for their own safety.

We pass the occasional group of revellers who, like us, are returning home after celebrating the turn of the new year at some party or other, but it's mostly just us and the silent flakes that fall softly from the sky. The world seems to have taken on a magical quality, every wall, garden, and chimney pot covered in a twinkling carpet of white.

As we climb the hill towards the centre of town, the wind intensifies. Whipping the snow up into flurries that swirl around our feet. I place my gloved hands over my frozen ears.

"Here." Gav pulls off his beanie hat and passes it to me.

"Are you sure? Are you not cold?"

"I'm fine. Take it."

"Thanks." I pull the wool hat over my head, feeling his warmth in the fibres, his heat transferring to me.

We continue walking along the snow-covered streets, mostly in silence, until about twenty minutes later we arrive at my front door.

As I slide my key into the lock, behind me Gav shuffles from foot to foot. Neither of us are sure how to end this brief, if heated, encounter.

What I do know is there ain't no way he's coming in for a nightcap.

After a very long and awkward pause, he's the first to break the stalemate. "It was nice meeting you, Victoria. Happy New Year."

"You too, Gavin. Goodnight," I say, not turning fully around to face him, instead holding my key in the lock and looking back over my shoulder at him.

"Goodnight." He takes a step back.

We don't kiss again and, as he didn't push for another date, it seems he's also happy to leave it there. It's only after I've closed the front door that I realise I'm still wearing his beanie hat. Pulling it off, I roll my finger over the logo at the front.

Well *that* wasn't how I expected tonight to have gone.

Chapter 3

I sleep through until the afternoon of New Year's Day, only waking when Leo decides to sit on my chest and purr like a tractor, kneading the duvet like a loaf of bread.

"Alright, alright. I'm getting up." I sit up, sweep my hair out of my eyes and catch my reflection staring back at me. I don't remember much from last night, but I'm surprised the mirror hasn't cracked. I touch my cheek and stretch the skin on my forehead. My lips are still stained red, but the colour has bled all over the bottom half of my face. The rouge in my cheeks has long gone, and my complexion looks sallow and washed-out. My signature smokey eye make-up now looks like I've done ten rounds with Mike Tyson. I look like a panda. A hungover washed-out panda at that.

Rubbing sleep and crusty mascara out of my eyes, I pull a sweat-shirt over my PJs and head down into the kitchen to feed Leo.

After a hot bacon sandwich, a hot mug of tea and an even hotter shower, I wrap up against the snow and ice, and walk back down the hill to Nessa's. I'm sure she'd appreciate the help in clearing up, and even though it's not my kitchen we congregate in anymore, it's always been our tradition to get together the day after a big night out and dissect all the previous evening's antics.

I'm hardly through the front door before two chocolate-covered, toothless grins plastered across two pudgy, smiling faces squeal loudly when they see me arrive.

My heart flips over inside my chest and I quickly throw my jacket onto the peg, my gloves and hat into a basket on the floor, and leave my snow boots by the door.

Hunkering down onto bent knees, my arms wide, I encourage Nessa's twins to crawl towards me. "And how's my favourite rug rats?" I say, clapping my hands. They gurgle and babble their way into my arms.

At eleven months old, Emily has begun taking a few tentative unaided steps, but Ethan, being slightly bigger, is still surfing around the edges of the furniture, dropping down onto all fours and crawling when he's decided he's had enough.

Sweeping them both up, I nestle one on each hip and carry them through to the kitchen, where seated around Nessa's trusty farm-house table, slurping tea, is my other bestie Becca, and my cousin Julie. Nessa has her rubber-gloved hands in the sink, and the telly in the corner is showing this year's New Year's Day family film: *Finding Nemo*.

'Oi oi," Becca says. "We were just talking about you. Wondering if you'd have the balls to show your face today."

"Why wouldn't I?" I crumple my brow.

"You're a bit late." Julie smiles. "We've been here for hours."

"I slept all day. Must have needed it. But I need to keep my cuddle quota up. I've missed these two." I gently pinch Ethan and Emily's legs, and they both squeal and kick their legs in delight. "What still needs doing?" I ask, looking around the pristine kitchen.

"All done." Nessa smiles at me, peeling off the yellow gloves and laying them over the side of the sink.

I seat the children in their highchairs and, without being asked, flick the switch on the kettle and make everyone a fresh round of tea. Behind me, Nessa collects a packet of Hobnobs from a cupboard.

"So come on then. Spill," Becca urges.

"Spill what?" I shrug.

"Oh, you gotta be kidding me." Becca rolls her eyes. "The last time I saw you, you were almost having sex with some stranger on the sofa."

Julie leans towards Emily's highchair, the one closest to her, and places her hands over the little girl's ears. "Ignore your Aunty Becca. She has no filter." Ethan, meanwhile, has tuned out from our conversation, as if he already knows this is *girl talk,* and is instead mesmerised by the film.

Passing round the fresh cups of tea, Nessa and I join the others at the table. With practised ease Nessa, chops a banana into bite size pieces, placing the chunks onto the high-chair trays in front of Ethan and Emily, who grasp them with podgy fingers and mush the fruit into their mouths.

"I think that's a *slight* exaggeration, Becks," I reply.

"Not from where I was sitting." Julie pulls her lips into a wry smile.

"Who was he?" Becca asks no one in particular. "Nobody seemed to know."

"He's new to the area," Nessa answers. "Not long started working with Anth. They call him Gav. Anth roped him in to help clear the drive and set up the fireworks yesterday afternoon. He wasn't planning on staying for the actual party, but I persuaded him."

"I bet Tor's pleased you did," Becca says, while I take a slow, considered sip of my tea. I'm quite happy for them to continue their analysis of mine and Gav's movements from the previous evening, as long as I don't have to participate.

"So what's he like?" Julie asks, looking at Nessa for an answer, appreciating that I'm refusing to be drawn.

"Nice. I think. He didn't say much. Seemed like a gentle giant. He only moved here a few weeks ago. Doesn't know anyone…"

"Except our Tor," Becca interjects with a wink in my direction.

I ignore her and continue drinking my tea.

"That's why I persuaded him to stay on for the evening," Nessa continues. "I got the impression parties are not usually his thing, and if I'd given him an out he'd have left long before the action started."

"Lucky for someone," Julie says.

"But what I want to know is what happened after you both left." Becca wraps her hands around her cup, and glares at me.

With three sets of eyeballs boring into me, I realise they're not going to let me off the hook without an explanation.

"Nothing." I shrug. "He walked me home. We said goodnight, and that was that."

"Bollocks!" Becca exclaims and Julie covers Emily's ears again, shaking her head.

"What's she like, Em."

Laughing, I add, "It's the truth. Nothing happened other than we walked home in the freezing cold, then said goodnight on my doorstep. The end."

"But is it?" Julie asks. "Surely you've made plans to see each other?"

"No," I baulk, as if she'd just asked me to run through the snow naked. "It was a snog at a New Year's Eve party. Nothing more."

"Shame." Julie hits me with one of her psychotherapist stares. The kind where she's all-knowing and wise while she waits for you to catch up. "It would be nice for you to meet someone new, Tor. Someone strong and kind. You deserve to find happiness."

"But I am happy. I have everything I want."

"Hmmm," she muses. "I think if you were to let him slip through your fingers, without at least exploring if there might be something more there, you could be missing out on something really great."

"To be honest," I continue. "I can't really remember what he looks like."

Everyone draws in a sharp breath, and Nessa's covers her cheeks with her hands as she shakes her head in disbelief.

"That's because you spent most of the evening glued to his face," Becca says pragmatically and everyone laughs.

I shake my head, amused. "Honestly girls, let it go. It was nothing. Now come on, what else did I miss last night?"

The following morning I'm upside down in my living room, holding a headstand on my yoga mat, when I hear my phone beep. Ignoring it, I continue my flow, until I'm ready to reengage with the world. Twenty minutes later, dabbing my neck with a towel whilst feeling suitably zen, I pick up my phone and read:

> Do you want to meet up for a coffee? You could give me my beanie back? Or if you don't want to that's okay as well. Gav

Staring at the screen, I walk through to the kitchen and fill a glass with water.

How the hell did he get my number? I reckon Nessa or Julie might have had something to do with that. Or did I give it to him? I honestly can't remember.

But the bigger question is...should I go? Meet him for coffee?

I think not. I'm not looking for a relationship. Granted, it was a nice night and I enjoyed his company, but apart from anything else, it's too close to home. He works with Anth, lives locally, has no other friends; if things went sour it could get really messy, really quick.

Post-divorce, all my dalliances with the opposite sex have purposefully been with men away from my hometown. Much easier to keep them at arm's length and away from my neat and tidy domesticity.

But what if I were to bump into him again? Either at Nessa's, or if he rocks up at the The Red Lion, and I don't recognise him. Surely that would be more embarrassing. We did get pretty hot and heavy on that sofa, and maybe that did mean something to him. Perhaps it would be better to meet for a quick drink, keep things casual, and make sure he understands that what happened at New Year doesn't mean I have any desire to take things further—at least emotionally.

But there's also something endearing in the way he's worded his message. *'Or if you don't want to that's okay as well'*. It's as if he's expecting an instant rejection, or he's giving me an out, or possibly he lacks confidence with the opposite sex, at least in the nuances of dating. I get the sense he's not a player and flirting isn't something he's had lots of practise with. There is, of course, the possibility he just wants his hat back.

I suck in a deep breath.

I suppose there's only one way to find out.

I punch out a quick text:

> Okay. But rather than coffee how about an early evening drink. We could head 'doon the toon'. Tomorrow night? V x

Before I hit send, I remove the kiss and change the V to Victoria. Best keep things formal. Don't want him thinking this is more than it is. Just an opportunity to say, "Thank you for walking me home," and a chance to return his hat. Meeting in a crowded bar, ironically, feels less intimate than a quiet coffee shop and rather than go anywhere local, down in Newcastle we'll be well away from prying eyes and wagging tongues.

> Great. I'll pick you up at 7

> Looking forward to it. Gav x

I let go of the breath I was holding before I spot the 'x' at the end of his last message.

Shit! He does think this is a date.

I hold my thumb over my phone, preparing to punch out an immediate reply and stipulate, *for the record,* that this is just two people meeting for casual drinks. But he'll find out soon enough.

Chapter 4

The following evening at seven o'clock on the dot, Gav pulls up outside my house in a black Ford Mondeo. He gets out of the car and begins to make his way around the back of it, but before he has a chance to hold the passenger door open for me, I rush down the path and open it myself. Hopping in, I leave him standing listlessly on the footpath. He double taps the roof of the car before returning to the driver's side.

"Right," he says, his back stiffening, as he climbs back inside.

"Hi," I say, as we both buckle up. "You good?"

He doesn't say anything, but nods tentatively, the tips of his ears turning pink.

"Before I forget," I say, adding extra cheer to my voice as I pass him his beanie hat. Hopefully my confidence can compensate for his obvious nerves. "Thanks for this. I think my ears would have fallen off without it."

"No problem."

He starts the car but doesn't put it into gear.

"I have a confession." He turns to look at me, and for the first time sober I see his face full on.

My first thought is that through my previous wine fog I don't remember him being so good looking. His hair is blond—yes blond;

I've never normally gone for blond dudes before, and although his hair is the colour of yellow straw now, it has the look of having been bleach white when he was a kid. He smiles, and I find myself unconsciously smiling in return. His soft hazel eyes crinkle in the corners, and although his frame fills the seat, he doesn't dominate it. Almost as if he's apologetic for his size. Everything about this guy oozes soft but strong. Indeed, as Nessa described, a gentle giant.

He coughs into his closed fist. "I feel embarrassed saying this, but I haven't a clue where's good for a drink."

"Of course. How would you?" I reply breezily, consciously wanting to put him at ease. It's not his fault he doesn't know the area. "Head to Osbourne Road in Jesmond. That way we can stick to the main roads. Don't want us getting stuck in the snow in any side streets. We can decide which bar once we get there."

He still doesn't move the car, slowly closing and opening his eyes.

Realising he doesn't know where I'm talking about, but is clearly embarrassed to ask again, I pat the back of his hand. "Newcastle. Head to Newcastle and I'll direct us from there."

Twenty minutes later, we park up on the street and head into the nearest bar, which is rammed to the rafters. Being the smarter side of town, most people are wearing suits or slacks with a blazer, and I spot Gav look down at his perfectly acceptable jeans, T-shirt and casual jacket; his wide eyes and nipped lips give away his obvious concern that he doesn't fit in.

I link my arm through his and lead him towards the bar. "Let me get the first round. As a thank you for walking me home the other night, and for lending me your hat. What's your poison?"

He exhales, clearly grateful for some guidance in this alien space. Nessa was right, he's obviously not the partying kind.

"Just a Diet Coke, please."

"Are you sure you don't want a pint?"

"No," he says without hesitation. "Not when I'm driving."

"Not even a half?"

"No." He shakes his head, his jaw set. "Or should I say, no thank you."

I think back to Craig's brother Rob, who was tragically killed by a drunk driver. A life cut short by someone else's irresponsibility.

"Well I admire your morals. I wish more people were like you, instead of taking their own and other people's lives into their hands. A Diet Coke it is."

I order our drinks, and he carries them to a quiet-ish corner of the bar, plonking them on an empty standing table.

Leaning against its top, I take a sip of my vodka and Coke. But rather than meet my gaze, Gav's eyes dart from corner to corner, like a trapped animal looking for an escape route.

I don't get it: he initiated this post-snog meet-up, but now that he's here, it feels like he can't wait to get away.

Is it me?

"Gav, can I ask you a question?"

"Uh?" he says, focusing on me for the first time since we arrived.

"When was the last time you went out for a drink? With a woman?" I add.

"Erm…" He pauses. "Honestly?"

"Of course."

"Would it seem weird if I said—never?"

I jerk my head back a smidgen.

"I saw that." He pulls his mouth into a lopsided smile. "See, I knew you'd think I was weird."

"No, not weird. I'm just curious how someone has managed to get to the ripe old age of…"

"Thirty-five."

"Thirty-five," I repeat, "without losing at least some of their life to the pub scene."

"It's just never been my thing," he says, meeting my eye contact. "If I've had to go out, it's only ever been for a specific event. Someone's birthday, a wedding, that sort of thing. I'm not a fan of crowds of any kind."

"Well I take my hat off to you. Most women my age complain that they're bar widows, while they stay home and mind the kids. I suppose there's no chance of that ever happening with you." I laugh, still consciously trying to put him at ease.

"I suppose not." He laughs as well, and his whole face lights up.

"So if this is not your usual *thang*, what is?"

"Getting outdoors. I like being physical. Making things, fixing things, or just going for long walks. I used to have a dog, but my ex-wife got custody."

"Oh I am sorry. That must have been hard." I place my hand on top of his and give it a little squeeze.

"I'm sorry," he replies, pinching the bridge of his nose. "It's hard to talk about."

"Then let's not. How are you with cats?" I take another sip of my drink.

"Can't stand them," he says quickly, then realising it was a loaded question smacks his forehead with his hand. "Oh god, I've just put my foot in it haven't I? As you can see, I'm not very good at seduction."

"Seduction?" I raise my eyebrows. "I thought we were just having a friendly chat."

"Yes. Yes," he says quickly, taking a sip of his drink. Buying himself some time. "That's what I meant."

It's clear he's out of his depth, but his inexperience and vulnerability make me warm to him.

"Can I ask you another question?"

He looks up.

"Do you like spag bol? Only I made a vat of it this morning which hasn't made it into the freezer yet. How would you like to get out of this place and come back to mine for a plate of home-cooked goodness?"

His shoulders drop and he lets go of a long exhale. "That sounds marvellous."

"Come on. Let's get out of here. And I won't tell Leo that you hate him. But then he hates all men, so be warned."

"Don't worry, all animals love me. I have that vibe." He waggles his fingers in a spooky kind of way, as I finish my drink and gather up my things.

⚜

To my surprise, Leo does not scratch Gav's eyes out when I introduce them. Rather the opposite. And Leo is a first-class judge of character. He jumps onto Gav's lap and purrs loudly, while I heat up the Bolognese and cook the pasta.

"How long have you had him?" Gav asks.

"About a year. He's a rescue." I don't add it was because I was in such a dark place after Craig left, that Julie suggested I get a pet, to give me something other than myself to focus on. And she was right.

"I did consider getting a dog, having grown up with dogs but cats are lower maintenance. And it wouldn't be fair to leave a dog locked up all day."

"When I saw him strut his way into the cat sitter's lounge," I continue, "I knew he was the one for me; or I him, depending on how you look at it. The cat sitter was looking after a rescued litter on behalf of the RSPCA, but he wasn't from the same litter as all the other kittens; a single cat, although still young, about nine months old, he meowed his arrival as if to say, *'Hey you lesser beings, stop what you're doing and look at me '"*

"So you're a diva, are you?" Gav says, giving the cat a tickle under his chin.

Being so low in self-belief and self-confidence at the time, I liked the idea of bringing home a creature who had an abundance of what I lacked. Maybe he could teach me something.

Very soon it became apparent he'd been mistreated, most likely by a man, as he'd snarl and spit his mistrust of any male that stepped across my threshold. I rather liked it. Leo, my own personal bodyguard who'd return any male guests' attempts of affection with a sharp warning scratch; to see him happily settled in Gav's lap is unusual to say the least.

I put a plate of food on the table in front of Gav, and he sets Leo down on the floor.

"Sorry buster, but you need to stay down there while we eat." Gav looks back up at me, and smiles. "Thanks for this. You didn't have to feed me."

"You're right, I didn't, but I felt bad for having taken you somewhere that made you feel so uncomfortable. And I'm so used to being on my own these days, and I know you haven't made any friends up here yet, I thought it might be nice."

"Is that how you see us? Just friends?" He raises an eyebrow as he looks at me, his face tilted downwards. "I only ask, as I don't remember ever kissing a friend the way we kissed the other night. In fact I don't think I've ever kissed anyone like that."

I can't help but smile. There's no doubt that he's not my usual type. All my relationships, and even the dalliances in the years following my divorce—which Becca has cheekily labelled the *The Durex Years*—were always with cocksure men. Blokes with silver tongues who had all the moves. I always knew their chat-up lines had been used a million times over, which is why, as I've gotten older, I've always taken everything that comes out of the mouth of a member of the opposite sex with a healthy pinch of salt. Whereas with Gav, it's clear this is unusual territory for him… and therefore unrehearsed and genuine. There's no front. He is who he is.

"Tell me something." I ignore his previous question. "If you don't go to bars, and you've never kissed anyone…" I pause, taking my time twirling a forkful of spaghetti around in my spoon, "… like we kissed at New Year, how on earth did you end up married? Were you betrothed at birth?" I purposefully exaggerate my last comment, wanting to keep things light.

"No, nothing like that." He takes a sip from his drink. Another Diet Coke, taken from my fridge. "Don't get me wrong, I wasn't just a passenger on a ride-along, but she made the first move. We met at work, otherwise I don't think we'd have crossed paths."

"She didn't drop into your lap then?" I tease.

"No. Only one girl has ever landed in my lap."

He looks at me again with those intense eyes, and a sense of calm settles in my stomach.

I smile and turn my attention back to my dinner.

Once we finish eating he helps me clear the plates, and as he loads the dishwasher I fill the Krups with fresh coffee. Although I drink tea like it's going out of fashion, on this occasion we share a freshly percolated pot of coffee, before he checks his watch.

"Thank you for dinner, but I think I should be making tracks." He reaches for my hand and we both look down at our interlaced fingers.

I'm rooted to the spot. The sensation of his skin touching mine, meshing us together.

Every other relationship I've ever had always started with a thunderbolt of desire that rushed through my core, whereas when Gav touches me a cloud of calmness descends over me. My heart rate literally slows down.

I've heard it said when you meet your soul mate, rather than feel giddy or lustful, a wave of familiarity washes through you. As if you've known them all your life even though you've only just met, and I have to acknowledge that's how I feel about the man who's standing in my kitchen holding my hand.

He reaches down and tenderly lifts my chin. Bending slowly he places a soft kiss on my cheek. "You're extraordinary, Victoria. I hope you know that."

"Call me Vicky, or Tor," I whisper. "Victoria is my Sunday name. Or the name my mam uses when I'm in trouble."

"How about Angel? 'Cause that's what you are."

Both of us snigger.

"See? I have no idea what I'm doing. That was my attempt at being romantic."

Despite what I may be feeling, every part of my logical brain is crystal clear: I do not have room in my life for this.

"It was lovely. But look, Gav—"

"Don't," he interrupts before I'm able to cool his intentions. "One thing you need to know about me," he continues, "is I'm always one-hundred-percent sincere. If I don't mean it, I don't say it. And what I say, I mean."

"Likewise," I reply, my giggles dissolving in the sincerity I see when I meet his gaze.

Shit! If I don't shut this down now, I'm in big trouble.

There's something about this guy that's totally discombobulating. I know complicating my life with another relationship is not what I want, yet I feel so good when I'm around him. It's like I'm more of myself, and being *that* woman is what I *do* want.

"Look, Gav." I pull my fingers away from his. "I need to be clear. I really don't have space in my life for anything complicated, okay?"

"I know," he says, his tone light, giving the impression he knows something I don't. "Like I said, it's time I made tracks."

I walk him to the front door.

"Okay then," he says as we smile once more and I softly close the door behind him, before collapsing back against it.

Bugger, bugger, bugger, I say to myself as I slide to the floor.

I'm in deep shit and I know it.

Chapter 5

GAVIN

*T*here's a reason Gavin Williams has always avoided living in the city. He never bought into the idea that their streets were paved with gold. Rather the opposite. He's always found densely urban areas overpriced, overcrowded, and lacking in nature, going against the natural rhythm of life. Why anyone would voluntarily choose that lifestyle is beyond him.

After their first *non-date* got off to such a disastrous start, and even after an easy intimate dinner she had tried to give him the brush-off, he was beyond relieved when Vicky agreed to a second *non-date* in a quiet and homely country pub, complete with roaring fire and resident gun dog stretched out in front of it.

Whilst tucking into roast beef with all the trimmings, the conversation—not for the first time—had flowed effortlessly, and, for Gavin at least, what had started as an out-of-character lustful urge that had overtaken his senses on New Year's Eve, in the glow of the pub fire and under the umbrella of their easy rapport was rapidly deepening into a serious attraction to this woman. He appreciates that she's fighting her own internal battle to remain unattached, for what reason he has no idea; he only hopes if they spend more time together he can gently soften that hard outer shell.

Today she's accepted a further invitation for another winter walk. This time she's taken him *'along the line'*, which he soon learned is the name the locals give to the now disused railway that cuts through the Derwent valley, joining the once industrial hubbub of Consett to the gateway city of Newcastle. Following the demise of the Consett steel works in the 1980s, the rails were eventually lifted, and the once industrial artery is now a popular trail for dog walkers and cyclists.

They joined *the line* at a disused station, its platform suspended eerily above the non-existent tracks, as if waiting for a ghost train that will never come, and walked east, under silent railway arches and over a viaduct that bridged a deep drop in the valley.

Gavin turns to admire the view, the snake of an ancient Roman road curling its way over the crest of the hill on the opposite side of the valley, an even earlier artery that once linked the barracks at York to the main fortress in Edinburgh.

"It's no Snowdon, but I've gotta admit it's still pretty stunning." He uses his hand to shade his eyes against the watery winter sun.

"Everyone says it's like living in Narnia up here. Snows all bloody year—which is partly true, but I love it." Vicky opens her mouth and catches a loose flake of snow on her tongue. Gav has to use all his self-control to stop himself pouncing on her, dipping her back and kissing the hell out of her.

What the hell is she doing to me? He thinks to himself. He's never been that forward with anyone–ever.

The sun is setting as they arrive back on Vicky's doorstep and just as on their previous *non-dates,* both of them shuffle uneasily from foot to foot, unsure how to end the encounter.

Gav, hands thrust deep into his pockets, shoulders rolled forward, eyes locked onto Vicky's face, tries desperately to convey his true feelings and judge whether she might reciprocate if he were to make a move.

But Vicky, feeling the intensity of his stare, turns her face away and looks down.

Gavin coughs into his closed fist. "Okay then. Thanks for the walk. See you soon?" he asks.

"Sure." Vicky shrugs. "I've got nothing on tomorrow. Fancy another walk?"

"Great," he replies. "See you tomorrow." Gav turns and heads back down the garden path, his heart lifting inside his chest.

On some level she must like me. But if I don't make a move soon, he thinks to himself, I'll end up in the friend-zone. And he definitely doesn't want to only be friends with Vicky.

He may not have known her long, but he can't stop thinking about her. He loves the way she unconsciously bites her bottom lip when she's concentrating really hard. Or how her blonde hair glistens in the weak winter sun. Or how she has the most ridiculous sneeze. She doesn't sneeze like a normal person. Her sneezes come in quick succession, multiple times over, building into a loud crescendo. Always ending in a very loud *ATCHOOOOOO...* leaving her looking dazed and ushering a quick apology, as if she can't quite believe her body's just made such a sound. It's endearing.

He can't remember the last time, if ever, he met a woman who has him equally intrigued by their very essence, whilst also sending him to bed holding his dick in his hand.

The next day the air bites as Vicky leads Gav up the steep path and through a carpet of pine needles. The frozen leaves crunch under their feet. They reach the top of the small knoll and Gav's heart skips a beat when the trees clear and reveal the vista beyond. The cold air burns at the back of his throat as he drinks in the view. A lone red kite swoops and hovers overhead. Its long, speckled wingtips spread out like fingers as it catches a thermal and flies away.

In front of them, nothing moves. The water of the Derwent Reservoir as still as a millpond, the afternoon light glistening off its surface as the sun dips low in the west. It'll be dark in a few hours, when the last rays slide behind the upper moors of Blanchland. A rural medieval village perched on the edge of the moors and named during the era when French was the official language of the UK

"You should see it in late summer." Vicky breaks the silence. "A carpet of purple heather as far as the eye can see. Very Cathy and Heathcliff."

"It's breathtaking," Gav replies. "Thank you for bringing me up here. I can see it's a special place. Reminds me of home."

"I've never been to Snowdonia, although I've always wanted to go."

"I'll take you." He pulls her gloved hand up to his lips and kisses the back of her fingers. Her eyes crinkle in their corners as she rolls her lips inwards, pressing them into a tight-lipped smile. "It's best to wait until spring though, otherwise Yr Wyddfa," Gav uses the Welsh word for Mount Snowdon, "likes to hide in the clouds."

"Have you climbed her?"

"Of course. I grew up looking out at her from my bedroom window."

"I know the tiny peaks of the Derwent valley can't quite compete, and I've personally had the privilege to travel all around the world and climb some of the most amazing peaks the world has to offer: Victoria Peak in Hong Kong, some of the best mountains in New Zealand; but there's something about this view." She places a hand over her heart. "It's in here. Home."

Gav turns and looks at her as she continues to gaze out over the reservoir.

"When I moved to London," she continues, "I thought it would be exciting. You know, bright lights, big city, but most of the time I felt like I was suffocating. I literally couldn't breathe."

Gav watches as she sucks air in through her nose, and her chest rises.

I wonder if it was the place or the person she was with who was suffocating her, he thinks to himself. Neither of them have divulged much more than headlines about their past relationships, but Gav suspects she's experienced a lot more heartache than she's told him.

"I know what you mean," he whispers, reaching for her hand to hold.

She returns the squeeze of his fingers. "Can I ask you a question?"

He turns to look at her.

"Was it you or her who ended your marriage?"

His eyes look in every direction, as if he's trying to find the right answer, before he mutters, "It was complicated."

"Isn't it always?"

"Technically I left, but only because she did something unforgivable."

Vicky's eyes stretch wide. "Really? I can't think of anything more unforgivable than my ex running off with a Thai bride."

"No!" Gav exclaims.

"Yes," Vicky replies in a matter-of-fact tone. "You couldn't make it up."

"Bloody hell. What the heck was he thinking?"

"Your guess is as good as mine. It made no sense at the time, and took me a long time to get over."

No wonder she's so guarded, Gav thinks to himself. And there was he thinking he'd been on the receiving end of the deepest betrayal one human could do to another.

<hr/>

Half an hour later they're back at Gavin's two-bed flat on the outskirts of town, furnished simply with two black leather sofas, a red rug in the middle of the lounge, and some black and white Ikea prints on the walls. Vicky is making herself comfortable in the living room while Gav knocks up a quick pasta dish in the tiny galley kitchen.

"Are you sure I can't help?" she hollers through to him.

"No, you're fine. There's not enough room to swing a cat in here."

"Why? Have you tried? Best not tell Leo." She chuckles.

"Put some music on. This won't be long."

Vicky dives for the cupboards underneath Gav's TV unit.

"You have quite an eclectic taste," she shouts, as she sifts through piles of CDs as diverse as Mozart, Haydn, Nigel Kennedy's recording of Vivaldi's Four Seasons, some Sam Cooke and Louis Armstrong, as well as albums from popular bands including Oasis, Green Day, and the Red Hot Chilli Peppers.

As it's her first time in Gav's bachelor pad, she continues riffling through his cupboards. Turning her attention to his film collection, she pauses when she reaches a particular DVD. Holding the red case in her hand, she walks through to the kitchen, hovering in the doorway. "Seriously?"

"Seriously what?" he muffles, the wooden spoon he's using to taste the sauce currently clamped between his lips.

"You own this?" She thrusts the DVD box out in front of her.

"That…" he uses the wooden spoon to point, "…second only to *The Shawshank Redemption,* is the best film ever made."

"You're kidding. *Moulin Rouge?*"

"What? Do you not like it?"

"Absolutely love it. Baz Luhrmann is a genius. I just don't think I've ever met a bloke who knows who he is, never mind loves his work. At least not a bloke from round here."

Gav raises an eyebrow and smirks.

"I once took my ex to the pictures to see Luhrmann's version of *Romeo and Juliet* when that first came out," she continues.

"Did he like it?"

"Hated it."

"Figures," Gav sniggers. "Yes, I have an eclectic taste. I like jazz and sometimes something classical. But I love *Moulin Rouge.* We should watch it together sometime."

Vicky rolls her eyes. "You can't be this perfect. There has to be something wrong with you."

"Does there? Can I not just be perfect," he replies, his eyes dancing with mischief.

"Which football team do you support?"

"Liverpool." He points to his oversized Liverpool coffee mug on the side.

"That's what's wrong with you." She wanders back into the living room, laughing to herself, as Gav's eyes track the gentle sway of her hips.

He lets out a long sigh.

After dinner they settle down on the sofa together, Elgar's "Salut d'Amour" playing softly in the background. The solo violinist lulling the pair of them into a state of relaxed comfort. Gav has lit the fire. Its soft flames illuminating their faces in profile.

Ever so slowly Gav reaches for Vicky's wine glass; lifting it out of her fingers he places it on the side table next to him. Turning back towards her he flicks her long blonde tresses back from her shoulders, looking deep into the green emeralds of her eyes, and rests his fingers on the curve in her neck where her throat meets her shoulder. The vintage necklace and solid gold orb she always wears stands proud from her décolletage. He traces the links of the gold chain around her neck and watches as she swallows hard.

"It was my grandfather's," she says, answering his unasked question.

"I've not seen you without it."

"It was his Masonic Orb. See, it opens." She pulls on a tiny lever at the back of the orb and it unfurls into a cross, the insides adorned with symbols and inscriptions. "I have no idea what any of it means, only that it means a lot to me. And this…" she points to the third finger of her right hand; a small pavé diamond ring, set to look like a delicate flower, "…was my granny's engagement ring. I like wearing them. It keeps them close." She looks up and meets his gaze once again. "It's why I've kept their surname: Fenwick. Some people couldn't understand why I didn't change back to Turnbull after my divorce, but I've never associated the surname Fenwick with Craig, even though I acquired it through my marriage to him. It was my maternal grandparents' name and I've always felt like that was the name I should have been born with. I can't really describe it. But it feels authentic."

"I never really knew my grandparents," Gav says, interlacing his fingers with hers, "but I wish you could have met my parents. They were amazing. My mother was strong. Feisty. Opinionated. Full of spirit. I see some of her in you. Whereas my father was a quiet man. Had the patience of a saint. This was his."

Gav slides off the signet ring he wears on the little finger of his left hand and passes it to her. She rolls the ring between her digits, admiring the engraving of the Welsh dragon on its top.

"I thought you wore it because of its Welshness."

"Well, that too. I've always identified with the spirit of the Red Dragon. History has not always been kind to us Welsh. Painting us as barbarians—always on the attack. Whereas if you look closely, the dragon is actually holding up his foot—in defence. He's actually a symbol of protection. Defending what is legitimately his. We're really a peaceful nation at heart. As long as you don't try and take what is rightfully ours. Then you'll meet the Dragon we all carry in our hearts."

"It's very you." She passes the ring back to him.

"Thanks. I like to think so." He slides it back on his finger. "Vicky," he says softly, his heart thumping so loud inside his chest he's convinced she must be able to hear it.

"U-hmmm."

"What are we doing?"

"What do you mean?"

"I mean, where is this going? I know you said you didn't have room in your life for anything complicated, but these past few weeks it kinda feels like things are getting more complicated. You must know I like you, and I think you like me, even if you don't want to admit it."

"Don't be silly. I wouldn't be here if I didn't enjoy hanging out with you. You're so easy to get on with."

He lets out a sigh. He knows she's deflecting.

"Yes but you know that's not what I mean. I like-like you. Not just like you… like I would a friend. I'd like to get to know *all* of you, you must realise that."

"I do," she breathes.

The air between them cackles with a palpable sexual tension, yet both of them remain reserved, holding each other's gaze, and Vicky watches as Gav's Adam's apple bobs in his throat.

Gav reaches up a hand and cups her jaw, and when she doesn't pull away, or change the subject, or try and make light of the situation by cracking a joke, he gently bends his head and kisses her. A slow, tender kiss. His lips moving gently, his tongue tracing the outline of her lips.

He hears her suck in a sharp intake of breath, her head lolling backwards, his hand taking its weight. She's surrendering to him. Finally letting go. It's the biggest turn-on and he goes hard instantly.

He deepens their kiss, using both hands now to cup her face, as she places her own hands over the top of his.

A slight moan escapes from deep within her at the moment their tongues meet. They remain locked together, their lips moving in unison, as she shuffles closer to him.

His arms slide around her back, pulling her into him, their torsos pressing against each other. If he could turn himself into a protective cloak to wrap around her, he would.

They remain like that for a long while, kissing and holding each other until eventually, pulling back from his kiss, she slides onto the floor in front of him, kneeling up, her eyes hooded with desire.

"What are you doing?" he whispers.

She ignores his question and silently undoes the buttons of her crisp white cotton shirt, peeling it from her body, holding it aloft before allowing it to fall to the floor.

Gav reaches for her, trying to pull her back onto his lap, but she untangles herself from his grip and, smiling brazenly, unclips her bra. Released from their confines, her smooth pale breasts jiggle gently as she purposefully sashays from side to side giving him a full frontal of her chest.

"Like what you see?" She opens her arms out to her sides and

ISABELLA WILES

shimmies her shoulders, making her breasts wobble like two mounds of jelly on a vertical plate.

Gav remains silent, drinking in the sight before him.

What the hell? He thinks to himself.

Of course he wants her, but this is not right.

She glides forward, her eyes cold and unfeeling as she straddles his lap. Sliding her hands inside his shirt, she peels it back over his shoulders. He winches as she digs her nails into the flesh of his chest, bending her head to lick the tip of his nipple.

Taking his hand, she guides his fingers over one of her hardened dusky pink rosebuds. His thumb touches her nipple and she throws her head back. "Oh god, yes," she moans.

But Gav freezes. "No, Vicky. Stop." He takes his hand away from her breast. "This is not what I want."

Her eyebrows pull together like a stitch. "But I thought you said you *like-liked* me. That you want to get to know all of me. Well, here I am."

"I do. But not like this. Stop, please."

She cocks her head to one side, trying to read him.

"Of course I want to take you to my bed, what full-blooded male wouldn't," Gav continues. "But not when you're putting on an act."

Her eyes glass over and her mouth twitches. Looking deeply into the green emerald pools of her irises, he searches for the truth. Her truth. When a single tear rolls unabated down her cheek, he tenderly wipes it away.

"I want the real you. The one you keep hidden."

The air between them hangs heavy, neither of them knowing what to say next.

"What on earth's happened to you, Angel? You don't have to hide your pain from me. You must know I'll never hurt you."

A little puff of air escapes from her nose, like a dog blowing away a seed that's tickling the inside of its nostril. "Don't say that to me, Gav. No one can promise that. You're no different from every other guy who's promised me the earth in order to take what they want, then run for the hills when the going gets tough. Well I'm not

42

falling for it again." She balls her hands into fists. "I refuse to fall for it again."

She tries to clamber off him, but he holds her still.

"I'm not bullshitting you, Vicky. I wouldn't know how, even if I wanted to. So don't bullshit me either. Your body is not a tool, yet you wear yours like a shield. Please don't mistreat it, and never use it to simply pleasure someone else. It's the vessel of your soul. There is so much more to you than this outer shell; I never want you to give yourself physically to me because you think you'll gain a modicum of affection, or validation, or whatever else you think *love is*, in return. Love cannot be earned, it must be given freely. Love is unconditional, not something you can tease out of me by showing me your body."

She wraps her arms around her torso, suddenly feeling more exposed than her mere nakedness, as if her skin is paper thin and he can see through her outer layers. Gav picks up her discarded shirt, returning her modesty. She shrugs into it, wrapping it around her body as if she were ice cold.

"I will never allow you to use your body as a weapon. At least not with me. I will not let you use sex to manipulate a situation. To manipulate me. Even in the short time we've known each other I know I want *you*, Vicky. More than I think you realise. But I will not take you like this."

"I think I should go." She rushes to gather up her things and makes her way out into the hallway.

"Let me take you home." Gav follows her.

"No it's okay. I'd rather call a cab." Her hand on the doorknob, she makes to leave, but Gav rushes up behind her, pressing his palms on the door above her head. The door slams shut. His weight leaning into her, holding her against the door, his breath hot in her ear. "Don't go. Please. I don't want you to leave," he whispers.

She turns to face him, her features contorted with pain. "I have to. You have to let me go. I can't give you want you want. Just let me go, Gav. Please."

"I don't think I can," he whispers, and as if to prove his point, he bends and kisses her—tenderly, and a tiny tear leaks out of the corner of her eye. Fighting her own internal turmoil, she relents and wraps her arms around his neck and kisses him back.

And in that moment, Gav feels a tiny crack break open in the stone she has wrapped around her heart. He knows he may have a long way to go yet before she'll open herself fully to him, but as they hold onto each other, both of them sucking air in urgently through their nostrils as their passion rises, she feels more real to him in that moment than any woman he's ever been with before.

Chapter 6

VICTORIA

1 week later, Saturday 24th January 2004

"Josh, man. Be careful will ya," Becca hollers after her rambunctious three-year-old who, having flown off the end of the kiddies' slide, is now charging through the snow towards the opposite side of the play park. "I swear that kid will be the death of me. Never listens, just like his bloody father."

Nessa and I exchange a look.

"You go. I can look after Livy." I take hold of Becca's pram, pushing it back and forth on the spot, encouraging her baby daughter, Olivia, who's neatly tucked up inside like a perfectly wrapped Christmas present, to remain in the land of nod.

"Thanks." Becca tramps off at a brisk march in the direction of her fearless son, her short legs sinking into the virgin snow almost up to her knees.

"Hi-yer, hi-yer," Emily, Nessa's daughter, squeals in her best attempts to communicate her demands. I push her higher on the swing, continuing to rock the angelic sleeping bairn in the pram beside me with my other hand.

"Me hi-yer." Ethan copies his sister, kicking his little legs as he demands his mother do the same for him. I suppose when you're a twin, everything is a competition.

"You okay, Becks?" I shout, laughing at the adult backside fast disappearing inside a crawl-through tunnel on the far side of the park.

"Yes, thank you," comes the sarcastic reply. "Just be grateful you don't have any rug rats, Tor. No one warns you how much the little shits ruin your bloody life."

Nessa looks at me and we share an eyeroll. We both know Becca doesn't mean it, even if she has been dealt a bit of a crap hand of late.

Having twins by IVF was no walk in the park for Nessa and Anth, but having two kids only three years apart, as is the case for Becca and Mark, is no joyride either. Especially when you consider that Mark, Becca's kind-hearted fiancé, is somewhat domestically challenged. His reluctance to give up his hobbies as a semi-professional bodybuilder and football fanatic have not helped Becca. Throw in a mother fighting breast cancer, and a small hairdressing business to run. Yup, it's fair to say Becca has a lot on her plate at the moment.

"You're a natural." Nessa nods at my impressive multitasking skills. "You know you can't put it off too much longer. Your eggs won't stay fresh forever."

"Oh, I think that ship's long since sailed."

Nessa jerks her head back. "I wouldn't quite say that. But you and I both know that once you reach our age, time isn't on your side anymore. All I am saying is if it's something you think you might want, you can't put it off forever."

"Firstly," I straighten up and adopt a business-like tone, "there's the matter of who would provide the sperm. Only seahorses, starfish, and some weird Amazonian lizard can reproduce on their own. Last time I checked I don't think I'm a seahorse."

"Gee-horse, gee-horse," Emily squeals; her podgy legs, encased in her bright pink snow suit, kick and wriggle as I push her as high as the swing will go.

"And secondly, I'm not sure I do want kids. Not now. If Craig and I had worked out, then yes, maybe. Before we married we floated the idea of having a baby, but I gave that dream up when he left me. The truth is I've worked too damn hard to put my life back together; I'm buggered if I'm going to let anyone or anything screw it all up again."

"And by anyone or anything, do you mean a man, or a baby?"

"Both." I give my head a flick, realising that's something I've just decided as of now. "The other thing no one tells you is, how great it is being everyone's favourite *Aunty Tor*. I get to do all the fun stuff with your kids, then hand the little darlings back. My house isn't—no disrespect—littered with plastic toys and kiddie paraphernalia, and Nessa, I know I haven't said this to you before, but the height of your ironing basket makes me want to cry. No, I love your two, as much as I love Becca's bairns, but I also love going home and sleeping a solid eight hours every night."

"God, I can't even remember what that's like," Nessa sighs.

I flash her a concerned look, noticing the permanent bags under her eyes that weren't there eighteen months ago. "How's it going… really? Now you're back at work and everything. How are you managing?"

Nessa took a full year off to be with her twins. Handling one newborn is hard enough, but I have no idea how she managed the sleep deprivation of two tiny terrors.

"I've got a few months left of my phased return, so while I'm only doing three days a week… it's okay. But I'm not looking forward to going back full-time. To be honest I wish I could give up completely. I know this past year has been full-on, but I've loved every minute of it. I hate the thought of missing out on so much. They'll only be this little once. But you know," she shrugs, "we need the money."

Nessa's never actually told me how much they spent on their multiple rounds of IVF, in fact they never let on that they were struggling to conceive at all until she was well into her second trimester with Ethan and Emily. However, their grand plans for a kitchen extension and a master suite over their garage all came to a grinding halt the year they were trying to get pregnant.

"Maybe in a few years if Anth's career keeps going the way it's looking, then maybe you can give up work. Either that or go part-time."

"That's what I'm hoping for. I mean, why have kids only to have someone else raise them. I wish I could stay home all the time. But needs must." She smiles, resigned. "But less about me." She gives me a wry smile. "How's it going with Mr Silent-but-sexy? You've kept a very low profile since New Year."

I roll my eyes. I have no idea whether Nessa is fishing for my side of the story to compare notes with what Gav might have told Anth at work, or whether she's genuinely in the dark.

"It isn't," I say blankly.

She raises a suspicious eyebrow. "Really?"

"Well, we've met up a couple of times. He's a nice guy…"

"And?" she interrupts.

"And nothing. I did agree to meet him again initially, but only so I could give him his beanie back."

I don't add that I also used the opportunity to remind myself of what he looked like. I internally slap myself for *that* faux pas. Serves me right for drinking far too much at New Year and snogging a man whose face I couldn't recall in the cold light of day.

"I suggested we go down the town for a drink," I continue. "Thinking it would be less intimate than a cosy dinner for two… I didn't want to give him the wrong impression, but he's like a fish out of water in loud spaces. After that, I felt sorry for him. He's new to the area and doesn't know his way around, which is why I suggested we go for a walk last weekend, which led to lunch at the Derwent Walk Inn—I was hungry." I give her a sideways glance, answering her accusatory snort. "He's easy to talk to and we have lots in common. He's also divorced, remember. Then on Sunday we went up Pow Hill, by the reservoir. But that's it. Like I said, he's a nice guy. Easy to talk to. We get on."

The squeak-squeak of the swings punctuates the freezing air as I wait for Nessa to either drop the subject or push me further. I wish I knew what she might have heard from Anth.

As I suspected, she's not satisfied with my explanation. "And?" she presses.

"And what?" I turn and glare at her. "There's nothing more to say. Honestly. I wouldn't even call us friends. Friend*ly* maybe."

My mind flits back to our passionate embrace last Sunday evening as I tried to leave. Our first since the protracted New Year's Eve make-out sesh. His body pressed up against mine, hot and wanting, and how—in that moment—I'd succumbed to my own primal desires. The flames inside me, licking up the inside of my gut. It had taken a mountain of willpower to pull back from *that* kiss, but eventually I'd had to. Peeling myself off his lips had been physically painful, but if I hadn't, I know I would have slept with him.

Ever the gentleman, once we'd regained our composure, he'd taken me home, with a promise to text me later in the week.

"Don't believe you." Nessa smirks, observing every micro emotion that trips across my face as I recall how it had felt when he kissed me. A part of me *really* wants to sleep with him. To feel the weight of his body on top of mine. To feel the heat of our bare skin touching; to feel him move inside me. But I know I can't let myself go there. If I do, I already know he's the kind of guy who could penetrate my walls, and I simply can't let that happen.

I suck in a cold breath to calm my inner desires, my exhalation blowing a cloud of condensation into the frosty air.

"Go on then, what have you heard?" I glare at Nessa.

"Oh, I don't know." She turns back to look over at the snow-covered trees on the far side of the park. I suspect to avoid my accusatory stare. "Only that *friends* don't accept invitations to go round to other friends' flats for something to eat, if they're only being *friendly*." She uses air quotes to emphasise the word 'friendly'.

"Of course they do."

"Not friends of the opposite sex who really *like-like* each other."

I turn sharply and walk slap bang into her smirk. She laid the trap and I fell right into it.

"Oh come on. Who are you kidding? It was obvious how much you were both into each other on New Year's Eve."

"That meant nothing. A drunken snog at the stroke of midnight."

"Well I've never had a snog that went on until four in the morning. Like Becca said, we all thought you were going to have sex with him, right there and then, on my sofa." She giggles at the memory. "So when you seeing him next?"

"I'm not."

"You can *not* be serious?"

I think back to the daily messages he's sent me since Sunday, urging me to fix another date, but I've cited commitments at work as the reason I've brushed him off. I'm not completely lying, I have had to work late every night this week, polishing and practising the multimillion-pound tender I'm due to present next week.

"I just don't have the time or energy for anything complicated right now," I repeat my mantra to Nessa.

The more I keep saying it, the more it will be true.

"That's utter bollocks and you know it."

Before I'm able to offer a retort, Joshua comes running towards us, Becca in his wake. "My turn, my turn," he chants, grabbing the other empty swing seat.

Becca lifts him into it and pushes him. "What's utter bollocks?" she asks.

"This one 'ere." Nessa jerks her head in my direction. "Only blowing off Mr Silent-but-sexy just because he like-likes her and pretending it's because she doesn't have room in her life for *anything complicated right now.*"

"Damn right." Becca nods her head in agreement. "I'd do the same if I were her."

"What the actual f—?"

"Not in front of the kids," Becca cuts Nessa off, covering Josh's ears with her mittened hands, a giggle in her tone.

The red ringlets that tumble out from underneath Nessa's hat swish in the air as she flicks her gaze back and forth between Becca, myself, then back to Becca again, like an umpire in a tennis match. "Am I the only sane one here? For the first time in years Tor's finally met what appears to be a half-decent bloke, who also happens to live on her doorstep." Nessa makes an indirect reference to my relationship with Chris which took me as far away as New Zealand and back again. "And you agree with her? You think she should blow him off?"

"Well I'm sure he'd enjoy that," Becca says, a conspiratorial look passing between us as I smirk silently, allowing the girls to continue the battle over my love life. As long as they keep me out of it.

"What the heck am I missing? Has he got a third nipple or something?" Nessa adds.

Becca shrugs. "I'm sure he's a canny bloke, but look at her." She points in my direction. "Miss Independent. Goes where she wants, when she wants, and with who she wants. She's got her shit together. Whereas look at us two…" Becca sweeps her hand over the top of the three bairns's heads, all swinging happily back and forth in front of us. "You're lumbered with one-year-old twins that take up every waking moment of your life, and I have a terror of a three-year-old that has me run ragged, and let's not forget the sleeping baby who will wake up any minute now and morph into a boob-demanding demon. Remember the crazy skiing holidays we all used to take together? Or the all-day drinking sessions in The Red Lion? You can't tell me you don't miss them."

"Not at all." Nessa smiles, ever the serene earth mother. "Sure it's a lot of work, but I'm happier now than I ever thought possible. I have everything I ever wanted and everything I didn't know I needed. I'll take the mess, the carnage, and the lack of sleep, for the joy, the laughter, and the love my ready-made family gives me. I wouldn't change a thing."

Becca and Nessa continue to argue over the pros and cons of family life. I ignore them. I refuse to be drawn into their heated discussion. Despite the tingles I felt when Gav kissed me, or the warm glow that spreads through my gut when I remember how the corners of his mouth pull into a dimple-revealing smile... I simply can't fall in love again.

Not now.

Not ever.

Even if I wanted to, I don't think I'm capable anymore. I've had two great loves in my life, even if neither of them were destined to be everlasting. Some people never have one. I'm truly grateful to both Chris and Craig and the relationships we had. The healing I was forced to go through as a result of those breakups—which forced me to look inward and truly heal my insecurities and co-dependant traits—is what has made me into the strong, independent woman I am today. Right now, my career is soaring. I'm financially secure. I live in a beautiful home, and most importantly, I love being me.

I don't need a man to give me anything I can't give myself.

Despite my base primal urges, why would I jeopardise all that simply to feel a few flutters in my gut every now and then?

A long-held memory surfaces from the back of my brain. A shared moment between myself and my good friend Tim, the morning after his Halloween party in London, over a decade ago.

'Fairy-tale endings only ever happen in, well... fairy tales. People are flawed and selfish', he'd said, tearing into his croissant. 'They let you down and only meet your needs when they've met their own. So why give them that chance? Love is a temporary emotional state and is not something upon which to build a life. It is fleeting. It will come and it will go, so my advice is stop putting your life on hold for someone else. Go after what you want. Money, security, career, hard work, those are the things you have within your control. Not some flimsy whimsical fleeting emotions stirred up by some hunky knight who arrived from a distant shore.'

Nessa turns to face me. "Well I think you're bonkers to push Gav away. I think he's just what the doctor ordered and you should give the poor bloke a chance. What have you got to lose? Nowt, in my opinion. I know you've got your work, and stuff. But what happens when you get older? You don't want to be known as the crazy old cat lady now, do you?"

"I don't agree." Becca raises her index finger in protest. "Your divorce was the making of you, and if you tie yourself down again, think of all the sacrifices you'll be forced to make. I think you should cut him loose, before he *really like-likes* you. Wouldn't you rather break things off gently than have to do it later when he's in a lot deeper? You of all people know what it feels like to love someone who doesn't love you back. You'd have to be really selfish to do that to the poor bloke."

I don't answer immediately, and instead focus my attention on my godchild in the swing seat in front of me. She's showing no signs of boredom or wanting to come out. So I carry on pushing her with one hand, while I rock Livy's pram with my other.

Eventually, I announce, "I agree, Becca. I think that's the kindest option. Especially when he works with Anth. You all remember how awkward it was when Craig and I split up. In the end it was a blessing when he moved to Asia."

Nessa shakes her head and lifts Ethan out of the bucket swing. "I think it's time we head back. These two must be getting hungry, and Livy's due a feed. If you don't wake her up soon Becca, you know she'll have you up all night."

"Come on little lady." I lift Emily out of her seat and settle her on my hip. "You heard your mammy."

As I buckle myself into the passenger seat of Nessa's car, the atmosphere is still stony between us. Clearly Nessa doesn't agree with my decision.

"I know you think I'm mad Ness, but I really think it's for the best. I don't want to cause him, or myself, any future heartache. And I guarantee it will only end in tears. It always does with me. And let's face it, you've got too much on your plate with these two to have to put me back together again, like you've always done in the past. You're lucky. You and Anth have been together since the first week of Freshers'. But I came to the realisation a long time ago, at least for me, love is not permanent. And I'm simply not prepared to

ISABELLA WILES

sacrifice myself anymore for maybe a few weeks, or even years, of loved-up-ness. Is that even a word?" I squeeze her knee, and she places her hand over mine and squeezes it back.

She gets it, however as she puts the car into gear and pulls away, my gut flips over like a snake.

I know I'm right, but it doesn't make cutting Gav loose any easier. A part of me has enjoyed his easy company these past few weeks. Another part of me also enjoyed the feeling of his breath hot against my neck, and his intoxicating masculinity when he slammed the door shut and pressed his body up against mine. And I know that wasn't just lust. It was something more. Something I thought had long since died.

And, if I'm honest, that thought absolutely terrifies me.

Chapter 7

"There's a call for you on line one," our office receptionist says down the telephone, the following Tuesday.

I glance at my watch, swivelling my chair and tearing my gaze away from the magnificent view up towards Grey's Monument as I spin back towards my desk. No matter how glum the weather, the beautiful Georgian architecture that curves and rises up Grainger Street, so named after the famed architect who envisioned this part of the city, never fails to inspire me.

"I haven't really got time, Cathy. Can you take a message?" I say into the handset.

"I can if you want, but he says he's calling from Hong Kong."

I let out an involuntary yelp of delight. I only know one person in Hong Kong.

"Put him through."

I hear the click on the line as Cathy presses the relevant buttons on her switchboard to connect the call.

"Well, well. Hello stranger. I trust you've been keeping yourself out of mischief now that I'm too far away to keep my eyes on you," the smooth velvet voice on the other end of the line drawls after I've said "Hello."

"Tim! Oh my God, how the devil are you?"

"Good. You?"

"Amazing. But look, I can't really talk."

My PA raps her knuckles against the doorframe to my office and mouths, "They're ready for you in the boardroom."

"Thanks. I'm coming now," I mouth back. "Tim, I've got a really big pitch I'm about to deliver. Can I call you later?"

"Since when was I relegated to second division? There was a time when you would move heaven and earth to speak to me."

Tim is one of my oldest friends, from my time living in Wootton Bassett when he was a bright but low-ranking accountant. Now he runs half the world for a global investment bank and he's rarely in one country long enough to catch up.

"Tim, you know I love you, but I've got clients waiting in the boardroom."

"All right, I get it. I'm no longer *that* important. But I only called to see if you might be around the weekend of the 20th March? I'm in London and I've got tickets for the England - Wales match at Twickenham. Well, when I say tickets, obviously I mean a box."

I quickly flip through my Filofax.

"Oh, that would be brilliant. I'm putting it in my diary now. I haven't seen you in so long, it'll be fab to catch up."

"Great, I'll fax you the details."

"Or you could email them to my work."

"You're on email now? My, my, we are moving up in the world aren't we," he says, teasing me as he always does. Tim is the older brother I never had. Someone who simultaneously pulls your pigtails whilst giving you a wedgie, then in the next breath decks a bully on your behalf.

I catch my PA's eyes as she glares at me and taps her watch with her index finger.

"Tim I *really* have to go, but stay on the line, Cathy will give you my email address. Bye for now. Looking forward to seeing you soon."

"Bye darling. And good luck with the pitch. Love you," he says in a throw away manner as I push the call back to reception with instructions to pass on my details.

"I'm coming," I say to my PA, who has now positioned herself in the doorframe to my office, her stress palpable.

Deep breath, I say to myself as I gather up my papers and turn my mind back to the job in hand. Our potential clients have flown up from London specifically to hear my presentation today. We're pitching for the whole of their business covering all of Europe, the Middle-East, and Africa, or what's known in the business world as EMEA, and they've never given that amount of work to an agency outside of London before. I know we're down to the last two in the tendering process, so I need to convince them we have the talent and the team capable of delivering their objectives, despite being in the provinces. I'm determined to show them we can deliver a far superior service at a more affordable price, and that being outside the capital is actually a competitive advantage.

We're winning this business today, no question.

"Ah, here she is. Our rising star." My managing director stands as I enter the glass-boxed boardroom. I smile and shake hands with all the suited occupants of the room.

"I know you're going to be bowled over with what Victoria has to share with you today," my MD continues.

"Gentlemen," I say, nodding at each of their faces in turn. "Shall we get started?"

Two hours later I'm virtually skipping back through reception. I knew we'd win. I could feel it in the ether while I was doing my wake-up yoga flow this morning. Something was fizzing in the air around me. And I was right. Even though it will take a further twenty-four hours to finalise the paperwork, we closed the meeting with warm handshakes and terms verbally agreed.

'Now the real work starts…' my MD's parting words as we waved the clients off into the lift.

As I walk back towards my office, I stop in my tracks and pause.

Covering my desk, and all the papers beneath it, is a stunning bouquet of roses, their colours as dramatic as a Caribbean sunset.

I bite my lip as I open the card.

Vicky,

Good luck today. I know you'll be amazing, and even if you don't want to see me again, I want you to know I'm thinking about you, and also to say thank you for making me feel so welcomed to your region.

Speak soon (hopefully)

Love Gav

xxx

Despite what I said to the girls last weekend, I haven't officially broken things off with Gav, I literally haven't had time, but it has been ten days now since we last spoke. I've deliberately been slower to respond to all his messages, and I've ignored any incoming calls. It seems he's taken the hint, so I'm surprised how disappointed I feel now that my attempts to shrug him off appear to have landed.

Hugging the bouquet to my chest, inhaling the sweet perfume of the perfectly ripe buds, I swivel my chair to look back out at the view. I roll his card over and over in my hand. As if rolling it between my fingers might help organise the turmoil of emotions that are whirring around my gut, like loose change that's come free from a jeans pocket inside a tumble dryer.

'...you'll be amazing, and even if you don't want to see me again, I wanted you to know that I'm thinking about you...'

His message today is so similar to the very first one he sent me:

'Do you want to meet up for a coffee? Or if you don't want to that's okay as well.'

Expectant. Hopeful. But without making any demands or setting any expectations of me.

'*Speak soon (hopefully),*' the brackets like an afterthought, as if although he would like to speak to or see me again, he'll also be okay if I don't want to.

This guy is emotionally sorted. Whatever his relationship past, I get the feeling he doesn't need to be one half of a couple in order to define himself, or to plug an emotional gap in his life.

Looking back over my previous relationships, the big loves of Chris and Craig as well as the smaller ones of Jeremy and Steve before them, I've always ended up morphing myself into the person I believed I needed to be, in order to make the relationship work.

I never found a way to be both authentic and in love.

But maybe that was because I was attracted to men who also had the same insecurities and hidden pain that I didn't know I was harbouring. And if that's the case, then is it possible that Gavin is also a reflection of who I am now?

He doesn't *need* to be in love, or in a relationship, in order to feel good about himself.

But that doesn't appear to stop him wanting to be with me either.

Or he could be just another wanker who's playing it cool and I'm in danger of falling for the same old shit all over again, and I won't realise that my world has fallen off its axis until I'm trying to drive off into the night, pissed out of my head, with a wine bottle clamped between my knees.

No, I vowed I would *never* allow a man to make me feel that low again. I hit the bottom of the barrel, then fell through it to an even deeper, darker place that I never want to visit ever again.

I get up and walk over to reception.

Cathy looks up. Her features all-knowing.

"Cathy, could you find a vase for these? I'm sure they'll look lovely on the corner of your desk."

I turn away from her crestfallen face, but when I get back to my office I tuck Gav's card inside the inner sleeve of my Filofax.

The next day, I receive another bouquet. This time the card reads:

Vicky,
I'm still thinking about you and have a feeling I
will be for a long time yet.
The Moulin Rouge invitation still stands.
Dav x

I ask Cathy to find another vase and she places this bouquet on the opposite side of the desk.

The day after that, the contracts with our new client are officially signed, and to celebrate of the largest account our firm has ever landed, my MD takes everyone involved in the bid out for a long lunch. When I return there's yet another bouquet waiting for me on my desk, and this one is accompanied by a gift-wrapped box. I inhale the pungent scent from the flowers, before pulling on the ribbon and lifting off the lid of the gift box. Inside is a stunning Villeroy and Boch crystal vase, together with a note:

Vicky,
Even if you never speak to me again, I thought
you might want to start your own tradition.
Your very own bowl to make your own pot pourri
and remind you of how much I like-liked you.
In fact, still like-like you.
Dav x

My heart stops, I'll admit. He doesn't give up easily, but then neither did Craig, or Chris before that. They both made their intentions clear, pursuing me until I gave in. Craig using his cool swagger and street-smarts to win me over, and Chris unleashing a heat in my body I'd never felt before. Both of them finding a weakness in my armour that elicited unguarded responses from me that became so addictive, I would do anything to chase that continued high.

It's only now when I reflect back that I realise it wasn't only the men I was in love with; they became the conduits for me to access deeper parts of myself. Parts of me that I was only able to reach if they unlocked and then held the door open for me. However, somehow in the process of allowing them in, I handed them the keys to that door. So when they withdrew their love, both figuratively and literally, I was distraught. Without them feeding my emotional needs, I had no way back to myself.

But that was then and this is now. And for the first time in my life—I feel whole. I no longer need a man to love me in order to love myself.

What if falling in love again—with anyone—means I fall out of love with myself? I never found a way to be simultaneously in love with myself and in love with someone else. I've always had to sacrifice myself in order to let love in, and no matter how good if felt at the beginning, it hurt twice as much in the end.

I ball my hands into fists and screw my eyes tight shut. I've fought too damn hard to get to where I am to let that happen again.

I won't allow it.

I simply won't.

I can't fall for him.

I pick up the bouquet. Cathy sees me walking towards her, her view partially obscured by the two enormous bouquets already on either side of her desk.

She stands up as I approach, halting me with her raised palm. "No way. No more. It's a good job I don't have hay fever. I can hardly see who's coming out of the lift as it is."

"Aww, but don't you think they look nice? I'm sure all our clients appreciate the colourful greeting. Reiterates the fact we give them the five-star treatment."

"Which is clearly what this guy wants to do for you." She glares back at me, her eyes stretched wide. "I have no idea what's going on in your private life, Victoria. Just call the poor soul, will you?

Please," she adds a beat later. "I don't know what you've done to deserve a bouquet of flowers every day this week, but I don't have any more room on my desk for your castoffs. My Eddie...God rest his soul," she makes the sign off the cross, touching her forehead, sternum, then each side of her ample bosom, "was anything but perfect, but then who is? However, he always said, '*Judge a man by his deeds not his words*' and based on this guy's behaviour I'd say he's a doer, not a bullshitter. And in my experience they're as rare as rocking horse shite. Whatever he's done, or not done as the case may be, I say... hang onto him."

She meets my gaze with a hard stare. "Or at least call the poor bugger and put him out of his misery."

"It's a bit more complicated than that, Cathy."

"It's only complicated if you make it complicated. Don't look for problems where they don't exist. This guy, whoever he is, must really like you. Why else would he go to all this effort?"

"Or in his case, like-likes me."

She tilts her head. Cathy, the unofficial mother hen of our office, takes her maternal role over all her baby hens very seriously. "Then what the heck are you playing at?"

I suck in a deep breath. "Actually Cathy, I think you're right. Can you make an international call for me, please? I need to talk to someone in Hong Kong."

She frowns. "These are from the guy who called the other day?"

"No, these are not from him, but I want to ask that *friend* a question."

She removes her glasses and knits her brows even tighter together.

"I simply want to ask if I can bring a plus one to the rugby in a few weeks' time."

She sits back down and begins to punch out Tim's number.

"And can you pass me those scissors please?"

Without overthinking it, I snip off the two most perfect rose heads, one from each bouquet, and carry the two single roses, together with today's bouquet, back to my office. I drop the clipped rose heads into the crystal bowl and set it in pride of place on my windowsill. From now on, I can enjoy the view outside my window and the one inside as well.

Still gazing out at the beautiful architecture I pick up my mobile and, before I can talk myself out of it, send Gav a string of quick texts:

> What can I say? The flowers are beautiful and it was extremely thoughtful of you, thank you
>
> We won the contract, so ...whoopee.
>
> Fancy helping me celebrate? Saturday night, Moulin Rouge? My turn to cook. Vicky x

I'm still terrified of all the *what-ifs,* but I agree with Cathy. I should be judging Gav's actions, and thus far he's acted like a true gentleman. Had I paid closer attention to the actions of my previous lovers, rather than hang my heart on their tirade of empty promises, perhaps I could have saved myself a tonne of heartache.

I'm still not sure I'm ready for a new relationship, and I'm definitely not ready to fall in love again, but I am prepared to give him some slack and see where this goes.

I mean, what could possibly go wrong?

Part II

Chapter 8

GAVIN

7 weeks later, Friday 19th March 2004

*G*av's eyes track the illuminated streetlights, the black expanse of green fields replaced by the dim glow of the city, as the train travels through the sprawling outer suburbs of London. Beside him Vicky gathers up her things as the train guard announces their imminent arrival at King's Cross.

"So, Tim?" Gav raises a quizzical eyebrow. "You sure you've never been more than *just good friends?*"

It wouldn't bother me if they had, Gav thinks to himself. I'd just rather know before I shake hands with the guy. There's a lot you need to communicate in that first handshake. Does it need to be a simple 'Hi, nice to meet you, thanks for your hospitality', or do I also need to communicate a subtle warning, a 'Whatever's happened in the past, she's with me now and I need you to respect that.'

"No, never." Vicky shakes her head before draining the dregs from her water bottle. "We're more like siblings. Constantly bickering, taking the piss out of each other. He can come across a bit full of his own self-importance sometimes, but that's just him. Despite his constant teasing he's one of the few people who's always come through for me. He once gave me a rent-free roof over my head when I was almost made homeless, and he looked after me when my marriage was turning to shit. He invited me to join him in Grand Cayman for a bit of respite. At the time, it was just what the doctor ordered. He never liked Craig, and it turns out his hunches were right. One of my only regrets in life is that when I was dating Chris, I allowed our friendship to wane."

"Why would you do that?"

Vicky lets out a long sigh and shakes her head. "Because Chris was insanely jealous. He never trusted Tim."

"U-hmmm." Gav's disapproving tone says everything he needs to communicate regarding Chris's previous cohesive hold over his girlfriend. He knows he will never be like that. If she says there's nothing romantic between her and Tim, then that's enough for him; even if he still intends to greet this *Tim* with a strong grip and a firm handshake.

Best to be clear, he thinks to himself.

"I know. You don't have to say it. Just another example of the shit sacrifices for the previous men in my life." She turns away and looks wistfully out of the train window at the distinct yellow-grey London brick as the arches of King's Cross come into view.

"Don't beat yourself up. Hindsight is a wonderful thing my angel. All part of growing up."

She turns back to look at him and the look in her eye makes Gav's heart expand inside his chest. He has so much love to give this woman, and like an empty well he wants to fill her up to overflowing, but despite her outward bravado and career success, she's so fragile it's like holding a damaged bird in his palm. If he's too heavy-handed with his emotions he could crush her, and he never wants to hurt her. Of that he is certain.

Gav holds out his hand to help her up as the train jolts to a final stop. "Well I'm very pleased you've rekindled your friendship, and I intend to take full advantage of his generous hospitality." Gav kisses his closed fist, then double taps the Welsh crest on his rugby shirt.

꙳

The next afternoon Vicky and Gav head down to Twickenham Stadium and Tim welcomes them into his corporate box with a warm smile and a glass of cold champagne.

"You're positively radiant." Tim smiles affectionately at Vicky. She dips her head and blushes at the compliment. Turning to Gav, a broad smile on his face, Tim adds, "So this is him…" leaving Gav to wonder what Vicky has told Tim about him.

"Apparently it is, Gav replies, mirroring Tim's upbeat tone. "It was very generous of you to include me in your invitation."

"Not at all; as soon as Victoria told me you were Welsh, how could I not? I thought you'd enjoy watching your side get properly thumped by our Lions," Tim laughs.

Vicky mouths an *excuse me* and backs away, whether to greet someone else she knows, or to allow Tim to give him the once-over without her being there, Gav's not sure. But he gives her a wink and a warm smile, before turning back to face Tim head on, squaring his shoulders. It's not just the two rugby teams that are about to go head-to-head.

"It's true this England side are a strong team, but it's not a foregone conclusion by any stretch," Gav counters.

Gav needs Tim to know that, despite Tim's longstanding friendship with Vicky, she has him to lean on as well now, and Tim needn't worry about her.

"Well, may the best team win." Tim raises his glass.

He's got the message.

"Here, here." Gav chinks his glass against Tim's as both men turn their gaze out over the pitch. Their eyes tracking each team as they warm up. The English in their all-white home kit, their shirts embossed with the red English rose, which contrast against the blood-red of the Welsh squad's tops, their shirts embossed with the Prince of Wales plumes across their hearts. The noise is deafening as the English fans sing "Swing Low, Sweet Chariot" at the top of their voices, while the Welsh counter equally loudly with "Bread of Heaven."

"I am glad you came today, I always like to vet the men in Victoria's life," Tim says. "She hasn't always made the best choices. In fact her choices thus far have been atrocious."

"Thanks. I think?"

"Oh, it is a compliment. From what she's told me, you seem different from the rest. But we'll see…"

Gav takes a slow sip from his drink. He knows Vicky's loyal to this guy, and that he's always looked out for her, but he can't work out whether it's genuine concern or possessiveness behind Tim's passive aggression.

Gav straightens up and raises his jaw just a smidgeon.

"Tim, I know you've known Vicky a lot longer than I have. And you've always been there for her, especially when all her previous relationships have turned sour, so I get why you want to make sure she's okay. But I assure you, she's safe with me. In fact I'm mad for her, and intend to spend the rest of my life making sure nothing bad happens to her. To us. I'm in this for the long haul. And we don't need a guardian inserting themselves where it's not needed."

Tim nods gently. "Glad to hear it. You're right, I do have a soft spot for her, and I'm so damn proud of what she's achieved and the woman she's become. Forgive my cynicism. I just don't want anyone to fuck it up for her… again. She's special, that one."

"You're right, she is."

Right on cue, Vicky comes bouncing back into the conversation.

"Gav, can I introduce you to Corrine, and her husband Peter."

Gav smiles at each of the strangers in turn, shaking the hands that are offered.

"We haven't seen each other since we were all in the Caymans, back in '96," Vicky adds.

"Gosh is it that long ago?" Corrine says. "I remember you were pining for your husband. Wasn't he in Asia or something?" Corrine takes a small step forward and locks eyes with Gav. "It's nice to finally meet him."

Gav almost chokes on his drink, amused, and Vicky draws in a sharp breath. "Err, no. This is definitely *not* my husband, but that's a story for another day. Suffice to say, Craig and I went our separate ways. This is Gavin Williams, my boyfriend."

Vicky's comment catches Gav by surprise and his heart flutters inside his chest. It's the first time she's publicly acknowledged him as her boyfriend, and in response he unconsciously puffs out his chest.

"Trust me to stick my foot in it. Oh, I'm so sorry," Corrine says.

"Don't be. You weren't to know," Gav says magnanimously.

Corrine smiles, then points at Vicky's right wrist. "I see you're still wearing it."

"Never taken it off. Not since the day I bought it."

Vicky lifts her arm, giving everyone a closer look at the bracelet wrapped around her wrist. Its diamonds sparkling in the light.

"It always did look better on you than me."

"Corrine was with me the day I bought this," Vicky explains to the men. "We'd been on a dive, then went shopping afterwards."

"To celebrate you surviving, I seem to remember," Corrine laughs, then says to Gav, "We thought she'd drowned. Completely lost her for a time. It was terrifying. Then as quickly as she'd disappeared, she reappeared over the top of The Wall. Bright as day as if nothing had happened."

Gavin recognises the reference to the famous Cayman Wall, a vertical shelf of coral off the north shore of Grand Cayman that plunges down into the depths of the Cayman Trench.

Vicky looks down at her shoes. "Yup. I'll never forget that day."

Gav suspects there's more to this story than Vicky's letting on, but before he has chance to quiz her further Tim indicates it's time for everyone to take their seats. Everyone shuffles their way outside just as an enormous roar erupts from the crowd and reverberates around the stadium, the referee having pulled the two team captains together for the coin toss.

Just as Vicky is about to take her seat next to him, Gav hears Tim whisper in her ear, "I like him."

Not that he needs Tim's endorsement, but Gav can't deny the warm feeling that spreads through his gut knowing he's gained Tim's approval.

Having supported Wales all his life, Gav has never missed a game that was televised, but this is the first time he's had the opportunity to see them play live, and nothing could have prepared him for the experience of watching his beloved national team battle it out in front of a packed stadium. The crowd collectively jeer, groan, and audibly suck air into their lungs at every pass, penalty, and drop kick. Each team attacks the other with a gladiatorial force. The sound of raw flesh slamming into one another thuds around the arena. It's a brutal match. After an early lead from England, Wales gallantly fight back, but at half-time the score remains 16-9 to England.

"See, I told you we'd give you a right good thumping," Tim says, topping up everyone's glasses.

"It's not over yet, Tim. I know my Welsh boys will come back fighting."

"Oh, who cares?" Vicky says, holding out her glass for Tim to refill.

"Are you kidding me?" Tim says. "My darling Victoria…"

Gav feels his hackles bristle again at Tim's over-familiarity.

Unaware, Tim continues, "Don't you realise sport is the only arena left where us men can take the very best specimens of our species and set them against each other in a battle for our fragile egos. It's basically legalised warfare."

"That sounds about right," Vicky says matter-of-factly.

"Why do men always have to be so competitive?" she continues. "Does it really matter who wins?"

Both men almost choke on their drinks.

"Says the most competitive female I know," Tim responds. "I don't know any other woman who's as career driven as you."

"That's different."

"Maybe. Maybe not. But when a man's pride is at stake…"

"Oh, I don't care. I came here to see you and enjoy a bit of light-hearted fun. Not start another war." Vicky slides an arm round Gav's waist, causing a rush of warmth to flood his body.

"Speaking of fun, how do you fancy another trip out to the Caymans sometime this summer?"

Both Gav and Vicky look wide-eyed at each other, absorbing Tim's invitation.

"I have to visit our office over there at least once a quarter, and you're both more than welcome. Victoria knows the rules. Pay your own way there, then the rest is on the company."

"Oh Tim, it was so great last time, it would be fantastic to have another opportunity to visit."

"Like I said. You're always welcome." Tim looks Gav directly in the eye. "Both of you. My villa has more than enough room."

"Your villa?" Vicky asks.

"I've bought my own place out there now. Still on Seven Mile Beach. I rent it back to the bank when I'm not using it, but there's still bags of room."

"Wow, that's an incredibly generous offer, Tim. I know this one here would love the chance to return to the Caribbean. She talks so fondly of the first time she visited. How could we ever thank you?"

Tim wraps his hand around Gav's in a vice-like grip.

"Thank me by keeping your promises," Tim says, his steely gaze locked onto Gav's. Turning back to Vicky, he adds, "See if you can hang onto this one, my dear. He's a keeper. Try not to fuck it up."

Vicky and Gav exchange a sideways glance.

"Now if you two lovebirds will excuse me, I have other guests to see to. See you in the Caymans sometime soon."

And with that, he air kisses Vicky and drifts off to talk to some of his other guests.

Chapter 9

5 months later, Tuesday 7th Sept 2004

Grand Cayman

*T*he balcony doors wide open, the thin voile curtains blow gently in the warm breeze that wafts over the dozing couple. A symphony of insects chirp in the darkness and the moon shines bright, as if the Caribbean air has somehow charged its glow. Off in the distance, waves crash and roll against the coral reef in a constant rhythmic reel. Closer to shore the surface of the lagoon lies still and flat, reflecting back the millions of bright stars that punctuate the heavens.

Vicky's skin feels hot next to Gav's, their legs interlaced, the cool cotton sheet draped loosely over their naked torsos; through the blackness Gav listens to the soft in and out of Vicky's breath.

As planned they spent their first week in Grand Cayman as Tim's guests in his villa on Seven Mile Beach. However, when he had to return to New York at short notice, they decided to continue their holiday on the other side of the island, renting a private beach hut in blissful seclusion away from the relative hubbub of George Town and the shared accommodation of other bank employees and their partners.

Looking out at the stars over the lagoon of the East End, Gav feels Vicky stir next to him.

"Go back to sleep, Angel. It's still early." He tenderly strokes the outside of her arm.

They lie in silence for a short while until Vicky mumbles, "Damn it, I'm wide awake now."

"Is something on your mind?"

"No, not really, although I have been thinking about that storm that seems to be on its way."

"Pfft. What's a bit of wind and rain? What is it Billy Connelly says, '*There's no such thing as bad weather, only bad clothes'.*"

"Billy Connelly did say that, but it was actually Wainwright who said it first… back in the 70s."

"Ooo get you. Mrs Knowledgeable." Gav gives her a little squeeze. "But that storm will blow itself out before it gets anywhere near us. They always do. Now go back to sleep."

But instead of resettling herself she throws her legs over the edge of the bed and pulls a loose beach cover-up over her naked form. "I think I'll go for a walk."

"What? Now?!" Gav shuffles up to a more seated position. "But it's the middle of the night sweetheart."

"Exactly. It's nice and cool and there's no one to disturb me."

"Hang on, I'll come with you."

Gav jumps out of bed and quickly pulls on a T-shirt and a pair of shorts. "Right, come on then, Little-Miss-Restless. A walk it is."

They stroll hand in hand along the pure white sand of the East End, the fine grains seeping between their toes. When they reach the far end of the beach, Gav leads Vicky towards one of the daybeds, strategically placed to allow the daytime sun worshippers the best view of the bay. She settles into the crook of his arm as they both look out over the millpond of the lagoon, the stars twinkling on its surface.

Gav sucks in a deep breath. He's been waiting for the perfect moment before he tells Vicky what's been on his mind, and he doubts it'll get more perfect than this.

"You know how much I love you, Angel," he says.

Gav declared his love for Vicky the night following the rugby match at Twickenham, a tender and gentle moment of sincerity after they'd made love. Vicky is yet to reciprocate with those exact words, but from her actions and deeds over the months since, he knows her feelings for him are deep and sincere. He doesn't need her to say she loves him when she demonstrates it to him every day.

"I know you do." Vicky rubs the outside of his arm. "And you know how much you mean to me."

"I do," Gav replies, sucking in another deep breath. "Because there's an important question I've been thinking about for some time now."

Vicky visibly stiffens.

"After the end of my marriage, I never thought I'd meet anyone ever again, at least not someone I envisioned spending the rest of my life with. I know it's still relatively early days in our relationship, but I can't ever imagine my life without you in it Vicky, and I'd like the rest of the world to know that."

Vicky sits up slowly, her features, despite her Caribbean suntan, as white as a sheet as she turns to look at him face on. "Gav, you must never ask me to marry you."

"Oh...kay?" He half-laughs, one corner of his mouth twisting upwards.

That was not the response I was expecting, he thinks to himself.

"I'm serious. Please don't ever ask me to be your wife." She closes her eyes. "I could never make that sacrifice again."

"Sacrifice?" He snorts a laugh out of the end of his nose. "The last time I checked, no virgins were slaughtered when a couple join in holy matrimony. At least not since medieval times."

"I know." She places her hand on his chest, forcing a distance between them and stopping him from sweeping her into his arms, which is what he wants to do.

"That's not what I meant. You know I'm not religious in the traditional sense, but I do believe there is some kind of higher force. An energy. Or some kind of karma. No matter how people interpret 'God', or what that might mean to them, for me when I stood in that church four years ago and made my vows to Craig I wasn't just making my vows to him; I was making them to the spirit that lies within me." She taps the ends of her fingertips against her sternum. "And I meant every goddamn word."

"I know. I felt the exact same way when I made my vows to Samantha." He leans forward and tucks a piece of stray hair behind Vicky's ear.

"For me, getting married meant that I would never give up," Vicky continues. "I internalised that to mean, '*I am prepared to do whatever it takes to make my marriage work — forever*'. Yet only a few months later, I found myself in an impossible situation."

Gav can see the glisten of moisture building up in the corner of her eyes. It physically pains him to know how much she's been hurt and betrayed in the past. She blinks a few times in quick succession. Gav reaches for her face and strokes her cheek with the back of his fingers. "It's okay. You don't have to relive it. I know how painful it was."

"I tried so damn hard, Gav. Believe me. I did everything I possibly could to make him love me, but he just kept pushing me away. I gave so much it nearly destroyed me. I never wanted to be the one to walk away. That would mean breaking my vows not just to him, but to myself."

Gavin watches Vicky's chest heave as she struggles to hold in her sobs.

"But in the end, I had to put myself first in order to survive. And in that moment I knew I could never marry again. I had broken the most sacred vow I could ever make, which is why marriage no longer holds any meaning for me. It doesn't mean I don't want you, or don't envision a future with you. Because I do."

She drops her head and bites her lip.

"But, Angel ..." Gav lifts her chin with his finger. "You know I'll never leave you like Craig did, or put you in an impossible position, like Chris did, where you're forced to choose between loving me or loving yourself."

"I know," she whispers, and he cups her face in his hand, landing the lightest of kisses on her soft, pillowy lips.

Gav holds her still while he contemplates what to say next.

If I truly love her, then I must give her what she needs. Her needs are my needs.

"If that means I never slide a ring on your finger as a way of proving how much I love you, then I'll never ask you to marry me."

"Oh Gav, that means so much." She releases a long sigh and falls into his arms.

They hug tightly, until she breaks from him and comes to kneel in front of him, her diamond bracelet glinting in the moonlight. Gav rolls the pads of his fingers over its surface, counting the twenty-one diamonds neatly aligned in an elegant channel setting.

"It's very pretty," he says.

"It's more than pretty. It's my personal memento to remind myself how strong I am. That I can survive anything. I've never taken it off since the day I bought it."

"With Corrine?"

"Yes, with Corrine," Vicky confirms. "See, it's made of triangles." She angles the side of the bracelet so he can see the line of triangles embedded in its setting.

"Triangles are the strongest shape in the universe," she continues, "they disperse pressure. With what I was going through with my marriage at the time, and after almost drowning that day, it seemed a fitting metaphor. It's my *warrior emblem*. Reminding me I'm stronger than I think."

"And of course, diamonds are a product of extreme pressure," Gav says.

"Exactly."

"It's stunning, and I'm exceedingly grateful that you're here telling me the tale, and not lying at the bottom of the ocean. But you shouldn't need to *survive* in order to *live*. When are you going to realise that? You don't need to survive me. Or survive my love. You just need to let me love you in the way you deserve to be loved."

She slowly closes and then reopens her eyes as she allows Gav's words to settle inside her.

"You don't get it do you?" Gav continues. "Victoria Fenwick née Turnbull, or whatever you want to call yourself, I'm in love with you. The real you. The authentic you. Not the façade you've created for the rest of the world to see. I know you try to keep the real you locked away, and that's okay. I understand. So however long it takes for those walls to come down, I'll be here... loving you."

She meets his gaze.

"You said you're not religious, but that you believe in a higher force of some kind. An energy that guides you. Well, I believe... no, I know, I was put on this earth to find you, to be with you, and to love and protect you. I never believed in the idea of soul mates until I met you. But you and I..." He sucks in a lung-filling breath, his exhalation coming out in staccato judders. "You've changed my life, Vicky. Being with you makes me want to be a better man. You inspire me. You're intelligent, driven, kind, courageous... I've never met anyone like you and I firmly believe we're destined to be together—forever. No matter what the future holds for us, my feelings for you will never change. I've known it from the moment you fell into my lap."

She continues to hold his gaze, but this time there is no smile on her face. Gav sees only virtue in her eyes and a sob catches in the back of his throat as he watches the shield behind her irises fall away.

Finally, there she is. Laid bare. Fully exposed. No pretence. No games. And he knows then, with absolute certainty... *Here is the woman I will spend the rest of my life with.*

His voice hardly a whisper, he looks directly into her soul. "It's okay. I've got you."

Her stunning green eyes turn to water, like swirling pools in an emerald lagoon. He knows she, too, is looking deep into his own soul, past any outer façade.

Gav's heartbeat slows as, kneeling before each other, the sound of the waves rolling up and down the beach mere metres away, they feel their souls connect. Gone is the powerful, glamorous goddess; instead, in front of him is a beautiful, vulnerable woman. A soul cracked wide open. Naked and exposed and completely trusting.

More than making love, more than taking her, or claiming her, or being inside her… all I want is to protect her, Gav says to himself.

Closing the gap between them, he pulls her in tight. "You're safe. I've got you," he says again.

Finally she allows her feelings to run free. Unguarded, her body begins to shudder as the tears from a decade of pain finally leave her body. Nuzzling into him, Gav feels her river of emotion run down his neck and pool in the triangle of muscle where his neck meets his torso.

"Shh, shh," Gav says, gently rocking her. "I've got you. I'm never going to let anyone hurt you ever again."

With each release he feels her core soften and her shoulders drop ever so slightly while he allows her the privacy to cry.

He's not sure how long he comforts her, but eventually, once her sobs subside, he loosens his embrace.

"Well! This is not how I expected this evening to go," she half-laughs, wiping her nose with the back of her hand. "God, what must I look like? A right blotchy, snotty mess."

"I think you are the most beautiful thing I've ever seen." He strokes the side of her face. His voice sincere.

"Hardly," she replies, sniffing loudly and rolling her knuckles under her eyes.

"Oh, but you are."

Her smile falls away and for the second time in as many minutes the veil behind her eyes dissolves once again. Her soul exposed and raw.

"Thank you," she whispers, and Gav knows, rather than batting away his compliment, she has allowed his loving words to break through her hardened outer shell and settle within her.

Despite craving love and affection, he believes she's never been able to accept love without condition, as that would mean she had to believe she was worthy of it. Something he suspects she's struggled with all her life. Why else would she have settled for such shitty relationships in the past? But perhaps for the first time in her life, she is allowing herself to be loved. Truly loved. By him. Meaning she loves herself enough to deem herself worthy. And that makes him love her even more.

Gav lies back on the daybed and pulls her up onto his stomach. Her hair falls over his face and he brushes it back. He's mesmerised by her beauty.

Without speaking, she leans forward and kisses him. Their lips connecting ever so lightly. Her feather-light touch causes millions of nerve-endings in Gav's skin to ripple with desire.

Both of them suck air in urgently through their nostrils as they unconsciously deepen their kiss.

It's never been like this before. Gav's mind races. Even with her, it's never felt like this.

Their tongues gently lick their way into each other's mouths and Vicky releases a light groan as her form moulds around his. Her fingers feathering his hair as Gav's hands travel up and down her back. The more she softens, the more he grows hard.

Gav's hands settle on her bare bottom. Their lips still connected, she arches her back, pushing her hips up into his hands. Every fibre in his body wants to claim her, to seal their union physically as well as spiritually, but he holds back. Treating her body with the same care and reverence he's shown her soul.

She pulls back from their kiss and kneels up, her thighs still straddled across him. He knows she's not wearing anything underneath her cover-up, and if he wasn't encased in his shorts he would be inside her, their bodies perfectly aligned.

Without breaking eye contact she peels off her smock. Tossing it aside her naked flesh shimmers in the moonlight.

Gav glances quickly to either side of them, double-checking that they are completely alone.

His hands caress her neck before tracing their way down her body, circling the curve of her breasts, over the flat of her stomach before settling between her legs. His fingers already familiar with every part of her body.

She throws her head back and gasps as he continues to stimulate the deepest part of her.

How different she looks now to the first time she tried to be intimate with him. That Sunday afternoon at his flat. Back then she was putting on a show. Trying to illicit a superficial response from him. But he didn't want her body, if that's all she was offering. She may have removed her clothing, but she revealed nothing of herself. Whereas now, she's not just naked, she's stripped bare and there's nothing separating them. Cloaked only in his love and the balmy Caribbean night air, she's surrendered her soul to him and he's gladly accepted it and offered his in return.

The sight of her raw vulnerability brings tears to Gav's eyes. "Oh Angel," he whispers.

This is all I ever wanted. She's finally given her whole self to me.

In one fluid movement Gav rolls Vicky onto her back and quickly sheds his own clothes, so that there is nothing physical left separating them.

Instinctively and without any effort their bodies join as one, almost of their own accord, cementing their union. Each grounding the other. No longer two separate beings, but two bodies and two souls, becoming one.

He interlaces his fingers with hers, kissing the back of her knuckles before holding their clasped hands above her head.

Her legs wrapped around his waist, she lifts her head and kisses him again. No words are needed; they both know that this moment is more than either of them have ever experienced before.

Gav's soul is floating above his head, intertwined with Vicky's in something both base, yet other-worldly and beautiful. A divine experience. Something neither of them could ever have anticipated, yet now it's happening it feels predestined.

Their bodies continue to move in gentle unison, as one, the blinding white heat growing in intensity as their passion for each other continues to spiral upwards. The world around them falls away, their awareness consumed by their emotions as they continue to give every part of themselves to the other.

Gently, reverently, eventually they both slide over the cliff together. Their bodies exploding into an energetic climax that dances and twirls above them, suspending all conscious thought, before they gently float back into their bodies, satiated and spent.

Droplets of sweat drip from Gav's torso and collect in small beads between Vicky's breasts as they both struggle to catch their breath. The air entering and leaving their bodies quivering and shaky.

Neither of them move. Gav holding his weight on his forearms as he gazes down onto Vicky's soft curves beneath him. Their eyes meet, communicating what their words cannot.

Vicky reaches up and slides her fingers through Gav's soft blond hair. He nuzzles his face against her palm.

Eventually he whispers, "I love you so much." His words almost painful to say, their meaning so much deeper than their mere sound.

She pauses, smiling up and him. "And I love you."

Gav's heart swells inside his chest as if someone has thrown a window open and a rush of fresh air is filling up a once stuffy room. "Oh, come here," he says, pulling her into his lap and wrapping his arms around her.

It's at this moment yet another tidal wave of suppressed emotion rises up and Vicky erupts into quiet sobs.

Gav knows that by peeling back her layers, she has no shield to hide behind anymore, and if she's to heal from her buried pain she must continue to exorcise any toxicity, until there is none left.

He continues to gently *shh* her, rocking her back and forth as each sob exits her body.

"It's okay," Gav says as he continues to rock her. "It'll all be okay. You're safe. I've got you now."

Eventually her tears subside and she pulls back from his embrace and looks at him. "I'm so sorry. I promise it's not you. I don't know what came over me—again."

"You've nothing to be sorry for," he says, sweeping her hair back off her face. "Whatever you need, I'll always be here for you."

He passes her her cover-up as he retrieves his T-shirt and shorts. They quickly pull on their clothes, then Gav reaches for both of Vicky's hands to hold.

"Whatever's happened to you in the past, whatever happens to us in the future, I'll always be here for you."

She meets his gaze. "And I, you. I know I said I don't want to marry you, but you must know that doesn't mean I'm not committed to you. To us. Because I am. In fact *not* being married to you feels like a bigger commitment. I'm in this not because a piece of paper binds us together, or because I'm afraid of leaving. We've both lived through that fear and come out the other side. No, you need to know I'm with you because I'm choosing to be with you. Every day. Does that make sense?"

"Today, tomorrow, always," Gav says reverently.

"Today, tomorrow, always," Vicky repeats.

They hold each other's gaze, allowing the shared commitment they've made to each other to settle within them. They both know their worlds have shifted tonight. From now on, life will be defined as before and after this moment.

"God, I love you." Gav cups Vicky's face and pulls her in for another kiss.

When he eventually pulls back, Vicky whispers, "And I love you too. Gawd knows why it took me so long to say it. I've been in love with you for so long. I mean, how could I not love a man whose favourite film is *Moulin Rouge*?"

"I've known you've loved me for ages," Gav teases. "I mean, how could you not love this?" He gestures up and down his body and she play punches him.

"Come on." Gav climbs off the daybed, holding out his hand. "Now we've got that cleared up, you've got the rest of your life to admire and love this perfect specimen."

Shaking her head, she follows his lead back down the beach.

Chapter 10

VICTORIA

*a*s our dive boat re-enters George Town Harbour, I spy Gavin sipping a rum cocktail in one of the waterfront bars. A Panama hat shading his freckled skin from the harsh Caribbean sun. His nose buried in his book: *The Last Juror* by John Grisham. As a Libran, he's a sucker for a principled protagonist.

"Is that him?" the woman sitting next to me asks.

"It sure is, Fi." I can't help but smile. My heart swells inside my chest just acknowledging to someone else that, yes—he is *the one*. The one I didn't know I needed but, it turns out, is the perfect one for me.

But it's more than that.

When we were on the beach two nights ago, I experienced something I've not felt before. Even in my most intimate moments with Chris or Craig, it never felt like it does with Gav.

I feel as if I've been uncorked. My true self unleashed. And love is bubbling up and through me as clear and clean as the waters of Te Waikoropupū Springs in New Zealand. And just like staring into the crystal clear clarity of the world's cleanest water, everything in my world has new depths and vibrancy.

I realise now, before I met Gav, I was living a half-life. Denying my own deepest needs to fit with my circumstances. When the truth is… all I've ever wanted is to love and be loved. But having been burnt more than once, I'd smothered that internal flame with the same story I'd told myself over and over: *'I'm happy. I have enough with my work, my life, my friends and their babies.'*

Six months ago, I wasn't looking for love. In fact, the opposite. I was rejecting it. Doing and saying anything and everything to push it away. Believing allowing myself that kind of love again would complicate my life in ways I didn't have time for. I realise now, those justifications were papering over deeper fears. *What if I fall in love, only to have my heart-broken all over again?*

Whereas now I've allowed Gav in, and told him how I truly feel, my life has turned from black and white into glorious technicolour. Everything around me seems amplified. Even the sounds of the birds and the scents of the flowers seem louder, more pungent. I'm feeling more. I even look forward to the low-level rumble of a Liverpool match filling the house every Saturday afternoon, punctuated by his celebratory bellows or shouts of anger, depending on how well they play; and my reluctance to shave my legs has been replaced by a joy of long candle-lit baths. Soaking in oils and preening myself.

When I've fallen in love previously, my axis always ended up being knocked off kilter. The more powerful my love for the other person, the more I ended up being pulled off centre. I found myself addicted to them. Constantly chasing an ever-diminishing high. And it was only afterwards I realised how inauthentic I'd become.

That cheesy line from Jerry Maguire pops into my brain. The one where Renée Zellweger's character turns to Tom Cruise and says, *'You complete me.'*

What utter bollocks.

I don't need Gav to complete me, or I him. We're both complete souls as we are, which is why this feels so different. Like two circles overlapping in a Venn diagram, we amplify the best in each other. He inspires me to be the best and most authentic version of myself. Yes, Gav is not my first *great love,* but he is the man who has made all my previous loves seem inconsequential.

Seeing our boat making its way back towards the dock, Gav stands and waves.

"He looks nice," Fiona says.

"I see we share the same taste in shirts," the guy on the other side of Fiona comments.

Mike and Fiona are not new friends. It was pure coincidence that during the check-in for today's dive I was reunited with the couple I've not seen in over a decade.

Mike originally met and bonded with Chris, when he and Fiona were on holiday in Santorini and Chris was backpacking around Greece. The men's shared love of Formula 1 cemented their friendship, but the couple were always Chris's friends first. When Chris and I broke up Fiona sent me a nice note asking if I was okay, but after I'd politely replied I let things lie. I didn't want them feeling they were caught in the middle. We never officially ended our friendship, but it was better for everyone to let things wane. However, bumping into each other again today, our friendship is as strong as it ever was.

Fiona had spotted me first. Squealing loudly, her hands flapping, she'd rushed to embrace me, and a decade evaporated instantly. Naturally we've spent every moment on the boat nattering and catching up.

I wave at Gav, who having spotted us returning is now leaning against one of the uprights on the dock. A wide smile across his face, revealing those sexy dimples.

God damn! They get me every time.

Originally wanting to take the opportunity to learn to dive Gav did take a Beginner's course earlier in the week, kneeling on the sand in the shallows of the lagoon over in the East End, but over dinner that night he admitted he didn't enjoy it.

'I know logically it's safe to breathe underwater, but the deeper we went I spent the whole time wondering if I could hold my breath long enough to reach the surface. But look, don't let me hold you back,' he'd added, 'you're a pro and you'll have a much better time if you're not worrying about me.'

The boat now tethered to the boardwalk, I jump ashore and throw my arms around Gav's neck. "Hey you."

His hands on my backside, he playfully nips my bum. "Good dive?"

"Really good. I've always wanted to dive Bonnie's Arch. We saw some wild turtles. But you'll never guess who else I've seen."

"Who?" he says, planting a smattering of kisses on my lips.

I slide my arm around his waist, turning back around to face the boat where everyone else is gathering up their gear. "Gav, I'd like you to meet two very old friends of mine. Fiona and Mike. We've not seen each other in years, but they happened to be on the same dive today. Fiona, Mike, this is Gavin."

"Good to meet you, mate." Mike simultaneously shakes Gav's hand whilst using it as leverage to climb out of the boat. "Vicky's done nothing but talk our ears off all morning about you. I was relieved to get underwater. My ears were almost bleeding." Mike gives me a wink before holding out his hand, helping his wife clamber up onto the dock.

"Very nice to meet you," Fiona says now that she's stepped up off the boat. "And take no notice of him." She gives Mike a backhand slap in the belly. "Can you believe it?" she adds, gesturing back and forth between the two of us. "What are the odds?"

"Long. And if I were a gambling man, not ones I'd take," Gav laughs.

Everyone grabs their gear and starts to make their way ashore. Gav takes my now empty oxygen tank, BCD and weight belt from me as we all trundle back down the boardwalk together.

"So how do you all know each other?" Gav asks, his eyes flicking between Mike and Fiona.

Of all of my friends, past and present, Mike and Fiona have never come up in conversation with Gav, so naturally he's curious as to our relationship.

Fiona and Mike look sideways at each other; determined to keep the mood light, I jump in to save them from any awkward explanations.

"We were really close when I was with Chris. Although they live up in Manchester, and we were down in London, there were far too many drunken weekends to recount." In my nervousness I accidentally snort-laugh, and Mike and Fiona nod enthusiastically, agreeing with my summation.

"Well I think we should continue that tradition, don't you?" Mike says, gesturing back towards the beach bar now that we've returned our gear to the dive hut.

Gav's gaze flirts from me to Mike and Fiona, then back again. His introversion and awkwardness in social groups, especially with people he doesn't know, still very much evident.

I watch as he sucks in a long breath. "That would be great," he says with a smile.

"I knew I liked you." Mike throws his arm over Gav's shoulder, either ignoring or unaware of Gav's nervousness around new people.

Mike steers us all back towards the palm-covered shack in the middle of the bar. "My round. What's everyone having?"

Chapter 11

Over the next few hours the laughs and memories, old and new, flow as easily as the rum cocktails we pour down our throats. Fiona and I have pulled on Tortuga dive T-shirts over the top of our swimsuits, and Mike is wearing a Hawaiian shirt, as equally garish as Gav's. Once they begin talking about their mutual love of sport it's clear the men are cut from the same cloth—literally.

"Fancy a mooch about the shops?" Fiona asks. "I've drunk so much, if I don't move soon I'll fall asleep."

We finish our drinks and wander south. The men disappear into the Hard Rock Café to buy the obligatory souvenirs, and Fiona and I disappear next door, invited in by the refreshing air-conditioning and glittering diamonds displayed in the windows of Gems International. Fiona and I smile at the friendly assistant, but shake our heads and say, "Just browsing," when she eagerly asks if we need any help.

I'm bent over a glass cabinet, my eyes not knowing which glittering collection of diamonds to settle on, when my energy is pulled like a magnet. I turn, already knowing Gav is behind me.

He slides his arm around my waist and rests his chin on my shoulder.

"See something you like?" he asks, planting a quick kiss on the side of my cheek.

"Oh, soooo many things."

"Isn't that your bracelet?" He points towards another bangle, similar in design to my precious warrior emblem.

"Almost. It's the same blend of yellow and white gold, but the setting is different. It's still nice though."

The bracelet is displayed alongside a matching three-stone diamond ring that must be at least a couple of carats, a matching eternity ring set in a similar channel setting to my bracelet, and a pair of elegant channel-set earrings that when worn would loop down and curve back underneath the earlobe.

"Would you like to try on the ring?" the sales assistant asks, noticing my gaze having rested on the humongous diamonds in the stunning piece of jewellery.

"Oh, no." I shake my head.

"What's the harm?" Gav insists. "It doesn't have to be an engagement ring."

"Exactly," the assistant says, picking up on my hesitancy. "It would make an equally stunning dress ring."

The sales assistant lays out a green velvet cloth on the top of the counter and unlocks the cabinet.

She pulls out the ring and, taking off my granny's delicate flowered engagement ring, I hold out my right hand, allowing her to slide it onto my fourth finger, but it's too big and it slips around.

"Try it on your middle finger," she suggests.

I slip the ring onto my third finger, where it fits perfectly. Stretching my fingers I angle my hand this way and that, watching the light as it bounces off the stones.

"It's stunning," Gav whispers in my ear.

Fiona and Mike wander over to join us.

"Isn't that on the wrong finger?" Fiona says bluntly, confirming my exact thoughts.

There's no denying it's a beautiful piece of jewellery, but no matter what anyone says it screams *engagement ring*.

I quickly slip it off and hand it back to the sales assistant. "Thanks. It's absolutely beautiful, but it's not for me."

Deciding that we all want to continue our day together, now that Gav has gotten over his own insecurities with new people, after returning back to our respective hotels, we agree a time to meet up.

At 8:00 p.m. we've reconvened at a dockside restaurant where, festooned all around the perimeter of the deck, twinkling fairy lights sway gently in the evening breeze. The air cloying on our skin and, just visible through cracks in the wooden deck boards, the sea, black as ink, moves in a constant swirling mass. Rising and falling. A calm but constant energy. The salt air, palatable on my tongue, mirrors the briny flavours I've consumed from my plate.

I take a moment and look slowly to each of the three other faces around the table.

This really has been an unbelievable holiday. Perfectly timed, and filled with magic.

As I expected, Gav has clicked with Mike and Fiona clicked— and vice versa—as easily as I had when I first met them.

"So nine years huh?" Gav says, topping up everyone's wine glass.

"Yup. Sixteen years as a couple. Nine married." Fiona nudges Mike in the ribs and he kisses the top of her head.

"That's so great." I nod my head across the table to each of them in turn. "I'm pleased you finally got your *happy ever after.*"

Mike was already married when he met Fi, and their relationship had started out as an affair. At the time Fiona was labelled *the home wrecker* and *the other woman.* Although Mike always stringently argued there wasn't a home, or a marriage left to wreck, it didn't make the beginning of their relationship any easier.

"Once I got pregnant," Fi says, "it seemed like the right time to make things officially official, so to speak. It's just a shame it's taken Mike this long to sort out a honeymoon."

Mike rolls his eyes.

"So while you're here, enjoying a belated honeymoon, who's looking after your kids?" Gav asks.

"Our parents," Fiona answers. "They've moved into our house for the duration. My parents were there last week, then they swapped with Mike's this week. They decided it was easier to look after two kids under five in situ."

"Either that, or they didn't fancy our sticky-fingered brats messing up their pristine show homes," Mike retorts. "So what about you two then? Do you think you'll bash out a couple of mini Gavs and Vickys at some point?"

I stiffen slightly, and Gav coughs into his closed fist.

This is not a conversation we've had yet. I've only just managed to trust the guy with my heart; whenever he's brought up the kids topic, I've changed the subject. Following my divorce I've put so much energy into believing it would never happen for me, that now there's a possibility it could if I wanted it to—assuming Gav wants it to as well—I haven't had the head space to process and figure out how I feel about the possibility.

If Gav does want a child, do I?

"There's plenty of time for that yet." Gav glances at me and I hope he can read my telepathic *thank you.*

"We're still enjoying getting to know each other at the moment," I add.

"Well if you do decide to have a family, good luck to the both of you," Mike says across to Gav. "Don't take this the wrong way, but I hope it takes you a really, *really* long time to conceive." Mike winks at Gav. "Trust me. Once your Mrs is *up the duff* and her body raging with pregnancy hormones, you're in for nine months of hell. And that's before the little nipper actually arrives. If you value sleep, man, I'm telling you, don't do it."

"Is that what you really think of our little family, Mike?" Fiona play-punches Mike's bicep. He pretends to be wounded by the blow.

"Never, my darling. Best decision we ever made." He places his hand under her chin and pulls her in for a kiss.

It's nice that they've not lost any of their sparkle, even after sixteen years together. Regardless of how their relationship started, they're clearly meant for each other.

"It's definitely life-changing," Fiona adds. "Being pregnant is the most magical feeling in the world."

"I can only imagine," I lie.

Only one other person in the world knows that I was pregnant —once.

Whether it's the memory of that time, or the mutual thread that ties Fiona, Mike, and myself together, I find myself asking, "Are you still in touch with him? Chris, I mean."

Gav's hand, which had been stroking my back, stills and settles into the curve just above my bum, the air around the table having cooled ever so slightly.

Mike glances at Fiona before answering. "I know who you mean." His tone warm but wary. It's clear his allegiance remains with Chris and he's grappling with how much information to share without being disloyal.

"Yes, we're still close," Mike continues. "More so now than ever actually. He was my best man."

"Oh? I see." My fingers fidget in my lap.

Mel still sends me a round robin newsletter in her Christmas card, and we write a couple of times a year, but we've become deft at avoiding any mention of her brother. Instead she fills the pages with news of her growing family and Karl's work. I still love her, but it's not the same since they moved back to New Zealand. I've not actually seen her since her wedding. In Spain, five years ago, which was also the last time I saw Chris.

"Obviously we only see each other every couple of years," Mike continues, "but we've both signed up to this new service called Skype. It's like a phone call, only it's transmitted over the internet. Way cheaper than BT. You should try it. We talk every couple of weeks or so. Usually moaning about the Grand Prix results. He's a massive Ferrari and Schumacher fan, whereas I obviously support Coulthard."

"Is he still dealing in cars then?"

"A bit, but he's moved into property development. The big thing over there is buying up old houses, sectioning the plots and sticking another house on the back. I've actually invested some cash with him to help him expand."

"Also he's godfather to our two," Fiona adds softly.

"Oh." I drop my head, not sure how I feel about this new piece of information. "Well that's nice." I manage to keep my voice level.

"We've been over to New Zealand a couple of times. Such a beautiful country," Mike continues, smiling at Gav, "and we sometimes meet somewhere in the middle and have a big family holiday. We all went to Hawaii last summer. Rented a villa on the beach. Great fun."

"All?" I can't hide the inquiry in my tone, but my gut rolls uncomfortably while I wait for their answer.

Eventually it's Fiona who locks eyes with me. "He's been in a relationship for some time now, Vicky. Someone he knew even before you. It was on and off again for years, and they're not married or anything, but they seem settled and happy now. We really like her."

I swallow hard. "Good," I stutter, my tongue sticking to the roof of my mouth.

"They've not long had a baby," Mike adds.

My back stiffens as if jolted by electricity, so much so I have to sit on my hands to stop anyone seeing them shaking.

One hand still in the nook of my back, Gav places his other on my thigh and gives it a gentle squeeze, sensing this is a shock.

"I see," I manage to mumble, my breath locked inside my lungs.

"A little boy," Fiona adds. "Three months old."

He has a son.

He's a father.

"In fact, he's coming to visit us this Christmas," Fiona continues. "He's planning a trip over to see his *rellies*, as he would say."

"Oh?" I reply, my voice hardly audible now. "His dad's parents are still alive then?"

"I believe so," Mike confirms.

A recollection of a garden party at his grandparents' house in Wiltshire rises up from the back of my mind. Fond memories of an afternoon drinking Pimms and eating strawberries, the air heavy with the scent of English roses, at a Williams family gathering.

"But knowing Chris," Fiona cuts in, "we'll get a message twenty-four hours before he rocks up on our drive in some flashy Porsche he's either bought or rented."

An involuntary guffaw of laughter escapes my lips at Fiona's accurate description of my ex. "Yup, that sounds like Chris." I suck in a deep breath, my body conscious of Gav's touch. His closeness keeping me grounded.

That was then, and this is now, I remind myself.

I straighten up in my chair. "Well when you do see him, please pass on my best. Tell him I'm glad he's happy."

"We will," Fiona says brightly. "And I know he'll be pleased to know you're happy as well." She raises her glass across the table at Gav, who nods politely in return.

"I am." I turn and smile at Gav, who's been patiently listening.

"I truly am," I say again. Leaning in and lightly kissing Gav on the lips.

Another man might have needed to shut down a conversation about their girlfriend's ex, but instead Gav calmed me with a steady hand in my back and a squeeze of my knee. Giving me strength when he sensed I might need it. Just another example of his own self-confidence and belief in us.

"We can see that," Mike adds. "And I think he is too, Vicky. Or at least as happy as Chris is capable of. I think a part of him will always hold a torch for you."

I turn my head sharply, glaring at Mike. My eyebrows knitted together.

Now why did he have to say that?

There was I, digesting all this new information, believing Chris had finally quelled his inner demons and found peace with a new love. Started a family. Settled down, despite his wanderlust soul and promises to love me forever.

Yet, with that one throwaway comment, Mike has filled my mind with a wave of unanswered questions.

Will there ever come a time he doesn't love me? Will Chris always be the 'what if' relationship of my life? The love without closure. The unfinished story?

Was the creation of an unborn life nine years ago the permanent thread that will always bind us together? Regardless of who we go on to love, or what continent we live on?

On some deep, intangible level, are we destined to be bound together forever?

Can I never be free of him?

If I could, do I even want to be free of him?

Unanswered questions continue to rattle around my brain as the man beside me continues to ground me with a loving hand in the small of my back.

"And when you do see him next," Gav says, his tone sterner than a moment ago, his eyes locking onto Mike's gaze, "be sure to emphasise how happy we *both* are?"

I release a long exhale.

Unknowingly, Gav has delivered the answer I didn't know I needed to hear but am grateful I have.

Chapter 12

GAVIN

"I'm sorry you had to sit through all of that," Victoria says, peeling the straps of her linen sundress from her sun-kissed shoulders as they get ready for bed. It falls softly to the floor and pools around her feet. Braless, she's naked except for her lacy white G-string which glows luminous in the dark, as if lit by ultraviolet light. Her cream breasts, now freed from their confines, bob and sway gently as she replaces her dress on its hanger. Their colour contrasting against the bronzed glow of her tanned limbs and torso.

Gav's eyes follow his naked girlfriend's every move. He may have fallen in love with the women Vicky is on the inside, but it doesn't stop him admiring her outer wrapper. He is human after all.

Wearing only their underwear they settle under the cool cotton sheet and she nestles into the crook of his arm, both of them staring up at the ceiling fan which turns silently in the darkness. Every rotation wafting a light breeze of cool air over their skin. A mild comfort in the oppressive heat.

"Why are you sorry? I had a great time," Gav says acknowledging Vicky's previous comment. "They're a lovely couple."

"I mean, I'm sorry you had to listen to stories about my past." She hesitates before continuing, "And to what's going on in Chris's life now."

Gav strokes the outside of her arm. "It's fun learning about your crazy life before you calmed down." Gav taps the end of her nose and she makes to play bite it.

If Gav is being honest, he wouldn't have minded hearing more. Seeing Vicky's reaction when the conversation turned to Chris, his sixth sense tells him there's something about that relationship she's not told him. She was fearful when his name came up. Shrinking back into her shell.

I mean, she had to slide her hands under her bum, they were shaking that much.

And that's not normal.

If only I knew why. What the hell did he do to her?

"Yeah, but still," Vicky says, "I'm not sure how I would feel if I'd had to sit through an evening of stories about your ex."

She places her hand on his torso, her fingers lazily outlining his pecs. The light touch of her nails setting off firecrackers of desire across his skin. A light groan escapes from the back of Gav's throat as the pressure builds inside his boxers.

"Tell me about her?" Vicky says.

"About who?"

"Your ex-wife. You know way more about my dark and dismal past, and I know virtually nothing about why your marriage ended. What was her name again?"

Any desire Gav was feeling dissipates like air escaping from a leaky rubber dingy.

"Samantha. What do you want to know?" he says nonchalantly.

"Why you fell in love. Why you fell out of love."

I really don't want her to know this, Gav thinks to himself.

He sucks in a deep breath. "When I met Sam I thought she was what I was looking for. But really we were too young, too naïve, and didn't know ourselves well enough to be a good husband and wife to each other."

"You've told me you met at work, but how did you actually get together?"

"It was a slow burn. There was definitely a spark, but we didn't want to make things complicated. Especially as she was my boss."

"She was your boss?" Vicky's eyes stretch wide.

"U-huh. But then she got another promotion and moved to a different branch of the company. That's when things got going. We stayed in touch. She invited me for a drink, and things went from there. We were happy for a time, but looking back I always had my doubts."

"I know you said she broke your trust, but what did she do?"

Gav shuffles in the bed and draws a long breath in through his nostrils.

He pauses before saying, "It's not something I like to talk about other than to say that I'm different from you in that regard. You assume someone's trust until they break it, whereas I'm more sceptical. You have to earn my trust, and once it's broken I find it impossible to trust that person ever again."

"But what did she do?" Vicky presses. "Was she unfaithful?"

"Not in the way you think."

"Then how?"

He pulls Vicky into his chest and kisses the top of her head. "It's not important, Angel. What is important is that I'm with you now. And all I care about is our future. I know you'll never break my trust. I trust you with my life."

"And you, with mine. As far as I'm concerned, this is it for me. Regardless of what Mike said tonight, I don't want to be with anyone else—ever. I choose you, remember. Today, tomorrow, always."

The ceiling fan continues to whirr over their heads.

Noticing the goosebumps on Vicky's arms, Gav pulls the sheet up over them. "Pleased to hear it." He nips her ear with his teeth, then quietly whispers, "Maybe then, we should talk seriously about if and when we might want to start a family."

"Do we have to do this now?" Vicky squirms in Gav's arms.

"I'm not saying we should do it right now, but is that something you've thought about?"

Realising she can't deflect her way out of this spotlight, Vicky stills and stares into nothingness while Gav waits patiently for an answer.

Eventually she whispers, "The thing is, Gav, there's something you need to know about me. About my past…" But before she's had a chance to say anything more, she's interrupted by a commotion outside.

Someone is running along the boardwalk in front of their beach hut; it sounds like they're banging on everyone's doors, screaming, "WAKE UP! WAKE UP!"

They haven't reached their door yet, but from the sound drifting in through the open balcony doors, they're getting closer.

The couple sit up in bed, listening.

"Wait here," Gavin says, hastily pulling on a T-shirt and shorts. "I'll go see."

"Maybe there's a fire or something. It sounds more serious than a few drunks stumbling back from the bar."

Heading downstairs and padding through their living room, Gav opens the door and is met by the complex manager, dressed in his uniform of chinos and monographed shirt.

"What's up?" Gav asks.

"Hurricane coming." He points to the sky. "Everyone must leave. Island not safe."

"What do you mean *hurricane coming?* I thought the storm that was forecast had been downgraded."

"No, it stronger now," the manager replies in his strong Caymanian dialect. "Category five. No longer safe to stay, Mr Williams. Island being evacuated. You must leave now. All guests go to the airport, IMMEDIATELY!"

"Are you serious? Right now? It's the middle of the night. Surely this can wait until morning."

More people peer out of their accommodation, listening to the exchange, also wanting answers to the same questions.

"No, everybody go now. We arrange for minibus to take all guests to the airport. Leave in one hour."

My God. Gav's mind is racing. It must be serious.

"We have a hire car," Gav replies. "We'll make our own way there. But thank you." Gav steps forward and shakes his hand. "Thank you for your hospitality and let's hope this all comes to nothing."

Gav walks back inside to find Vicky now dressed in a kimono, the telly remote in her hand.

On the screen, a male reporter dressed in waterproofs, leaning into the wind and rain, shouts into his microphone, "Hurricane Ivan has been upgraded to a category five, making it the strongest hurricane to enter the southern Caribbean for fifty years."

The scrolling ticker tape at the bottom of the screen reads:

THE WINWARD ISLANDS BEGIN CLEANING UP AFTER HURRICANE IVAN.

AT LEAST 12 DEAD ON GRENADA. NINETY PERCENT OF HOMES DAMAGED.

AN UNKNOWN NUMBER OF CONVICTS ESCAPE AFTER JAIL DESTROYED.
500,000 PEOPLE ORDERED AWAY FROM COASTAL AREAS IN JAMAICA.

DAMAGE SO FAR ESTIMATED AT $6BILLION AND EXPECTED TO RISE TO $20BILLION AS IVAN CONTINUES ITS PATH OF DESTRUCTION.

The screen changes to an animated graphic showing the predicted pathway of the storm, which is due to pass over Jamaica in twenty-four hours' time, before a straight line trajectory and direct hit on the low-lying Cayman Islands.

Vicky, her face ashen, turns and looks at Gav.

"Angel. Go pack. We need to leave right now."

Chapter 13

VICTORIA

"What do you mean there are no flights?" I watch as Gav shakes his head in frustration. Our airline tickets and passports clenched in his hand.

"I'm really sorry sir." The apologetic customer service agent smiles weakly.

I look around the airport, crowded with hundreds of people all in the same predicament.

Dawn broke while we were queuing, snaking back and forth in an orderly fashion. A calm but palpable tension in the air. By the time we reached the front, all available airline seats were gone, and with all inbound flights cancelled, no amount of banging frustrated fists on counters is going to magic a jumbo out of the sky to rescue us.

It hasn't escaped my consciousness that in the midst of a category five hurricane threat, our Caymanian hosts are doing everything they can to help their island guests leave, without any thought for their own safety.

If this scenario were playing out back in the UK, I know I would want to be at home, battening down the hatches or keeping my loved ones close, not helping some ungrateful tourists escape the impending mayhem.

"Come," Gav instructs, grabbing our bags and turning to make his way out of the terminal. "We'll head to the harbour; find a boat."

"Can we do that?"

"We have to try."

                              ✳

"It's impossible," the harbour master says to Gav.

"All the big boats have already left, and small yachts cannot outrun a hurricane. Trust me, when it comes you are safer on land than out there." He points out towards the horizon.

Gone is the blazing sunshine from earlier in the week; now the sky is overcast and ominously grey. Even the clouds mirroring the impending danger. My skin is covered in a fine layer of sweat thanks to the thick, muggy air.

"Sweetheart, I think we should return to the beach house," I offer. "I think we're going to have to sit it out with the locals. We should help them prepare. I don't think we have any other option."

His hands on his hips, his shoulders slouched, Gav looks around the dock.

"Let's stop at the shops on the way back and pick up some emergency supplies. I can't believe we're actually seriously preparing for a hurricane."

"I know. Me neither. But we come from tough stock you and I. You're a Geordie and I'm Welsh. Hell, if we can survive our winters, I'm sure gale-force winds will be a walk in the park."

I crumple my mouth into a wry smile.

"That's the spirit. It'll be an adventure," he continues. "And it's gonna make one helluva dinner party story."

I rock up on my tippy toes and peck him on the lips. "Come on. Let's go and grab whatever's left in the shops."

                              ✳

Gav leaves me to pack the boot of the car with the bottled water and other supplies we've been able to find, and that we've agreed to take back to our hotel, ready to stay there for however long we need.

Gav checks his watch. "Stay here. I have an errand to run."

"An errand?" I cock my head to one side. "What on earth do you have to do now? It's already midday and the forecast says it'll start sometime tonight. We don't know what we're going to find when we get back over to the East End. We really should get going."

"I know, but this won't take more than ten minutes. There's something else I need to pick up."

His hands on my shoulders, he kisses my cheek before running across the supermarket car park and down into George Town.

I finish putting the groceries in the car, climb in the passenger seat and switch on the radio:

'Winds of 160mph recorded in the Antilles as Hurricane Ivan continues its destructive path through the Caribbean. Jamaica is ordering a mandatory coastal evacuation as high winds and storm surges of up to ten metres are expected in the next twenty-four hours. Those with means are being urged to leave the low-lying Cayman Islands, which are in danger of being completely swamped by high waves.'

I turn the dial, searching for music. Settling on a pop station, I thrust my head back against the headrest.

'...And up next we have another hit from the English singer/songwriter. Here's Will Young with 'Think I'd better leave right now.'

No shit Sherlock!

I turn the radio off and close my eyes. Where is Gav? What on earth is so important that he had to rush off now? He wasn't bothered an hour ago when we were at the airport. It must be something he's got wind of that will help in the hurricane.

My phone in my hand, I feel it vibrate. Flipping it open, I read the text:

> Have you made it out safely? I hope so. Reply to me in next 15mins, otherwise I'll assume you're in the air and on your way to Miami. Tim x

> No Tim. We're stuck here.

> No flights. No boats

> We're planning to sit it out. No other option. V x

> Shit. Get to the airport NOW!

> We have a charter leaving in an hour bringing the last of our guys home.

> I'll let them know to expect you

> Stay safe. T x

Oh my God. Once again Tim has metaphorically arrived to save the day. Saving my bacon just when things seem hopeless.

I look across the car park.

Where the hell is Gav?

It's been fifteen minutes. I call him, but after three rings his voicemail kicks in.

"Gav pick up. We need to get back to the airport immediately. Tim's just messaged me. He's got us a ride out of here. A private charter but we need to go now or else we'll miss it. Where are you? Whatever it is you're doing, just forget it. Nothing is more important than this. Please honey. Just get back here now!"

I twiddle my fingers and my knees bob incessantly. Obviously there's no way I'd ever leave Gav behind, but every second that ticks by is pure torture. Watching the numbers click over on the dashboard clock feels like sand running through the timer on our lives. Each agonising minute that passes, our chance of escape grows ever slimmer.

I hop over to the driver's seat and turn the key in the ignition. The engine purrs, poised and ready for a fast getaway.

My heart beats furiously in my chest, and the sound of my blood pumping whooshes in my ears. I look in the rearview mirror, praying for the sight of Gav's big, strong six-foot-four frame walking nonchalantly across the tarmac, but I only see other stranded tourists and locals frantically emptying the supermarket of every last supply.

I slam the car into reverse and charge backwards out of the parking space. Slamming the gears again, I turn the vehicle around in readiness to tear back to the airport.

I try his mobile once more, but he must have it on silent.

Come on Gav. Where are you?

My right foot unconsciously presses the accelerator, and the engine revs in response.

Finally I see him. Walking, as I expected, nonchalantly back across the tarmac in the distance. His wide shoulders and loose swagger unaware of the urgency needed.

The engine still running, I open the door and stand with one leg out of the car.

"Gav. Quickly! We need to go NOW!"

He breaks into a jog, a serious look on his face.

Jumping into the car next to me he asks, "What's the sudden urgency? It won't take more than half an hour to back to the other side of the island."

"More like, where the hell have you been?" Slamming the gears again, I pull away, wheels spinning as the velocity throws us both backwards in our seats.

"Whoa there, Angel. What's the rush?"

"I wouldn't have to rush if you hadn't disappeared. You still haven't told me where you've been."

"And you still haven't told me what's the rush."

"I'll explain on the way."

Dashing through the now empty airport, all the other stranded tourists having left to find shelter, we run towards the charter desk where one lonely customer service agent is preparing to shut up shop.

After giving us our instructions, Gav slides the keys to the hire car across the desk.

"Here. It's parked right outside and it's packed full of supplies. Water. Tinned food. Anything we could buy. Take it. Use it, give it to anyone else who needs it."

Her eyes heavy with sadness, she replies, "Thank you."

His face equally sad, he clasps both of his hands around hers. "Good luck. Stay safe."

"Thank you. But you two need to go. That way." She points in the direction of the now deserted airport security. Something tells me no one will care what we may or may not be carrying on board.

Grabbing my hand, Gav and I dash across the terminal.

"We've only got ten minutes, Vicky. We'll have to run."

We quicken our pace, zipping in and out the last few people wandering aimlessly about the place, presumably also hoping for a last-minute miracle.

Out of the corner of my eye, I spot a couple hugging. The woman is crying on the man's shoulder. Their bags at their feet, obviously they have no place else to go

"Stop! Wait." I turn and look at the couple.

"Come on, Vicky. We don't have time."

"It's Fiona and Mike. They're still here. They haven't made it out either."

At the sound of my voice, Fiona lifts her head off Mike's shoulder. "Oh Vicky. It's hopeless. What are we all going to do?"

"Grab your bags," I say. "You're coming with us."

"Yes, a friend has managed to wangle us seats on the last charter jet out of here," Gav adds. "They're just going to have to make room for two more."

"Really?" Mike says, unable to hide the hope in his voice.

"Come on," Gav says. "We haven't got time for niceties. We've only a few minutes before it takes off."

The four of us bolt through the airport and out of the open Gate door onto the tarmac. A twin-engine Gulfstream jet is preparing to leave. We run to the bottom of the steps just as the stewardess is about to pull them up.

"Wait," I say urgently. "We're friends of Tim. He told us you had space for us."

She looks inside the aircraft then back out to us. "We've only room for two, not four."

"But these are our friends. We can't leave them here," I plead.

The captain appears in the doorway, his hat under his arm. He comes down the steps and onto the tarmac, all the while the roar of the engines increases as their rotation speeds up.

"Victoria Fenwick, is it?" He holds out his hand.

"Yes." I step forward, shaking the hand that is offered. "And this is my boyfriend Gavin and our friends Mike and Fiona."

"I'm Captain Montgomery. This is all highly irregular, but then this is a highly irregular situation. Technically we're only insured for company personnel, but Tim's our CEO so if he says it's okay, it's okay."

"I sense a *but* coming." Gav looks directly at the captain.

"I may be able to bend company rules, but what I can't do is bend the laws of physics. In order to take off safely, I can carry a maximum of twenty-two people on board, and that includes our four crew members. By agreeing to take two additional passengers, I'm already pushing that weight capacity to twenty-four. That I can do. What I can't do is risk the lives of everyone on board by carrying twenty-six people."

He drops his head. "I'm very sorry."

"I see." Gav nods. "So, let me get this straight. You *can* take two people, but not four."

"Exactly," he replies, replacing his hat on his head, squaring it slightly. "And I'm also sorry, but we need to leave in the next five minutes, otherwise our flight path will need to be resubmitted, and I don't need to tell you we don't have time for that."

I stare at everyone's face in turn. The colour simultaneously draining from everyone's cheeks at the hideousness of the situation dawns on us all.

"Well then. It's been nice knowing you." Mike makes to shake my hand while silent tears roll down Fiona's face.

"No, that's not right," Gav interjects. "The women should go."

"No, you guys go," Mike protests. "They were your seats. We have no right to take them. We'll be fine, won't we sweetheart?" He wraps his arm around his wife who turns and buries her head in his shoulder.

"Err, I hate to rush you," the Captain says. "But I'm about to walk back up those steps, and the doors will close behind me. Once they do, they will not reopen. I need you to decide now."

Gav answers him. "The decision is made Captain. The women will leave with you."

"Oh Gav." Salty tears sting in the corner of my eyes.

I wrap my arms around him and bury my head in his chest. I don't want to leave him behind, but what other choice do we have? It's too cruel. What if the unthinkable happens and I never see him again?

"I'll be fine, Angel," he whispers in my ear. "I'll find us some shelter somehow. Like you said—it'll be an adventure. We'll be fine. I promise."

"Take care of the kids," I hear Mike whisper to Fiona.

Jesus, the men are preparing us for the worst.

"Here. I want you to have this." Gav slides his signet ring from his finger and reaches for my hand.

"No Gav. I don't want it. You keep it."

"But I want you to have it. Just in case."

"Just in case what?" I say, panic rising in my voice.

"Nothing. Forget I said that. But I'll feel better if I know my dragon heart is watching over you. Keeping you safe." He closes my fingers around the ring in my palm.

"But it's you who needs to stay safe," I cry.

"I'll be fine. Just take it… please."

I won't let this be the end, I think to myself, my fists scrunched into balls by the side of my body. "Okay, I'll keep it safe," I whisper, my arms back around his waist, my head buried in his torso. "I suspect it'll only be a few days before I can either fly back down here and we can go home together, or you get a flight up to the states."

"That's right. I'll see you in a few days."

"*Ahem*," the Captain coughs into his closed fist. "I'm sorry but I'm going to have to rush you. Everyone else on board has also had to leave someone behind, whether it's a housekeeper, an employee, a loved one."

Holding my shoulders, Gav kisses me on the forehead. My throat burns at the emotion I'm holding in, but I refuse to allow his parting image of me to be one of my face crumpled into an ugly cry.

Mike has already walked Fiona towards the aircraft.

Gripping my hand tightly, Gav leads me to the bottom of the aircraft stairs and as I step up onto the first step, he slaps my bum lightly. "Now get going and I'll see you soon."

I climb the steps and turn one last time, mouthing, "I love you."

He blows me a kiss, and I mime catching it in my hand and squashing it into my heart, before the stewardess pulls up the stairs and locks the aircraft door.

Fiona and I take our seats, and as the aircraft taxis its way to the runway our gaze remains glued to the solitary figures of our men, standing by the terminal building, waving us goodbye.

Potentially forever.

Chapter 14

Four and a half hours after leaving Owens International on Grand Cayman, we touch down at Teterboro Airport in New Jersey, where, along with the other well-heeled members of New York society, Tim houses their company's private jet.

After explaining to the exhausted and thankfully disinterested sole US customs guard that we have no intention of staying illegally, despite having no US dollars in our pockets, onward flight tickets, or confirmed hotel reservations, I collapse into Tim's waiting arms as soon as the screen doors open in Arrivals.

"Hello stranger," he says warmly. "Fancy seeing you here."

"Oh god, Tim. You have no idea how happy I am to see you."

"I know. I tend to have that effect on folks." He looks around behind me to where Fiona is loitering, waiting to be introduced. "Where's Gavin?"

"It's a long story, but this is my friend Fiona. She came with me. Captain Montgomery insisted there was only room for two more passengers so we had to leave Gav, and Fiona's husband, Mike, behind. Oh, Tim, it's just too horrible."

"Oh, I hadn't realised. Well then you'd both better come back to mine, while we figure everything out."

• • •

Tim's chauffeur drives the three of us back to his penthouse on Bleecker Street, on the border between Greenwich Village and Soho, and over a glass of Chablis I update him on our predicament.

"We don't know where they are now. Gav and I had stocked up on emergency supplies and were planning to go back to the hotel, but then he gave them all away along with our hire car, so he won't have had any way to get back there. Even without all the chaos, it's about forty-five minutes to drive back over to the East End."

"I can't bear the thought of what's going to happen in the next twenty-four hours." Fiona buries the heels of her hands into her closed eyes, wiping away her tears. "The thought of my kids losing their father…" She trails off.

I rub her back, knowing it will bring her little comfort.

"Okay. One thing at a time ladies." Tim raises his hand. "The networks may be jammed, which I suspect is why we can't reach the guys on their mobiles, but my team here in New York are still in touch with our office down there. Thank goodness for good old-fashioned telex. I still own property and have employees on the island, remember. Locals who didn't want to leave. We've put the word out and we'll find them. Try not to worry." He looks at each of us in turn. His calm tone at odds with the concern in his eyes. "I know that's impossible. But hurricanes in the Caribbean are fairly common and the islanders are pretty adept at dealing with them."

"Yeah, but even you have to admit this one's different, Tim. It's a monster."

Clutching her phone in both hands, Fiona screams, "I've got a text."

"So've I." I exhale, seeing Gav's name light up on my screen.

An image of them both, their fingers permanently hitting the resend button on their phones comes to mind.

> Hello Angel.

> Couldn't get back to the hotel

> We've been sent to one of the emergency shelters in the gym of the George Hicks High School

We're just helping out at the moment, making up sandbags and boarding up the windows. Battening down the hatches — literally.

Let me know that you've made it to New York safely.

I'm assuming Tim's able to put you up, or you've found a hotel.

I love you. Today. Tomorrow. Always. Gav x

I punch out a swift reply, telling him that Fiona and I are staying with Tim and that he's not to worry about us, but to focus on staying safe.

He sends another reply, saying he's going to switch his phone off to conserve the battery. I quickly type back:

Good idea.

I love you too.

Today. Tomorrow. Always. V x

I hit send, but the message remains undelivered. I slowly close then reopen my eyes.

Even if he can't see my words, I hope he can feel them and that they keep him safe until this nightmare is over.

✳

Sixty-six hours later and that message remains undelivered.

"It's the not knowing that's killing me," I say across to both Tim and Fiona on Sunday morning, while we continue to wait for news. Any news.

Pressing the button on Tim's coffee grinder, the machine whirrs into life. The sound of the beans being pulverised forcing a temporary halt to my conversation.

Fiona picks up the remote to Tim's flat-screen TV. Flicking through the channels, she stops when she lands on a twenty-four-hour news programme. An impeccably dressed anchorwoman with glistening white teeth and perfectly coiffured bleached-blonde hair is reporting on the news of the day. After an update of the top stories in the US, the screen changes to images taken from a helicopter. It's of an island hillside. All its vegetation, buildings, and infrastructure obliterated.

"That's Jamaica," I shout across to Fiona. "Quick. Turn it up!"

"Jamaica is waking up this morning counting the cost of the devastation from Hurricane Ivan that continues to bring havoc to the southern Caribbean." The anchor woman delivers the horrific update in a professional but monotone report. *"The repair bill on Jamaica alone is estimated to be as much as $500 million. Reports are unconfirmed, but an estimated seventeen people have lost their lives on the island. Some from mudslides and flooding caused by the torrential rain that accompanied the high winds. That brings Ivan's death toll so far to sixty-one. Thirty-nine on the island of Grenada alone."*

Acid bile rises up the back of my throat and I cover my mouth with my hand. I resist the urge to vomit and force myself to keep watching.

"The eye of the storm passed twenty miles south of Jamaica during the early hours of Saturday night. Winds as high as 170mph were reported, with some gusts reaching as high as 200mph. What is known is that the devastation to buildings and infrastructure will be long-lasting. Let's go now to Michael Price who's on the ground in Pensacola, finding out how businesses and residents in the US are preparing for its arrival sometime in the next few days."

The screen changes to a reporter outside a Wallmart in a US suburb. In the background people wheel trolleys stacked high with bottles of water and other supplies towards their cars and pickup trucks.

"Thanks Suzanna. Yes, we may be in the middle of hurricane season, but everyone here in the Panhandle and as far west as Louisiana are all preparing for the worst."

"What about the bloody Caymans?!" I scream at the telly.

Tim comes and puts his arms around me, meanwhile Fiona stares into nothingness. Struck dumb by fear and uncertainty.

I look outside, through the floor-to-ceiling windows of Tim's stark industrial penthouse. The open-plan kitchen, dining, and sunken lounge area filling an entire floor of the converted printing factory. The sun rising outside into a clear cobalt blue sky. A deceiving mistruth.

"It must be there right now. This very moment," I say, pinching the bridge of my nose.

"All we can do is pray." Fiona wraps her arms around her own body.

"I'm supposed to be back at work tomorrow." I snort out a dry laugh.

Work. Life. England. They all seem so far away right now, whilst we're stuck in the middle of an unimaginable alternate universe.

"That's the last thing you need worry about," Tim says. "I'm sure they must have an HR policy for unavoidable absences. And I reckon getting caught up in a natural disaster counts as an unavoidable absence. Worst case scenario they'll doc your wages for unauthorised leave. Same for you, Fiona." He looks over to where she's still sitting on the sofa, staring at the ongoing news report.

Tim picks up his phone. "My Blackberry is pinging every two minutes. Everyone with someone still down there wanting updates. None of the agencies are open until tomorrow, so we'll all just have to sit tight. My PA's already on it. The storm will definitely have passed by then and the clean-up will have started. I'll contact the Governor, the Red Cross, the military… and I promise you we'll get your guys home. We're British, remember. One thing we're good at is coping in a crisis."

I bury my head in Tim's shirt. "So if we're British, Tim…"

"Yes?" he asks, his voice muffled as he kisses the top of my head.

"Then why the fuck do you not have any tea in this apartment? Forcing us to have to drink your shit American coffee."

"There now, Victoria—that's the spirit."

Chapter 15

"*I* know you won't be able to pick this up, but I'm leaving you another message anyway, just in case ..." I whimper into my phone handset.

It's 5:45 a.m. on Monday morning, another agonising day of no news having passed. I'm in Tim's guest bathroom, sitting on the closed toilet seat lid, the ceiling spotlights dimmed to their lowest level. I know Gav isn't picking up any messages, but I can't sleep so I'm leaving yet another voicemail. It gives me the faint hope that we're still connected on some ethereal level.

"Oh Gav, I'm praying you're safe. Please get in touch as soon as you can. I keep reliving every last moment on the tarmac. Like a rerun of a really bad movie. I'm ashamed to say it, but a part of me wishes we hadn't bumped into Mike and Fiona. Gosh, that's really bad isn't it? They're parents for fuck's sake... but if we hadn't seen them in the airport, then you would be here safe. With me. Oh, why wasn't there room for all of us on that damn plane?" My tone becoming increasingly desperate with every syllable.

I turn and look in the mirror. My tanned face and arms shine back at me with a healthy glow, but the pain in my face gives away the truth of our situation.

"I love you so much. Not knowing where you are or being able to reach you hurts so much." I clutch my chest. "And it's made me realise something. That last night, lying in bed together, you asked me a really important question—and even though you may never hear this..." Hot tears spring into the corner of my eyes. I sniff loudly. "... Now I've had time to think about it, I know exactly what I want and I want to tell you my answ—"

Beep. The answerphone cuts me off.

With shaking fingers and tears rolling down my face, I frantically punch out his number again, but this time I'm greeted by an automated message.

"This mailbox is now full. Please try again later."

"Nooooo!" I scream, staring at the phone clasped in my hand.

Tossing the handset into a folded pile of towels on the floor, I bend double with the physical pain that rips through my gut.

Seconds later, my phone buzzes and I dive for it. Hoping upon hope that somehow the communication gods have sent me a message from Gav and he's safe.

Hey Goose,

A cold shiver ripples across my skin. Only one person in the entire world calls me that.

How you doing?

I had a message off Mike a couple of days ago and he told me about the horrific situation you're all in.

Mad that you bumped into them after all this time. God I hope he's okay. And your fella too of course. I've not heard anything since. Have you?

Funny. You were the one person I wanted to message when I heard. Thank god you managed to escape.

Always in my heart. Chris x

I stare dumbstruck at the phone. What the actual...? Of all the people I expected to hear from, Chris wasn't even on the list.

Of course he came up in conversation the other night, but that was to be expected considering who I was with. Rarely do I think of him now. All my memories of that period of my life are safely tucked away in the wooden ballerina box I keep stored at the back of my cupboard. Hidden there are the stunning yellow diamond earrings he returned to me after we saw each other again at Mel's wedding in Denia five years ago. The black velvet box remains nestled amongst all the letters he's ever written, together with the odd postcard he sent from far-flung exotic locations. I have considered throwing it all away—minus the diamonds, obviously, but that would feel like throwing a part of myself away too. So I've kept it all, even if I have no intention of ever opening that wound again, which is why hearing from him now, and in such traumatic circumstances, is so jarring.

I think carefully about how to reply. Part of me wants to pour my heart into the message. Tell him how dreadful I feel and how desperate the situation is. But I know he'd interpret that as an open doorway. He never did have any boundaries where I was concerned.

Eventually I punch out:

> Hey Chris, I wasn't expecting to hear from you, but I appreciate your concern. We're still waiting for news. Fi & I are just hoping and praying they're okay. Vicky

No *love Vicky*. Not even a kiss after my name. All very matter of fact. Nothing he could misinterpret.

I'm still staring at the screen, processing everything, when there's a soft knocking at the bathroom door. It opens a fraction, allowing in a chink of light.

"Hey Vicky. Are you okay in there?"

It's Fiona. She pushes the door open some more. The dawn light behind her shines like an aura, making it impossible to see her features.

I squint. "Not really. You?"

"Same," she replies, coming into the room. "Couldn't sleep." She sits down on the rim of the bathtub and reaches for my hand.

"Me neither," I reply.

"I've put some coffee on… in the absence of any bloody tea."

We both look at each other. Our grim smiles sitting beneath bloodshot eyes, puffy and swollen from three days of intermittent crying.

"Come on." She stands up. "We'll get through this. I don't know how… but somehow we will. We have to."

The rich smell of roasted coffee wafts through the apartment and draws us out into the kitchen where we find Tim, fully dressed in a pinstripe suit, his eyes glued to the TV screen.

The sound off, the ticker tape along the bottom of the screen reads:

TWO DEAD IN THE CAYMAN ISLANDS AS STORM SURGES FROM HURRICANE IVAN COMPLETELY SWAMP THE ISLAND

"Nooooooooo," Fiona screams, covering her mouth with her hands.

I fall to my knees, my body no longer able to support my weight.

"Okay. Nobody panic," Tim says in a military-like fashion. "I'm heading into the office now. I've called an emergency meeting for 6:30 a.m. and I'll update you as soon as I know anything concrete. Stay by your phones. And look at me… both of you."

Holding onto each other, Fiona and I pick ourselves up and lean on the kitchen island in front of us.

Tim looks us straight in the eyes. "It's not them. The fatalities. Trust me. They're fine. Maybe a bit wet, but wherever they are, they're fine."

"You don't know that, Tim," I mewl.

"No. You're right. I don't," he answers truthfully, dropping his gaze to the floor. "But I feel it in my gut; it's not them. Stay by your phones."

He heads out, slamming the heavy metal door behind him. A dead echo reverberates straight through my heart and around the apartment.

★

The rest of the day passes painfully slowly, as if someone has added weights to all my limbs and replaced the oxygen in the air with soup. The muted TV has been left permanently on, even though it's showing the same, now old, newsreel of the devastation on Jamaica, but Fiona and I remain glued to it. Desperate for any new updates. Meanwhile, we take turns to watch over our mobiles while the other takes a shower, or nips to the loo.

Fresh coffee in hand, we watch as the news report changes; we cling to each other like baby gibbons watching the first grainy aerial shots of the devastation on Grand Cayman in stunned silence. I pick up the remote and turn up the volume. The pictures show once perfect palm-lined beaches, fringed by luxury villas and personal docks for millionaire's boats, now completely flattened; the boats lying upturned and ripped to shreds on the roads behind the villas, giving some indication as to the height of the storm surge. The newsreader says:

"With all on-the-ground communication and infrastructure wiped out, there is no firm news from Grand Cayman, only speculation, but it's fair to say the residents of The Cayman Islands are waking up this morning to a very different world than the one they remember."

"Early reports say waves of up to thirty feet battered the low-lying main island. Cayman Brac and Little Cayman appear to have fared slightly better. No single building has been left undamaged and the repair bill is estimated to run into billions. It is believed the island is without running water and electricity, and looting is widespread."

"A large scale humanitarian rescue is underway. The Department for International Development is sending three million water purification

122

tablets, as well as 50 chainsaws, 500 camp cots and plastic sheeting to the island."

"Switch it off," Fiona shouts. "It's not helping. It's as bad as it could possibly be."

"We just need to hope that they remained in the shelter and that they're okay."

"I've never felt so helpless," she says. "Everyone back home wants an update. But what do I tell them? The kids are asking to speak to their daddy and I don't even know if he's alive or d—"

Dropping her head into her hands, she breaks down into heavy sobs once again. I too have been ignoring all the messages from my family and friends. I called Nessa two days ago and gave her a brief update, and asked if Anth could update Gav's work so I didn't have to. I've emailed my own managing director and told him I won't be in work tomorrow and he's emailed back his support. I've sent brief texts to my mother, Julie, and Becca, but kept the details scant and asked that they don't call, promising I'd let them know as soon as I hear more. It's too upsetting to have to repeat the same story over and over.

"Here." I pass Fi her coffee. We seem to be living on the stuff at the moment. "We have to trust that Tim will find out what's going on. The governor is his personal friend. We couldn't have anyone better in our corner. There are no other agencies or resources we can turn to that Tim isn't already all over." I let out a long sigh. "All we can do, Fi, is wait."

"But for how much longer?" she wails. "I don't know how much more of this I can take."

I open the fridge. "I think we should eat something. How about some eggs?"

My phone starts vibrating, jumping about the worktop. I dive across the kitchen island and flip it over.

On the screen is a message from Tim.

Two words:

They're alive!

Shrieking, I show the message to Fiona and she leaps up and hugs me. We're still dancing and screaming around the kitchen when he calls.

"They're fine." Even Tim sounds elated. "A bit wet, as I predicted, but alive and fine."

I can't speak, the torrent of emotions that floods through my veins rendering me mute. I put the phone on loud speaker.

"The team down there are working on a plan to get them out, together with the injured and any other remaining tourists. The place is completely wiped out," Tim continues.

"We know. We've just seen the news. It looks like total devastation," Fiona says.

"It is," Tim confirms.

"Thank you, Tim. Thank you, thank you, thank you," I splutter, now I've re-found my voice.

"You don't have anything to thank me for, Victoria. But I need to be brief. I have to keep this line open."

"Of course."

"We think they'll come into Miami." Tim shares what little he knows. "We don't know when, but when we do I'll send the jet down for them and the other company employees or their relatives we're bringing out. There's no firm timescale yet. The harbour is full of debris, literally boats sunk all over the place, so no large ships can dock, and the airport is completely destroyed. It's a logistical nightmare. Just hang tight, Victoria. Be patient. This is an international incident on a major scale and we're to be mindful that there's an entire island of people who need help."

"I know, and we will. And Tim... thank you so much for all of this. I don't know what I would have done without you."

"It's fine. What are friends for?"

Hanging up, Fiona and I collapse into each other's arms, sobbing.

Eventually our sobs turn into laughter and we step back from each other, wiping our happy tears from our cheeks with the pads of our fingers.

I reopen the fridge.

"Fuck the eggs, Fi. I think this warrants cracking open the bubbly."

＊

Five days later, Fiona and I are waiting nervously at Teterboro Airport. Hopping from foot to foot and biting our nails while we wait for the opaque doors in the arrivals hall to open. Then as abruptly as our men were taken from us, they are here. Rescued by a combination of the US Navy followed by Tim's help flying them up from Miami.

We rush into our respective partners' arms.

"Angel," is all Gav says, burying his face in my hair.

My cheek pressed against the side of his neck, his familiar musky smell rushes up my nostrils and suddenly the world starts turning again.

He breathes me in as we hold each other tight. The feeling of his strong body enveloping me once again only emphasises how much I've missed him. I never want to be parted from this man again.

"I thought I'd lost you." I smile up at him as we look deep into each other's eyes.

"Never. You think a bit of wind and rain could keep me from you? It'll take a lot more than a big fuck off storm to delete me out of your life," he jests.

I reach for his hand and slide his signet ring back onto his little finger. "Here. Time to be reunited with your dragon."

He holds my face in his hands and lands a gentle kiss on my lips. "Vicky, all I've done this past week is hope and pray for this moment. I've had lots of time to plan out how I want to do this, and inside a soulless grey airport arrivals hall wasn't top of the list, but damn it, I can't wait a moment longer before I ask you this. You know you mean the world to me…"

"And you to me," I interject.

He smiles a tentative smile, before becoming serious once again. "And I want the rest of the world to know that too."

He pulls out a small black velvet box from the pocket of his now grubby shorts, the same ones he was wearing the last time I saw him.

My stomach does a full cartwheel, like a washing machine on a spin cycle, when I look down at the jewellery box in his hands.

No, my internal voice screams, don't ask me. Don't make me reject you. Not when we've just been reunited.

He angles the box in such a way that when he pops the lid, I'll see what's inside.

I hold my breath, waiting for him to drop to one knee, but he remains standing. "As horrific as this past week has been, the vision of you waiting for me, just as you are, is what's kept me going. And I'm never letting you go again—ever.

This is it. He's about to pop the question.

"I heard you when you said you didn't want me to propose, because to get married you feel you'd have to sacrifice a part of yourself." He glances down at the diamonds on my wrist, before locking eye contact with me again. "Vicky, I never want you to have to make any sacrifices for me, or to feel like you have to survive us. I want you to live a full and happy life. One filled with an abundance of love, where you wake up every morning and feel you are enough. Because you are. If this past week has taught me anything, it's that life can be snatched away in a heartbeat." He snaps his fingers, the sound cracking like a whip around the hollow terminal hall. "And more than just living a life together, Vicky, I want us to create a glorious one. I know we'll be together for ever, but..."

I hold my breath. He still hasn't dropped down onto one knee; instead he stands firm and flips open the lid of the box. Inside are a pair of stunning diamond earrings, the ones from the set I admired in Gems International. That's what he must have rushed back for when we were preparing to leave. Made of two-tone gold, they're shaped into a channel setting of a half hoop of diamonds. Not overly ostentatious. Simple. Chic and utterly *me*.

I gasp, my gaze flicking back and forth between the earrings and Gav's softened features.

He sucks in an enormous breath, making his shoulders rise. "Vicky, will you have a baby with me? Will you be the mother of my child?"

His hands shake while he waits for my answer.

This is as far from the proposal I was dreading as you could get. As always, Gav has gone one better. He's given me the perfect proposal I didn't know I needed.

Bubbles of excitement and love pop inside of me as I realise this *is* what I've been wanting for so long. I didn't want to commit to marrying Gav for fear of losing a part of myself all over again, but a baby is something different. I'd be giving a part of myself, to create a whole new life. We'd magnify the love we have for each other, and having a baby together feels like a much more meaningful commitment than saying *yes* to marriage.

Jumping up and down on the spot, I squeal, "Of course, yes. Let's do it. Let's make a baby."

I quickly remove the plain gold studs I'm wearing, and replace them with my new diamond earrings. A symbol that Gav and I are committed not just to each other, but to the life we've yet to create.

Gav pulls me into a hug so tight I fear my lungs might burst. "Oh Vicky. I love you so much."

"And I love you." I beam. "But can I be honest?"

"Of course, what is it?" he says, holding me at arm's length again, so he can look into my eyes.

"Could you take a shower before we start trying? You absolutely honk."

Throwing his head back he releases a loud belly laugh. "Come on." He grabs my hand to hold, while throwing the only bag he has with him over his other shoulder—presumably our original suitcases and clothes we took on holiday are all long gone. He walks us towards where Mike and Fiona are waiting for us, before we step inside Tim's sleek black limo.

I'm the happiest I can ever remember being—Gav is safe, we're reunited, and we're ready to start a family—yet my gut has just flipped over like a snake.

What if I can't have kids? What if I can't give this man everything he wants?

I know he says he loves me and he'd never leave me, but what if the decision I made all those years ago, long before I even knew him, has jeopardised our future happiness, and then he decides I'm not enough.

Then what?

Part III

Chapter 16

GAVIN

3 months later, Friday 17th December 2004

*T*ing.

The lift doors open and Gav's eyes adjust to the soft sepia lighting that casts shadows around the grey lobby. Accents of purple and fuchsia catch his eye. Purple chairs. A purple sofa. A piece of abstract art with flashes of shocking pink hangs on the wall. His shoes sink into the plush carpet as he walks towards the friendly eyes that peek over the top of the walnut reception desk. A spray of oversized Birds of Paradise spill out of the top of a tall vase filled with pink and purple glass beads. Next to them, a framed notice announces a routine fire alarm test at 10:00 a.m. on Monday.

"Hello Gavin. Aww… she's going to love them." The receptionist points to the bouquet of multicoloured roses Gav is cradling in the nook of his arm. Glancing down, presumably at some checklist of pre-booked visitors, she asks, "Is she expecting you? I don't have you on my list today."

"No, Cathy. I thought I would rock up unannounced. Surprise her. Help her carry her box out."

"I know. It's really sad. I can't believe she's actually going. A proper canny lass that one."

A snort of involuntary laughter escapes from Gav's nose.

"What's so funny?" The laughter lines around Cathy's eyes crinkle as she smiles.

"*A canny lass.* I don't think I'll ever get used to some of your Geordie sayings."

"Sweetheart, I'm old enough to be everybody's mother around here; you're all *canny lasses* or *lads* to me. I tell you, it's a sad day when your doctor is younger than your own last-born!"

Gav pulls out a red rose from the bouquet, leans forward and lays it across her keyboard.

"Cathy, you're ageless in my eyes."

"Oh give over. You're such a charmer." She picks up the rose and inhales its scent. "I shall miss you too. Coming in here most evenings and brightening my day." Her eyes glass over as she looks at the rose. "It's been ten years since my Eddie passed. He always gave me red roses."

Gav leans over the desk and grips her hand, giving it a little squeeze. "Then imagine this one is from Eddie too."

"I swear, if I was forty years younger," she mumbles, shaking her head and smiling.

Gav gives her a wink and points down the corridor in the direction of Vicky's soon-to-be-vacated office. Cathy nods, confirming that she's somewhere in that direction.

Gav turns the corner and walks into the open-plan office space. Banks of desks, each workstation separated by a blue divider screen, are laid out in pods of eight on either side of the room. This engine room houses around sixty people, but rather than focusing on their individual computer screens, everyone's attention is turned towards the end of the room. They've either swivelled their chairs around, or found a place to stand around the periphery with a clear line of sight towards the row of Directors' offices, where the leaders of the company have begun to gather. Not wanting to disturb the impending huddle, Gav hangs at the back.

Vicky's managing director appears from his office and begins the informal lineup together with the rest of the directors, along with Vicky.

Looking back towards all the pairs of expectant eyes, the managing director raises his hand and a hush falls over the room.

"Today is bittersweet, as we say goodbye to one of our most valued colleagues—Victoria Fenwick. For the past eight years she has given her all to this company, but now it's time for us to wish her well as she embarks on her own entrepreneurial adventure."

The crowd show their appreciation by applauding until he raises his hand once again. Vicky leans casually against the doorframe of her own office which, as second in command to the MD, is immediately next to his.

"I'm sure we all have our own memories of working with this incredibly talented young woman; in fact some of those stories, especially the ones involving alcohol at our Christmas parties, she should take with her…"

A ripple of laughter flows through the crowd. Gav looks over everyone's heads, but Vicky, her eyes downcast, has yet to spot him at the back of the room.

"But what I shall always remember about Victoria is the moment eight years ago when this ambitious young lady came in for her first interview. She made myself *and* the rest of the management team sit up and pay attention. It felt like she was interviewing us."

Another ripple of laughter spreads like a Mexican wave in a stadium.

"… Exactly." The MD acknowledges the irony of an interviewee giving a potential employer such a detailed grilling. "We hadn't even offered her the role at that point, but she wanted us to guarantee the budget and resources she'd outlined if she was going to deliver the results we expected. Nobody before or since has ever interviewed like that."

Vicky, still leaning against her doorframe, her eyes fixed on the floor, crosses her Louis Vuitton encased feet. Her stocking-covered calves disappear under a pencil skirt, and her waist looks tiny, nipped in with a fitted suit jacket. Vicky is not a naturally heavy-breasted woman, but somehow today her shape seems more voluptuous. The blue silk shirt, open at the neck, reveals a deep cleavage; Gav feels a familiar stirring inside his boxers, knowing he will be the one later to slowly undo those silk buttons and dip his head between those perfectly shaped mounds. He inhales, and as well as the sweet smell of the roses in his arms he can already smell the intoxicating oriental scent of the Coco Channel perfume he'll find there.

"We knew then what a sharp cookie she was, and that we had to have her, and it's fair to say we've never looked back."

Vicky looks over to her boss and smiles in recollection.

"I know she will be super successful as she launches her own business and training company, partly as she's already managed to retain us as her first client. The first of many, I'm sure."

They lock eyes momentarily and smile affectionately at each other.

"I'm sure you'll all agree she has an impeccable work ethic, a creative brain, and is a brilliant and fair leader, but most of all… she's a really decent human being, and I for one will miss her."

This time the crowd break into spontaneous applause. Vicky looks up for the first time, nodding in appreciation at the thanks being offered by her colleagues. As her gaze drifts around the room she clocks Gav at the back and smiles.

Gav watches as Victoria's eyes continue to roam the room, connecting and smiling with familiar faces.

It doesn't seem like three months since they'd returned from New York and she'd outlined her plans to start her own business on the flight home. Even before they'd landed, she'd written her business plan, outlined her brand promise, and created a marketing plan.

Gav hasn't told her all the horrors he witnessed during the hurricane itself.

What would be the point? It was traumatic enough to live through, he doesn't need her to be haunted by those images too.

He'll never forget how helpless he felt huddled together with Mike, like two lab rats in a metal can, hoping that the gymnasium roof would hold. Everyone trying to silence the sound of the destruction outside by pressing their hands over their ears. Howling winds and relentless rain. Trees cracking and crashing to the ground. Glass smashing. Metal twisting and grinding as cars and even boats were picked up by the storm surge and dumped hundreds of yards inland. The sandbags he'd helped to stack across the gym entrance did little to prevent the thirty-foot storm surge that completely obliterated the island. Even after the waves subsided, everyone was left wading through knee deep sludge.

But if living through the storm wasn't bad enough, nothing could have prepared them for the horrors in the week that followed. Emerging wet and thirsty from the storm shelter, everywhere they looked everything was destroyed. Buildings torn apart, roads ripped up, everything damaged beyond repair. The beautiful island from weeks before replaced by an unrecognisable war zone.

As night fell on that first day, Gav will forever by haunted by the helpless wails of the children separated from their parents. Others shaking and crying, having lost everything.

Over the days that followed, as two strong able-bodied men, they helped out where they could. Clearing debris by hand, creating burial piles for the hundreds of dead wild animals and family pets who didn't survive. But as food and water stocks diminished and tensions rose, he was more than relieved to be evacuated with other non-residents, and eventually reunited with Vicky in New York.

Something like that changes you, he thinks to himself, which is why he's so proud Vicky is following her professional dream and starting her own company.

"In true Victoria style," the managing director continues, "rather than a leaving gift, she has asked that we all make a donation to The Cayman Islands National Recovery Fund."

Another round of applause ripples throughout the room and someone curls their index finger and thumb into their mouth, blowing a loud appreciative wolf whistle.

"Having discussed it with my fellow directors, we've decided to double the amount you all generously donated. So Victoria, on behalf of everyone here, it gives me great pleasure to give you this."

He hands Vicky a sealed white envelope, and everyone claps loudly.

She rips open the envelope, looks at the cheque inside, and covers her mouth with her hand.

"Oh my goodness," she splutters. Looking up at the expectant eyes in the room, she sucks a deep breath in, and gathers herself.

The MD steps back and gives her the floor.

She clears her throat. "When my partner Gavin and I holidayed in Grand Cayman back in September, we could never have appreciated what a life-changing three weeks it would be. I know this very generous donation will make a massive difference to those who are having to rebuild their lives—literally. So on behalf of the people of the Cayman Islands, thank you."

The applause continues but everyone now rises to their feet, giving her a full standing ovation. Gav watches as a red flush rises up her neck and into her cheeks. She places her right hand over her heart, and bows her head.

Her MD steps forward and vigorously shakes her hand before turning to the assembled company. "Alright everyone." He checks his watch. "Thank you, and back to work."

A couple of people nod their heads in recognition as Gav walks through the dispersing crowd to her office on the other side of the room. After a couple of handshakes with the team members who have stepped forward to say a few final personal goodbyes, Vicky slinks back inside closes the door. A cardboard box containing her personal effects sits in the middle of her desk.

"For you." Gav passes her the flowers and lands a kiss on her cheek.

"Thank you, hon." Instinctively she bends and inhales their pungent scent.

Gav knows the best bud will end up clipped and added to her

growing bowl of pot pourri on the sideboard back at their home, continuing the tradition his tad started with his mam.

Agreeing to try for a baby, and Vicky starting her own business aren't the only decisions the couple made on their return to the UK Gav moved in. To be fair, he was spending more of his time at Vicky's than back in his flat, which, rather than sell, he's rented out. Having decided to keep it as an investment.

"Ready?" Gav picks up the storage box from her desk.

Turning slowly, she takes one last look around.

"Ready." She throws the strap of her laptop bag over her shoulder, and picks up her handbag. "Let's go. We don't want to keep the gang waiting."

It takes another thirty minutes to finally leave the building, everyone wanting to give her a hug and a final goodbye. Despite the monetary donation, the storage box is overflowing with cards, gifts, and boxes of chocolates.

Back in the privacy of the lift, Gav asks, "How much?"

Turning to him, her face beaming, she replies, "Three fucking grand! Can you believe that?"

"Knowing what people think of you my angel, yes, actually, I can."

Chapter 17

*V*icky slides into Gav's Mondeo and turns on the electric seat warmer.

"We'll be there before it's had a chance to warm up." He squeezes her thigh affectionately.

"Maybe, but my nether regions are freezing. I think my butt warms up faster if it believes it's being warmed up."

He glances sideways at her. "You okay?"

"Yup. It's just a lot, that's all. The last time I left a job was when I left London and moved to New Zealand. I've worked here ever since I came back to the UK. I shall miss them. They've been good to me."

"True. But you've been good to them too. It's nice that you're going out on a high. And just think of all the new adventures to come."

"I know. But now it's really happening… it's all a bit scary. Like stepping off a cliff and hoping your parachute will open."

"I haven't showed you the additions I've made to your website this week. I've managed to squeeze in a few more sneaky hours' work. Our place is dead at the moment. Unless they pick up some new business soon, I can't imagine they'll need to keep everyone on. But no reason to worry about that right now. Your branding, however, is super hot, and you're more than ready for your press launch next month."

"Well, I've got four months before my savings run out, so I'd better land a couple of clients by then, or else I'll be applying to the Cayman Islands National Recovery Fund and asking for my cheque back."

"You won't need to, Angel. You'll be fine."

Gav parks up outside Cafe 21 on Queen Street in the heart of the Newcastle Quayside.

"Come on. Everyone's waiting."

~☆~

Gav pulls opens the restaurant door and a rush of warm air greets them. Rivulets of condensation run down the insides of the windows, obliterating the view back out onto the street which is teeming with revellers and pre-Christmas cheer.

"SURPRISE!" the gang all scream in unison when they spy Vicky and Gav arrive.

On the back of one of the two vacant chairs around the table set for eight, someone has tied a nest of party balloons. They bob and fight with each other every time a draught from the kitchen blows through. Vicky's place setting is obliterated by silver confetti containing hearts, stars, and the word 'congratulations'.

"Have you no shame, you guys? This is a classy joint." Vicky laughs good-naturedly.

"All Becca's idea," Nessa pipes up.

"Aye, that'll be right. Blame all the good ideas on me," Becca replies.

"Well it's a lovely thought." Vicky smiles at everyone in turn.

A waiter appears behind them, takes Gav and Vicky's coats, and they each slip into their chairs.

Vicky has previously explained to Gav that *Black Eye Friday*, the last Friday of the working year, is always one of the biggest drinking days in Newcastle, the hordes building up in the Bigg

Market from lunchtime onwards, before rolling down Dean Street onto the Quayside by nightfall. He's grateful he's met everyone at a time in their lives when the fancy-dress pub crawl has been replaced by a more civilised sit-down meal. Attending that first New Year's Eve party at Anth and Nessa's pushed him to the edge of his social anxiety comfort-zone, and no amount of Christmas cheer would make him join them on a pub crawl. Especially if he was required to dress-up as a snowman.

"But tonight isn't just about me and my new venture. It's about all of us." Vicky gesticulates to the three other couples that make up this tight-knit friendship group.

Gav nods at Nessa and Anth, the couple out of the other three they're the most close to and spend the most time with. Partly because Vanessa and Vicky went to secondary school together, and Anth and Gav work in the same company, albeit in different departments.

Next to them are Julie and Paul, or as everyone calls him, *Clarky*, on account of his surname: Clark. Julie is Vicky's cousin, and the women are bound together through a history of childhood memories.

The other married couple are the ones Gav knows the least. Mark is an electrician and Becca a hairdresser, although since having their kids she's set up her own mobile hairdressing business. They bicker endlessly, but appear deeply committed to one another.

Despite knowing these people for less than a year, they've accepted him as one of their own. Learning all his quirks and teasing him relentlessly, just as they do everyone else.

The waiter hovers around the table topping up everyone's wine glasses.

Julie slides her hand over the top of her glass. "Not for me, thanks. I'm fine on water."

"Water! Really... is everything alright? You're not *up the duff* are ya?" Mark hollers, and Julie blushes.

Julie and Clarky make the most unlikely looking couple. Clarky is tall and lanky, and although in middle age he hasn't completely shed his *Goth* roots: the leather straps around his wrist, the drain-pipe black jeans and winklepicker shoes. Julie is much more demure. Like Vicky and Gav, they're not married, but it's easy to see the depth of their connection.

All the girls stare and wait for Julie to respond.

When she doesn't, Becca demands, "Come on Jules. Don't leave us hanging. You haven't denied it… so, are you?"

Clarky slides his arm around Julie's back. "Well we weren't planning on telling anyone just yet, but it looks like you've just outed us."

Nessa and Becca cover their mouths and shriek in unison.

"Calm down, will you. It's still early days, but yes, we're seven weeks and counting," Julie adds, beaming. "I have my first scan in two weeks."

While Nessa and Becca shriek with delight, Vicky remains quiet.

"You okay?" Gav whispers.

She turns and smiles meekly.

"It'll be our turn soon." He kisses the side of her cheek.

Regaining her composure, she picks up some of the confetti from the tablecloth.

"You should have some of this too." She sprinkles the glitter across Julie's place setting.

Nessa raises her glass. "Congratulations. You're also ending the year on a high." Nessa winks at Vicky. "Yes, two thousand and four was definitely the year to score."

"*Chees-y.*" Anth jabs his finger into his wife's shoulder, before whipping his head back to look across the table at Gav and Vicky. "But totally accurate. You definitely *pulled a cracker* last New Year," Anth says, cocking his head in Gav's direction.

"And you call me *cheesy,*" Nessa retorts.

"Enough, you two," Mark cuts in. "Jeez, talk about old-marrieds."

He taps the side of his glass with his knife, and other restaurant patrons turn in their direction at the sound.

"I'd like to propose a toast," he says, raising his glass.

"Two thousand and four may have been the year to score." He turns and winks at Vicky and Gav, and then across to Julie and Clarky. "But I have a feeling two thousand and five is going to be the year to be alive."

"Ahhh! That's terrible." Becca tugs on his arm, while everyone else guffaws and laughs at the terrible line.

"Actually I think I can go one better," Gav butts in. "What with new babies and new businesses to look forward to, I think two thousand and five is going to be the year to *thrive*."

"Aww that's even worse, Gav." Nessa groans and everyone else throws their head back and laughs.

Meanwhile Mark tears off a hunk of bread and chucks it at Gav. It bounces off Gav's forehead, before he catches it and plonks it back on the table.

Opening a menu, Gav says, "Alright, alright. Shall we eat, before Mark chucks anymore of his food at me?"

Chapter 18

8 weeks later, Saturday 12th February 2005

Bangor, Wales

Gav bends down on one knee and places a single red rose on the headstone in front of him. Standing behind him, I lay a sympathetic hand on his shoulder.

The final resting place of his parents is a quiet corner of a small churchyard that overlooks the glistening Menai Strait. If his parents were as gentle and strong as their son, this peaceful corner of the world is perfect for them.

"They would have loved you," he says, stepping back and breathing in the thick green mountainous air.

I slide my arms around his waist and rest my head against his shoulder. "I'm sure I would have loved them too."

After another few moments of reflection, we begin a slow walk back to the car.

"Hold up." I pull on his hand. "I like reading the headstones."

He chuckles. "Only you."

"When I lived in London, there was this Victorian cemetery

across from our flat. I would spend hours in there. Wandering amongst the ancient oaks and sycamores, reading the headstones."

"Not creepy at all," Gav teases.

"I know, weird right? But I've always liked graveyards. I find them cathartic. Not in some sadistic devil-worshipping kind of way, I find them peaceful, contemplative places. I like to image the lives of the people buried there. Who were they? What kind of life did they have?"

"Whereas to me, they're sad and depressing places. Reminders of who you've lost." Gav stops walking, dropping one hand to his hip and nipping the bridge of his nose with the other.

"Oh I'm so sorry, that was insensitive of me."

"It's okay, Angel. I love the fact you find the positive in everything."

"Even graveyards?"

"Even graveyards."

I take a few steps off the path to a cluster of headstones marked out by a small lip of perimeter stones, infilled with purple shale.

"See this here. You've got mum and dad and four children all in the same plot. But then if you look at the dates, mum was left to raise the four children after her husband died. One of the children died when they were only days old. And... *oh look* ... Mum died around the same time. Aww, that's really sad; she must have died in childbirth and the baby either passed away as a result of some birth trauma or because there was no one to nurse it. Gosh ... those poor children left orphaned. I wonder what happened to them."

"My point exactly. There's nothing positive about graveyards, and any *normal* person would just want to get out of here. But then you're not *normal* are you?" He reaches for my hand and gives it a little squeeze. "I have no idea why you find all this cathartic."

"Maybe I just have an overactive imagination, because I can already picture them."

I point at the family plot. "Hard-working. Wholesome. They had a tenanted farm until mum and dad died..."

I twirl my fingers around my temple as the pictures come thick and fast. "But they had a sympathetic landlord who allowed them to stay on in the property."

I snap my fingers as another thread of the story appears in my imagination. "The father had an unmarried sister and she took on the three orphaned children and raised them as her own. The family that she never had." I turn to meet Gav's gaze. "See, it doesn't always have to have a tragic ending."

"You and your overactive imagination. It's a nice story and I hope that's what happened to that poor family." He pauses. "But I'm not sure I could take on someone else's child. It's not that I don't like other people's children, I've just always wanted to raise my own flesh and blood. Surely part of the fascination of parenthood is watching a version of your own DNA grow up in front of your very eyes. I mean I admire anyone who fosters, adopts, or takes in a child that isn't biologically their own, it's just something I know I couldn't do."

That snake in my gut flips over again. I never knew that was how he felt about adoption or any of the alternative ways to bring a child into your family.

"Well, fingers crossed we'll have our very own squawking, puking and pooing mini version of us sometime soon."

Gav and I lock eyes and he presses his lips together into a thin line, while behind my back I secretly cross my fingers.

"I can't wait," he says.

The warm spring sun bathes my cheek with defused rays and I close my eyes against its glare. I sense Gav leaning into me, our auras blending together before our physical bodies connect. The softest brush of his lips against mine. I open my mouth to receive him and he takes the invitation, sucking air in through his nostrils as our passion rises, our reverent lips demanding more.

He wraps me in his arms and I soften against his firm chest. The familiar warmth floods my veins as a pool of desire sinks down from the pit of my stomach, settling between my thighs. I feel his own passion hard and erect against my hip. Cradling the back of my head with his hands we remain locked inside our passion, unaware of the world beyond our kiss.

"*A-hem*," someone coughs in the background.

Breaking our kiss, Gav releases me.

A modestly dressed couple aged around their mid-sixties stand in the path up ahead. The woman is holding a bouquet of lilies. Her eyes, puffy and sore, are the same puce colour as the end of the man's nose.

"I'm not sure that kind of behaviour is appropriate in here." The woman's voice is curt and clipped.

"I agree," Gav replies diplomatically. "We were just leaving."

"I should think so too," the man mutters under his breath.

"My apologies," I say quietly as we head towards the gate. "We meant no disrespect."

She *humphs* as she passes us, and Gav rolls his eyes.

"Shall we?" Gav says once we're back in the car, more as a confirmation than a question, before he rams the gears and heads inland, into the Snowdonia mountain range.

We wind our way up through the Pen-y-Pass and the road rises up to greet us. On either side dramatic hills, treeless and rugged, simultaneously touch both heaven and earth. Each twist in the road reveals yet another breathtaking vista. Hillsides covered with a carpet of spring bluebells are sliced through with interlocking valleys. Their bottoms filled with lakes of glass.

My hair blows in the wind and I pull my scarf more tightly around me. My little two-seater MG may be almost ten years old now, and I drive a sensible Audi A4 on a day-to-day basis, but I've kept my little sports car for fun days out like this. I've never lost the pleasure of driving through open countryside with the top down.

Flopping my head back against the headrest, driving through this landscape I could just as easily be back in New Zealand. Driving the Haast Pass in the Southern Alps, on our way to the Tasman Sea from Wanaka. The similarity is astonishing.

The only difference being the rustic browns and moss greens of the Welsh hillsides are occasionally sliced open from now derelict slate mines. Open wounds, their jagged scars revealing the purple gold buried within these beautiful mountains.

The road continues its twisting route up through the mountain pass and just when I think the peaks can't get any more dramatic, each bend reveals another breathtaking view. The hillsides growing ever steeper, the peaks ever higher as the landscape continues to grow in magnitude. It's like entering a magical kingdom through a secret unmarked route.

We finally park up in Llanberis, at the foot of the steam railway that snakes its way up to the summit of Mount Snowdon. Her snow-capped peak looming ominously in front of us.

"Are you sure you don't want to walk to the top?" Gav asks. "It's knackering, but worth it when you get there."

"Err, no thank you," I reply.

"I was joking." He shakes his head, laughing. "It takes about five hours and you'd never make it in them." He points down at my white trainers.

This is only the second time he's brought me to Wales. The first was a quick day trip to Bangor, his hometown, not long after we started dating. It was my suggestion we come back for Valentine's weekend, so that he can show me more of the country he grew up in.

The bright winter's day has brought many tourists to the mountain, so we wait patiently for our turn to chug our way up to the summit on the steam train.

Once there, we scramble up the last few snow-covered steps to the highest point, marked by a stone circle topped off with a brass plate, and take in the breathtaking three-sixty views. The second highest peak in the British Isles, and the highest mountain in Wales, it really does feel like we're standing on top of the world.

Gav stands behind me, nestling his chin on my right shoulder, his arms wrapped around my waist as we look out over the Irish Sea, the coast of the Emerald Isle just visible in the distance. Turn south and the coastline curves inwards to Cardigan Bay, down past the beaches of Aberystwyth. Look to the east and England's green and pleasant hills roll on as far as the eye can see.

There is no need to speak. Standing atop this mountain with my Celtic lover standing protectively behind me, I'm filled with love and gratitude.

Growing up, how could Gav not be inspired by the view from his bedroom window, a framed vista of this magnificent mountain. This quiet unassuming man mirrors the quiet unassuming reverence of this strong masculine landscape. I hear him suck in air before he releases a slow, cleansing out breath. Being here with him makes total sense and I understand his affiliation to this land.

This is *his* place and he is home.

"Room for one more?" a man with an extremely strong Welsh accent asks, holding his wife's hand as they both step up onto the uneven peak platform.

The summit itself is only capable of housing a handful of people at any one time.

"Wrth gwrs," Gav replies in Welsh, presumably telling them 'yes', and we shuffle along to make room.

That's the other thing about being here in Wales. It gives Gav an opportunity to speak his mother tongue.

"Ydych chi'n lleol?" the man asks.

I assume he's asking if Gav grew up around here, or where he learnt to speak Welsh.

"Yes, I grew up just down there," Gav says, switching back into English and pointing in the direction of Bangor.

"Hi, I'm Victoria," I say by way of introduction, raising my hand in a tentative wave.

"Oh hello. I'd assumed you must be Welsh too," the man remarks.

"No, sorry. One hundred percent English I'm afraid. But don't switch to English on my behalf. I could listen to the rhythm and timbre of your beautiful language all day long."

"Has he not taught you any?" The man cocks his head in Gav's direction.

"Only one word," I reply. "Paned!"

The man and his wife both laugh. "Well it's always good to know how to ask for a cup of *tea*," the wife says.

"Lovely to meet you both," I say, squeezing past them.

I take the first tentative step on the path back down, but my foot slips in the snow, twisting my ankle and shooting it over the edge of the slab of stone that acts as a step. With no handrail to grasp onto I jerk forward, unable to find my footing, and the momentum pulls me backwards. In an attempt to right myself, I overcompensate and swing violently forwards. My arms flailing in the air, desperately searching for something to grab onto.

Somewhere behind me I hear Gav shouting *"VICTORIA!"*, but I'm already off balance and with nothing sturdy to stop me, I'm falling. Down. Down.

My right wrist makes contact with the ground first, before my temple smashes bluntly into the hard earth as I continue to tumble down the steps. Rolling over and over. Head over heels. Knees, hands, and hips banging into the hard ground, I roll on and on.

Eventually I come to a halt, face down, my mouth full of grit mixed with a warm metallic taste. Pain shoots through my right wrist, my right hip bone, and the side of my face. I feel like something has kicked me hard in my ankle bone and smacked me around the head with a metal frying pan.

Even before I've caught my breath, Gav is there. Crouching down beside me. One hand in the centre of my back while I lie head first down the slope. I can only open one eye, the other pressed into the mixture of freezing snow and hard earth. I try to speak, but no words form. Only a few grunts of pain.

"It's okay, Angel. I'm here. Stay still. Don't move. Help is coming."

His voice is calm but laced with an undertone of concern. All around us people are shouting and running out of the cafe a few hundred yards away.

"Oww!" I whisper, spitting out the mixture of gravel, saliva, and blood from my mouth. I try and move, but I can't bear any weight on my right hand. Seeing my attempts to right myself, and realising I haven't broken my neck, Gav helps me up to a seated position. Cradling me in his lap, he nuzzles into my hair.

"It's okay," he says softly. "I think you got away with it. Nobody noticed."

I try to chuckle, but laughing hurts my ribs and I slap him lightly with my left hand. "Don't make me laugh," I whisper. "It hurts."

★

Two hours later, inside a curtained cubicle of Bangor Accident and Emergency department, a sympathetic nurse is rinsing the laceration on my head with saline solution. She's already cleaned up the nasty graze on my lip. Gav sits on a plastic chair next to the bed.

A Junior Doctor in light blue scrubs comes into the cubicle and picks up the clipboard of notes that were hung over the end of the bed.

"Okay," he says brusquely. "Looks like you took a bit of a tumble."

"More like a spectacular face plant," I say with a lisp on account of my fat lip, my sense of humour marginally restored after the lovely nurse jabbed me with a shot of morphine.

"Righto." He avoids any eye contact, as if acknowledging me would slow down the treatment of his overly full patient quota. "Well, it doesn't look like you'll need any stitches in that head wound, just some Steri-Strips, although I suspect you're going to have a severe headache and a corker of a black-eye for the next few days. We'll get you down to X-ray as soon as possible and then we'll know what we're dealing with in your hip and wrist."

"I don't want an X-ray," I say urgently.

Pausing, the doctor looks up.

Before he's even had a chance to ask me why I would refuse any treatment, I blurt, "Just bandage me up. Put one of those Velcro splint thingies on it and I'll be fine."

"It's important we know whether you've damaged your pelvis, although I suspect you've just given it a right good bang. I'm not so sure about your wrist. I think it may be fractured. We also need to do a CT scan of your head. Again, just to be on the safe side."

"Can't you just treat me as if I had experienced the worst? Patch me up and let me out of here?"

"Errr... Ms Fenwick," he says, double-checking the clipboard for my name, "it doesn't work like that. Treatment follows diagnosis, not the other way round."

I glance sideways and catch Gav's eye. He's not happy, and as confused as everyone else. I wince as the nurse applies iodine to my head wound.

"Sorry dear. This will sting, but only for a minute." She puts the cardboard tray down and meets my gaze. "Is there a chance you might be pregnant?"

I squeeze Gav's hand.

"We're trying for a family, and I've not done a test yet." I turn and look at Gav. "I was due on today, so not technically late yet, but I was hoping..."

Gav, his eyes wide—this is news to him to too—smiles, lifts my hand to his lips and kisses the back of it.

"Well then, do you think you can manage a little sample for me, and we'll find out one way or the other," the kindly nurse asks.

"Okay then," the Junior Doctor says. "I'll come back once we know for sure. It just means we'll do an ultrasound rather than an X-ray."

"It should be fine to do a urine test, but do you know what..." the nurse continues, "if it comes up negative I'll do a blood test as well. Just to be doubly sure. We can detect hCG in blood about five days before it shows up in urine, so there's no harm in taking a belt and braces approach now is there."

Gav steps out of the cubicle while the nurse helps wrestle me onto a bed pan.

Oh the glamour.

She subtly looks the other way while I wee, then diligently using a pipette drops a couple of tear-shaped droplets of the warm straw-coloured liquid into the absorbent window of a white plastic pregnancy test.

She checks her watch then announces, "You can come back in, dear." Gav reappears and takes the seat next to the bed. "We'll know in two minutes." She sits on the other side of the bed and all three of us fall into an awkward silence.

When I'd imagined the moment Gav and I would be waiting for the stick to turn blue I hadn't envisaged a nurse in purple scrubs also in the picture. I'd assumed we'd be at home in our bathroom, sitting cross-legged on the floor like giggling teenagers. Instead we find ourselves in a sterile hospital environment with a third, albeit friendly, person unexpectedly on the scene.

Gav and I avoid each other's eye. Looking at each other would mean unconsciously admitting to this stranger we've had sex. Instead I methodically count the rings on the curtain rail at the end of the cubicle, while we all listen to the monotonous *tick, tick, tick* of the clock on the wall.

"Not be long now." She pats the back of my hand.

She spots me looking at her name badge: Seren.

"It means 'star' in Welsh. After five boys, my tad always said I was his shining star."

We smile warmly at each other.

She checks her watch again, then the test, before announcing matter-of-factly, "Congratulations. You're going to have a baby."

"Oh Angel." Gav leaps up and kisses me. "That's brilliant."

I wince in pain, but I don't care. "Happy Valentine's Day," I reply, my heart overflowing with love for him and our unborn child.

And just like that, he and I are expecting.

Chapter 19

3 weeks later, Saturday 5th March 2005

J think you'll find the cups in here." Clarky plonks a cardboard box down on the black granite worktop of their new kitchen and heads back outside to help Gav unload the rest of the boxes and furniture from the removal truck.

"Right, let's get this kettle on. Time to christen our new home with a round of tea," Julie says, flicking the kettle on. "You dig out the mugs and I'll find the tea bags."

Using my one good arm, the other still encased in a plaster cast while my fracture heals, I try my best to rip open the top of the box marked '*Kitchen*'.

"Here, let me help you." Julie steps in.

"I warned you I'd be as much use as a chocolate teapot today."

"Yup. You may be useless, but your man has two good arms and legs, so at least we'll get our money's worth out of him."

"This is such a lovely home Jules." I glance around the large kitchen/diner. "I think the three of you are going to be very happy here."

"I think so too." She strokes her rounded belly, her waistline having thickened over the past few months, and pours boiling water into the four waiting mugs. "We're lucky we could pool our equity."

She lifts another heavy box up onto the work surface and starts filling an empty cupboard with tea bags, coffee, salt, sugar, and other store cupboard staples, before placing her hands in the crook of her back and leaning back to stretch.

"You think you're useless? At least you don't have *this* getting in the way. We must be mad. I get heartburn every time I bend down and when I do bend down, I need a hand back up again. Honestly Tor, everyone talks about pregnancy as this beautiful and womanly time in your life, but growing another human is hard work."

"I know, but it's so exciting for you and Paul. Finally, after all this time, you and Clarky moving in together. We all thought you would carry on living separately, even after the baby's born. Your weird set-up seems to have worked for you all these years."

Although they've been together for almost six years they initially hid their relationship, and only came clean a couple of years ago.

She pats her stomach affectionately and continues, "It seemed the right time to bring our lives together, in every sense."

I smile coyly and unconsciously place a protective hand over my own still-flat tummy, knowing that I too am growing a tiny human and that our lives are also coming together in new ways.

Julie glares wide-eyed at my instinctive motherly action. Her eyes darting from my face, to the hand on my stomach, and back up to my face again.

"You're not, are you?"

I avoid her stare, looking down at the floor. She waits for an answer. I nod almost imperceptibly. She shrieks with delight, does a little jig on the spot, before pulling me in for a bear hug.

"Shhh will you." I laugh. "Keep your voice down. We didn't want to tell anyone just yet. At least not until I'm out of the first trimester, but I'm so excited Jules. Finally, it's my turn and I can't wait."

"Oh my God. This is *soooo* exciting. How far on are you?"

"Only eight weeks. We go for our first scan on Friday."

"When did you find out? I want all the details." She sits down at the table, wriggling in the seat with excitement.

Wrapping my hands around the steaming mug of tea, I take the seat opposite and fill her in on the events of the past few weeks.

"I had this funny taste on my tongue, I could smell fish and chips at three miles, and my boobs ached like you wouldn't believe."

"And what was Gav's reaction when he found out?" she asks.

"Pure unadulterated joy." I laugh. "His heart is full to bursting. Honestly, you'd think he was the only man to have successfully impregnated his woman. He's been strutting around like a proud peacock."

"Paul too," she laughs. "It must be some primal masculine thing."

"Gav's been super attentive. Bringing me tea and ginger biscuits every morning. To be fair I haven't been much use domestically these past few weeks since breaking my wrist, but still…"

"Make the most of it Tor. You never know how long it might last. Wait until your hormones start raging, he may tire of fussing over you then."

"I doubt it," I interject. "This is Gavin we're talking about."

"True. He really is a good egg." She leans forward and squeezes my hand. "I'm so happy that after all the turmoil you've been through, you've finally found your Prince Charming."

"Me too."

"So what does this make them?" Julie asks.

"What do you mean?"

"These two." She points back and forth between our bellies. "Will they be half cousins or cousins once removed?"

"Second cousins. I've already checked," I reply.

"Oh this is so exciting. They'll only be a few months apart in age and we can do all the baby things together. Take them to Swimming Babies. Enrol them in the same playgroups. We can message each other in the middle of the night when we can't get them to sleep, or they start teething. It'll be like they're siblings."

My heart flips over in my chest. With no siblings of my own, the idea of Julie and I bringing up our children together fills me with warmth.

I can already imagine shared caravan holidays to Bamburgh. The kids playing on the beach at The Wyndings. Making sandcastles or holding hands while they jump the waves in the shallows, their pudgy little limbs slick white with Factor 50 suncream. Later being rewarded with 99s from the ice-cream van that parks up in the car park. Their tongues unable to lick the drips fast enough to stop them running down the backs of their hands, before they wipe their sticky paws across the front of their T-shirts.

My future continues to flash before me like a movie.

The men laughing and joking whilst teaching their respective offspring to ride bikes. Then the children waving innocently, hands held as they turn and walk into school together on their first day. Jules and I consoling each other, snivelling quietly in the playground.

"When they're older we could take them to Disney, in Florida," she continues.

Another image of us all staying in adjoining hotel rooms flits through my mind. The children's eyes wide with wonder the first time they spy Cinderella's castle, or their shrieks, loud and carefree, as they plunge down Splash Mountain, their cheeky grins and freckled faces soaking up every ounce of joy.

Julie's right: after all of the turmoil and heartache of the last decade, all I can see in my future is happiness, joy, and an abundance of love.

"Well it doesn't look like there's been much unpacking going on in here." Clarky appears in the kitchen doorway, his brow dripping with sweat. He uses the bottom of his T-shirt to wipe it away. "What have you two been gassing about?"

"Nothing," Julie answers a tad too sharply, her eyes acknowledging our shared secret.

"Oh it's alright. You can tell him." I roll my eyes.

"Tell me what?" Clarky asks.

Gav appears in the doorway behind Paul, and smirks. "I knew you wouldn't be able to hold your piss. You've been dying to tell someone." He picks up one of the cups of tea and comes to stand next to where I'm sitting; laying his arm protectively across my shoulders, he kisses the top of my head.

Julie meets Clarky's gaze. "Gavin and Tor are pregnant too."

Clarky doesn't hesitate before he reaches across and offers Gav a firm handshake. "Congratulations mate. That's superb news. Well done."

I look at Julie across the table and we both roll our eyes.

"Why do men always feel the need to congratulate each other as if they've just climbed Mount Kilimanjaro or something, when in fact all they've done is deposit their soldiers in the right place at the right time," I say.

Gav suppresses a giggle. "Exactly. A difficult task that should never be underestimated."

"I'm feeling the need to make a toast," I say, raising my mug.

"Actually, before you do, Tor," Julie interjects. "Paul and I have a little announcement of our own."

"Oh?" I raise my eyebrows and I feel Gav's hand still on my shoulder.

They gaze lovingly at each other before Julie turns back towards us.

"Are you two doing anything next Saturday?" she asks.

"About 1pm?" Clarky adds.

Gav and I look at each other, neither of us believing we have any prior commitments, before Gav confirms, "Not that we can think of."

"In that case," Julie continues. "Would you be witnesses at our wedding?"

"Oh my God!" I leap up out of my chair and run around the table to hug her. "Like you need ask. And I thought we'd trumped you today."

"Well I could argue that your news is equally as exciting, but

Paul and I don't want any fuss. Which is why we're keeping it low-key. Just us, our parents…"

"And now you two," Clarky says.

"… and a registrar," Julie adds.

"I'm happy for you, mate." Gav shakes Clarky's hand. "A new home, a baby on the way, and now you're getting married as well."

"Thank you." Clarky returns the handshake. "Yes. I'm very happy. A very happy man indeed."

"You deserve it. Both of you," Gav replies.

"As do you." Julie stands next to her beau, her head resting on his shoulder. "Maybe it's about time you made an honest woman out of our Tor as well." She smiles, dipping her head but maintaining Gav's eye contact while she sips her tea.

"Maybe," he deflects, turning to look at me, his eyes full of love, "…but it's not something we're that bothered about."

"To everyone's dreams coming true." I raise my mug, still holding Gav's gaze.

"To dreams coming true," Julie repeats, and the men raise their mugs and repeat the toast in unison.

Chapter 20

*G*av grips Vicky's hand with both of his own as the pair of them remain glued to the screen, waiting. The sonographer remains deathly silent, moving the wand every which way over Vicky's tummy.

Everyone can see the grainy black and white outline on the screen: a small oval-shaped sac with something inside. It may not look like a fully formed human yet, but there's definitely the beginning of a baby's head and a body.

Why's she not saying anything? Gav thinks to himself.

When she does speak, she utters the two words most expectant parents fear the most — "Wait here," — before giving them a sympathetic smile, her lips pressed together. "Try not to worry. I'll be back in a bit."

Vicky flashes Gav a terrified look. He lifts her hand to his lips and kisses the back of her knuckles. "It'll be fine. Everything's fine."

"You don't know that." She shuts her eyes in frustration. "Something's wrong. I know it."

Before they have a chance to say anything more, the sonographer returns with a doctor. The doctor introduces herself then turns her attention to the screen. Keeping her eyes locked on the images, before picking up the wand and rolling it over Vicky's tummy again, making her own scans of the insides of Vicky's womb.

The second hand on the wall clock ticks loudly, emphasising each agonising minute that passes while Gav and Vicky wait nervously for the professionals to say something.

Eventually the doctor turns to them both. "I'm very sorry to tell you, your baby has no heartbeat."

"What?" Gav says quickly. "How can that be?"

The sonographer subtly passes Vicky a box of tissues while the doctor answers Gav's direct question. "It means the pregnancy has miscarried. I'm very sorry, and appreciate this is an awful shock, but it's surprisingly common, especially in women approaching middle-age."

No! This can't be happening, Gav's internal voice screams.

"Are you sure?" Vicky whimpers. "Is there any chance you might be wrong? Can you check again… please?"

"I'm afraid there's no mistake," the sonographer says, squeezing Vicky's leg.

"What happens now?" Gav says, his face tortured with pain.

"Although the pregnancy has failed," the doctor says in a flat tone, unaware how her words slice Gav's skin with a thousand cuts, "the pregnancy sac has yet to pass."

"Oh god." Vicky covers her face with her hands, the shock acting as a dam to her tears.

"The best thing to do now is go home and allow nature to take its course. Most likely you'll start to bleed in the next two weeks," the doctor says.

"What? That's it." Gav sounds incredulous, his voice rising. "Go home and bleed."

"I appreciate this is a shock…" she looks down briefly at Vicky's pregnancy file, noting the name at the top, then looks back at Gav, "… Mr Fenwick."

"Mr Williams. I'm Mr Williams," he says through gritted teeth. "We're not married. Mr Fenwick was her first husband."

"Oh, my apologies Mr Williams. I meant no offence. However,

for early miscarriages like this, *expectant management* is the best course of treatment."

"What does that mean?" Vicky says, her voice hardly audible.

The doctor turns her attention back to Vicky. "It simply means we let Mother Nature do what Mother Nature does best. We'd rather not interfere if it can at all be helped. You'll need some heavy flow pads; I suggest you stock up on actual maternity pads rather than period pads, don't use tampons, and you can take paracetamol and ibuprofen for any cramps or pain. It'll most likely feel like a nasty, heavy period. If you develop a fever, any severe pain, or the bleeding hasn't stopped in two weeks after you start, then you'll need to come back in. Otherwise the best thing to do is go home and try to rest."

Vicky reaches for Gav's hand to hold. "I can't believe this is happening. Did I do something wrong?"

The sonographer steps forward. "You didn't do anything to cause this Victoria. You can't think like that."

"But I had a nasty fall the day I found out I was pregnant? Could that have harmed the baby? Caused the miscarriage?"

"Miscarriage is very common," the doctor interjects, "and most likely caused by an abnormality with the foetus. It's nature's form of natural selection. Here, take these with you." She passes Vicky a handful of leaflets. "There's some more information in these, and some helpline numbers if you think you might need to talk to someone. It's natural to grieve your loss."

"I'm very sorry," the sonographer says. "Take as much time as you need. There's no rush. We don't need the room back for another hour."

And with that the pair quietly close the door as they leave.

Gav breaks down instantly while Vicky remains stoic. Burying his face in Vicky's lap while she remains prostrate on the hospital bed.

"Shhh, shhh," she says softly, stroking his hair.

How can I be the one to fall apart? Gav feels as if someone has reached inside his chest and ripped his heart out. *But why is this happening to me again,* he cries internally.

"Oh Angel, I'm so sorry." He looks up at her, his eyeballs streaked with red lines. "I can't believe our baby has gone."

"I know. I don't want to believe it either." Vicky cradles her non-existent bump. "But our baby has gone, Gav." A single tear rolls down her cheek. Locking eye contact with him, she pleads, "Take me home. I just want to go home."

The next day a subdued Gav holds open the car door. "You look ravishing," he says, whilst thinking, *despite everything that's happening.*

Vicky swings her long legs, clad in a pair of Wolford nude stockings and matching nude heels, down onto the pavement. He helps her up and she brushes away the non-existent wrinkles from her dusty pink frock coat, the cuff of her right arm loosened to allow room for her cast. Her hair is pinned in place by a matching silk fascinator, worn at a jaunty angle. Gav has tucked a handkerchief in the exact shade of Vicky's outfit into the top pocket of his sharp navy suit.

Leaning forward he kisses the back of her hand as he slams the car door shut. "Shall we?" he says, linking his arm through hers and leading her in the direction of Hexham Registry Office.

They take the shortcut that runs through the centre of Hexham Park and behind the 12th-century abbey, its clock showing twelve thirty. Thirty minutes before Julie and Clarky's booked slot.

The park is littered with white snowdrops and purple crocuses that poke their heads up through the neatly mowed lawns, and the air still carries the scent of fresh morning dew. Spring has definitely sprung.

They follow the path as it winds its way through the spindly trees, covered in virginal leaves and bright green buds that push through the once barren bark. In another six weeks the ground will be covered in pink and white blossom, blowing around in the wind like confetti.

The sound of children laughing drifts on the breeze from the direction of the play park. Vicky stiffens and misses her footing. Gav steadies her. "You okay?"

She looks at him, her puffy eyes disguised by perfectly applied make-up. No one has any idea the pain they're both going through. Knowing the inevitable is yet to happen doesn't make waiting for it to start any easier.

Smiling weakly she replies, "I've been better, but today is not about us."

"Exactly. Let's stay focused on Julie and Paul's happiness."

Outside the registry office Gav air-kisses Vicky's aunt and uncle and shakes hands with both of Clarky's parents.

"Well this is a turn-up for the books," Vicky says to her aunt, who is shuffling her weight from foot to foot.

The sun may be high in the sky, but this early in the year it carries no heat and the air remains sharp. The fan of vibrant yellow daffodils around the edges of the manicured lawn of the registry office a reminder that it is still only March.

"Isn't it just. Although it's about time if you ask me," Vickys's uncle says to the small gathering.

"I have to say I am pleased Julie and Paul have decided to do the right thing before my grandchild arrives," her aunt adds. "Call me old-fashioned, but in my day we did things in the right order. We would never have considered living together before we were married, never mind contemplating starting a family."

"I know. But times are different now, are they not?" Vicky asks.

"Perhaps. Nevertheless I'm just happy they're making it all official, even if my Julie is denying me a big white wedding. It's what I would have wanted for her."

"I know you would," Vicky placates her aunt, "but a lavish

wedding doesn't guarantee a successful marriage. I'm the poster girl for that, remember."

"Well yes," her aunt replies, "that's true."

Gav squeezes Vicky's hand, sending her supportive vibes. Like Vicky, his first wedding was a lavish affair—inside a Welsh castle, but even the two-metre-thick walls couldn't insulate him from the hurt and betrayal caused by his first wife.

If only I'd known before the wedding what I found out later, would I have still married her? he's often asked himself.

"I regret how much it all cost," Vicky continues. "If I was doing it again, I'd much prefer something simple and small like this."

"But then the trick, Tor, is marrying the right person in the first place," Julie says, tapping Vicky's bum cheek in greeting.

Vicky jumps, turns, smiles and hugs her cousin as Julie and Paul appear behind everyone.

"Oi oi." Gav slaps Clarky on the back. "I thought it was bad luck to see your bride before your nuptials, never mind rock up to the venue together?"

"Like we're superstitious." Clarky shrugs.

"And can we have no more talk about *marriages failing* today please. Paul and I may be unconventional but I'm determined that nothing is going to spoil my *perfectly formed and practically perfect in every way* wedding day," Julie adds.

"I agree." Gav air-kisses Julie on both cheeks.

Stepping back, Victoria opens Julie's arms so that she can appraise her wedding dress. "You look absolutely amazeballs."

"Thanks," Julie laughs.

Julie's crepe cream dress is trimmed with delicate lace and cut in a flattering empire style. Nipped in below her bust and flaring out in gentle folds that fall softly over her rounded tummy. Her shoulders are covered in a faux fur wrap, her arms in full-length white gloves, and her outfit is topped off in a neat Jackie Onassis pillbox style hat, complete with a half veil that covers the right side of her face. In her left hand she clutches a small posy of lily of the valley flowers. Clarky is wearing a matching buttonhole in the top left lapel of his three-piece suit. He's wearing stick thin drainpipe suit trousers, his long hair pulled back into a tight ponytail; his beard has been shaped to within an inch of its life, and he may not be wearing winklepickers on his feet, but he's managed to find the pointiest black shoes that could pass as *smart suit shoes.*

"Once a Goth, always a Goth," he's told Gav previously.

"How you feeling?" Gav hears Julie whisper to Vicky. He watches as Vicky swallows hard, her spine straightening almost imperceptibly.

"We're fine," Gav interjects, suspecting Vicky doesn't trust herself to speak and not burst into tears. "But today is all about you, Jules. Or should I say, soon to be Mrs Clark."

"And on that note…" Clarky checks his watch. "It's time we got this show on the road. There's some *I do's* to be said, then plenty of beer to be drunk."

The ceremony passes without incident, and twenty minutes later Julie and Paul emerge back outside under a shower of confetti as the new Mr and Mrs Clark. Throughout the nuptials Vicky remained subdued.

"Not long now," Gav whispers, sliding his arm around her waist while they all pose for photographs.

"Not long for what?" She looks at him, her eyes heavy with sadness.

"I know. It's hideous," he whispers back. "I meant not long before we can go home. At least you'll be more comfortable there… when it does start."

After the meal of smoked salmon, roast beef, and sticky toffee pudding in a gastro pub in the middle of the pretty market town, Vicky disappears to the ladies, and returns ten minutes later, looking ashen.

Sitting back down around the intimate table of eight, she remains quiet, her hands folded in her lap.

Gav interlaces his fingers with hers.

He looks at her and she nods quietly. It's started. Every fibre of his being wants to pick her up and run out of there, but leaving early would mean admitting something is wrong.

Thankfully, the bride and groom have broken with another tradition and foregone any formal speeches, but it's another hour before coffees are served and wedding cake is handed out.

Vicky merely moves hers around the plate, before disappearing to the toilet again.

When she returns, Gav can wait no longer. "Julie, Paul, congratulations. It's been a wonderful day, but I know Vicky has a very heavy week coming up…"

At least that part's true. But not in the way they think.

"… So if you don't mind I think we'll start making tracks."

"Oh thank goodness," Julie says. She swings her legs up and lays them across Clarky's lap. "I'm absolutely cream-crackered." Clarky slips off her shoes and massages her feet. Her ankles look like puddings, having stood in heels all day. "I'm dying to go home and get an early night."

"You need your beauty sleep, Mrs Clark," Clarky says, smiling. "We've a long drive tomorrow."

Both couples say goodnight to the 'olds' who are now two sheets to the wind, the men having hit the whiskey and the women the gin even before the first course was served.

Outside on the pavement the girls hug.

"Thank you for coming. Are you okay?" Julie asks. "You've been very quiet all day."

"I'm fine Jules. Just tired, that's all."

"Yup. No one tells you how knackered you are during the first trimester."

And that's when Vicky's emotions finally spill over. The first proper tears she's shed since the scan yesterday.

Gav wraps his arms around her as Julie looks on, concerned.

"Is everything alright? I've not had a chance to ask you how your scan went."

Gav bites his lip and looks away, and Vicky locks eye contact with Julie.

One look at Vicky's face and Julie understands immediately. Intuitively she knows what's happened.

Julie pulls Vicky into her. "Oh Tor, why on earth didn't you say something? You didn't have to do this for us today. I could have asked Nessa and Anth to be witnesses."

"But I wanted to be here. For you," Vicky whimpers. "I didn't want anything to spoil your day."

Clarky lays a supportive hand on Gav's shoulder. "Some things in life are more important. Is there anything we can do?"

"Not really, but thanks for asking," Gav says. "It's the worst kind of waiting game at the moment. I just need to get her home and into a nice warm bath."

A ball of dread lands heavy on Gav's chest as he imagines what's in store for them over the next two to three days.

Vicky smiles meekly at the newlyweds. "Enjoy your mini-moon in the Highlands, and try not to worry about me. I'll be fine."

"I hardly think so, but you've got Gav to take care of you."

"Yes, she has," Gav says. "Take care the pair of you and we'll see you when you're back."

He scoops Vicky up into his arms and, cradling her like the baby she's loosing, carries her back to the car.

Chapter 21

*N*either of us speak on the journey home, but Gav lays his hand on my knee while keeping his eyes firmly fixed on the road ahead. I look out the passenger window. The world outside continues to move forward, the countryside whizzing past at speed while my own world crumbles and dies.

I'm stuck in a horrible limbo.

A cramp catches me unawares and I bend forward, grunting, my hands clutching my stomach.

Gav squeezes my knee but says nothing.

Once back home, I take a shower, make up a hot-water bottle, shut the curtains and curl up in bed. Leo jumps on the duvet. Purring and nuzzling into my chin, demanding I stroke him. I'd love to think he senses something is wrong, but the reality is it's most likely his bowl his empty.

"At least I'll always have you," I say, stroking his arching back, "... as long as I keep feeding you."

Gav is noticeable by his distance, but I haven't the physical strength or emotional capacity to worry about his feelings right now.

I hear him quietly close the spare room door. We've not yet set it up as a full-blown nursery—we've only known about the baby for four weeks, but it hadn't stopped us talking about our plans for the room and for the little person we anticipated would occupy it. We'd decided on a lilac and mint green colour scheme, and Gav had bought the paint last week. We'd chosen our nursery furniture, even if we'd not yet purchased it.

However, I couldn't stop myself picking up a few things this past week. A packet of muslins and a cute snuggle blanket that I'd seen on offer in Mammas and Pappas. Their carrier bags lying untouched, heaped in the corner of our bedroom. The receipts still inside.

I suppose I'll need to decide whether to return them, or keep them for the next time.

Will there even be a next time?

I grip my stomach as another cramp rips through me, followed by a warm wet oozing between my legs. It's definitely getting heavier.

I can already feel the change in my body. Yesterday I felt pregnant, now I don't, and right now I'd do anything to replace that indescribable pregnancy feeling.

As I close my eyes, willing sleep to numb me from the pain, I hear the sound of Gav's muffled tears as he deals with his own grief in the room next door.

⭐

Over the next few weeks, on the surface at least, our life returns to normal. Gav stayed off the Monday after I began to miscarry, but returned to work the day after that. Meanwhile I retreated into the attic, where I've set up my home office while I get my fledgling business off the ground. No point spending unnecessary money on office space until I have a team big enough to justify the outlay.

I've landed a couple of small clients since starting my entrepreneurial journey at the beginning of the year, so although I'm not cash positive on a monthly basis at the moment, it does mean I'm burning through my savings at a slower rate. However, I have lots of irons in lots of fires, including a big keynote I've been booked to deliver at a conference in San Diego in a week's time. The opportunity had landed unexpectedly on my desk the week after the miscarriage and it was too big to turn down.

If only I could persuade Gav to come with me it could give us the opportunity to process our grief together, as opposed to separately, as we are now.

"Please come. We could make a little holiday of it," I plead while Gav sits on the end of the bed watching me pack. "California is somewhere you've always wanted to go. You're owed loads of lieu time and I've got stacks of Air Miles to use up. Why not come out this coming Wednesday or Thursday? The conference finishes at noon on Thursday after my closing keynote, so I'll be free by the afternoon. We could stay on until the following weekend." I sit down on the bed next to him, leaning my head against his shoulder. "I've checked the long-range weather report and there are no hurricanes forecast," I add, hoping my attempt at humour will draw him out of his grump.

He *humphs* a puff of air out of his nose. "You've got it all worked out haven't you, Little Miss Organised?" He crumples his mouth into a half-smile and rolls his eyes.

The truth is, I'd prefer not to go to the conference in San Diego at all. Losing this baby has created a wedge between us, and I could never have predicted how distant he's become in the weeks since. But I'm being paid a handsome fee and the cash injection will go a long way in my current cash flow.

Placing my hand on his thigh and looking straight ahead, avoiding his eye, I continue, "I think after what's…" I suck in a shuddery breath, "… what's happened, a trip away would do us both the world of good. Give us some breathing space. Time away without any distractions. Time to adjust back to being *just us* again."

He winces.

I wait patiently for him to speak.

"There's a lot going on at work you don't know about. I can't justify the time away," he says eventually.

Sucking in a long breath, I stand up and walk towards my wardrobe. "I get it. Well maybe the time apart will give us time to process what's happened."

Pretending to look at my clothes, my back ramrod straight, I slowly close my eyes. I desperately want him to rush over, wrap me in his arms and tell me it'll be alright. That we'll be alright, but instead I hear him quietly leave and close the bedroom door behind him.

⁂

Six hours later and somewhere high above the Atlantic, I swallow down the last morsel of tasteless chicken from the vacuum-packed plastic tray, and reach inside my tote bag. Rummaging past my laptop, my travel wallet containing my passport and the few toiletries I've brought on board, I pull out my latest Moleskine journal.

I'm not as religious in journaling as I once was, but I still find it cathartic to write down my thoughts when I'm struggling to make sense of my feelings.

If only I had someone to talk to. Someone who could understand how I'm feeling. Someone who knows what it's like to have lost something precious. Someone who's also lost a baby.

Chewing on the end of my pen I attempt to organise the swirl of emotions in my gut, hoping to turn them into words I can articulate down onto paper. I turn to a fresh page, note the date at the top and, without censoring my thoughts, scribble them down as they tumble out of my brain.

I pour onto the page my anger at losing the baby. This one had arrived at the right time in my life and I was ready to become its mother. My pen almost pushes through the paper as my fury flies across the page. How dare the universe take it away from me. And how dare Gav turn away from me when I need him the most. How dare he choose to deal with his emotions alone instead of turning towards me.

I am strong and I can handle it, but at this stage of my life I never thought I'd have to. I thought I'd have an equal partner that I could lean into, not have to stand alone as I've become so adept at doing.

Resting the journal on my knee, the airplane hits an air pocket, jolting me in my seat and spewing the random postcards and notes from the back of the diary onto the floor. I lean forward into the tight footwell and gather up the spilled contents, just as the airplane hits another air pocket and I bang my head on the back of the seat in front of me. The passenger in front turns and glares at me through the gap between the seats.

"Sorry." I offer a weak smile of apology, whilst rubbing my noggin.

What the hell? Why the fuck should I apologise? It's not my fault the plane jolted unexpectedly. I sniff loudly and set my jaw.

Fuck you, universe! Fuck everything about this shitty situation.

I pull my knees up and cross my legs into the best lotus pose the airline seat will allow. Forming a circle with each thumb and forefinger, I turn my palms upwards and allow the backs of my hands to rest on the tops of my knees. My gaze naturally softens as I turn my focus inwards. Becoming conscious of the air entering and leaving my body.

Calm, Victoria, I say to myself. This is no one's fault.

I remain in my makeshift yoga position until I feel the anger dissipate.

Why does everyone around me seem to have their families sorted, yet every time I try to embrace life and live it to the full, I get knocked back? As if by daring to stretch for more out of life, events conspire to hold me in my place.

Feeling calmer, I reorganise the notes and letters stuffed into the back of my Moleskin, my fingers involuntarily pausing when I find myself staring at a blank postcard. It has no message. Only my name and address on its reverse and a postmark from Fiji. I turn it over and study the picture of the deserted beach at night. The sky a deep purple except for the bright moon that throws rippling shadows across the surface of the sea, and the single shooting star that darts across the sky. Its burning tail blazing through the image.

After my marriage to Craig had ended, Chris had sent me this message. Letting me know he hadn't forgotten our conversation at the top of the mountain in Denia, the night of his sister's wedding.

'Do you know what I think every time I see a shooting star?' he'd said whilst we'd been wrapped in a passionate clinch watching the sun rise over the Mediterranean. 'That's our baby girl, Vicky. Reminding us that she's still out there. Still waiting to be born.'

I cover my mouth with the postcard and squeeze away the tears that pool in the corners of my eyes.

I remember clearly what I'd said to him during that conversation: 'And how is that ever going to happen, Chris? ... We had our chance and we couldn't make it work. No matter how hard we tried. We always ended up hurting each other. It's too late for us. We can't undo what's already been done.'

He'd wanted me to run away with him then. Give up Craig and the life I'd built back in the UK and run off into the sunset with him. Despite the love that passed between us in that moment, I didn't. I chose Craig. I chose what I thought was an everlasting love and stability over what Chris offered: passion and instability.

And look how that turned out.

How different my life might have been if I'd chosen the alternate path. Taken Chris's hand and allowed him to lead me off the mountain and back into his life, and his bed. Might the daughter he foretold, a star unborn in the night sky, be a living breathing bairn in my arms by now?

Who knows?

But as I'm processing my thoughts, I'm also thinking about the other child that never was. The child from ten years ago.

Not a day goes by where I don't harbour the shame that comes from having had an abortion. Even today, a decade later, I've never told a soul.

Only Chris knows the truth of what happened.

Chapter 22

*A*fter landing in San Diego I take a taxi to the hotel, check in, take a long soak in the bath, and eat the meal I've ordered from room service.

I check my watch. It's 8:00 p.m. Sunday which means it's only 4:00 a.m. back home and Gav won't be awake for another few hours. I've already sent him a text to let him know I've landed safely, although I'm not expecting a reply. He's still stuck in his own mental cave, grieving in his own way, which seems to be… away from me.

I let out a long exhale.

The only other people who know about what we're going through are Julie and Clarky, and that's only because it coincided with their wedding, but no matter how desperate I am to talk to someone, I wouldn't dream of waking Julie up at this ungodly hour.

I bite my nail as an idea pops into my head.

No. I couldn't possibly.

What time would it be over there at the moment?

I quickly do the calculations in my head.

4:00 p.m. on Monday afternoon. No chance he'd be in bed asleep, then.

Should I? I can almost guarantee he'd be happy to hear from me.

I pace the floor for the next ten minutes, second-guessing myself, before diving across the bed and picking up my phone. I punch out a quick text:

> Hey Chris. What you up to? I'm currently in San Diego, preparing to speak at a conference at the Marriott Marina in a few days' time. I've been having a bit of a tough time of late and wondered who might be awake at this ungodly hour.
>
> Trust everything is good with you. Vicky x

I hit send and don't even have time to pick up the telly remote before my phone is ringing in my hand. I look down at the screen and of course it's his name flashing back at me.

Dropping the phone like a hot potato, I shuffle away from it.

What have I done? This is a big can of worms that I vowed I would never reopen, yet here I am with my finger on the ring pull.

The phone goes silent, the call having cut off to voicemail, but seconds later it rings again. When I don't answer it a second time, a minute later it buzzes with a text:

> Hey Goose, you'd better text me back and let me know you're okay.
>
> If you don't, I'm coming to San Diego to check on you in person.
>
> I'm already checking flights.
>
> Always in my heart. Chris x

Shit! I slowly close then reopen my eyes, realising I've definitely yanked that ring pull open.

Reaching for my phone I hit the call button. The line doesn't even ring once before it connects.

Not even waiting for him to speak I blurt out, "You don't need to fly to San Diego you muppet. I'm fine."

"Then why the cryptic message, ya daft old goose?"

The tone and timbre of his voice is as familiar as slipping into a warm bath, and with that one reply it feels as if I last spoke to him this morning, not six years ago.

I dip my head and close my eyes.

When I don't answer, he continues, his tone laced with concern, "Hey, hey. Are you okay? What's going on?"

I squeeze my eyes tight as my throat burns with the tears I'm holding in.

I will not fall apart. I will not cry.

"You're not dying or anything are you?" he says in a jokey way that makes me snort out a puff of laughter.

"No, nothing like that, Chris. I'm fine, honestly."

"Well clearly you're not, or else you wouldn't have texted me out of the blue. Whatever it is, you can tell me. You can tell me anything."

I can't hold in my emotions any longer and begin to cry softly. He listens, but I can hear the muffled sounds of him moving things around in the background.

"Okay, you've got two minutes to explain what's happened and why you're so upset, or else you can tell me in person tomorrow. I'm packing a bag as we speak."

"No Chris. I'm fine, really."

"That's the second time you've said that without telling me what the problem is. Clearly you're not fine."

"Oh it's too awful, I don't want to say it. Saying it out loud makes it real and I'm not ready for it to be real."

He goes quiet on the other end of the line, waiting patiently for me to unburden myself.

"I've lost another baby, Chris."

"Oh, Vicky." He sounds as heartbroken as I feel. "You poor, poor thing."

The line falls quiet again. Only interspersed by the soft sounds of my quiet weeping.

"If I could reach through the airways and give you a big hug I would. You sound like you desperately need a cuddle. In fact, close your eyes and imagine I'm wrapping my arms around you right now."

I hear him suck in a deep breath.

"Thanks. I appreciate that," I whimper, imagining the feeling of his arms wrapped around me.

"Mike's told me all about your latest fella. It's Gavin, isn't it? Said he really liked the guy and that he's good for you."

"He's hardly *the latest,* Chris." I don't mean to sound quite so defensive. "We've been together over a year now."

"Whatever," Chris says breezily, "but I gather it was his?"

"Who else's would it be?"

He ignores my brusque tone and continues, "Okay. Start at the beginning and tell me everything."

Over the next couple of hours, and after we switch from a phone call to Skyping each other on our respective laptops, I tell Chris everything. How Gav and I met. How amazing everything's been. At least, until this happened.

It feels good to unburden myself and have someone listen to how I'm feeling. Especially someone who doesn't know Gav personally.

The more we talk, the more the miles between us disappear. We may not be in a romantic relationship anymore, but we have a level of intimacy that only comes from having shared your soul with someone.

When jet lag finally claims me and I fall into deep twelve-hour sleep, I wake up the next morning to two texts. One from Gav. The other from Chris.

I read Gav's message first:

> Hey Angel, I'm pleased you've arrived safe. The house already seems so empty without you. I've been such an arse and I'm sorry.

> I've been at Anth and Nessa's for Sunday lunch and they could tell something was up. I didn't go into details, but alluded to what's happened and they gave me a right good talking to. Made me realise what a shit I've been.

> Give me a call when you wake up, so I can apologise properly.

> I love you so much, and I know we'll get through this — together.

> I'm here for you (even if it seems like I haven't been lately.)

> Love you,

> Today, tomorrow, always,

> Gav x

My breath settles in my gut. That's all I've been waiting for. A bit of reassurance. And I know we will come through this — together, and I know this episode of our lives will pass and in the long run it'll only make us stronger as a couple.

Rolling out of bed, I throw open the curtains and the blistering west coast sunlight streams into the room. Pottering around in bare feet, my phone still in my hand, I flick on the switch for the kettle.

My finger hovers over Chris's message, before I open it:

> Hey Goose, so good to talk last night. Thanks for calling me and I'm glad you're feeling better.

> You mean the world to me and will always have a special place in my heart. Always here if you need me. Love you, Chris xxx

I stare at the message.

Love you and three kisses. *Holy f—*

As I feared, I've inadvertently opened the can and worms are wriggling all over my life once again.

I quickly punch out a reply:

> Morning Chris, or evening where you are. Yes it was good to catch up and I'm feeling much better now. Thanks, Vicky

Thanks and no kisses. I couldn't be any more formal.

I drop my phone into my dressing gown pocket and take my cup of tea out onto the balcony which overlooks the marina and San Diego Bay beyond. I've only taken one sip of my tea when I feel the handset buzz in my pocket. Taking it out, I read:

> That's my girl. I'm so proud of you.

> No matter what path our lives take, you know I'd do anything for you. You will always be the one true love of my life and I'm a fucking idiot for having letting you go. Love you, C x

Bloody hell! I suck air into my lungs and blink slowly. I punch out a reply:

> Thanks Chris. I appreciate you being there for me, but you must know, even if I was your girl once, I'm Gav's girl now. Take care, Vicky

Turning my phone face down on the bistro table in front of me, I take long slow sips of tea. Allowing the warm sweet liquid to flow over my tongue. It tastes of home.

What the hell have I done?

I may have been the one to initiate the contact, but I've not been unfaithful or anything like that. We only had a conversation and despite Chris's explicit declaration of love in his follow up texts, I've made it clear his feelings are not reciprocated. Not anymore.

So why does reaching out to Chris after all these years feel like I've betrayed Gav in some way?

Is it because in some deep buried corner of my heart, a part of me does still love him?

Chapter 23

The next four days pass in a blur of meetings, keynotes, and press junkets. The business organisation who brought me over to the states are connecting me with their European counterparts, and as I've just published my first non-fiction business book, their local PR agent seems determined to help me use this platform as a way to leverage my business offering. There's no doubt the exposure has been amazing.

On the final day, the conference room is packed with two thousand business owners and sales executives wanting to hear my final session and I'm building up to the final point, when I completely lose my train of thought.

Standing at the back of the room, leaning nonchalantly against one of the pillars, is a familiar figure.

Oh my god he's here. He actually came.

I sense the energy in the room shift as for a nanosecond the audience lose confidence in me, the pause in my presentation feeling marginally longer than seems comfortable.

Unable to contain my huge smile, I subtly purse my lips and blow him a kiss, and he mimes catching it and melting it into his heart, before I suck in a large breath, refocus, and continue my presentation. The audience audibly exhales.

When it's over I step off stage and am escorted back to the green room. Before the engineer is able to unhook my mic I rush into Gav's arms, leaping up onto him and throwing my arms and legs around him.

"You came!" I exclaim.

"How could I not. You were magnificent." He lands a kiss on my lips. "They were hanging on your every word."

"Was I okay?" I climb down off him, still clutching his hand.

"Are you kidding? Can you not hear that applause?"

"How long are you here for? And why did you not tell me you were coming?"

"What would be the fun in that? Wouldn't you much rather be surprised?"

"You know I hate surprises."

"You, Angel, only hate surprises you don't like… and I knew you'd like this one." He kisses me again. "I'm here until a week on Sunday. And before you ask, I've changed your flight as well. We've got the next ten days to ourselves. No distractions. No interruptions. Just time for you and I."

"Sounds perfect."

★

Over the next few days, to keep our costs down, we stay in a motel on Mission Beach, while we chill on the sand with the surfer crowd.

However, for one night only we're pushing the boat out and we've come across the bay to the famous Hotel del Coronado, or as the locals affectionately call it, 'The Del.'

'I mean, how could you come to San Diego and not stay in one of the most iconic buildings in North America?' Gav had said as we were checking in.

'*Quite,*' the check-in clerk had replied whilst charging Gav's Amex card the eye-watering amount.

The hotel's layers of white wooden balconies, nestled beneath a distinctive rotund red tiled roof, have shaped the architecture of the Coronado Peninsula since the 1880s.

'The whole building could be mistaken for a wedding cake on top of a cruise ship sailing off over the horizon of the Pacific,' I'd added, as the porter had led us to our room.

Later that evening, we're seated inside the dark oak-panelled Prince of Wales Grill, the room where local folklore claims the then Prince of Wales met and fell in love with the infamous American divorcee Wallis Simpson, the demure waiters hover around us with the same kind of discreet attentiveness with which I'm sure their predecessors tended to their society guests back in the 1920s.

"What's Kobe beef?" Gav asks our server.

"The very best steak in the entire world, sir," the white-gloved waiter replies. "The meat comes from a small herd in Japan. They're fed on a rich diet of corn and grains, which gives the cut a unique texture and taste. Every day the herd are massaged, to ensure their loins are supple and soft. I guarantee sir, your knife will slide through the steak like a hot knife through butter."

"Sounds perfect." Gav slams the menu shut.

"And how would you like it cooked, sir?"

"Medium-rare please."

"And for you madam?" He turns, smiling at me.

"The lobster please."

"Excellent choice. It was flown in fresh this morning from Maine."

He nods politely and slopes off into the darkness.

"Are you sure we can afford this?" I lean in and whisper out of the corner of my mouth.

"What's one night of luxury worth?" Gav reaches up and strokes my face with the back of his fingers. "It's just nice to see you smile again."

Barefoot, Gav and I walk along the beach after dinner. Our toes sinking into the cool sand with each step.

"So, how do you feel my angel?" He squeezes my hand.

"About what, specifically?"

"About Prince Charles' wedding last Saturday to Camilla. What do you think I mean?"

I roll my eyes. Gav always finds a way to make a serious situation lighthearted.

"Well, to answer your first question, I think it's bloody brilliant. And to think that it was in this *very* place," I turn and point back to the hotel which is lit up like a Christmas tree, "that his great uncle, the future Edward VIII, met the infamous Mrs Simpson. And here we are less than a hundred years later and the future King of England is being allowed to marry for love *and* keep the throne, even if they're both now divorcees."

"I agree. I wonder what other attitudes will evolve in the next hundred years?"

"More equality for women would be a good start."

Gav squeezes my hand.

Beside us the waves roll small stones up and down the shallow beach. I breathe in the salt air and pull my pashmina tighter around my shoulders.

Turning to look out over the ocean, Gav pulls me into him and I rest my head against his shoulder. I feel the gentle touch of his fingers brushing the outside of my cheek and I tilt my head. The full moon reflects back in the soft hazel of his irises.

"Thank you for flying over," I say.

"Sorry for being so obstinate. I was trying so hard to keep my own emotions under control, I didn't see how much that was hurting you. Especially when you were already hurting so much. Can you forgive me?"

"There isn't anything to forgive. You're here now. But you shouldn't feel you have to hide your emotions from me. I'm your partner, girlfriend, whatever you want to label us as; I should be the person you turn towards, not turn away from."

"I realise that now. I was just so damn angry."

"And I wasn't?"

"Yes, but I was angry at myself. It's my job to keep you safe and I wasn't able to protect you from this hideous thing that happened."

"But it wasn't your fault."

I don't share that I'm hoping it wasn't my fault either. That this wasn't karma's payback for the decision I made ten years ago.

I really want to tell him the truth, tell him all the dark secrets from my past. But even as I think about that first child that never was, and all the circumstances surrounding that time in my life, that hideous snake in my gut flips over. Something is telling me to hold back, so I bite my lip and hold my tongue. One thing I do know is Gav is innocent in all of this.

He shrugs his shoulders. "Maybe."

"What do you mean? Of course it wasn't your fault."

"Oh I don't know," he says. "I'm so mixed up. One minute I feel fine. Resigned to what's happened. Then the next, I want to lash out. Beat my palms against my chest until I bleed. Then in the next minute, I'm overwhelmed with grief and want to collapse into a deep dark hole and not come out again. Then once I'm through that, the sadness is replaced with gratitude. I remember how blessed I am and how much I have to be grateful for."

He tucks a stray strand of hair behind my ear.

"And in case you can't decode my ramblings," he continues, "what I really mean is—I'm immeasurably grateful for you, V."

"I know. I am pretty amazing aren't I?" I lightly punch him in his gut and he fake recoils.

"And what about you?" he asks, serious once again. "How are you feeling?"

"Same as you really. I'm flip-flopping between feeling sad, angry, resentful." I let out a long sigh. "But right now, I'm also grateful to have you."

"Oh Angel." Gav pulls me into him. "I'm so damn lucky to have you. Regardless of what I've been through this past month, it's you that's been put through the mill."

"I can handle it, as long as I know we're good."

"We're good," he repeats, both his arms wrapped around my

back as he holds me close. "We're always good. And we can always try again."

I look away.

"Maybe," I say quietly, secretly crossing my fingers behind my back.

Chapter 24

The waves reach our ankles. Submerging our feet before dragging the sand away from our heels as the water slinks back into the ocean. Instinctively we step back from the rising tide. Above us the stars shine bright like a twinkling blanket of candles draped protectively around the earth.

Regardless of our own turmoil, the world around us continues to turn. The tide will continue to rise and fall. Day will follow night, and night follow day. When you strip everything away, we're two inconsequential beings in the vast universe that surrounds us.

"Look," Gav points. "A shooting star. Quick, make a wish my angel."

He squeezes my waist and I lay my head against his shoulder, wishing that I could turn the clock back.

"I don't think you need to be a genius to know what you wished for," he whispers out into the blackness.

I place my finger on his lips. "Shhh, don't say anything more. If you tell, it won't come true. But yes, darling—let's try again soon."

I watch as his eyes sparkle and his lips crumple into a grateful smile. I close my own heavy lids as he pulls me into an embrace and gently kisses the side of my neck.

I love this man with all my heart, and I feel his love for me. If only we could complete our family, then everything would be perfect, and I could finally lay my past to rest.

✦

Back inside our room, the melodic sound of a jazz band playing down on the terrace below drifts up on the warm evening air and through the open balcony doors. The mournful lyrics of Sam Cooke's "A change is Gonna Come" wrap around us like a soothing comfort blanket.

The moonlight casts a shadow over Gav's square jaw and powerful physique as he stands in front of me. He reaches for my face. Like a blind man suddenly seeing for the first time. He tenderly feels his way from the centre of my brow, around the outside of my eyes, feeling his way over my cheekbones, his thumbs tracing the Cupid's bow of my lips, all the while his gaze is locked with mine. His stare melting my core. I feel my body soften and my knees grow weak.

He sucks air into his lungs and pauses momentarily.

Peeling his hands away from my face, I cup them together and kiss each of his palms, tasting the slight tang of salt on his skin. He's nervous and waiting for me to give consent.

"It's okay baby," I say softly. "I'm okay."

He exhales and closes then opens his eyelids in a slow grateful blink.

He takes my hand and wraps it around his body, placing it on his back, and clasping my other hand into his. Pulling me into a close ballroom hold, we sway gently together in time to the music, our feet sinking into the deep pile of the plush carpet; without my heels on, he seems taller than his six feet four inches.

I lay my head against his chest and inhale deeply. The smell of his fresh cotton shirt mixes with the sensual amber scent of his cologne as it dances up my nostrils. The dull methodical rhythm of his heart beating gives me comfort. In his arms, I feel safe.

Tears spring at the corner of my eyes, that we've reconciled, but I hold them back. I've cried enough this past month. However, I know these are not tears of pain, or grief, or loss, as all the others have been. These are the tears of love. Of connection. Of vulnerability. These are the tears of hope.

I slide my hand down his back, feeling my way over the hollow in the base of his spine, until my palm rests on the brawn of his backside. He breathes out again and releases a deep guttural groan.

Very gently he peels the strap of my Hervé Léger bandage dress away from my shoulder. It rests provocatively over my upper arm. Leaning forward, he kisses the length of my collarbone. Light butterfly kisses; his breath hot but calm, one after another until he's nuzzling the sensitive spot just below my ear.

My head falls back and I feel the spark between my legs ignite. A sensation I've not felt since losing our baby. For the first time since that day, my body no longer feels like a vessel for another life. Clinical. Asexual. A host. Tonight I am all woman.

He continues to kiss my neck and nibble my ear, the fire between my thighs smouldering and burning upwards into the pit of my stomach where it settles into a dark pool of hot desire.

I too release a deep guttural groan and squeeze his backside with the hand I still have placed there.

"You smell gorgeous," he whispers.

I want to reply but find myself mute, as if the sensory overload from his touch has stripped me of the power of speech.

Below us, the jazz singer begins a new song. I grind my body in time to the smouldering beat, and I feel Gav's hardness pressing against my hip as the dulcet notes of "At Last" drift into the room.

He covers my mouth with his own, our tongues gently exploring and twisting together. I taste the remnants of red wine and warm coffee on his breath, all the while we continue to rock in time to the slow beat of the music.

The intensity of his kiss deepens and my lips tingle and yearn for him. Out of the corner of my eyes I see his cheeks darken to a deep crimson as the flush of his own arousal rises up his body. His hard pecs press against my soft curves.

ISABELLA WILES

Still moving in unison, he guides me backwards towards the enormous queen-sized bed.

Our lips still locked together, he reaches behind me and seductively undoes the zipper of my dress. Easing my shoulders out of the fabric, I shimmer myself free. My dress drops to the floor and pools around my feet. I step out of it and Gav breaks our kiss, leans down and picks it up.

"I know you won't want this left in a crumpled mess... too expensive." He turns and lays the garment over an armchair.

I smile. Only he would anticipate that's what I was thinking.

Turning back towards me, he reaches over his head and in one swift movement pulls off his shirt and throws it into the corner of the room.

"That, however, doesn't need any special care." He shrugs, placing his hands gently on my waist.

Taking the initiative I unhook his belt buckle, allowing his suit trousers to fall to the floor.

He steps out of them, folds them methodically and lays them neatly over the arm of the chair. "But they are a bitch if they get creased."

I shake my head and suppress a giggle. "Only you would worry about the state of your trousers when you're about to get laid."

"Well these things are important." He steps forward and grips the outsides of my shoulders, the intensity of his stare disarming me once more. "Now, where were we?"

Leaning forward he nibbles my neck, while his other hand unclips my bra clasp and the lacy garnet pings free. His mouth still connected to my skin, he peels the straps from my body and allows it to drop silently to the floor. I hear him suck air in between his teeth as he looks down at my perfectly round breasts.

My connection with Gav is so much more than skin deep, but knowing that he still finds my physical appearance a turn-on gives me a warm glow.

Holding my girls gently in each hand he rolls his thumbs over my nipples and they tighten instantly, sending a thunderbolt of

190

desire down to between my legs. Now it's my turn to suck air in through clenched teeth.

My knees weak from the shock of it, I wobble backwards and in one swift movement he picks me up. Cradling me in his arms he lays me down on the bed like a treasured possession, where I sink backwards against the soft down of the pillows.

Kneeling over me he kisses me again. Firmer this time and I return his kiss with an equal amount of ardour. Threading my fingers through his hair, I pull him down onto me and enjoy the feeling of his body weight pressing me into the mattress.

The music changes again. The sound of "It's a Wonderful World" fills the air and Gav pulls back from kissing me.

"I absolutely love this tune," he says wistfully.

Wrapped in each other's arms we listen together as the jazz singer rasps out the lyrics: seeing trees of green and red roses too.

"He's no Louis Armstrong, but he's pretty good," Gav says, humming the tune, before saying the next two lines: "The bright blessed day, the dark sacred night… and I think to myself, what a wonderful world."

"You make my world wonderful," I reply, staring deep into his kind hazel eyes.

"But that's where you're wrong, Victoria. I'm the lucky one here," he says, silencing me with another kiss.

We make love for hours. All the while, the jazz singer below continues to serenade us. I lose track of time. I'm only conscious of Gav's touch on my skin and the feel of his lips on mine. Both heightening the pleasure and desire in my body until I can hold back no more.

"I need you in me," I say urgently.

"Are you sure, Angel? We don't have to do this just yet."

"No. I need you. Now," I reply more insistently, scratching my fingernails down his back, causing him to kiss me more fervently.

"Are you sure you're ready, or do you want me to wear a condom?" he whispers into my mouth.

"Do you have one?" I ask, surprised.

"Good point. I may have one in the back of my wallet, but I couldn't testify as to its use-by date," he laughs, brushing my fringe away from my face. "Do you want me to go and check?"

"Only if you want to. Or we could roll the dice of fate once more," I whisper.

"Dice it is. What will be, will be."

When he slides into me, my world is complete once more. He fills the void within and I find myself gripping the cotton sheet with both hands at the intensity of our coupling.

Our hips move in unison and my mind detaches from my body as our rhythm and intensity increases. Up and up. Each thrust causing the swirl within me to rise, and just when I don't think I can take any more he yells out, "Oh God, I love you," as his body begins to spasm and shake, before he collapses on top of me. The comfort of his weight on my body pushing me over my own cliff edge.

"I love you more," I reply, as the waves of my climax bring me crashing back down to earth. Down. Down. I'm falling and unable to stop, but I know he's there to catch me. My body in spasm and every nerve ending heightened, my brain shuts down except for the raging sensations pulsing through me and the contact of Gav's body against my own.

Seconds later, drenched and satiated we lie together, our bodies a mass of tangled limbs, conscious only of the soft sound of our breath and the synchronised rise and fall of our ribs. Eventually he kisses the end of my nose and rolls onto his back, pulling me into the crook of his arm. He strokes my hair and I trace lazy patterns on his torso with my index finger.

"We needed that," he says softly, his voice wobbling. "I love you so damn much V, sometimes it hurts."

I can hear the emotion in his voice.

"Thank you," I reply quietly.

"Thank you? What for?"

Now it's my turn to cry. Happy tears pooling in the corner of my eyes. "For loving me. For knowing me better than I know myself. For your unconditional love. For never giving up on me," I say.

"Giving up on you? Thank *you* for putting up with *me.*"

Below us, we hear the band announce, *"Thank you ladies and gentleman, you've been a lovely audience this evening."* A ripple of applause radiates upwards as they introduce their last song.

Moments later Gav is humming the tune of Marvin Gaye's "I heard it through the grapevine," into the crook of my neck, just as I spot another shooting star dart across the sky. A flash of brilliant white light blazing across the ink-black curtain of night before it dies and disappears, as if it never existed in the first place.

Except for that one fleeting moment, it did.

Chapter 25

The next morning, I wake up first.

Our room looks west, out over the ocean, and all night the comforting sounds of the never-ending waves of the Pacific lapping the shore soothed us both to sleep. Not that we needed any help to fall asleep after our mammoth love-making session, both of us eventually collapsing against the crisp cotton sheets, completely spent. I smile inwardly at the memory.

The sun is rising on the other side of the hotel, therefore rather than harsh rays throwing shapes against our bedroom walls, they reflect back off the ocean and light our room in a soft ethereal glow. A gentle awakening. The soft voile drapes flutter in the light breeze, having been left open all night.

Beside me Gavin sleeps on. His firm naked body wrapped around mine as I spoon into his. I feel his chest rising and falling in perfect sync with the sound of the waves rolling and churning outside. I tenderly stroke the arm he has lain across me. The pads of my fingers rolling over the soft down of hair on his forearm.

I gently extrapolate myself and throw on my workout gear. Grabbing my yoga mat, I head out onto the balcony. I feel the sinews in my body lengthen as I begin my sun salutation flow. It feels good to stretch. To let go of the last residuals of tension and breathe fresh air into my lungs.

As I continue my yoga routine, whatever darkness has been clouding over me, today feels more than a new day. It feels like a new dawn. As if the universe is finally shining down on me once again, and I've entered a new phase of my life.

I have my eyes closed in Tadasana, my hands in prayer position while I finish my yoga routine with some deep breaths. My mind clear, an image pops into it. I'm in a garden, cradling a child in my arms and walking down a red carpet lain over the grass, its surface strewn with white rose petals. At the end of the carpet is a smartly dressed man, his back towards me. He begins to turn, but I can't yet see who it is, then—

"Boo." Gav rips me out of my visualisation by tickling me under my armpits. "This is where you're hiding."

Smiling, I throw my arms around his neck. "Morning. I didn't want to disturb you."

"You didn't, I slept like a baby. I'm gonna take a shower, or do you want to jump in first? Or we could jump in together," he says, a twinkle in his eye.

Tap-tap-tap. Someone knocks at the bedroom door.

"That'll be breakfast." I pull away from him and playfully pull his hotel robe open. "And you'd better tighten that belt if you don't want the whole world to see your morning glory."

He gives my bum a light spank as I flounce past him.

Opening the door, I'm greeted by two smartly dressed room attendants holding a tray each, both stacked high with cloches.

"Would you like us to set these up on the balcony, madam?"

"Yes please." I step aside and follow them through the room and out onto the veranda. "It's a beautiful morning."

"Best climate stateside, madam," one of them adds. "Low humidity, a comfortable seventy-degree average temperature all year and a blessed three hundred and thirty-five days of sunshine."

"Yes, you are very lucky. It wouldn't be a hard decision to leave the grey wet gloom of Blighty and come and live here."

They smile politely at my small talk, passing me the chit to sign before leaving in silence.

Gav rejoins me on the veranda, a pair of sunglasses shading his eyes. "How much did I have to drink last night? My head's pounding."

"A couple of bottles of wine, maybe. Not too much."

"Wine! Why did you let me drink wine? That's why I'm so hungover."

"What you need is some of this." I lift one of the cloches. The plate underneath is stacked high with pancakes, bacon, and maple syrup. Still warm, their delicious sweet smell bursts out from underneath the lid.

"Hold that thought." He clamps his hand over his mouth. "Back in a bit."

"Maybe just some water to start then," I shout after him as he rushes to the bathroom.

Grabbing a fork, I stuff a slice of delicious fluffy pancake covered with salty bacon and sweet syrup into my mouth. The mix of flavours explodes on my tongue and I close my eyes, enjoying the indulgent richness of the breakfast. Just then a familiar *beep-beep* disrupts the tranquillity. I walk inside to the table where both our mobiles and my laptop are all on charge.

"You have a message," I holler into the bathroom, noticing that it's Gav's phone screen that has illuminated.

I hear the sound of the toilet flushing. "You check it," he shouts from behind the half closed door.

I open Gav's messages. "It's from Mark," I shout. "He's asking you to pick up some duty-free."

He and Becca are in charge of the not-so-secret arrangements for Mr and Mrs Clark's belated wedding celebrations next month.

"Cool," he says easily, taking the phone from me as he emerges from the bathroom looking distinctly fresher than he did a few moments ago.

⭐

We soak up the morning view together as we enjoy our breakfast, and only when the tea has gone cold do I announce, "Right, I'm going for a shower."

I'm still wearing my workout gear and I haven't yet showered since our mammoth love-making session last night.

Turning on the faucet, I allow the steaming water to blast away the sweat and salt off my skin. Closing my eyes and opening my mouth, the water rolls over my tongue and cleanses my palate.

From outside the bathroom I hear Gav shout, "You've had a text."

"You check it," I holler back. "It's probably my mam asking me to pick up some duty-free perfume for her."

I finish showering and, after wrapping myself in a fresh fluffy robe, I open the bathroom door and walk smack into Gav's stony grey face.

He's standing stock still in the middle of the room, my phone in his hand.

"What is it? What's happened?"

When he doesn't answer, I take the phone from him. Staring at the screen, a cannonball of dread lands heavy on my chest.

> Hey Goose, how you feeling today? I'm around if
> you want to talk some more. I've not been able to
> stop thinking about you all week. No matter what
> you say, or who you're with, you'll always be my
> girl. Always in my heart. Love you, Chris x

I look from the phone to Gav's face, his jaw slack, his eyes crumpled with pain and confusion.

"Let me explain," I blurt. "It's not what you think."

He jerks his head back, his eyes wide. "Then please enlighten me, because from where I'm stood it looks exactly like you think it might."

I flop down on the end of the bed and pat the space next to me, but Gav takes one of the armchairs facing the bed. Steepling his fingers under his chin, it feels like he's prepping for an interrogation.

"Start talking," he hisses through gritted teeth. "Because right now I'm ready to explode."

I suck in a deep breath. "It's hard to explain."

"Try."

I look down at my brightly painted toenails but say nothing.

"I don't even understand how you have his number," he says, the veins in his neck popping.

"He messaged me out of the blue when I was in New York, waiting on news of you. Mike had contacted him before the storm hit. And I've had the same mobile number all my life, so he took a punt. He was concerned, that's all."

"I see. Go on," Gav gestures.

"Honestly, this isn't what it seems. It's not like we've been in contact every week or anything like that."

"But you are in touch with him, and you didn't tell me?"

"I've not heard from him since the hurricane, well not up until this past week."

"So what's happened this past week that's suddenly prompted him to get in touch? Last time I checked there weren't any hurricanes due."

"Honestly, Gav. You're blowing this all out of proportion." I laugh nervously. "I called him, to catch up. That's all. It was no more than two mates having a chat."

"But you're not two mates, are you? You're anything but mates."

I turn my gaze to look out of the window, my eyes glazing over.

"No, we're not just mates," I say softly. "We mean more to each other than that, but I promise you, I'm not in love with him or anything."

"Well clearly he feels differently."

"So it seems," I reply, my voice hardly audible.

"But what I don't understand is, why talk to him? Surely, that's all in your past. Why bring it into your present if it doesn't mean something to you now?"

"I can't explain it," I say again.

"Well you're gonna have to try, because right now I'm at a loss to understand why you would even want to talk to this guy. From what you've said he did nothing but hurt you. Is this some kind of Stockholm syndrome? Either that or, despite what you're telling me, you do want to start things up again."

"No Gav. I definitely don't. I did love Chris once... with all my heart, and I had an opportunity to go back to him once, six years ago. I didn't."

"So what is it? Why stir all this up again now? Why talk to him and not me?"

I scrunch my eyes tight and ball my fists. "Because we lost a baby too!"

I open my eyes and see Gav's incredulous face staring back at me.

"I'm sorry, okay? I've been feeling so alone, and even you've admitted you've been an arse this past month, and I don't blame you, you were dealing with your own emotions the best way you could, but I needed someone to talk to. Someone who also understood what this feels like."

"I never knew. You never told me."

"Yeah, well, that's the reason. But if you want to read all the other messages from this past week, here..." I hold out my phone. "I know Chris still holds a torch for me, but I've been clear that his feelings are not reciprocated. Yes, he is someone special to me, because we made a baby together. And that feels like a bond that can't ever be broken. But it doesn't change how I feel about you, or that you're the one I want to share my life with."

He reaches for my hand to hold, his eyes softening. "I'm sorry I wasn't there for you when you needed me, but I'm here for you now." I watch as he draws in a breath. "But there's something I've never told you either. You see, I've also lost a baby before."

I tilt my head and draw my eyebrows together. "Really? With who?"

"With Samantha. Well, when I say we lost a baby, that's not strictly true... the bitch aborted our child without telling me."

My hand flies up to my mouth as my eyes stretch wide.

"Yup, I know. Shocking, isn't it. I didn't find out until years later. She robbed me of the chance of fatherhood without my knowledge or consent."

"Is that why your marriage ended?"

"Partly. When it all came out, let's just say it was the final nail in the coffin. It turns out she was pregnant in the lead-up to our wedding, and was worried she wouldn't fit into her dress. Or so she says."

I'm so shocked my jaw drops open and all my words fly away, like caged birds flying free after someone leaves their door open.

"Surely that can't be true," I say, my voice having returned.

"That's what she told me. Said she wanted to have time to adjust to being married before we had a baby. Although, there were rumours."

"Rumours?"

"That it wasn't mine."

Having never told a soul the real circumstances of the loss of mine and Chris's child, I know now is the moment to finally share that truth with the one person who means the world to me.

No more secrets. No more barriers between us. Once Gav knows this, he'll finally know all of me.

But before I have a chance to say anything more, he adds, the venom rattling in his voice, "Yeah, I'll never forgive her for taking that life before it even had the chance to live. I mean, what kind of monster does that? Absolutely unforgivable."

And in that moment my breath suspends inside my lungs and my world stops turning.

I break eye contact. "I see," I whisper, knowing that I can never reveal my truth to him now.

It will remain the secret that continues to bind Chris and I together and simultaneously stop Gav knowing the whole of me.

Chapter 26

1 month later, Tuesday 10th May 2005

*G*av passes me a glass of wine, glances at the myriad of numbers on my laptop screen and sympathetically squeezes my shoulder.

"Can't you leave that and come back to it tomorrow? You've been poring over spreadsheets ever since we got back from the states. Take the night off."

He settles himself next to me on the sofa, crosses his feet on the coffee table and picks up the TV remote. "Leave it and watch a bit of mindless telly."

"I wish I could hon, but I have to get these numbers right before I see the bank in the morning."

"Is everything alright?" he asks, an edge of concern in his voice. "With the numbers, I mean."

"If you mean is our new-business pipeline looking good and are our current clients happy with what we're doing for them, then the answer is a resounding 'yes'. However, if you're asking whether we have positive cash flow for the foreseeable future, then my report would be... could do better."

Setting his glass down, he turns and eyeballs me. "Oh? I thought things were going well with the business, at least that's the impression you've given. You've been working every hour god sends for the past five months. I thought things were beginning to pick up."

"They are, darling. Especially after San Diego. I've had a flood of new enquiries, but it takes time for all of that to turn into cash in the bank. I just need the bank to extend my overdraft and we'll be back on track, which is why I need these projections to include all of that optimism. I'm in a bit of a Catch-22. I needed to hire Clive and Angela, otherwise there simply aren't enough hours in the day for me to deliver our current client contracts, as well as pitch for all the new business that's coming in, on top of managing the finances and all of the client relationships as well. And although finding Helen to be our office manager was a stroke of luck, she's probably arrived a couple of months too early, but now she's here, the business wouldn't function without her. However, all of these increased overheads put pressure on cash."

It's true that our expansion over the last couple of months has been faster than I predicted in my original business plan, and bringing on the team has skyrocketed both my operational and capital expenditure. I've had to rent office space while I split my time between working in the office and working from home, and I'd completely underestimated how much it costs to sit someone at a desk, with a phone, a computer, and a chair!

"Anything I can do to help?" Gav asks. "I have some spare money tucked away in an old ISA if you need a loan."

Lifting my head from my laptop screen, I look over towards him. "Sweetheart that's so generous and… unnecessary. I appreciate the gesture, I really do. However, this is something I have to do on my own. I hope you understand?"

"It's your business V. I would never suggest anything different, but you know I'll always support you in any way I can."

"I know. And your website-building skills have saved me a tonne I'd have paid a marketing agency to create my digital presence."

"No worries," he says easily. "But the offer remains open."

Closing the laptop I snuggle into the crook of his arm. "Thanks, and I may change my tune tomorrow, if the bank turn me down."

※

Raising my face to the sky, the early morning sun warms my skin. All around, people rush past. Their heads down and eyes focused. Dashing back to work after a few snatched moments outside, grabbing a mid-morning coffee or a sneaky sausage roll from Greggs.

Grey's Monument looms majestically behind me. The famous Earl Grey looking out from the top of the one-hundred-and-thirty-foot column where he presides over Grainger Town.

This part of Newcastle is so beautiful. Its Georgian architecture curving majestically down past the Theatre Royal and down Grey Street towards the Quayside. Glance right and the historic Newcastle Central Station is just visible at the bottom of Clayton Street, down in the direction where my old office was based.

It's hard to believe there was a time when I couldn't wait to leave this beautiful city, having found the decay and deprivation that followed the collapse of heavy industry in the late 80s just too depressing. Now I feel akin to the regeneration and renewed hope of this renewed city. Like me, it has risen from the ashes and reinvented itself. The energy that surrounds me today mirrors the bubbles of excitement that pop and dance in my gut.

Today is a good day.

Thankfully the bank have approved the extension to my overdraft, even if I did have to sign a personal guarantee, but fifty thousand pounds will be more than enough to see us through until something drops in from the pipeline.

But I have another reason to be glowing today. My period is a week late, and although I haven't taken a test or told Gav yet, I know my body well enough now to recognise the early signs of pregnancy. The metallic taste in my mouth, the soreness in my breasts, the water retention and slight bloating in my tummy. I place my hand on my belly and smile inwardly.

Here we go again, little one. I promise Mammy's going to take care of you.

I check my watch.

Shit. I'd better get a wiggle on.

I don't want to be late for my meeting in Leeds, a two-hour drive away. If luck really does come in threes, then I'll finish today with a new client in the bag as well.

☆

The reception of the Malmaison Hotel in Leeds city centre is an intentionally dark and intimate space. Black velvet sofas strategically grouped together around low coffee tables are intermingled with high-backed purple armchairs that could have come straight out of *Alice in Wonderland*.

It's around one of these coffee tables that, four hours later, my client meeting draws to a close.

"That's excellent, gentleman. I'm so delighted to have the opportunity to work with you." I rise from my chair, extending my hand for a deal-closing handshake.

The two businessmen rise together and I shake their hands one after the other.

"We're delighted too, Victoria," the first businessman says.

"Your services are exactly what our business needs, and I can't wait to see the results that you and your team can bring," the second gentleman says.

"*Will* bring," I say with a confident smile. "Thank you for placing your trust in me. I never take that for granted, and I'm committed to ensuring we surpass your expectations." They both nod their agreement. "Helen will send the contract over this afternoon, and then Clive will follow up with you to discuss start dates."

They gather their things and leave. I wait until I'm sure I'm out of their eyesight and earshot before I punch the air and skip on the

A Star Unborn

spot, letting out a celebratory "*Yessss!*" followed very quickly by, "*Sorry,*" when I realise four other businessmen have paused their conversation and are looking at me, perplexed.

I dip my head as I feel the heat of a flush creep up my neck. "Just closed a deal," I offer as way of an explanation and they all nod and smile in acknowledgement, before returning to their own discussions.

Only yesterday whilst poring over my spreadsheets I'd had to prepare myself for the fact that if the bank hadn't supported me I would have had to let either Clive or Angela go, and today I've secured our cash flow, landed a new client, and tonight I will take a pregnancy test with Gav by my side and confirm my suspicions.

Life is good.

I send Helen a quick text telling her to prepare the contract, then I message Gav:

Put the champagne on ice babes.

Sounds like it went well then?

Something like that x

Let him think I'm referring to business success.

With a spring in my step, I go back to the car. Turning left out of the multistorey car park, I join the throng of traffic on the inner ring road and that's when I drive smack-bang into my past. Craig is walking nonchalantly across the pedestrian crossing.

The sight of my ex-husband right in front of me after all this time causes me to freeze in my seat. My breath suspends inside my body.

He is the last person on the planet I expected to see walking in front of my car, especially as he lives in Thailand now with the second wife and new baby Clarky has alluded to. Out of respect, the boys don't talk about him in front of me, but I know they're still in touch with him and have the odd drink in the Red Lion whenever he comes back north to visit his parents. I may be closer to them all now, but when Craig and I got married Clarky was our best man and Mark and Anth our ushers.

I take in the familiar gait and relaxed manner as Craig steps up onto the opposite kerb, and watch out of my rearview mirror as he turns left down the pavement, walking away, unaware of my presence. In that split second I realise if I don't act now this opportunity will be lost forever, and I have one unanswered question from our marriage that I'm damn well going to get an answer to.

⭐

That evening back at home, Gav and I work side by side in the kitchen. He chops up peppers and mushrooms while I tip diced onions into the hot oil in the wok. Gav reaches above me and switches on the extractor fan which whirrs into life. Sucking up the steam from the sizzling onions.

"You'll never guess who crossed my path today—literally," I say, stealing a piece of raw pepper from his chopping board.

He puts his knife down and turns to look at me. "Now, before I answer that, is this one of your *man tests?* Where everything you say is in code and no matter what I say, it'll be the wrong answer?"

Standing with one hand on his hip, he continues, "Like asking *'What do you think?'* when you're deciding what to wear. Dearest, I've fallen into that trap before and I ain't doing it again."

I laugh out loud. "No, but have a guess."

"I know you don't want me to guess and you're really just bursting to tell me."

I plant a peck on his cheek. His three-day stubble prickling my lips. "You're so right. As always."

"So Victoria," he resumes his chopping, "did you meet anybody interesting today? Anyone walk across your path—literally. Pray, do tell."

"Craig."

"Craig? Craig… *The* Craig? The ex-husband Craig?"

"The very same. Walked right in front of me while I was at a pedestrian crossing."

"And did you accelerate?"

"No," I laugh.

"What?! It didn't even occur to you to run him over?"

"Never crossed my mind. If anything, I froze at the shock of seeing him again."

"Then you have more self-control than me. I would have slammed my foot to the floor without even thinking about it." He raises his eyebrows before continuing, "Seems like all your exes are crawling out of the woodwork at the moment."

Gav may have accepted my explanation in San Diego as to the reason why I reached out to Chris, but from his little dig just now it's obvious it's still niggling away at him. Hopefully the good news I have to share this evening will wash away any of those lingering thoughts.

I know lots of people whose relationships started out as friends before developing into something more, just look at Julie and Clarky, but is it possible for a relationship to go the other way? To start out as lovers and end up being *just good friends?* I suppose it might be possible if one of them wasn't still in love with the other. But for Chris it seems I'll always be *the one that got away.*

"Ha-ha. Very funny." I make light of his little dig.

"So if you didn't run him over, what did you do?"

I remind myself we're talking about Craig, even if my mind had momentarily drifted back to Chris.

"Pulled over, hollered down the street like a fishwife. Then stood on the pavement and chatted awkwardly for five minutes."

"And?"

"It was very cathartic, actually. I got some straight answers that made a lot of sense."

"Such as?"

"Well, he finally admitted that he had had an affair. Something I always suspected, but was unable to prove at the time. Although that was never the real reason behind our breakup, it all kinda makes sense now."

I pause, while continuing to stir the sizzling onions. Sensing I have more to add, Gav listens intently.

"Plus he apologised… for hurting me."

"And so he bloody should. What he did to you was unforgivable. Although if he hadn't left, then you wouldn't be mine now."

He stops chopping his vegetables and comes to stand behind me, wrapping his arms around me and resting his chin on my shoulder. "And how did it feel? Hearing an apology."

"Not how I expected it to. It made me realise I didn't need it, and that I stopped loving him a long time ago."

He squeezes my waist and kisses the side of my neck. I close my eyes and sigh.

Turning, I wrap my arms around Gav's neck. "Sweetheart," I beam, "I was going to wait until after dinner, but I have something to tell you."

"Oh?"

I reach into my jeans pocket and pull out the white plastic tube, two clear blue lines showing in the test window.

Rolling my lips inwards and pressing them together, I hold the test up in front of my face.

Gav's eyes flick between me and the pregnancy test as he registers what it means.

"But… but…" he stutters. "You've not even had a period since the miscarriage."

"I know. But you can ovulate as soon as two weeks after. So it seems our little mini-moon in San Diego did the trick."

He picks me up and spins me round. "Oh Angel, that's the best news. Now then little one," he talks down to my stomach, having set me back on my feet again, "This is your dad talking. I need you to promise me you'll stay in there and keep cooking for the next nine months."

"I love you," I say, pecking Gav on the lips.

"And I love you and our little one here more than you could ever know."

Could my life be any more full than this moment right here?

My heart swells to overflowing with gratitude. I have the love of my life right here with me, my business has just turned a corner, and Gav and I are about to become parents.

We may have travelled out to San Diego as two individuals rebuilding their relationship, but unknowingly we returned as an expectant family once more.

Chapter 27

GAVIN

3 days later, Friday 13th May 2005

*T*he tyres of Vicky's beloved but now vintage MG crunch on the gravel drive as Gav and Vicky arrive at the Lakeside lodge.

Gav applies the handbrake and leans over to give her a peck on the cheek. "Now, Angel. Are you sure you're going to be able to keep schtum this weekend?"

She beams back at him, patting his knee. "Of course. It's far too early to say anything yet. Plus, I'm enjoying it being our little secret for a wee while longer. This weekend is all about celebrating with the new Mr & Mrs Clark."

"You say that now, but I know what you're like when you get with your girls. You'll be bursting to tell them."

"I'm more concerned about hiding my morning sickness from everyone." On cue, she covers her mouth as a sicky burp erupts from the back of her throat. "Which right now seems to be all-bloody-day-sickness."

"Delightful," he says, laughing whilst opening his car door. "Just as well I packed an extra packet of ginger biscuits."

Gav lifts their weekend cases out of the tiny boot and carries them in through the lodge's ornate oak front door. He blinks a few times in quick succession, his eyes adjusting to the dark austere interior.

This may be the last chance we have to enjoy the MG, Gav thinks to himself, knowing that once their little one arrives they may have to tighten their belts and sell the impractical sports car. Which only made the twisty drive over the spine of Britain and down into the Lake District —the top down, Vicky's hair blowing in the wind, the stereo blasting the beats of *NOW 2004*—pure, utter joy.

"Hats off to Becca. This place looks amazing," Vicky says, looking around the hallway of the private hunting lodge they've collectively hired for the weekend. "I used to be the designated team travel agent, but she's nailed it."

Gav plonks their cases down on the flagstone floor and a welcoming clerk looks up from the small reception desk that is positioned to one side of the carved stone fireplace. Despite it being May, a welcoming fire glows in its grate. The warm welcome from both the staff member and the burning flames is only tainted by the stony-eyed stag's head mounted above the fireplace.

"Checking in?" the clerk asks.

"Gavin Williams and Victoria Fenwick," Gav replies.

"Ah yes, Mr Williams and Miss Fenwick. We have you in the Ullswater suite. Peter will show you the way."

"Actually it's *Ms* Fenwick," Vicky corrects him before turning to Gav. "Not to be pedantic or anything."

"Oh but you are." He smiles, following the porter up the carved oak staircase. "There's a way to solve that problem you know. Just take my name."

"Never," she whispers good-heartedly back at him and he slaps her lightly on the bum as they climb the stairs together.

Opening the door to their suite, the porter announces, "You're the last of the party to arrive. Everyone else is enjoying a drink in the library."

"Thank you," Gav says. "We'll be down as soon as we've freshened up."

The room is sumptuous. High ceilings, ornate coving, a tartan covered four-poster bed, and sash windows that lead out onto a balcony with an uninterrupted view of Derwentwater. The bed is so tall it has wooden steps on either side.

Vicky climbs up onto the bed, meanwhile Gav takes a running jump and they both flop back onto the soft pillows, laughing.

"So when you said *freshen up*, what exactly did you mean?" Vicky cocks her head.

"I think you know exactly what I meant." Gav pulls her into his arms and kisses her hard on the lips.

"Okay, but be gentle; we don't want to upset the little one." Vicky puts a protective hand over her tummy.

"No chance. We'll just rock him or her gently to sleep," Gav growls.

An hour later, after they've showered and freshened up, they make their way downstairs and into the wood-panelled library.

"About bloody time!" Mark exclaims. "We saw your car pull up hours ago. What the hell have you guys been up to?" He raises his hand. "Don't answer that. It's obvious from Tor's rosy glow."

"Eurgh. Too much information." Becca crumples her face in disgust before embracing Vicky, air-kissing her on both cheeks. "But it is lovely to see you looking more like your old self Tor," she adds. "We've all been very worried about you."

"Yeah, everyone's really sorry to hear about what happened," Mark says.

"It's bloody shite, is what it is," Becca adds, air-kissing Gav. "And on the day of Jules's and Tall Man's wedding as well. It doesn't get more shit. I have no idea how you held it together." She reaches forward and clasps Vicky's hand.

Vicky looks over Becca's shoulder and catches Gav's gaze,

smiling knowingly. Gav places his index finger to his lips, miming a *shhh*.

She's never gonna make it through the whole weekend, he thinks to himself.

"Thanks Becca, but I'm doing much better."

"Good," Becca replies.

"Where's everyone else?" Gav asks Mark.

"Outside. We just came back in for top-ups."

Becca holds up her own almost empty wine glass. "What you having Tor? Vodka and Coke? Gin and tonic? Or you just going to get stuck into the wine. I highly recommend the Chablis, it's delish."

"Just a Diet Coke for me. I've had a hard week back at work and I'm likely to fall asleep if I start drinking straight away."

"Diet Coke?! You've gotta be kidding me?! It's a free bar." Becca juts out her chin.

"Actually I think I'll have a Diet Coke as well." Gav slides a protective arm around Vicky's waist. "Just for now."

Mark and Becca stare at the couple as if they'd just asked for *diarrhoea over crushed ice.*

"We've both had a hard week and my body clock's still not right after San Diego." Gav gives Vicky a sideways wink and she smiles appreciatively.

The bartender starts filling two glasses with ice.

"Another Stella for me please," Mark asks, "and a Chablis for the Mrs."

Rebecca and Mark have been engaged for eight years and may not be officially 'married' but it's perfectly natural for Mark to refer to Becca as his 'missus'. They've been together the longest out of everyone, having met on their first day at college, aged sixteen.

Gav picks up the two glasses of Coke, passing one to Vicky. The sweet nectar feels cold and wet and slides easily down his gullet. Mark collects his and Becca's drinks and the four of them make their way through the open patio doors.

"Look who we found loitering with intent," Becca shouts.

Seated around two adjacent patio tables are the rest of the group: Anth and Nessa, Clarky and a very pregnant Julie.

"Wahey!" The communal cheer goes up when Gav and Vicky appear. Their party now complete.

Beyond the patio the immaculately manicured lawn rolls uninhibited down to the shoreline of the lake. Behind them, the moderately low peak (by Lake District standards) of Cat Bells offers protection from any harsh westerly winds, and out in front the dense pines of St Herbert's Island rise mysteriously from the middle the lake. It's not hard to believe that this location was the inspiration for Beatrix Potter's *Tale of Squirrel Nutkin*.

Clarky and Anth extend their hands and Gav shakes each of them in turn, before turning and air-kissing Nessa and Julie on the cheek.

"Don't get up," Vicky says to her cousin, as Julie makes to stand in greeting. "You look proper washed out. Are you sure you're okay?"

"I'm fine," Julie replies, stroking her distended belly affectionately. "Well, if you don't count these." She lifts a leg to show her painfully swollen ankles.

She's definitely retaining a lot of water.

"And I've got a wicked headache. Even my face has gotten fatter these past few weeks, and I've still got ten weeks left. I keep thinking I can't possibly get any bigger. Then I do."

"I think you look glorious." Vicky bends and kisses Julie's cheek. "Pregnancy is a marvellous thing."

Gav smiles. Knowing her comments are also a reflection of her own condition.

"Right. Sup up lads," Mark says, checking his watch. "Taxi's due in ten minutes. Time to get this stag do on the road."

Clarky shakes his head in amusement. "Mark, I accept I denied you all the opportunity of throwing me a stag party before getting hitched, but doesn't it feel a bit like closing the stable door after the horse has bolted, having one now?"

"Hadaway'n shite, ya geet big lanky lad," Mark says in pure

Geordie, slapping him on the back. "Tomorrow night's your belated 'wedding breakfast' for all us common folk you chose to exclude from your *actual* wedding breakfast." Anth rolls his eyes, as Mark continues, "But tonight is your pretend last night of freedom."

Clarky and Julie lock eye contact and shake their heads in amusement. Everyone knows Mark is kidding, but he wasn't going to let the opportunity pass without an official 'boys' night.'

"But let's face it," Anth says, necking the last of his beer, "there's not much choice in the way of strip clubs in Keswick, so I think you're safe, Paul."

"Yes, bugger off you lot." Becca waves her hand. "We have things of our own planned for the evening… for the *virgin* bride." She turns back towards Nessa, her face plastered with a mock smile.

"Hardly," Julie laughs, stroking her belly.

"Irrelevant." Becca holds up a palm to *shhh* her. "I haven't spent all those years training as a hairdresser slash beauty therapist to not pull in some favours. We're gonna pamper the shite out of you, girl… as soon as this lot bugger off. Even you Gav." She wags her finger in Gav's direction, knowing his natural instincts to want to avoid any loud crowded spaces. "It's all arranged. Why do you think I've kept you all out of the lounge?"

"Come on then boys. Time to leave the ladies to it," Clarky says, downing the last of his drink.

※

"So how are you doing, really?" Anth asks Gav an hour later while they push their way to the bar in the Dog and Gun. "You looked like a wet dishrag at ours the other Sunday, before you came to your senses and flew out to the states."

"I'm much better, thank you. I didn't realise it at the time, how much I needed that little pep talk."

"Anytime." Anth squeezes Gav's shoulder. "When the pair of you walked out onto the lawn just before, you looked like a pair of newlyweds. All loved up and happy again."

"Yes, we are. Something shifted in San Diego and we came back different people in more ways than one." Gav smiles inwardly.

"Same again?" the barmaid asks, and when Gav and Anth both nod, she plonks down two pints of beer, their sides wet from the foam sliding down the outside of the glass.

The men add the drinks to their tab, before walking back towards Clarky and Mark.

Gav slows his pace. Anth stops and turns.

"Actually there was one thing I wanted to ask your opinion on," Gav says.

"Go on," Anth encourages, indicating towards two armchairs by the fire, out of earshot of the other men.

They sit down, placing their pints on the low table in front of them. Gav hunches forward, rolling his clasped hands over and over in his lap, while Anth sits patiently opposite, waiting for him to speak.

Gav coughs into his closed fist, clearing his throat. "Hypothetically, how would you feel if you found out Vanessa had been corresponding with an old flame?"

Anth's eyes widen.

"Just on text, mind you, or at least that's what you believe. Although, again hypothetically, you had no reason to believe there's any romantic connection on her side, but it's blatantly obvious that this guy still loves her."

Anth sucks air in through his clenched teeth, buying himself some time before replying. He takes a slow, considered sip of beer, wiping away the foam moustache that settles on his top lip with the back of his hand.

Looking Gav directly in the eye, he asks. "Craig?"

Gav shakes his head. "No. Chris."

"Chris?" Anth jerks his head back sharply. "The guy from New Zealand?"

"The very same."

"But that was over, what…?"

"… Ten years ago." Gav finishes his sentence for him. "And she was married to Craig after that."

Anth pauses, as if contemplating the right thing to say. "Okay, but before I give you my opinion, tell me what you know."

Gav fills Anth in on the details, as he understands them.

"Has she given any indication that she has any feelings towards him?" Anth asks.

"Not that I'm aware. She showed me the messages where she's explicitly said she's with me now. But it hasn't stopped him expressing his feelings for her."

"Then my advice would be… trust her. Vicky's a good woman and she's crazy about you, and wouldn't do anything to jeopardise what you guys have. Everyone has a first love. The person who took up special residence in your heart, and we all have fond memories of who that person was for us. But that doesn't make the love you have today, for the partner you're with now, any less. If this Chris hasn't moved on in over a decade, that's his problem not yours… or hers. I say, let it lie."

"Thanks Anth. I appreciate that." Gav rubs his chin with his palm, while he allows Anth's words to sink in.

"Take it as a compliment mate." Anth smiles. "A bit of healthy competition might keep you on your toes."

"Well, there is that."

His conscious mind may agree with his friend's sage advice, meanwhile his sixth sense is screaming: But what if it's more than healthy competition? What if there's something deeper that keeps them connected? An unfulfilled destiny, like an ethereal thread in the universe that is more powerful than the love I have for her?

"You good?" Anth says when he can see Gav's eyes have stopped flicking from side to side, and his mind has quietened once more.

"Yup. Let's go find the lads."

• • •

Gav and Anth find seats next to Mark and Clarky, just as a couple of wrinkly faced locals pull out a wooden box filled with an ancient and well-used set of dominoes.

"Who needs strip clubs and Jägerbombs when you can play dominoes on your stag do?" Mark grips Clarky's shoulder.

Gav straightens the dominoes he's been dealt just as his phone buzzes in his back pocket. He fishes it out and sees a message from Vicky.

Mark rolls his eyes. "Oh here we go. We've only been away for a couple of hours and already the women can't manage without us."

The old guys mumble in agreement with Mark.

But Gav's body floods with adrenaline, his eyes stretching wide as he leaps up from his seat and he reads:

CALL ME STAT! We're waiting for an ambulance. It's the baby.

"Guys, I need to take this. Re-deal my dominoes. Play this one without me," Gav says, already pushing his way through the throng inside the pub.

"Spoilsport." Mark throws his hands up in the air.

Stumbling outside Gav gulps down lumps of fresh air. His fingers quivering, he punches out Vicky's number. Holding his breath, his heart is hammering inside his chest while he waits for the line to connect.

Chapter 28

*W*hat's up?" Gav's voice sounds strained and crackly through my car phone connection as I take a particularly tight corner at speed. "What's the matter? Are you okay?"

"Yes, I'm fine. It's not me," I reply, realising I didn't make that clear in my message. "It's Jules. And it's bad."

"I'll go get Paul," Gav says without hesitation.

Down the line I hear him push open a door, releasing the background noise of jovial drinking and general merriment onto the line.

Poor Paul is amongst that crowd. Completely unaware his life is about to change.

"No listen, there's no time," I say quickly. "The paramedics had already arrived as I left. They're taking her to West Cumberland Hospital in Whitehaven. I'm already on my way into Keswick to pick up Clarky. I'm the only one who can drive as I'm obviously not drinking."

"I've only had a few sips of beer myself, so I'll be fine to drive."

"Fine. But I'm in the MG so there's only one spare seat. Get a taxi back to the lodge with the others and then you can drive Paul's car through to Whitehaven. Meet us there. The girls are putting together an overnight bag for Julie as we speak. You can bring that through for her. We don't know yet whether they'll keep her in, or what might happen next."

"Why? What on earth's happened V?"

I suck in a deep breath. "She's gone into labour."

"Shit! But she's only…"

"… Twenty-nine weeks." I finish the sentence for him. "I know. Look. Try not to worry Clarky too much. She's in good hands, but we're not the experts. I'm on the ring road now. Where are you?"

"The Dog and Gun. Meet me at traffic lights at the top of Bank Street, by the war memorial. I'll have Paul there in five minutes."

"Try not to worry," I repeat to a grey-faced Clarky five minutes later. Despite his size, his long gangly legs squished into the footwell of my small sports car, he seems small. Childlike.

"I knew this weekend was a bad idea," he mutters. "Too strenuous. She should be at home putting her feet up. Enjoying these last three months. Not expending unnecessary energy."

"Don't blame yourself. No one knows why these things happen, Paul. I'm sure everything will be okay," I say, even though I know full well no one can make those type of guarantees. Ramming the gears, I slam my foot to the floor. "At least this little car was designed for roads like this. I'll have you there in no time."

☆

Forty-five minutes later we pull into the hospital car park and I screech into the drop-off zone.

"You go. I'll come find you." I wave him out of the car and he dashes off towards the main entrance.

Once inside I'm directed to a family waiting room on the labour ward where I find Clarky, pacing back and forth, opening and closing his clenched fists.

"Where is she now?" I ask.

"In theatre. I haven't seen her. They'd already taken her down before we arrived. I've just been told to wait and someone will find us when there's some news."

I reach for his hand and give it a little squeeze. He looks at me and smiles appreciatively, but his eyes are full of fear. He towers over me, but when I wrap my arms around him he leans forward and rests his head on my shoulder and weeps like a baby.

I rub his back. "She's in the best place. Just hang in there."

The room around us is bare, except for a handful of white plastic chairs and a grey Formica table stained with sticky coffee rings. In the centre a pile of dog-eared weekly chat magazines lie untouched; next to them is a square box of multicoloured tissues.

Tactful. I wonder if they're there to catch tears of grief rather than tears of joy.

The walls are plastered with various posters advertising the benefits of breastfeeding, and listing helplines for 'Abuse during pregnancy.'

Considering this is the space where new life is brought into the world, you'd think they'd make it a bit more welcoming.

For the sake of Paul, I hold in my own emotions. Someone needs to be strong, and right now — that's my job.

In the corridor outside, midwives and resident doctors in green scrubs march up and down relentlessly. Silently walking with purpose and intent. Glancing at charts and whispering in riddles to each other. These are busy people who give off an air of not wanting to be interrupted by pointless questions, but I need to know what is going on.

I check my phone.

There's a message from Julie's mam saying she's on her way and will be here in a matter of hours. Another one from Nessa saying that Gav left half an hour ago and do I have an update for everyone back at the lodge.

"Wait here," I instruct Paul. "I'll see if there's any news."

I walk towards the nurses' station, plastering my widest I'm-not-going-to-be-fobbed-off smile across my face, and make eye contact with the frosty midwife behind the desk. She sees me approach but keeps her eyes on the screen in front of her.

"Hi there," I say, ensuring my smile can also be heard. "I know how busy you all are, but I'm just wondering if there is an update on Mrs Clark. I'm her cousin, and her husband is waiting with me." I point back towards the family room. "We've not been told anything other than she's in theatre. We're past ourselves with worry. Is there anyone at all who can give us an update?"

She taps away at her keyboard before answering abruptly, "Follow me."

I beckon to Paul and we fall in step behind the midwife as she frogmarches us down the corridor, depositing us in a small side office, furnished only with an old wooden desk, the kind used in schools in the 1970s, a blank computer screen, and two 'patient' chairs. We sit beside each other in the chairs and wait.

Twenty more minutes pass before a grey-haired gentleman enters, wearing a white coat over his scrubs. He extends his hand and we each shake it in turn. I notice his manicured fingers and the absence of a wedding ring.

Doctor's hands, I think to myself.

"Mr Clark?" the doctor asks, and Paul nods. "… And you are?"

"Victoria Fenwick. Julie's cousin."

The doctor bobs his head, his stoic features giving nothing away. I hold my breath as the knot in my stomach tightens.

"I'm Senior House Officer Dr Woodward." He directs his monologue to Paul. I may be Julie's cousin but in these matters I'm superfluous to needs. "Mr Clark, your wife is gravely ill. Dangerously so. It's a good job you called an ambulance when you did."

"Actually I didn't," Paul says. "It was our friends who dialled 999."

Still holding my breath, the sound of my own blood pumps loudly in my ears.

The doctor ignores Paul's last remark. He's a busy man and who called the emergency services adds no value to the conversation.

"The good news is we've managed to stop the contractions… for now."

Paul visibly exhales.

"But we need to deliver your baby in the next twenty-four hours. Your wife's life depends on it."

All the colour drains from Paul's face. The doctor pauses, allowing us to absorb the seriousness of what he's just said. I reach over to Paul and give his back a supportive rub.

At least the baby is still alive. That had been my worst fear, but I never considered we might lose Julie as well.

"Your wife has pre-eclampsia. Sudden onset and very serious. Her blood pressure is dangerously high. The only cure is to deliver your baby."

"Is the baby alright?" Paul asks, his voice wobbling.

"For now. Yes. But I don't need to tell you the risks of delivering a baby this early. Having said that if left untreated your wife's pre-eclampsia would develop into eclampsia, which would result in a whole host of other problems, including seizures, kidney failure, blood clots, and create a much bigger risk to both mother and child. But delivering at twenty-nine weeks is also not without risk."

I listen intently as the doctor goes on to explain the long list of complications for a child born eleven weeks early. Heart problems, brain bleeds, Cerebral Palsy, gastro issues, and that's before you add in the immediate challenges of breathing, hypothermia, and risk of infection that could afflict the poor mite as soon as it were born.

"We've already administered corticosteroid injections to help mature your baby's lungs. We'll need to give your wife a second dose in twelve hours' time, then I'm recommending we deliver your baby tomorrow night. Twenty-four hours from now."

"Well, Saturday the fourteenth has a better ring to it than Friday the thirteenth," I quip, before realising that my attempt at a light-hearted joke did not land as I expected. "Sorry," I mumble under my breath, dropping my head.

Paul squeezes my hand. At least he appreciated the attempt to lighten the mood.

"Will the baby be born here? In Cumbria?" Paul asks.

"That's up to you." The SHO sits back in his seat. Having delivered the hardest part of the conversation, he now visibly relaxes.

"We'll keep Mrs Clark in overnight, administer the second corticosteroid injection tomorrow morning, together with some magnesium sulphate. That's a relatively new procedure, but recent studies have shown it helps protect brain function in both mother and baby when we're dealing with such high blood pressure. Then assuming your wife shows no further signs of labour or worsening complications, I'm happy for you to travel the two and a half hours back to the RVI in Newcastle if you'd prefer. Either way you and your wife will be spending a lot of time in the NICU over the next few months and I'm sure you'd rather be closer to home if at all possible."

"Yes. I see," Paul says, his eyes glazing over. I can tell this is a lot of information to take in. It's probably just as well I'm here. I can remind him of some of the finer details later.

"But you don't have to make that decision right now. Talk it over with your wife. We have space here in our NICU and providing the RVI have beds in their neonatal unit, there'll be no issue transferring care. Assuming she's deemed well enough to manage the journey. She'll travel by ambulance of course, but that's a decision we'll reassess in the morning."

"Can I see her?" Paul asks.

"Yes of course. She's had a sedative, so may be a bit sleepy, but a good night's sleep is probably the best medicine for her right now."

We follow the doctor out of his office and down the corridor just as a familiar face barges through the double doors at the end and rushes up to the nurses' station.

"Vicky," Gav says, just slightly too loud for the hushed tones of a hospital ward, earning him some disapproving looks from the feisty midwife behind the desk. Gav hugs me briefly and grips Paul's shoulder in a mutual show of support.

"This way," the doctor urges. He clearly has other matters to attend to and doesn't have time to waste while we all bring each other up to speed.

He pushes open a door to a private room that contains only one bed, one large, plastic, patient armchair, and a couple of plastic visitors' chairs stacked in the corner. The light is dim, the blinds drawn, and the rooms smells of disinfectant. Wearing only a hospital gown, her hand hooked up to a drip, her face ashen, her bump visible under the pale blue hospital blankets, lies Julie, half-asleep.

"Jules. Are you awake?" Paul rushes to her bedside, while Gav and I hang back.

"I am now," she replies, her eyelids still closed.

"How you feeling, sweetheart?"

"I've been better." She opens her eyes slightly and smiles weakly. "Sorry to have caused such a fuss." She looks over in my direction.

"Don't be silly. It's more important that you and baby are okay."

Instinctively she rubs her belly. Checking that her bump is still where it should be.

"Have they told you what's going on?" Paul asks.

"Only that I have pre-eclampsia, life-threatening high blood pressure and early onset labour." She turns her head and looks lovingly at her husband, her voice hardly audible. "Did I miss anything?"

"No. I think that pretty much covers it." He strokes her hair and kisses her forehead.

"Here." Gav steps forward. "Nessa and Becca packed some things for you. They had a feeling you might be here overnight." He passes the bag to Paul.

"Did they pack anything for me? I don't think I'll be going anywhere soon," Paul half-laughs.

"I think you two know each other well enough to share a toothbrush," I quip, feeling more confident that my light-hearted joke is better-timed this time around.

"And here's your car keys." Gav passes the key fob to Paul. "You can't miss it. I've parked in the first row as soon as you walk out of the main door."

"What a bloomin' disaster." Julie uses her non-cannula'd hand to nip the bridge of her nose. "Becca went to such trouble to find that place, and all the organising of everything. The whole weekend's ruined."

"Hardly the priority right now," Clarky says.

Julie looks at me again. "You all should stay on. Enjoy the rest of the weekend and the dinner tomorrow night. Tell me all about it in a few days' time."

"I think you're kinda more the priority at the moment, Jules," I say. "Plus who's gonna want to be stuck on the side of a beautiful lake, sipping free wine and enjoying the delicious treats of a private chef when you're about to have a baby. I know where I'd rather be."

"Well let's just hope that this drama isn't a sign of things to come. That this little one doesn't turn out to be a demanding diva."

"Oh but let's hope they are," I half-laugh. "Whatever star sign they were meant to be, they're going to be born a Taurian. Stubborn as a bull. But it's a good strong sign." I lean over and kiss her forehead. "Just think, in a matter of hours you guys are going to be parents." I clap my hands like a seal. Trying to eke out the tiniest bit of positivity from this horrific situation that all of us are powerless to change.

Gav wraps his arm around my waist. "I think we should let Julie get some rest." Turning to Clarky he adds, "We'll hang around here for another half an hour or so. Go and grab a coffee, in case there's anything else you need before we head back."

"I'll come straight back in the morning." I smile at them both.

Gav and I leave arm in arm. It's only in the safety of the hospital cafeteria that the adrenaline finally leeches out of my system, rendering me a shaking, quivering wreck.

Gav holds me tight and strokes my hair. "Try not to worry, Angel. It'll all be alright."

"You can't say that for sure."

"No. I can't. But Julie's strong. Like you. And I'm sure they'll both come through this and out the other side."

Looking up to meet his gaze, I reply, "What other choice do they have? God, damn it Gav. Why does becoming a parent have to be so bloody hard?"

Chapter 29

Forty-eight hours later, I push Julie's wheelchair along the 4th floor of the Leazes Wing of the RVI and through the security doors into the Special Care Baby Unit.

"Wait until you see him," she says excitedly. "He's so tiny, but he's a real fighter."

"Can't wait," I reply, smiling.

"In here." She points towards an incubator next to a plethora of machines. Their screens all beeping and flashing. Keeping track of the health of the incubator's tiny occupant.

She stands gingerly. The pain from her recent C-section obvious. I support her as she shuffles forwards, peering into the fish tank that houses her son. Her face softens into a mixture of pride and undeniable motherly love and my heart flips over in my chest just watching her.

"I desperately want to hold him," she says wistfully, placing her palm on the side of the plastic incubator. "The nurses have said maybe tomorrow. As long as he has a good night tonight."

"He's beautiful," I say, peering into the incubator.

It's hard to ignore all the wires and monitors, but inside all that tangled mess is a tiny premature bright pink scrawny infant. His miniature face only just visible underneath a white knitted bobble hat and the ginormous nappy that seems to swamp half his body.

"Isn't he?" Julie gushes. "Considering he's so early he's doing really well."

"How much did he weigh in the end?"

"Just over a kilogram."

"…And what's that in old money?"

"Two and a half pounds. About one bag of sugar."

"Gosh that is tiny. But he's all there. Ten fingers. Ten toes. He just needs to grow a bit; I'm sure he'll beef up in no time."

"He will." She sounds more confident than the circumstances would suggest. He's her little miracle.

It's also a miracle that, thus far at least, he's not suffered any major trauma, even if he has a long road ahead of him.

I've not done a whole lot of research on preemie babies born this early, but you only have to look around the department at the enormous amount of equipment keeping them alive to know that these are very sick children, and without the support of modern medicine they would not be here.

A nurse wanders over, and seeing Julie touching the side of the incubator asks, "Would you like to touch him?"

Julie's face lights up. "Oh, yes please. I've not yet held him."

The nurse smiles warmly and unhooks one of the circular ports on the side of the fish tank. "Have you washed and disinfected your hands?"

"Yes. As soon as we came in."

"Okay then. Be careful of his IV and the central line, and his breathing tube, obviously, but you can talk to him and stroke his little leg, or an arm. It's good for him to hear your voice. He'll recognise it from being inside you."

The nurse hovers a while, until she's certain Julie is confident reaching inside the incubator and is not going to accidentally disturb any of the life-giving equipment.

Julie sniffs up a snivel and I gently put my arm around her waist in support as we both peer inside the fish tank. When Julie touches her son, he twitches his arms and legs in a startle reflex.

"He can feel your touch, Jules," I say softly. "Have you thought of a name yet?"

"Jonathan. It means *Gift from God,*" she replies, her eyes never leaving her son. "Jonathan Paul Clark."

"Ooh I like that. JP for short," I say softly.

"Actually I hadn't thought of that as a nickname, but that's quite cool. JP Clark."

I kiss the side of her cheek. "It's perfect."

"Hey there JP," she sing-songs in that motherly tone all new mothers use. "Now you listen to your mammy here. You've only got one job to do—okay? You need to promise me you'll stay healthy and grow up to be big and tall like your daddy. Can you do that for me?"

She wipes away another snivel with the back of her other hand. The stress must be unimaginable.

"Now this here is your Aunty Victoria, or Aunty Tor as you'll probably call her. She's a bit nuts, but we all love her for it."

"Hey," I say, faking offence. "Don't be slagging me off in front of your son. Don't take any notice of your mother, JP, she doesn't know what she's talking about."

"I need to sit down," Julie says, looking behind her for the wheelchair.

"It's okay. Take it easy." I wheel the chair towards her and she flumps back into it, gripping her stomach. "You're overdoing it honey. It's easy to forget how much you've been through as well these past two days."

She closes her eyes and takes a few deep breaths.

"Can I get you anything? Water? Pain killers?"

"A glass of water would be great, Tor. I went all light-headed there. Thought I was going to faint."

"I'm not surprised. You had a massive operation bringing that little mite into the world, and let's not forget how poorly you were the day before that. Vomiting, blurry vision; properly poorly. In the last forty-eight hours your body's been through massive trauma. I'm surprised you're even standing up."

I return a few minutes later with a plastic cup of water and a packet of Maltesers that I've picked up from the vending machine.

"Here. For the sugar."

She takes them from me and looks blankly at the packet. I realise she doesn't even have the strength to open them. I rip into them and pass the open packet back to her. She smiles feebly and pops a Malteser into her mouth, sucking slowly.

"You need to rest, Jules." My tone more serious. "I think I should take you back to the ward. You need a nap. I'll stay with JP if you like. Keep him company. Make sure he doesn't flirt with any of the nurses."

She snorts a light laugh and smiles weakly. "Actually I need to express some more breast milk for him. Would you wheel me into the breastfeeding room? Then you can come back and sit with him. I'd like that."

"Of course. I was born for wheelchair chauffeuring."

I settle Julie with one of the midwives, and return to the side of the incubator.

"Well kiddo. It looks like it's just you and me. So here's the deal. You just lie there and focus on getting stronger, meanwhile I'm going to stuff my face with this Wispa bar, because your little cousin in here is zapping me of all my energy. Oh no. I've said too much." I chuckle to myself. "So JP you have to promise to keep my secret. This is between you and me okay? And Uncle Gav, obviously. Just for a little while longer. But in another seven months you're going to have a little playmate, so you'd better be strong and healthy by then."

I settle back into the plastic chair and I'm about to wrap my chops around the chocolate bar when I feel a familiar pair of hands squeeze my shoulders.

"They told me I'd find you here." Gav leans over, kisses my cheek and simultaneously steals my chocolate bar out of my fingers.

"Oi! That was mine."

He smiles, takes a bite then passes it back to me. "Sorry I took so long. The car park's rammed. Where's Jules?"

"Expressing." He looks at me quizzically. "Breast milk," I add.

"Okaaaay. I definitely don't need to see that."

"Don't be squeamish. It's perfectly natural." I lightly slap him. "She'll be back in a bit. But I think she should be resting. She looks dreadful, Gav. I'm really worried about her. Her skin's almost translucent she's so pale."

"I'm sure they'll be closely monitoring her. She's in the best place… as is this little guy." Gav peeks inside the incubator and his eyes soften into a sympathetic gaze. "So this is him? Do you know how much trouble you've caused young man?"

I stand up and wrap my arms round Gav's waist while both of us look into the incubator.

"Yup. Meet Jonathan Paul Clark. JP for short."

"Hey little guy. I'm your uncle Gav." After a beat, he continues. "God, it's horrific isn't it. He looks so small and helpless, all wired up. Like a little lab rat. I think if he were mine, I'd just want to pick him up and run away."

"The whole situation is horrific, babes. *Or* you could say he's a little miracle. It's not that long ago that he wouldn't have stood a chance. Which is worse? Seeing him like this, or him not being here at all?"

We stare in silence. Both of us gazing into the incubator. I know Gav is thinking the same thing as me. *What if this was our child? Our helpless little baby. How would we cope?* JP may not be my son but he's already earned a special place in my heart. Technically he's my second cousin, but labels aside, he's family. I suppose if it were Gav and I in this situation, we'd just have to find a way to cope. You'd have no choice. You'd have to let the rest of the world fall away and focus minute by minute, hour by hour, day by day on the health of your precious tiny baby.

"I can't imagine how Julie and Paul are feeling," Gav says.

"I suspect like two people who became parents three months too early," I reply. "In shock. Not quite ready. Relieved and, in Julie's case, very sore."

"Yup. Clarky was telling me that he hasn't even finished painting the nursery yet."

"I think he'll have at least a couple more months to worry about that. I don't think JP will be going home anytime soon."

I swallow hard. I already love this pathetic little mite and will do anything in my power to help him and his parents through these next few months. Lifts to the hospital. A freezer full of home-cooked wholesome meals. A shoulder to cry on when they need it. Anything. I'll be there.

Life isn't about keeping score, but I owe Julie so much. She's always been there for me, especially when I was teetering on the edge of a breakdown when my marriage to Craig fell apart. She took charge when I was too weak to think clearly. Her kindness and compassion pulling me back from the brink more than once. Now it's my turn to be strong for her.

Gav kisses the top of my head while he stands behind me leaning on the back of my chair. There's nothing more either of us can say. JP is a very premature baby. He has a long road ahead of him and all we can do is hope.

Just then, an alarm goes off. Gav and I both look across at the machine that's buzzing loudly, a red light flashing on its dashboard. Gav's face grey, he looks back at me and then at JP, who's lying motionless in the crib, unaware of the danger surrounding him.

Within seconds an army of doctors and nurses surround the incubator. They slip into a well-rehearsed rhythm. Checking the monitors, checking JP's lines and discussing his condition in hushed tones. Someone gently manoeuvres us back from the crisis unfolding in front of us.

"Give the doctors some space to work," the kindly nurse instructs.

"What's happening? What's wrong with him?" Gav asks.

"The doctor will come and update you as soon as we've stabilised him, but it looks like his blood pressure dropped suddenly. Try not to worry." She steps away and returns to the rest of the medical team.

"I'll go get Julie," I announce to no one in particular. "You stay here," I say to Gav, "Tell the doctors I've gone to get his mother."

I rush down the corridor, but the knot in my stomach turns into a crippling cramp, forcing me to bend double. Unable to catch my breath from the sudden force of the pain, clutching my stomach, I lean, still bent double, against the side of the wall. I consciously revert to my well-practised yoga breathing, trying to still my racing heart and get on top of the pain, but I grip my tummy tighter as the cramp intensifies. It feels as if my womb has been placed in an ever tightening vice, and no matter what I try, I can't control my breath. I'm unable to move as the pain spreads out from my womb. Like shards of glass splintering up my spine, into my back and down through my hips into my legs. I slide down the wall behind me onto the floor, where a warm puddle of blood leaks from between my legs and pools around me.

"No! No! Not again!" I cry out.

Chapter 30

GAVIN

*I*n the midst of all the panic, with JP's alarms ringing, when Vicky doesn't return with Julie as expected Gavin runs out into the corridor just in time to see her being helped into a patient toilet by one of the nurses, a trail of blood running down the inside of her legs and pooling on the floor around her feet. At the exact same time Julie hobbles out of the breastfeeding room.

Seeing the trail of blood, Julie, her face ashen and her hand flying up to her mouth, looks first at Gav, then Vicky. "No, Vicky. It can't be…"

In the middle of the panic, everyone freezes.

Both women need me. Who do I go to first? Gav's internal voice screams.

In the end Vicky makes the decision for him, shouting, "Gav, take Jules to JP. Go now! She needs to be with him."

"But you're not okay?" Gav says.

"There's nothing you can do to help me. Go! Take Julie to her son."

The midwife helping Vicky waves Gav away. "Do what you need to. We'll sort this out."

"What's going on, Gav? Is Vicky having another miscarriage?"

Julie asks as he comes up behind her, grabs her elbow and manhandles her towards the nearest wheelchair.

"No time to explain. You need to come with me. NOW!"

It doesn't escape Gav's consciousness that in the moment of crisis Vicky has done what any mother would do... she's sacrificed herself for the child. Even if in this case it wasn't her child; their child. She sacrificed her own needs for the sake of the child who is still alive, and fighting for his life.

Twenty-four hours later Gavin quietly pushes open the bathroom door at home; if it wasn't for the few air bubbles escaping from the end of her nose, he'd think Vicky had drowned herself in the tub. She looks like a beautiful naked water nymph. Her eyes closed and hair waving like seaweed in an outgoing tide. He could hardly blame her if she'd decided to check out from this world, which has done nothing but cause her pain and heartache.

Despite everything, she's never looked more beautiful, he thinks to himself as his heart expands inside his chest.

She reappears out of the water with a *whoosh,* like a goddess emerging from the ocean. Water running in rivulets over her face, her hair hanging like a sleek curtain down her back.

At the side of the tub, a flickering candle bathes the room in a soft glow. The pungent scent of lavender and geranium hanging in the air.

"Here." Gav passes her a cup of camomile tea.

"Thanks hon." She takes a sip. "I don't suppose we have any booze? After the day I've had I could murder something stronger."

"I think the wine fridge is empty, but I'll have a look in the cellar. See what I can rustle up."

"Do you mind? Probably the only good thing from today is the lifting of my teetotal status."

Their eyes connect in a knowing sadness.

These past three days have been a rollercoaster of emotion for everyone.

Three days ago everyone was looking forward to a weekend of fun at the belated celebrations of Julie and Clarky's nuptials. Julie and Paul were expecting a baby and, secretly, so were Gavin and Vicky. Now Gav and Vicky are back at home, Julie is in hospital after almost dying, Julie and Paul are parents, albeit to a very premature and sick baby, while Gav and Vicky are once again baby-less.

Gav returns to the bathroom with two glasses of Baileys.

"Oooh… and over ice." Vicky takes a sip and smacks her lips together. "Now *this* is what the doctor ordered."

Gav lands a peck on her lips, tasting the whiskey and vanilla that lingers there, before he sits down on the closed toilet seat lid next to the bath, cupping his own glass in his hands.

"How you feeling, Angel?"

They lock eye contact, and he can see the steely resolution behind her irises. She may be trying to hide it, but he can tell she's angry.

"Fine," she says flatly. "The one benefit of having a miscarriage in hospital is the easy access to maternity pads." She snorts out an ironic laugh as the ice tinkles in her glass as she swirls it around. "I'm fine Gav, honestly," she adds, smiling weakly. "I'm not unaware of what's just happened, but right now with JP fighting for his life, our situation kinda seems less of a priority. Today at least."

"I don't disagree, but it doesn't take away from what's just happened to you. To us. Again." He swallows down the lump that's formed in the back of his throat. "Once JP is out of the woods, I think you and I need both time and space to process what's happened."

"I know," she says quietly. "It's fucking shite, and if you want the truth … I'm fucking raging. I want to smash something I'm so angry. It's all so unfair. I was just getting used to the idea again. Just thinking how amazing our little San Diego miracle was. Beginning to imagine what our lives would be like once he or she was here."

Her bottom lip quivers.

She takes another sip of her drink and visibly regains her composure. "The one blessing is that we hadn't told anyone. I'm not sure I could cope with all of the sympathetic don't-know-what-to-say looks all over again."

"Except Julie knows," Gavin corrects her.

Taking another sip of her Baileys, Vicky continues, "I know. She didn't need to see that. She's got enough on her plate right now. But I'm learning that miscarriages happen at the most inopportune moments and there isn't a damn thing you can do about it." She drops her head. When she speaks again her voice is no more than a whisper. "And that one came on so suddenly. It was so violent. I had no inkling. No warning or bleeding or anything. One minute I was pregnant and the next I wasn't."

Gav reaches over the rim of the bathtub and clasps her warm wet fingers in his own. She squeezes his hand in return.

"But tomorrow I shall pick myself back up again, hold my head high and focus on what Julie and Paul need. That's what we need to do right now."

"You're right." Gavin sighs.

"I knew instantly the minute my stomach cramped, you know…"

He furrows his brow, listening.

"I knew instantly that our baby was gone, but all I cared about in that moment… was JP living. It's almost as if our baby gave up its own life to save JP's." She turns to look at him, sucking in a large gulp of air. "That may seem a bit fanciful, but that's how it felt. At least, in that moment. He or she gave up their life to save the life of another."

"Well if that's true, they did manage to stabilise JP's blood pressure. Let's hope he doesn't have any more complications. It's just so sad. He's got such a long road ahead of him."

"I know he has, and right now that's all I can think about." Her eyes steely, she continues, "I'm not saying 'never', but right now Gav I want to be able to focus on Julie and JP, and I can't do that if I'm worrying about my cycle all the time, or thinking if I might be pregnant, or if I do get pregnant that I'm going to lose it—again. I think it's best if I go back on the pill… for the foreseeable future, at least."

Gav gives her fingers another squeeze. His heart feels heavy. Weighed down by grief and loss of hope.

If there was a way I could take on all of her pain, so she doesn't have to, I'd do it in a heartbeat, Gav thinks to himself. I'd do anything to stop her pain. She doesn't deserve any of this.

"You know I'll support you, Angel. It doesn't stop me wanting a child with you. But you need time to recover. Both mentally as well as physically. And when you feel strong enough, I'll be here."

She pats the back of his hand.

"And when that time comes, I'll make sure all my soldiers are lined up and ready for action."

That makes her smile.

She takes another sip of Baileys. "You really are my solid trunk."

"Pardon?"

"The trunk to my blossom tree." She laughs, and Gav's heart lifts just to see her mood lighten. "I'm the blossom. Always got a million different things going on in a million different directions all at once. Fizzy, dizzy, and putting it out there." She's put her glass down and is twirling her hands in the air. "But when the strong winds come and blow my blossom to the ground, I can pick myself up and carry on because of the strong, stable tree trunk beneath me. It's your roots that keep me grounded and that anchor us both. And it's your tree trunk that holds me up. The trunk beneath my blossom."

"That's beautiful, Angel."

"And if our baby had to give up its life so that JP could live," she continues, "I'd go through it again in a heartbeat, because I know you'd be there to hold me up." A silent tear rolls down her cheek.

Gav holds Vicky's gaze, his own eyes burning with unshed emotions as he registers the tears pooling in the corner of her emerald green eyes.

Both of them acknowledging the grief in the other.

Eventually Vicky turns and looks out of the window and sniffs loudly. "I'll get Helen to re-arrange my schedule for this next week. Julie will need clean clothes and I'll take her some books to read. She's going to have a lot of hours to kill."

Gav notices that she's shifted the conversation to more practical matters. Making lists doesn't require any emotional energy. "We should invite Clarky round for tea one night this week. Make sure he's eating properly."

"How long is he planning to take off work?"

"I don't know. He hasn't said."

Their conversation is interrupted by the sound of Vicky's phone vibrating. It starts dancing along the side of the sink. Gav picks it up and looks at the screen. "It's Julie. Do you want to take it?"

He watches the thoughts race across Victoria's face.

Is Julie calling to give us an update on JP, good or bad? Is she calling to ask for help in some way? Or is she calling to ask how Vicky's doing?

It's the latter that he knows Vicky won't want to discuss.

She holds out her hand and Gav passes her the phone.

"Hey," she says into the handset, faking a smile. "What's up?"

There's a pause while Julie speaks at the other end.

"No, not at all. I was just having a nice soak in the bath."

Another pause.

"Honestly Jules. Don't worry about me. I'm absolutely fine. I was only a couple of weeks along. We'd hardly got used to the idea. Right now we're both more concerned about you and JP. How's he doing?"

She pauses again.

"Oh that's great news. I am pleased. He gave us all a real scare there." She looks across to Gavin and gives him a thumbs up. He nods in reply.

There's a longer pause in the conversation this time. Vicky turns to look at Gav and he tries to read her face. Her smile widens as she listens.

"Oh my goodness. Of course—yes. I'd be absolutely delighted

Jules. What an honour. Thank you. Yes. Yes, he's here. Do you want to speak to him too?"

She passes the phone to Gavin, along with a side wink.

"Hello," Gav says.

"Hi Gav. How you doing? What a day... for all of us," Julie says tactfully.

"Indeed. As V says, we're more worried about you and the little fella. You don't need to worry about us. We'll be fine—eventually. So how are you? You were napping and Clarky was crashed out in the chair when we left. You both looked exhausted."

"I'm feeling much better, thank you. Getting stronger, as is JP. He's stable, which is all we can hope for at the moment."

"Good. Let's hope he stays that way."

"Actually that's why I was calling. Paul and I have talked it over and wanted to ask if you and Victoria would be his godparents. Victoria was already a shoe-in for godmother, but both Paul and I are massively grateful for all the support and help you've given us, and we couldn't think of a better role model for godfather than you."

Gav looks up. Vicky is beaming and now he realises why.

"Oh Julie, of course. I'd be honoured. Someone needs to keep him on the straight and narrow if you've asked Vicky to be his other godparent."

Vicky gives Gav a wet slap on the arm.

"Honestly Jules. After the day we've all had, this is the best possible news. That, and knowing that JP is doing well and you're on the mend."

"Because of his condition, we're getting him christened tomorrow. The chaplain is holding a special service for him. I hope that's going to be okay."

"Of course. I already had tomorrow booked off work anyhow, on account of our long weekend." Gav keeps his voice upbeat, but having a baby christened in hospital doesn't bode well for his long-term prospects.

"Well, we'll see you tomorrow …" Julie pauses before adding, "and I am sorry for your loss—again."

"Thanks," Gav replies, his tone softening. "But right now, you just need to focus on you and your family. I'll take care of V, I promise."

Vicky smiles gratefully in Gav's direction.

"Oh, and Jules? No one else knew …" Gavin pauses before continuing, "… about the baby, and both of us would appreciate it if you could keep this to yourself. It's just easier that way."

"Of course. Goes without saying. Although she gave me such a shock when I saw her on her floor, blood all down the insides of her legs."

"Well, you know our Tor. Never does anything by halves." Gav half-laughs, even though it's not a laughing matter.

"Indeed. Everyone's mad Aunty Tor." Julie laughs down the line. "Okay well have a good night's rest, and the service, if you can call it that, will be at 2:00 p.m. tomorrow."

"Well V's planning on coming through in the morning anyway, so text her if there's anything you need."

They sign off and Gav places Vicky's phone back on the side.

Reaching for both her hands he gazes deeply into her glassy eyes. "It'll be our turn soon. I promise."

"But what if it's not," she whispers. "What if it's never our turn, Gav?"

"It will be. One day, Angel. I promise."

Breaking his gaze she sucks up air through her nose, and her chest rises as her lungs fill to capacity.

"Please don't make promises you can't guarantee. I love you, but I've had too many men in my life make promises they can't keep. Please don't be another one of them."

✴

Five months after JP was christened in hospital, Vicky and Gav are dressed in their Sunday best and take their places around the font at the back of the tiny medieval church on the outskirts of town.

JP, wrapped in a handmade white shawl, is nestled securely under the vicar's arm. His eyes wide, he takes in everything around him. Julie and Clarky look on lovingly as the vicar addresses the congregation.

"We rejoice today with the family of Jonathan as they thank God for the gift of life."

Having already been official christened, today's service, although still a religious ceremony, is an unofficial alternative with slightly different wording. A way for Julie and Paul to include their wider circle of friends and family in the celebration of Jonathan's life. Neither Vicky nor any of her friends are particularly religious, being more part of the 'births, marriages and deaths' church brigade, but for the sake of tradition they'll gladly fall into line and follow the protocols laid out by the generation before them.

The vicar opens his arms and raises his voice. "We welcome Jonathan, who has been baptised and now comes to take his place in the company of God's people."

Under his instruction, Paul, Julie, Vicky and Gavin all make their pledges to support JP in his life, before the vicar passes JP to Victoria to hold, as is the custom, while he lights a candle and hands it to Julie.

"God has delivered us from the dominion of darkness and has given us a place with the saints in light," the vicar continues while Gav looks sideways at Vicky and gives her an imperceptible smile. "You have received the light of Christ; walk in this light all the days of your life."

JP meanwhile is mesmerised by the candle. His eyes fixated by the flickering flame.

Gav slides his arm around Vicky's waist and gives her a little squeeze. He is beyond proud of how she's conducted herself these past five months.

She did everything she said she would.

Supporting Julie and JP, through every high and low of his journey from a tiny helpless preemie to the bouncing, energetic five-month-old he is today. He may be small for his age, being the size and weight he would have been had he been born on his due date, but as Vicky predicted he's as stubborn as a bull. Fighting back against every complication and setback that has beset his short life.

He's battled against a heart murmur, breathing problems, and challenges with his underdeveloped digestive system. And all the while, Vicky was there in support. She was by Julie's side when they celebrated the day he came off the ventilator and only needed CPAP support. She held Julie's hand while they waited anxiously for the results on his brain development, his vision and hearing. And she was waiting for them with a warm home-cooked meal in their oven the day the proud parents brought their son home.

Despite his difficult start, he seems to have made it through the first five months of life with flying colours, and today is the culmination of all of his achievements thus far.

'An old soul,' Gavin had said to Julie one day when the pair were staring into his crib in hospital while Vicky had dragged Clarky off to get something to eat. The bags under his eyes a telltale sign of the exhaustion and build-up of stress.

'Indeed. I feel he's teaching me,' Julie had replied. 'I've often thought life gives you what you need, never what you want. I wanted a healthy baby, like everyone would, but I never realised until JP came into the world in the way that he did, that that was what I really needed. As dark and as difficult as this period of our lives has been, it's been equally uplifting and full of love. Without his struggles I would never have received all of that love. And it's made me stop, slow down, and really appreciate what I have. You guys, and all of the nurses and medical staff here, have been amazing. Because of him I have a new appreciation of life. He's made me realise what's really important. Family and love. And that's it.'

As the vicar draws the service to a close, Gavin knows the moment is fast approaching when Vicky will have to hand JP back to his mother; his heart constricts inside his chest.

Too many times now I've watched her hand babies back to their rightful owners, he thinks to himself. Vanessa's twins. Rebecca's two. And now Julie's precious baby boy. Is she destined to only love babies that she has to give back and never allowed to hold onto permanently? God, I hope not.

Vicky smiles magnanimously at the people gathered around the font, but when her eyes connect with JP's, he giggles in recognition, chewing on his closed fists.

Gav's breath catches in the back of his throat.

This is not right. If there is a God up there, I hope you're looking down on us and seeing what this beautiful woman deserves. She needs this. Please God give her a child of her own to hold.

Chapter 31

VICTORIA

Saturday 31st December 2005

*T*he snow falls silently outside while the fire hisses and cracks in the grate. Our Christmas tree lights flash on their timed sequence and the Christmas present I gave to Gav, a watercolour of Mount Snowdon under a crisp winter's sky, hangs in pride of place over the fireplace. On either side of the fireplace lie two crystal bowls filled with pot pourri. One his father gave to his mother, and my own bowl of love, filled with the dried petals from every bouquet he's ever given me.

At the rate I'm filling it, I'm going to need a bigger bowl.

Plumping the cushions next to me on the couch, I cross my sock-enclosed feet on the pouffe and pull my long woolly cardigan tighter around my body.

This is the first New Year's Eve I can ever remember staying home, or not hosting a party. Gav and I did offer to have one, but with everyone now raising small children, dragging kids out on a cold winter's night and keeping them up past their bedtimes seems more hassle than it's worth.

'Honestly Tor,' Nessa had said, 'now the kids are older, it's not worth the pain that comes with breaking their bedtime routine. Trust me, one grouchy toddler is a handful, two is pure anarchy. You'll understand one day,' she'd added before realising her faux pas. Dipping her head and mumbling an apology, before I'd replied with my standard smile and an, 'It's fine, nothing to apologise for.'

She's not the only one who's tripped over themselves in the past few months. I'm used to it. Despite our attempts to keep my second miscarriage a secret, it had leaked out, and after the usual *we're so sorry for your loss*'s, and *it'll happen when it's meant too*'s, my life more or less returned to normal. I resumed my role as nutty Aunty Tor to all my friends' children. Gav returned to work with gusto and I threw myself into my business, which has continued to grow. Cash flow is still tight as I roll all the profits into further expansion, but we have a good book of solid clients and our reputation continues to build.

"Hurry up," I shout through to Gav who's rustling up some snacks and drinks in the kitchen.

"Coming," he hollers back. He reappears with a bottle of Bollinger in one hand and two champagne glasses in the other. "Someone's impatient." He plants a kiss on my cheek.

"Bolly? Any particular reason?"

He pops the cork and pours two glasses of fizz, passing one to me.

"Happy second anniversary my love."

I check my watch. "You're about two hours too early. I believe it was more like 10:00 p.m. when I spectacularly crash-landed in your lap."

"Mere semantics. Sup up and enjoy."

I chink my glass against his, smiling. "Happy second anniversary Gavin. I may not tell you enough, but I'm very grateful to have you in my life."

"Yes. You're very lucky," he replies, a twinkle in his eye.

The refreshing notes of apple, peach, and walnut slide over my pallet and down my throat. "Hmm, nice." I smack my lips together.

"I love you, Angel," he says more seriously and my heart flutters open. "Okay, so what do you want to watch," he asks, flicking through our DVD collection. "Your choices are *Moulin Rouge*…"

"Always a favourite."

"… *Love Actually*, *Die Hard*…" He looks at me. "Which is not a Christmas movie."

"Really? You want to have that conversation again?"

Refusing to take the bait, he continues, "Or *It's a Wonderful Life*."

"Ooh, let's go with *It's a Wonderful Life*. I haven't watched that since I was a little girl. Such a lovely film. It kinda restores your faith in humanity."

He slides the DVD into the machine, picks up the remote and settles himself back next to me on the settee.

The opening credits have only begun to scroll up the screen when we're interrupted by the sound of the doorbell. We both look at each other, perplexed.

"I'll go," he says.

"Whoever it is … invite them in. We'll have a party," I joke.

Two seconds later Julie and Paul burst through the lounge door. Carrying a sleeping JP in his car seat. His button nose just poking out from the pale blue Winnie-the-Pooh snowsuit that makes him look like a mini-Michelin man.

"Surprise!" Julie gives me her best jazz hands. "We were sat at home on our tod and it just didn't seem right to not be spending it with you… so here we are."

I leap up and hug Julie and Clarky in turn. Gavin returns from the kitchen with two more champagne glasses.

"What are we toasting?" Clarky asks.

"This little fella." I raise my glass in the direction of the cocooned baby. "Two thousand and five was a year of highs and some horrendous lows, but little JP was definitely everyone's high."

"I second that." Julie puts down her glass momentarily and, in a well-rehearsed move, releases him from his snowsuit before he overheats. JP, none the wiser, sleeps on. The very image of an angelic bairn.

"To Jonathan Paul Clark." Gav raises his glass.

"To JP," we all reply in unison.

Ding-dong.

The doorbell goes again. Gav and I glance at each other. I shrug and he heads out of the room to answer it.

I hear the commotion in the hallway before I see the cause of it. An elated Ethan rushes into the room and wraps himself around one of my legs. Looking up at me, he beams. "Aunty Tor. 'Appy New Year!"

"Why thank you Ethan. And Happy New Year to you too." I smile down at his chubby round face and my heart flips over.

He's followed seconds later by his sister who, seeing her brother, decides to attach herself to my other leg. I'm now wearing a pair of toddler tights.

"Happy New Year Emily." I stroke the little girl's bright red curls. Ethan may be blond but Emily has inherited her mother's distinctive hair colour.

"Aunty Tor?" Her voice is high-pitched and innocent, like a squeaky toy.

"Yes Little 'Em." Little 'Em has become my nickname for Nessa's daughter, another one of my godchildren.

"I w'ove you."

My heart wants to burst out of my chest.

I've often heard parents say to each other, especially when they're expecting their second or third child, "What if I don't have enough love for this child as well," or, "I don't think I could love another one as much as my first." But if I've learnt one thing from all the children I'm blessed to have in my life, it's that love is not finite. It's boundless. Each child brings with them a new capacity to love more, and these children have brought more love into my life than I ever thought possible.

"And I love you too sweetheart," I say down to Little 'Em.

"And me?" Ethan demands. "You w'ove me too?"

"Yes and you too," I assure him, winking at Nessa and Anth who have removed their coats and also joined us in the living room.

"We were sat at home and the kids were desperate to see Aunty

Tor and Uncle Gav, so we thought, why the hell not? To hell with their bedtime routines," Nessa says.

"I figured you can babysit them tomorrow if they become too hard to handle," Anth teases.

"Ah… they'll be fine. You've got a two-day bank holiday to get them right again. Let them stay up, I say," Gav says.

"I think we'll need it. They're hyper already," Anth says, taking a sip of the champagne Gav has just passed him. "Anyway, cheers," he adds, raising his glass.

"Cheers," Everyone says in unison.

"You know who else should be here," Julie says, looking round the room.

"Already texted them," Gav interjects. "They're on their way."

Twenty minutes later Becca and Mark turn up with their two offspring in tow. A five-year-old Joshua struts into the room in full *Star Wars* regalia, complete with glowing lightsaber, and mimics the electronic schvrmm-schvrmm sound as he waves it around the room.

"We've not been able to get him out of it since Santa delivered it on Christmas Day," Mark offers as way of explanation. "We'll have to peel it off him in his sleep. Either that or shove him in the washing machine fully dressed."

Becca follows behind with Olivia on her hip. Born six months after the twins, the little girl is a mini-me of her mother. Petite but feisty, and with the same auburn hair and dark brown eyes that make her mother such a stunner. And just like Becca, Livy is also a woman who knows what she wants and will take no shit until she gets it.

'A right little fucking madam,' Becca has said of her daughter on more than one occasion.

To which Nessa and I always reply, *'Like mother, like daughter.'*

"Well this is turning out to be the best New Year's Eve ever," I say to everyone gathered in the room.

"Definitely the best spontaneous New Year ever," Anth confirms.

Gav picks up the TV remote and flicks it onto the kids' channels.

He finds a showing of *Madagascar* and like bees round a honey pot all the children gravitate towards the screen.

"Let me see what I can rustle up in the way of food." I down my drink and head into the kitchen, while the noise level continues to rise in the lounge behind me. Everyone sharing stories about their respective Christmases.

Half an hour later, I've managed to serve up two Margherita pizzas from the freezer, a bowl of oven chips, together with some nachos and dips. For the children I've knocked together a picnic of cucumber sticks, cheese squares, bowls of crisps, ham sandwiches, all finished off with a tub of Ben & Jerry's Phish Food ice-cream. Happy Days.

By eleven thirty, Olivia and Joshua have been put to bed in our spare room, having finally given in to their tantrums of tiredness. Emily and Ethan are still awake, quietly playing with building blocks on the floor, and I'm giving JP his bottle. The rest of the adults are scattered around the sofas and chairs, chatting quietly while a rerun of the *French and Saunders Christmas Special* plays on the telly in the corner.

Meanwhile I'm lost in JP's face. His 'dream feed' is my favourite bottle of the day. Hardly awake, he guzzles his eight ounces before dropping off into an even deeper sleep. He always looks so content, it's hard to believe the fight that he's had to go through to get here. Yet he bears no grudge or self-pity, he simply drinks his milk and sleeps.

I love the smell of him too. That distinctive smell of sweet milky baby that's so intoxicating, particularly on the spot behind his ear. Sometimes when I've been babysitting him and the time comes to hand him back, rather than kiss him goodbye, I simply sniff the top of his head.

The door pushes open and Leo slinks into the room, announcing his arrival with a snooty meow. He wraps himself around Gav's leg, purring and arching his back as Gav unconsciously strokes him.

"Happy?" Gav whispers in my ear.

"More than you'll ever know." I look around the room and a

warm glow seeps through my veins like a hot toddy on a cold winter's day.

"I've been thinking, Angel. What with the new year just around the corner, two thousand and six might be our year. Time for a new beginning. And I wanted to ask... if you might feel ready again. You know. To try for one of these of our own?" He gently strokes the top of JP's head with his cupped palm.

On the telly, the countdown to midnight has begun. The BBC flicks between skyline shots of various London landmarks. Big Ben, the British Airways London Eye, Trafalgar Square and the Embankment, all packed with crowds wrapped up tight against the cold. Clare Balding's voiceover giving a round-up of the year's events. The successful London bid to host the 2012 Olympics, the horrific London bombings only days later. The wedding of Prince Charles to the Duchess of Cornwall in the spring, the two hundredth anniversary of the Battle of Trafalgar. Yet my year was very different.

Two thousand and five was the year I started my own business, taking charge of my own professional and financial destiny. It's also the year that one past love was laid to rest, while another rumbles on. Coming face-to-face with Craig on a busy street in Leeds gave me definite closure from our marriage, yet the thread of texts between Chris and I means that connection lingers on. This year was also the year I lost two babies yet got to hold one of the most precious ones in my arms.

Despite the struggles, two thousand and five is the year I've definitely been the most settled, the most content, and the happiest I've ever been—and that is largely due to the man by my side.

I look up and he's right there. His face full of love, smiling warmly as I cradle my cousin's child in my arms. Like me, I know he's happy but missing something. It makes me happy to make him happy, and the one thing I know he wants is to become a father. Something he too has been denied all his life.

But can I put myself through it all again? I know I'm strong, but strong enough to cope with another loss, if that were to happen?

The TV focuses on a wide shot of Big Ben's illuminated clock face, its hands creeping ever closer to the vertical, meanwhile the digital BBC clock in the corner of the screen counts down the last few seconds before midnight.

Ten, nine, eight… Gavin turns the volume up and everyone stands, drinks in hand. Julie looks over to where JP is fast asleep in my arms, a warm smile on her face. I lift my arms, gesturing that she can take him back if she wants to hold him at the turn of the year. She shakes her head, knowing her son is fast asleep and in safe hands.

Seven, six, five… Gav quickly tops up my glass and passes it to me.

Four, three, two, one… "Happy New Year," Clare Balding shouts as the familiar bongs of Big Ben chime in two thousand and six.

At the exact stroke of midnight I feel a sudden bolt of energy shoot through my body, catching me by surprise. It feels like I've stepped onto an invisible vortex, just like it did on my wedding day when I heard myself called Victoria *Fenwick* for the first time.

My spirit rises up, out of the top of my head, like I'm being pulled upwards. Turning and spinning, until I look down at JP's sleeping face and I'm grounded once again.

The firework display begins over the capital as Big Ben's final bongs fade, and all the couples lean into their partners and share an embrace. Nessa and Anth scoop their sleepy children up into their arms in a tight family group hug. Meanwhile Becca and Mark, and Julie and Clarky, kiss and hold onto each other.

With JP nestled between us, Gav leans his forehead against mine. "Happy New Year my angel," he whispers.

I tilt my head and invite a kiss. "Happy New Year my love. And by the way, the answer is yes. I'm ready if you are. Let's surrender to whatever two thousand and six has in store for us. Whatever it brings, I know I can handle it … because I have you."

"I'll be the tree trunk," he says, and I giggle.

"And I'll be the blossom."

"I'm so glad, V. I really feel like this is the year we'll finally get what we need, not just what we want. Great things are coming." His lips pull into a wide smile, making his dimples extra deep, and I allow his love to settle within my gut.

It was exactly ten years ago I was in the Coromandel in New Zealand, and my life couldn't have been more different. Chris and I were camping with his brother's family, and our relationship was in crisis. Over the dying embers of the campfire I'd set the spirit of Chris and I's' unborn child free, and I'd felt the earth shift around me, just as it did a few moments ago. That evening triggered a whole sequence of events that brought me back to the UK, to Craig, and ultimately to Gav.

Tonight, in the warmth of my own living room and surrounded by all the people I love, I feel that same movement in the ether. Something powerful is shifting, an opportunity opening up like a path laid out before me, one leading towards my destiny, should I choose to take it.

I am brave. I am strong, and I can do anything I want, I repeat internally to myself like a mantra.

No longer will I allow my fears over what might happen hold me back. To hell with what might or might not happen. I'm someone who takes control and *makes* shit happen. And I can't do that if I continue to fear the unknown.

I'm going to grasp this nettle, and with Gav by my side, do it anyway.

Two thousand and six is going to be my year.

I'm going to make damn well sure it is.

Part IV

Chapter 32

GAVIN

15 weeks later, Monday 10th April 2006

*D*rop your pants, babes. It's ovulation day."

Victoria throws her arms up in the air as if she's just jumped out of a cake.

"Angel, it's not even 6:00 a.m.," Gav groans.

"Exactly." She rolls on top of him, laughing. "Time to make hay before the sun shines." She kisses him enthusiastically, sliding one hand down inside his boxers.

Gav sighs, but with Vicky's hand wrapped around him, and a bit more coaxing from her, he gets himself into the mood sufficiently to be able to perform as required. It's all over in less than three minutes.

"That was so *gooood*." Vicky pecks Gav lightly on the lips before rolling off him and sliding a pillow under her bum, delicately turning herself around and sliding her legs up the headboard, her feet touching the wall above the bed.

"I suppose that depends on your definition of good," Gav says as a throwaway comment over his shoulder, whilst heading towards the shower.

Vicky is oblivious, having already slipped earphones over her lugs and spun her iPod to the required track. Some hocus-pocus meditation that's supposed to aid fertility through the visualisation of Gav's sperm meeting her egg.

In the shower Gav turns the faucet on to full strength and relishes the feeling of the water running over his body, but the warmth does little to take away the chill in his veins.

These past four months, Vicky has tackled the Fenwick-Williams baby-making plan like a business project. She has spreadsheets a go-go tracking her basal temperature, a schedule of the peak days to have sex, which she's cross-referenced against their respective work diaries.

"We need to plan our schedules around the best times to conceive,"she'd justified when she'd spotted Gav's raised eyebrow during her explanation.

"In any given month the window for conception is only ever forty-eight to seventy-two hours—max. Surely it makes sense that we should at least be together during those crucial few days."

A rigid healthy meal plan is now pinned to the front of their fridge. "Extra veggies for both of us," has become her dinnertime mantra. And each morning she lays out his zinc and iron supplements, while she swallows down her pre-pregnancy vitamins with added folic acid. "Don't you want to make sure all your soldiers are super-strong and swimming in the right direction?"

Gav had smiled resolutely as she'd babbled on about the latest fertility tips she'd read on Netmums. He'd had to draw the line though at a PowerPoint presentation when she'd wanted to share all that she'd researched.

"I never knew getting a sperm to meet an egg was such a complicated process," Gav had joked one evening over dinner. "And there was me thinking all it took was one decent shag." That little comment earnt him a hard Paddington Bear-esque stare in return.

"I hardly think that's the point, Gavin."

He knew he was in trouble. She never called him by his full name. It's always Gav, hon, babes, or sometimes sweetheart.

"You and, more importantly—I—are not getting any younger. It's a fact. Given my age, biology is against me. So why wouldn't I want to do anything and everything I can to boost our chances of getting pregnant, and more importantly staying pregnant." She'd dropped her eyes. "I'm only trying to stack the odds in our favour."

"I get that, Angel. But stress is also a known factor in reducing fertility. And I worry that you're over stressing. Putting waaaaay too much pressure on the whole thing."

"I'm not stressed," she'd replied through gritted teeth. "But we've missed three cycles now, and every month that passes is another month my eggs are not getting any fresher."

"I know, but don't you think we ought to relax a little?"

"We can relax Gavin, when we're holding our baby in our arms."

It's pointless arguing. She's on a mission and anyone who knows Vicky will tell you, once she's made her mind up there's no going back. She will achieve her aim, by hell or high water.

"Okay then." Gav kisses her cheek, having now showered, dressed and readied himself to leave. She's still flat on her back. Her legs up the wall.

Pulling a headphone off her ear, she looks surprised. "Off already?"

"Yup, early meeting at work. But I should be home normal time tonight."

"Okay cool. Don't forget your supplements," she adds, before sliding her headphone back over her ear and closing her eyes.

Grabbing a travel mug of coffee and those damned pills, Gav sups the warm liquid as he pulls off the drive, and once he's turned the car out of their street he hurls the bloody pills out of the car window, where they catch in the wind and disappear into thin air.

☆

"So as you can see, our first-quarter profits are the weakest we've had for three years." Mr Callaghan, the managing director of Integratas, the software business where both Anth and Gav work, points to the downward trending line on the PowerPoint slide.

The eleven people seated around the boardroom table all shuffle uncomfortably. The four other directors look on stoically. This is not news to them, but to Gavin and the other five heads of departments this is a stark reality check.

"Jeez," Anth, who's seated next to Gav, whispers in his ear. "I knew we've been a bit quiet but still…"

"After asking a lot of very hard questions of ourselves," Mr Callaghan continues, "we believe this has been caused by a combination of changes in the marketplace and reduced customer demand. Together with increased competition in our space and poor productivity on our part."

A rumble of nods flow around the table like a Mexican wave.

"No one can deny that when we launched Integratas ten years ago," Callaghan continues, "we had a unique niche in our space. However, since then the number of competitors has grown faster than the size of the market, meaning we have to compete on price in a way that we didn't have to back then, or even five or three years ago. This obviously has had a huge impact on our win rate and project margin."

There's a collective intake of breath around the table.

"In addition, in more recent years we experimented and expanded into areas outside of our core expertise. Namely digital content creation, web development and UX."

Now it's Gav who shuffles uncomfortably in his seat. This is his department Callaghan is referring to.

"And despite some great work and huge client satisfaction on the projects we've delivered, we've failed to make any real profit in that space," Callaghan says.

Gav looks across at Dave, Head of Sales, who's purposefully avoiding his gaze. Although he would never admit it, Dave is largely responsible for the company's current financial situation.

Gav detests the guy, having butted heads on more than one occasion. Dave has told Gav that he believes Gav's team are a 'nice to have' rather than a crucial part of any complex project delivery. Whereas Gav firmly believes the future of any digital technology and its adoption will hinge on how good the user interface is, and Gav's team are at the forefront of how future consumers will want to make purchases and engage with online retailers.

If only he believed that too, he would never undercut our margins, Gav thinks to himself while Dave continues to dodge his glare. It's my team that take the complex coding from Anth's team of programmers and wrap that in a user-friendly layout.

It's Gav's team who understand how the customer thinks, how they want the software to look, feel, and work, which ultimately affects its rates of adoption and therefore its overall success, but Dave and his team don't see the value in just 'making things look pretty.' Therefore they always end up underselling Gav's team's services. Pricing their part of any project at zero margin, or sometimes at a loss, and it drives Gav potty.

'Sometimes Gavin, you have to catch a sprat in order to catch a mackerel,' Dave would say if Gav questioned his maths. 'Gavin, you're not in sales. You wouldn't understand. Just let me do my job and I'll leave you to do yours.' Another one of his patronising Dave-isms.

Dave tilts his head while he listens to Callaghan's presentation, like a proper teacher's pet. Gav suspects he's had a preview prior to today's senior leadership team meeting.

Mr Callaghan moves the presentation on to the next slide, which simply reads: What's next?

"So you're probably wondering what The Board plans to do to reverse this downward trajectory? Well, following extensive discussions with Dave and his team…"

Dave nods his head and smiles to the rest of the room.

Smug bastard. How much I'd give to punch his lights right out.

"…he assures me that our pipeline is strong and we will achieve our long-term growth plan. Having said that, we do still need to tighten our belts in the short-term. At board level we are taking a good hard look at all our customers. Who are the ones that make us money? Who is costing us money, or making hardly any margin? Which sectors are we strong in and where do we sit in those sectors against the competition in that space? We're also considering beefing up our competence and manpower in some emerging technologies, specifically Artificial Intelligence, and of course we're listening to our customers, asking them what it is they want and how we can potentially partner with them for the long-term. All of these things combined will allow us to narrow our focus and be laser sharp in our approach to the next six months."

Everyone around the table exhales.

"Having said that, we haven't ruled out cutting heads."

Everyone re-inhales and this time holds their breath.

"In the next few weeks, as Department Heads you will be asked to review every single member of your team, using a competency framework we've devised. This will help you evaluate everyone's contribution against a number of factors, including the value they bring to the business. Now is not the time for us to be carrying any dead weight, so regardless of anyone's competence, if they are deemed to be superfluous to needs, under the current business climate we cannot afford to keep them."

"Letting good people go. Every manager's nightmare," Anth whispers.

"I hear ya mate," Gav whispers back.

"There will also be a company-wide spending review. We're aiming to cut overheads by ten percent… at least. To ease the burden on short-term cash flow. So expect to see large purchase orders declined, and we have put in place an indefinite freeze on any CapEx expenditure, and I've lowered our automatic authorised spending limit right down to £50. Anything more than that will require board sign-off. I know it's harsh, but cash is tight. Extremely tight, in fact. The rule is, if you don't need it, don't buy it. And I expect you all to communicate the same message to your teams."

There's another ripple of agreement around the table, Gav

suspects more out of fear of everyone keeping their jobs than the impact of having to get a stationery order signed off by the board.

"But it's not all doom and gloom." Callaghan moves to the next slide, which is filled with company logos. "We are in the final stages of negotiation with all of these businesses."

Dave nods his head again and smiles once more.

"A couple of them for multimillion pound deals. If any one of these lands in the next twelve weeks, it will be a very different picture than the one I've just painted. Anything you want to add, Dave?"

"No sir."

What a prick. Who calls their boss 'sir' in this day and age?

"Just that my team are beavering away to dig us out of this hole, so I'd appreciate any support from my colleagues around the table, prioritising technical input into any complicated proposals and the like."

Digging us out of this hole! Is he for real? It's his fault we're in this mess. If he hadn't over-estimated his projections or missed his sales targets for the last three quarters concurrently, we wouldn't be in the shit.

"Goes without saying." Callaghan adds his support to Dave's request. "Sales *is* and absolutely must remain our top priority, until directed otherwise. Likewise, any existing contracts you or your teams may be working on where there is any opportunity to extend, or pitch for more work, please ensure that your teams understand that *sales is not a department,* rather—it's a culture."

Gav watches Dave sit up tall in his chair. He would rather be the hero that saves the sinking ship, walk away with all the glory for himself and his team, than make this a collaborative turnaround.

"Err … just adding to that," Dave butts in. "If you do have any emerging opportunities with existing clients, I'd be grateful if you would pass them back into my team to manage."

I can't stand this anymore. I have to say something.

"But aren't you targeted only on new business, Dave?" Gav pipes up. Everyone turns their heads away from the presentation and down to the bottom of the board table where Anth and Gavin are sitting side by side.

"Brave," Anth coughs into his hand.

"And surely your time would be better spent landing those big deals that Mr Callaghan has just highlighted?" Gav continues. "Rather than taking over existing client relationships where me and many of my colleagues around the table have strong and trusted rapport."

There are a few wide eyes around the room. Gav knows he's made a valid point, but nobody ever stands up against Dave-the-wanker.

"True, but I hardly think that's the point Gavin, now, is it?" Dave replies, his passive aggressive smile causing his eyes to narrow into slits. "As Mr Callaghan has just outlined, we're all in this together and we need to do whatever it takes to ensure we trade out of this sticky patch."

Gavin nods, whilst under his breath mutters, "The sticky patch created by you and your own team's incompetence."

⁂

A few days later, while Gav and Vicky have joined their friends at the park for an Easter family fair, Anth and Gavin walk in step.

"You were brave last Monday. Challenging Dave like that. And in front of the board," Anth says.

"Brave or stupid. I haven't decided which."

"Daddy. Come. Help." Ethan runs up to his father and attempts to drag Anth away.

Emily is not far behind her brother, her face painted with orange and black stripes. *"Roar."* She holds her hands up like paws. "Look Daddy. I a tiger."

"And a very scary one." He laughs.

"Daddy. Come. I go find Easter eggs." Ethan tugs at his father's shirt. They've already been around every stall in the park and spent more on raffle tickets and fairy cakes than the gross domestic product of a small country.

"Eth-*an*. Em-*i-ly*," Nessa shouts from the other side of the grass. "Look what Aunty Tor's got you."

Vicky has knelt down and is holding out two massive ice-cream cones, each topped with a flake and strawberry sauce.

As fast as the twins appeared, they run back in the opposite direction. Lured away by the universal attraction of sugar and dairy.

"All I'm saying, Gav, is be careful," Anth continues, "Dave's a slippery bastard and I wouldn't want to be on the wrong side of him."

"That may be so, but it boils my piss that he's still in a job when others are going to lose theirs."

"Callaghan thinks the sun shines out of his arse. He can do no wrong in Callaghan's eyes."

"Then Callaghan is a fool." Out of his peripheral vision, Gav notices Anth's raised eyebrow. "I know it's his company and he grew it from the ground up, but Dave and I started there around the same time, and all I've seen from him in the last two and a half years is hot air and bullshit. The bulk of the revenue still comes from the existing client relationships that we all maintain. As far as I can see, Dave and his team just drive around in their fancy cars, running up huge expenses, and deliver bugger all in return. I have zero confidence that any of those multimillion pound contracts Callaghan said were 'in the pipeline' will ever materialise. They've been *in the pipeline* forever."

"Perhaps. But all I'm saying is, Dave has Callaghan in his pocket." Anth slaps Gavin on the back and squeezes his shoulder. "Just keep your nose clean, that's all. You're a good man and I'd hate to see your head on the chopping block just because you ruffled the wrong feathers."

"I'd rather ruffle feathers than sit on the sidelines and watch that snake get away with blue murder."

"Who's been committing blue murder?" Vicky asks, now that the men have rejoined them near the ice-cream van.

"No one," Anth interjects.

"So what've you both been gassing about?" Nessa reaches up and kisses her husband on the cheek. "That looked like a heavy conversation you were having."

"Just boring shop-talk," Anth replies. "There's a bit of upheaval at work, that's all."

"Nothing serious I hope?" Vicky looks at Gav.

"Nothing that directly affects Anth or me," Gav appeases her.

"Okay good, because someone here has done nothing but ask when his daddy is going to do the Easter egg hunt with him," Nessa says.

Ethan flashes his father a big toothy grin.

"Err, Ness. Pass me a wet wipe. I think I need to clean him up first."

Everyone looks at Ethan and laughs. Both the twins are a smeared mess of ice-cream, chocolate, and snot. Nessa pulls a wet wipe from the nappy bag slung across the double stroller in front of her, and starts cleaning them up.

"Was that nice, Ethan?" Gav asks.

"U-hum." The little boy nods his agreement.

"Emily would you like to do the Easter egg hunt with me? I don't want to be left out." Vicky holds out her hand and Little Em takes it willingly.

Vicky picks her up and sits her on her hip, whispering in her ear, "What shall we get you if we win?"

"Another ice-cream?" she asks.

"If you want."

Gav watches Vicky throw her head back, laughing. Her blonde tresses tumbling down her back; his heart skips a beat. In that moment, he remembers how important it is he sticks to the baby-making plan.

No more whining when she asks me to take my vitamins or perform on schedule. I want her to have this for herself. For us. Nothing is more important than Vicky having the child she so desperately deserves.

Chapter 33

VICTORIA

Two Fridays later, Becca lies back on her daybed, crosses her fluffy slipper-encased feet and takes a slow languorous sip from her champagne flute. "Girls, remind me why we don't do this more often?"

"I couldn't agree more." I lean over from my own daybed and chink my glass against hers, while Julie and Nessa look on and smile.

We're spending the day at Seaham Hall Spa now that Fridays have become our new Sunday mornings. Everyone's lives are so consumed with the constant juggle of kids, childcare, jobs, and family lives, so we don't get together every week, but on the occasional Friday morning, we're able to eke out a few hours for a coffee and a catch-up.

Julie is back to work part-time, having decided to resign from her NHS role in favour of building up her private psychotherapy practice; so, like me, she can set her own hours and keep Friday mornings free.

Becca alternates her days off around her team in her busy salon. Having built up a solid clientele for her mobile hairdressing business long before Josh and Olivia were born, she's recently taken the plunge and leased a small shop in the centre of town.

And Nessa seems to have settled back into her role as finance manager of a large manufacturing firm on the Team Valley, now that she's successfully negotiated a four-day-week contract which suits her much better and means she's always off on a Friday, even if a day out still means she has to palm the kids off with her mam or sort out alternative childcare.

"When was the last time we had a kid-free girlie day all together?" Nessa asks.

"My hen do?" I offer. "And I've been divorced for four years, so that gives you some idea how long ago it was."

"No, that can't be it?" Julie exclaims. "What about our cheeky weekend away in The Lakes?"

"Nope, doesn't count. For two reasons," I reply. "One—you weren't drinking."

"Neither were you," Becca counters, and everyone dips her head.

Although the others know I've lost another baby, the secret having leaked out at some point, no one — other than Julie — knows the details, and the rest of the gang have respected mine and Gav's choice not to talk about it. Although I suspect they've likely discussed it amongst themselves at some point.

"Well anyway," I acknowledge Becca's comment about my tee-totalling status during our weekend away in The Lakes, "but second," I continue, swallowing down my emotions. *I will not cry.* "You spoilt all our plans by going into labour." I point my glass in Julie's direction.

"Hardly Julie's fault," Nessa adds. "But it's true. I was right in the middle of a pedicure when madam over there decided to faint. Do you know how long I walked around with only one set of bright and shiny nails?" She slips her foot out of her slipper and raises her leg in the air as if to make her point.

"No, but I've a feeling you're going to tell us." Becca takes another sip of her drink.

"Four flippin' weeks. That's the madness of my life now. Can't even find ten minutes to paint five toenails."

"Well we need to make sure you walk out of here today with ten perfectly manicured little piggies," I say.

"You're on," Nessa replies, and everyone laughs.

Until today, I hadn't appreciated how much I needed a break. I've been working non-stop. Taking meetings at all hours. Travelling the three hours up and down to London most weeks, often staying away for a couple of nights at a time, and on top of this Gav and I are trying to conceive. If I'm not careful I'll burn out. I inhale and relax back on my lounger.

Closing my eyes, I say to no one in particular, "We should definitely do this more often. I don't know about you lot, but I bloody well deserve this."

"Defo," Julie answers.

"Rebecca and Victoria?" A beautician, dressed in all-white culottes and tunic, a monogram of the spa logo over her left breast, wafts over and asks of our group.

"That'll be thee and me." Becca points back and forth between us. "Come on glamour-puss, time for your torture."

Laughing, we link arms and follow the beautician out of the pool area and down the dimly lit corridor into an even dimmer side room where two Thai masseuses wait patiently for us, their heads bowed and hands clasped in front of them.

Two towel-covered massage beds fill the space in the middle of the room, and the smell of incense hangs heavy in the air. Becca and I disrobe, and taking a bed each, the Thai girls cover our modesty with strategically placed towels before they begin massaging our feet. All the while a meditative CD plays in the background. The hypnotic tinkling of running water is overlaid with an incandescent vocal and the occasional *bongs* of Nepalese singing bowls.

"So how have you been?" Becca asks softly, and my insides freeze.

What does she mean? I hope she's not trying to draw me into a conversation about Gav and I trying for a baby — once again we've not told anyone of our latest efforts — or Gav and I losing babies.

I relax when she continues, "I feel like I've hardly seen you at all this year. Do you know it's been over four months since New Year's Eve?"

"I know. Ridiculous isn't it," I say, whilst trying to control my breathing as the masseuse has worked her way up my calves. I really shouldn't wear such high heels. My muscles are knotted to hell.

"When did the world get so busy? We used to hang out multiple times a week. In and out of each other's houses all the time. Spending every spare minute in The Red Lion or *doon the toon*," Becca says.

"Followed by a bacon sarnie at mine and Craig's most Sunday mornings." I laugh.

"God, that's right. But that's only because you live closest to The Red Lion. We'd scoff our bacon sarnies then head back to the pub for the next round. How the hell did our livers cope?"

"Fuck knows, but I suppose we all grow up at some point. Mortgages. Kids. Marriages. Everyone's settled down. That's what's happens."

"Hmmm," she mumbles. "I guess so."

"Except I'm missing the kids bit."

I let out a long exhale while, with one foot in the middle of my back, the masseuse pulls both my arms backwards and my spine pops.

"I've always envied you though," Becca says. "I mean I know you've not always had it easy, but once Craig left, after you'd wallowed for a bit, you rose like a phoenix. Everything in your life got better and better, whereas mine trundles on. Year in, year out, more or less the same, ever since I first met Mark."

"I know your life isn't perfect and you've had some of your own shit to deal with. Losing your mam and stuff…" Becca's mam lost her battle with breast cancer eighteen months ago, "but look at you guys now. I'd love to have your life. You've got your own business, two amazing kids, and you and Mark were childhood sweethearts."

"Hmm, yeah, well. Don't believe the façade."

My ears prick up, but before I can push her further there's a forced interval in our conversation as the two masseuses hold up our towels and signal for us to shuffle over onto our backs. We resettle ourselves as the Thai girls re-tuck us in and begin working their way up the fronts of our legs.

I twist my head and look at Becca. She's lying prostrate. Face towards the ceiling, her eyes closed. "Right Mrs. You don't get to drop a bombshell like that then stay quiet. Spill."

Still with her eyes closed, she replies, "Oh it's nothing. Only I do wonder what my life would be like if I hadn't settled for the first guy that came along."

"But you love Mark. You always have."

"Maybe, but I've nothing to compare it with. He was, and is, my first and only love. Do you remember what it was like to be in love in your twenties, Tor?"

"Actually I do." An image of Chris and our hot steamy love-making flashes through my mind. "But then we grow up. Even if I was still with the same guy I was with in my twenties I can't imagine our relationship wouldn't change over time."

"I remember meeting your Kiwi fella once, and thinking he was as hot as hell. Chris, wasn't it?"

"Yeah, that's him."

"Well, given the opportunity, I would have climbed him like a tree."

"Becca." I shake my head, stifling a giggle. "Only you would say that."

"I bet he could make my toes curl," she says, turning back to look at the ceiling and closing her eyes again. "I can't remember the last time Mark made my toes curl. Just be grateful, Tor, you don't have kids; they kill your sex life."

Even trying to make one can kill your sex life, I think to myself.

Becca flashes me an apologetic look, realising what she's just said. "I'm so sorry hon." She reaches her hand across the chasm between our two beds. "I didn't think."

"It's okay." I take her hand in mine and we give each other's fingers a mutual squeeze. "I know you didn't. But I will say this. Hug your children, Becks. Every day. And be grateful for what you do have. There are plenty of women like me, who would give their right arm to have just one beautiful bairn to call their own. Even if being a parent does turn your world upside down."

"I know, and don't get me wrong, I am grateful. But our kids arrived on their own schedule. We weren't trying when I fell pregnant with Josh, then once we had him we didn't want a massive gap between siblings so we just sort of cracked on, and boom, along came Livy. I only wish someone had told me how hard it would be. There are some days I sit on the sofa, surrounded by chaos, and I catch myself looking at the clock, counting the hours until the day's over. Sometimes I'm so worn out being their mam, I don't know how to be Becca anymore."

"Which is why today is doubly important," I offer, but she hasn't heard me. She's in her head.

"What with Josh's challenges at school…"

Her eldest started Reception last September and has struggled with the transition up to 'Big School.' Every day is a battle to get him through the school gates. He's been labelled as disruptive and there is talk he may be on the spectrum.

"… And Olivia hasn't slept since the day she was born," she continues, "regardless of what time I put her to bed, or how carefully I monitor her daytime naps, she's awake at 4:30 every bloody morning. And not because she's hungry, but because she's up and wants to start her day."

"I can only image how hard it is," I say sympathetically.

"…Add in all her allergies and skin problems."

Poor Olivia was born with severe eczema and a whole host of other allergies and, unlike many babies, didn't grow out of them.

"… And I know I've said this before, but Mark's about as much use as a chocolate teapot."

I snort out a laugh at her turn of phrase.

"Plus money's been tight this past year. I've poured all our savings into the salon and Mark's been bounced from one contract to the next. There's always demand for sparkies but without a permanent contract he has no job security and it's been impossible to replace our savings. We're always only one unexpected bill away from disaster." She lets out a long exhale. "In order to replace the hole in our savings I need to make the salon work, and to do that I need to put more hours in, but to do that I need Mark to pick up more of the slack at home. And he does nothing. I mean I do everything for the kids, and all the shopping, all the washing, and all the housework, as well as working full time, *and* he still expects me to have his tea on the table at 6.00 p.m. every night.

"Wow. I had no idea. He's always seemed such a family man."

"That's what I mean... don't believe the façade. Since I've opened the salon, he's had to pick up his share of morning routines —running Josh to school and Livy to nursery—and he will do the occasional bath and bedtime, but only after I've nagged him to death or we've had a big bust up the night before. It's so wearing. I'm not sure how much longer I can continue like this."

"Oh Becks, you should have told us."

I think about how much support I've offered Julie and Clarky this past year, yet I had no idea one of my other friends was having such a tough time. I internally vow to lend more of a hand. I make a mean lasagne and my chilli con carne is famous... well, famous amongst our lot at least. All meals I can batch cook and Becca can shove them in the freezer until they're needed. And I'm sure I could persuade Gav to babysit with me on a couple of occasions. Give Mark and Becca a night off. They could even go away for a cheeky mini-break in a hotel, if their finances could stretch that far. But it's no hardship for us to give them the opportunity for a date night at least.

"And to top it off," Becca continues, "I think he may be having an affair."

I jerk my head to the side. "What, Mark? Surely not?!"

"Oh, I don't know. It just seems that when I need him home early, he always has an excuse to be late. Saying he's stuck on some particular job or other."

"Or maybe he's just trying to shirk his responsibilities. Delay coming home for a few more hours. I had a husband once who ran away to Thailand to shirk his marital responsibilities." I roll my eyes in her direction and she guffaws under her breath.

"Maybe. Either way, it's all on my shoulders."

"No it's not, Becks. We're all here for you."

"I know. But look at us girls. It's taken nearly four months to coordinate one single day together."

"True. But I'm only ever a phone call away, and assuming I'm not away on business, I'd be there in a flash if you needed me. Especially since your mam..." I trail off.

"What? Even when Olivia's done a stinky nappy, Josh is having one of his meltdowns and has thrown his dinner all over the kitchen floor, the sink is overflowing with dirty dishes, the beds haven't been changed in weeks, the washing machine needs emptying, we've run out of milk and Mark's gone AWOL — does that constitute an emergency?" She laughs hoarsely.

"Abso-blummin-lutely. That's exactly the type of emergency when you should call. The least I can do is rock up with wine."

Laughing, she replies, "Oh Tor. You're a good friend and the perfect tonic. Sometimes I wish I could be you."

"Why on earth would you want to be me?"

"Because you've got your shit together. You're always so well turned out. Perfectly highlighted hair, perfect nails, and your clothes are always creased in all the right places, as opposed to always looking like you need an iron. You've travelled the world and always have such amazing stories to tell, whereas I've never been further than the Costas. Even now you travel to all these exotic places and stay in the nicest hotels. Your business seems to be flying while I'm struggling to get mine out of first gear. And now you've found a decent fella who absolutely dotes on you. I'm telling ya, you've got your shit together and I think you're amazing."

"Except I'm missing the one thing that you, Nessa, and Jules all have."

The masseuses have moved to our arms now. Extending them out from under our towels. Pulling and stretching our limbs as they release the tension held in our muscles.

"And how is the baby-making plan going?"

I suck in a long breath. I might as well be honest. "It's going. But without much success at the moment."

"Have you ever considered adoption?" she asks matter-of-factly.

"I haven't ruled it out, but Gav's not keen. Thinks he'd struggle to love a child that isn't genetically his. Plus, call me selfish but I want the whole shebang. Pregnancy. Birth. Breastfeeding. If I'm gonna do it, I want to experience the whole thing."

"It's not all it's cracked up to be, you know. You've missed off your list; back ache, swollen feet, stretch marks, and let's not forget cracked and bleeding nipples. Honestly my body will never be the same again. My belly button was stretched so much with Livy, it now looks like an upside down frown."

Laughing, I reply, "Maybe so, but I'm not ready to give up on that dream just yet."

"It's funny. I envy so much of your life, yet having babies isn't something I've ever struggled with. I only had to forget one pill, then nine months later out popped Josh."

My insides give an involuntary shiver.

One of the Thai girls clangs together two tiny cymbals that ring out and vibrate in the room. They clasp their hands together in the prayer position, bow their heads, and say "Namaste" in unison.

"Namaste," Becca and I say together, having now stood and re-robed in the spa dressing gowns.

"I'm sure it'll all work out, Tor," she says, as she slides her feet inside the fluffy slippers, before linking her arm through mine and leading me back down the dimly lit corridor.

"Likewise," I reply, patting the back of her hand.

We walk past the famous elephant statue and rejoin the others,

275

who are exactly where we left them. Lying on daybeds by the side of the pool.

"Have fun ladies?" Julie asks.

"I think I might be two inches taller," Becca replies.

"Nah. You're still a short-arse," I tease, turning to her and giving her a cheeky wink.

Chapter 34

GAVIN

3 weeks later, Sunday 14th May 2006

The sun warms the side of Gavin's cheek, while the cold beer slides down his gullet.

"Ready for another?" Mark asks.

"Go on then." Gav tips the can of Stella to his lips, draining it in one.

Anth shakes his head. "Not yet, mate."

Mark takes Gav's empty can from him and disappears through the patio doors and back into Clarky and Julie's kitchen, leaving Anth and Gav seated under the pergola in the garden.

"So how hard has the surgeon's knife had to cut in your department?" Anth turns to Gav and asks.

"That's the weird thing mate. Every other department has announced one or two redundancies, but so far in my department they've not cut a single head. At least not yet."

"What? No one?"

"No. I did the full team assessment as asked, and as much as it pained me to have to do it, I put my suggestions forward."

"Who did you pick?" Anth asks.

"It wasn't really a question of *picking*. Everyone in my team had great scores in performance and productivity, so it came down to *last in, first out*. I'll be sad to let Nancy and Peter go though. They were just settling in and beginning to produce some great work."

"I know, it's horrible. Like being asked to choose your favourite child."

"Well only you would know about that." Gav smiles wryly at him, and Anth bobs his head in sympathetic acknowledgement.

The men may not discuss their feelings like the women do, but everyone is aware of Gav and Vicky's desire to have a child.

"So when do you think they'll be told?" Anth asks, taking a sip from his beer.

"Not sure. I've got to go in first thing tomorrow for an 8:00 a.m. meeting with Callaghan and the finance director, so I suspect I'll know more then."

Anth slaps Gav on the shoulder and gives him a supportive squeeze. "I'll be thinking of you. I've just been through it this past week with my own team. We've lost four. Team morale is in the toilet. I only hope we can all recover from this."

Mark returns with two beers and Clarky, who has JP sitting on his hip.

Gav stands up and shakes Paul's hand, before tickling JP under his chin. JP kicks his pudgy legs in delight. "Who'd have thought it mate," Gav says to the infant, "one year ago when I first saw you all wired up like a lab rat, that I'd be helping you celebrate. Happy Birthday little fella."

"I know. A year ago it was hard to imagine getting to this point," Clarky says.

"Ahh, he's a little fighter. He was always going to make it." Gav slaps Clarky on the shoulder, before taking the beer from Mark. It opens with a fizz.

"It's been a hard year, but I'm so proud of him," Clarky says.

"If you think it's hard now," Mark says, "try looking after an autistic six-year-old and an almost-three-year-old that screams half the night."

"That's true," Anth says. "But I bet you wouldn't be without the little rascals?"

"Wouldn't I?" Mark replies, looking down into his can.

As if on cue, Becca stomps into the garden, passes a wailing Olivia to Mark and drops an oversized nappy bag at his feet. The smell that accompanies Olivia reveals the reason for her tears.

"You know, Mark, a little bit of help wouldn't go amiss. Why should I have to nag you all the time? I'm dealing with a Josh meltdown in the lounge. He's just thrown his blackcurrant juice all over Emily who is now bawling her eyes out."

Anth looks on, concerned. "Does Nessa need any help?"

"She's fine," Becca exhales. "Tor's calming Josh down while Nessa cleans Emily up, but I need to sort out the carpet, or else my first birthday gift to JP will be a lasting stain in his mam's front room."

Paul looks lovingly down at his child and sing-songs, "Don't you listen to them. You're not going to cause anybody any trouble when you grow up because you're just too perfect."

Becca storms off, leaving Mark no option but to pick up the nappy bag and console his wailing daughter. He passes Gav his tin of beer. "Here. Hold this. Back in a bit."

A short while later Vicky appears through the patio doors, balancing a number of tea plates in her hands. "Who wants cake?" She passes out the plates, and pulls a handful of forks, she's had tucked into her back pocket, out of her skinny jeans.

Clarky carries a sleepy JP back into the house to put him down somewhere quiet. Anth and Mark wander off in search of more beer; seeing Gav on his own, Vicky sidles up to him.

"It's a year ago today." She looks off into the distance.

"I know." Gav wraps an arm around her waist and kisses the top of her head. Her hair smells of shampoo and hairspray. "You okay? I know you're happy for JP and everything, but it's still okay to grieve as well."

"I know."

Gav watches as she draws in a deep breath.

"But maybe we won't need to grieve much longer." She meets his gaze and a tentative smile creeps across her face.

"You mean…?" He beams.

"Maybe. I haven't taken a test yet. I'm three days late, but I know my body well enough now."

Gav pulls her into him, squeezing the tears out of the corner of his eyes as tightly as he squeezes the breath out of her body.

"Careful," she laughs. "If I am, you know…"

Neither of them are confident enough to even say the word. At least not yet.

"… You don't want to harm the little mite before it has a chance to cling on."

Gav is about to say something else, but his thoughts are interrupted by Becca, who appears at the patio doors, manhandling her kicking and screaming son.

"Joshua Heron. Get outside now. You know that is not nice behaviour. I don't want to see you in here until you're ready to apologise."

Becca dumps him on the back doorstep, turns and matches back inside, leaving a bereft Josh, his arms outstretched, wailing for his mother.

"Wait here." Vicky passes Gav her unfinished plate of cake. "Becca's at her wits' end, and Mark's doing nothing to share the burden."

Gavin watches on as Vicky crouches down next to Joshua. The little boy wraps his arms around her neck and hugs into her. In one swift movement she stands up and he wraps his legs tightly around her waist.

"Would you like to come and play in the sandpit with me?" she asks.

"Yes please, Aunty Tor," he manages to say in between his heaving sobs.

"We could make a big fortress and then show it to your mammy. I'm sure she'll be really impressed." She turns and winks at Gav.

Gav holds up the plate of half-eaten cake, gesturing if she wants it. She smiles, shrugs, and holds up two sand-covered hands, before blowing Gav a kiss. He pretends to catch it and squish it into his heart.

Watching her play with Josh, who only moments ago was crying like his world had ended, and who is now explaining in great detail the huge fortress he's building, it's clear that her mothering instinct is as strong as any woman who's birthed their own bairn. Maybe, just maybe, her time has finally arrived.

Please God make it true, Gav thinks to himself. She deserves to do this with one of her own.

⁂

"Sorry to have pulled you in so early," Callaghan begins, "but we felt it was best to do this before the rest of your team get here."

Both Callaghan and the finance director sit bolt upright on the opposite side of the board table, faces stern, hands clasped in front of them.

"No problem," Gav replies. "Actually I'm a little surprised you haven't requested this meeting before now. I'm aware I'm the only department head who hasn't yet had the opportunity to discuss my recommendations for cutbacks and potential redundancies."

"Yes, well, that's why we asked you here." Callaghan purses his lips together before sucking in a lungful of air.

Gavin shuffles in his chair. He's prepared, and as difficult as it is letting Nancy and Peter go—Peter is saving for a deposit on a house, his first home with his long-term girlfriend, and as Nancy got married last year Gav suspects she's working towards her two years of employment at Integratas so she'll qualify for full maternity benefits—he understands that every department has been asked to make cutbacks and his team are no exception.

"So here's the thing," Callaghan continues, "and there's no easy way to say this, but you know how things have been lately and how tight our margins currently are, so after much thought and deep discussion we've decided to cut the whole of your department."

Callaghan pauses, allowing Gav time to absorb what he's just said.

"What, all six of my team?!" Gav exclaims.

"Actually, all seven," the finance director interjects. "Your six team members *and* yourself Gavin." He looks Gav directly in the eye. "I'm so very sorry."

Gav sucks in a deep breath, composing himself.

Don't lose your shit. That won't help anyone.

"I understand," he says, forcing himself to keep his tone level. "However, I'd appreciate it if you could explain the rationale behind this decision."

Callaghan picks up the thread from his colleague. "We've had many tough decisions to debate at board level, Gavin, and trust me this decision wasn't made lightly or without looking at every other possible option. But when we reviewed what services are currently selling, and where we make the deepest margin, the numbers don't lie. Your department—as talented and loyal as you all are—contributes the least to profit. It was purely a decision based on metrics."

"But surely you must see the value in what my department brings. We may be a high cost to the business at the moment, but the way things are moving in the market, the need to be able to create customer-centric user interfaces will become an integral part of *every* project, if not *the* deciding factor when customers are choosing to engage with us. I believe our skills will become critical in winning new business in the next five years."

"That's not the opinion shared by Dave," Callaghan counters.

That fucking snake. Anth was right.

"Well, for the record I categorically disagree. I appreciate your decision, gentlemen, but I think you're making a mistake. A big mistake, and one that you'll look back on and regret."

"You may well be right," the stony-eyed FD adds, "but it's our mistake to make. You will of course receive your due severance of six weeks' wages, made up of one month's payment in lieu of notice plus one additional week for each full year of employment. Once you've packed up your things you're free to leave."

"I see. I guess you're not asking me to work out my notice period then?"

"We find in these types of situations it's best for the remaining employees if we don't draw things out," the finance director confirms.

"You will of course have until the end of the day to update any files, give a courtesy call to any clients. We're suggesting you hand any existing client relationships over to Anthony and his team, so it would be helpful if you could facilitate an introduction. Then you'll be asked to surrender your company property and obviously all access to our systems," Callaghan adds, as if Gav should be thankful they're giving him the opportunity to do any sort of handover despite being made redundant.

He drops his eyes to hide the anger that rages there.

"When do we tell the team?" he hisses through gritted teeth.

"At nine o'clock. It's your call as to how long they need to clear their desks, but we're assuming they can all pack up by lunchtime."

"Who else knows?" Gav eyeballs Callaghan.

"Only the other directors."

"… and Dave."

Gav can't help making *that* little dig.

"Well, actually, we believe this reshuffle is the perfect time to announce Dave's promotion to Sales Director." Callaghan fluffs out his feathers and bobs his head from side to side, like a child who's just received praise from a parent.

Great. So when I'm out on my ear, that termite gets a promotion.

"I see. Gentleman …" Gav is the first to stand. He may not be able to control the termination of his employment, but he can control the end of the meeting.

The directors scrape their chairs back as they too stand, offering their hands to shake.

Gav narrows his eyes as he stares at the two outstretched hands. Really?!

"I believe I have some pressing matters to attend to and a very limited amount of time to tie up any loose ends, so if you'll excuse me," he says, relenting and shaking each of their hands in turn.

"Gavin." Callaghan clasps his other hand over the top of the younger man's, regaining control again and prohibiting Gav's exit. "You do know this wasn't personal. You've been a great asset to our organisation these past two years and I wish you every success in the future. Do keep in touch."

Gav extracts his hand, purses his lips into an acrid smile and walks out of the room with his shoulders pulled back and his head held high, even if he has no idea what he's going to do next. But he needs to do something, and quick.

Especially now that we're pregnant, he thinks to himself.

Chapter 35

VICTORIA

4 weeks later, Wednesday 28th June 2006

*C*old gel," the sonographer announces as brusquely as if she were a station guard waving off a departing train. She squirts my exposed belly with gloopy mucus which shoots out of the tube with a fart, before rolling the transducer over my tummy. My skin tingles from the mild electrical current and I can taste metal on my tongue. Having dutifully consumed the required one and a half litres of water just before my scan appointment, my bladder is fit to burst, so as the sonographer pushes and twists the ultrasound wand over my abdomen, applying what some might consider *more than necessary pressure*, I'm seriously wishing I'd worn some TENA Lady this morning.

Gav hunches forward, his eyes focused on the grainy black and white screen in front of the sonographer. I have to squeeze my eyes tight shut. The suspense too painful.

"There," the sonographer says. "There's baby. And that little flicker is baby's heartbeat."

I hear Gav exhale as he squeezes my hand. I open my eyes and follow the line of the sonographer's extended finger. On the screen is the grainy outline of a black peanut-shaped sack with a little alien inside. Its head three times the size of its body. What appear to be the beginning of arms and legs float and wave around aimlessly, but inside its abdomen is the unmistakable flutter of a tiny heartbeat, and I know then, with absolute certainty—I'm in love.

This is my fourth pregnancy, but the first time I've seen any of my babies with a life-affirming heartbeat.

It's alive. It's real. This is really going to happen.

Gav lifts our clasped hands to his lips and kisses the backs of my fingers. "Oh, Vicky," he says, his voice wobbling with emotion.

"I know," I whisper in reply. "Is it healthy?" I ask the sonographer, more formally. The pace and tone of my words communicating my concerns.

Finally she turns away from the screen, locks her gaze with mine and, woman-to-woman, gives me a reassuring smile. "Everything looks absolutely fine, Victoria. Now sit back and relax while I take all the necessary measurements."

I smile at Gavin and finally allow myself to exhale.

The sonographer moves the wand around my tummy, looking at the foetal sack from different angles. "There's baby's head and body." She points out the various parts of our child's anatomy on the screen. "Its limbs are not fully formed yet, but those two hollows are its eyes. See, it's looking at you. Say hello to Mammy and Daddy," she sing-songs as the tiny foetus wriggles and rolls around the screen.

My emotions continue to erupt and my heart bursts wide open. Everyone talks about the overwhelming love that rushes through you for your child, yet I never expected to fall instantly in love with a grainy black and white image on an ultrasound screen. I always assumed that feeling would come the first time I get to hold my bairn in my arms.

"And just hold still for a moment," the sonographer says as she freezes the screen.

"Why, is there something wrong?" I ask, trying to sit up, and doing the complete opposite of what she's just asked.

"No not at all." She turns and her smile reassures me once again. "We just want to ensure we have your correct dates."

She uses a digital ruler and begins noting a series of measurements. The length of the sac. The circumference of the baby's head.

Gav looks at me and his eyes are full of love. "There was a part of me that thought we'd never get here," he says.

"Don't you be admitting that to me now!" I lightly slap the back of his hand. "You're my tree trunk, remember. When the rest of the world turns to shit, I rely on you to be strong and keep the faith.

"But we're here now," he says.

"Yes. We're here now."

"Okay, Victoria. I can confirm that you are ten weeks and six days pregnant," the sonographer announces.

"Can you tell the sex?" Gav asks.

"Not yet. But if you ask again at your twenty-week scan, assuming baby is lying the right way, you should be able to find out then. Do you have any preference?"

"Not really. It would be nice to be prepared that's all," Gav replies.

"Would you like a scan photograph to keep?"

"Definitely," both Gavin and I say in unison.

She passes me a handful of paper towels and I begin to wipe the gel off my belly, meanwhile the machine spits out a three-inch square still of our baby. She slides it inside a tiny paper photo frame and passes it to Gav. "Congratulations."

"Happy Birthday, my angel." Gav leans over the bed, kisses me lightly on the lips and passes me the scan photograph. We both gaze at it together. Both of us hopelessly in love.

"Oh, I should have realised from your notes that it was your birthday." She checks the date on my file. "Thirty-six today. Well, Happy Birthday. Here, have another scan, just for luck." She hits the button again and another scan spits out of the machine.

"For luck?" I flash her another concerned look.

She leans forward and pats the back of my hand. "It's just a saying Ms Fenwick. Your baby looks fine, as far as we can tell at this stage. It's healthy, as are you. I know it's been a long road for you to get this far, but try and relax as much as you can."

Finally, all my emotions collide and like a crater of a volcano erupting to release the pressure from within, tears finally fall from my face. My veins flood with a mix of joy, relief, and an overwhelming love that Gav and I are finally to have the baby we've wanted for so long.

"Why am I weeping?" I throw my arms up and shake my head, half-laughing, half-crying.

Gav wraps his arms around me and whispers, "Because it's an emotional moment. Neither of us can change the past. What's done is done and it's okay to let it all out."

"Not quite. I daren't let it all out here." I smile through my snivels. Turning to the sonographer I ask, "Can you point me in the direction of the nearest loo? I'm about to pee myself."

Laughing, she points. "Right across the hall."

I don't wait for any further instruction. Jumping down from the bed, I bolt out of the room.

※

"I wish you'd have let me take you out for dinner," Gav says, twirling his spaghetti around his fork.

Tonight's birthday tea is a simple home-cooked meal with just the two of us and our baby scan propped up in the middle of the table between us. The other scan is already pinned to the fridge with a magnet. Laid beside the baby photo is a single red rose. When dinner was ready he'd appeared in the kitchen doorway, two plates filled with spaghetti bolognese, and the rose clamped between his teeth, mumbling, "Happy Birthday."

"Honestly, it's fine," I say. "When you're past the age of thirty-five, only tombola birthdays are worth celebrating."

"Tombola birthdays?" Gav jerks his head back a smidge and furrows his brows.

"Yeah," I reply, tearing into the garlic bread on the platter in the middle of the table. "If it doesn't end in a zero or a five, it's not worth worrying about."

"If you say so," he replies, laughing.

"Plus right now we need to be saving every penny we have. You can take me out for a slap-up meal at Café 21 once this little one is safely here. It'll be our little treat." I simultaneously point at our scan whilst stroking my tummy with the other hand.

It's true. We need to watch every penny. Since being made redundant Gav has been doing his best to secure another position, but there are no senior roles in the job market for someone with his specific skill set; this Friday he'll receive his final pay check from Integratas, then that's it. We're relying on our savings to make up the deficit in our household income. My drawings, although growing, have some way to go before they reach the level I was on in my last job. Still, I don't regret becoming my own boss and, thus far at least, we've always found a way to manage.

As of today, Gav has a few irons in the fire, but no visibility on anything concrete and no firm interviews lined up. In all honesty, the timing couldn't be any worse. Babies are expensive and in six months' time I'm going to have to take maternity leave and pass the day-to-day reins of the business over to the team, which, depending on cash flow at the time, could mean taking a further hit on my drawings. I haven't even thought about how I'm going to juggle motherhood once the baby is here. That's a puzzle for another day.

I do know I have no intention of giving up the company. It's another part of my life I've worked too damn hard to let go now. No, the priority is securing Gav another job as quickly as possible, but I'm cautious of pushing him too hard. I tried that with Craig and look where that got me. Abandoned by a husband who fled to Thailand to 'find himself.'

However, the harsh reality is unless my company wins some big deals in the next six months, my savings will be gone, and unless Gav is bringing in some additional income by then, financially we'll be in an unsustainable position.

"I have something to tell you," I say, more formally.

"Oh?" Gav replies, sitting up straight in his chair.

"I had a really interesting email land in my inbox yesterday. I didn't want to say anything initially as I thought it might be a hoax, but I've had another reply today and it's a genuine opportunity."

"Go on." Gav nods.

"So it appears the D.I.T... the Department for International Trade," I add, picking up on Gav's confused look. "Anyway there's this major international trade coming up at the Suntec Centre in Singapore, and they would like me to be the headline speaker on behalf of UK industry."

"Oh my God V. That's amazing."

"I know. It's a big deal. I'd be there representing the UK, inspiring UK businesses to invest in Asia, whilst promoting the benefits of inward investing. Apparently they're inspired by my entrepreneurial journey and want me to be the poster girl for British business overseas."

"This is incredible. What an opportunity. So why do I sense a 'but' coming?"

"It's in four weeks' time." I lock eye contact with Gav, trying to read him. "If it had been a couple of months ago I'd be snapping their hand off. But now, in my condition, I'm just worried if it's, you know...safe."

"How far on will that make you?"

"Fifteen weeks. Well past the first trimester and the so-called danger period, but still." I look into his eyes again. "I don't know what's for the best. I'm worried about the stress on my body. All the travel and stuff."

"When's your next midwife appointment?"

"Friday."

"I reckon you should discuss it with her. If she says you're safe to fly, then she's the expert. And if not, then you can gracefully say 'maybe next time'."

"True. But the fee's twenty grand, babes."

Gav chokes on a mouthful of spaghetti. "Holy shit V. How much?"

"I know. Plus they'll cover Business Class airfares and are planning to put me up in Raffles. If I fly BA, they have flat beds on their Singapore route, and I know I'll be well looked after for the whole trip. It's just…" I shrug. "I don't know. It seems so far away."

"Surely that's not worrying you. You've travelled halfway around the globe and back again on your Jack Jones. That's not something that's ever concerned you before."

"Not normally, no. But I've never flown abroad when I'm pregnant."

"If you're that concerned, couldn't Clive or Angela go in your place?"

"No, that was one of the questions I asked. They want the person who's published, not a stand-in."

I've recently had my first business book published by a major publisher, and it's shot to the top of the business charts, which has vastly increased my notoriety in business circles. "I wish there was a way you could come too. But I've asked that question as well, and they won't cover your airfare. I don't have any more Air Miles left, so we'd have to fund your ticket ourselves. It doesn't help that Heathrow to Singapore is one of the most expensive airfares in the world."

"You know I'd be there in a heartbeat, but like you say, it makes no sense to spend half the fee on my airfare. Not when we're tightening our belts. Makes much more sense to bank the full twenty grand which, quite frankly, couldn't have come at a better time."

I pause and take a slow sip on my elderflower juice, a pregnancy alternative to wine. "I know I'll be fine. There's just something in my gut telling me I'd rather have company on this trip."

He reaches across the table and clasps my hand. "That'll be all the pregnancy hormones zooming around your body. All those mammy vibes wanting to keep you and Peanut safe."

"Peanut," I repeat softly.

Gav picks up the pregnancy scan and points at it. "Can you think of a better name?"

Laughing, I reply, "I bloody well hope so. I'm not taking responsibility for he or she being bullied at school with a name like that. But for now, I guess they do look like a peanut."

Gav's eyes stretch and he snaps his fingers. "I have an idea. Why don't you email Tim? See if there's any chance he could come down from Hong Kong for a few days. I'm sure he'd love to see you, and knowing you'll have someone with you, for part of the week at least, will stop your mammy worries going into overdrive."

"That… is a genius idea. Why didn't I think of it?" I pick up my Blackberry and fire off an email to Tim. Within minutes my Blackberry buzzes. "Jeez, he must be working really late. Either that, or he's at a corporate bash. It must be two o'clock in the morning over there."

"That's assuming he's in Hong Kong," Gav replies. "Knowing Tim, he could be anywhere in the world right now."

"True." I quickly scan the email. "He's free. Says he was planning to be in Singapore the Wednesday and Thursday of that week anyhow. Oh," I continue reading, my eyes zipping from left to right over the electronic text, "he has a dinner at the embassy on Wednesday evening and has invited me to go as his plus one."

"See?" Gav smiles. "It's all coming together. Assuming the midwife gives you the all-clear, it looks like you're about to be the poster girl for British business." He raises his glass. "Here's to you, and your amazing success."

I raise my glass in return. "Here's to us and everything finally coming together."

"I'll drink to that."

I lean across the table and plant a smooch on his lips. "And while I'm gone I'll have all my fingers and toes crossed that one of these interviews comes through for you too. You deserve it."

"Now who's being the tree trunk," he says, kissing me back, the picture of our unborn baby on the table between us.

Chapter 36

1 month later, Wednesday 16th July 2006

*F*ive weeks later I'm standing in line with the other invited dinner guests at the gatehouse of Eden Hall, the official residence of the British High Commissioner to the Republic of Singapore, on Nassim Road.

Those ahead of us are systemically stripped of their passports, mobile phones, and any digital cameras by the British Army on guard.

"You're essentially going through passport control," Tim whispers in my ear. "On the other side of that gate is top-secret British soil."

"As long as they don't strip-search me. You have no idea how long it took to wrestle these knickers on." I twang the elastic waistband of the ginormous maternity pants that begin just below my bra line and fully encompass my thickened waist. "Jeez, it's so damn hot," I say, fanning myself with my invitation as my armpits grow damp with sweat.

"Err, excuse me gentlemen." Tim signals to one of the soldiers. "I wonder if we might politely jump the queue? My friend here is fifteen weeks pregnant and suffering dreadfully in this heat. I really should get her inside. She needs to sit down with a glass of water."

"Yes, of course, sir." The captain signals for us to come forward.

A few moments later we're walking up the drive towards the immaculate stucco building, its light grey render inlayed with intricate white carvings in similar patterns to the ornate plasterwork you'd find inside any Georgian mansion back home. Only here it's all on the outside.

"I've never seen anything like it," I say to Tim, blinking as we step under the impressive portcullis and towards the main entrance.

"Ah yes. Beautiful Eden Hall. Built by the same architect who designed Raffles and Goodwood Park Hotels. Once the home of an Indian opium trader, now the official residence of the British Ambassador."

"It's magnificent," I reply, momentarily closing my eyes and raising my face to the cool breeze from the ceiling fan inside the entrance hall. Inhaling the fresh air, my nose picks up a familiar scent. Jasmine? Rose, perhaps? Opening my eyes I spy an impressive display of burnt orange calla lilies on one of the highly polished side tables.

Of course.

"What do you think?" Tim extends an upturned palm around the impressive but intimate hallway hung with portraits of leaders past.

"Not too shabby," I reply as we glide through to the drawing room and Tim grabs two tall flutes from a liveried waiter on our way past. His filled with champagne, mine orange juice.

I take a welcome sip of the sweet tangy liquid.

Mmmm. Freshly squeezed.

As soon as the liquid slides over my tongue I realise how thirsty I am, and throwing my head back, down the drink in one. I've hardly had a chance to swallow before an unexpected and very unladylike burp escapes from my mouth. Catching me and everyone around me by surprise.

Shocked by my unfiltered bodily noise, I cough into my closed fist to try and cover up my faux pas, but I've already gleaned the attention of everyone in the room.

Brilliant! What a way to make an entrance.

Giggling under his breath, Tim says, "Another for the lady? Well… I say *lady…*"

"Stop it," I mutter, my cheeks turning puce from embarrassment as I mouth my apologies to those who have turned to see who let the rabble in.

The drawing room is light and airy, painted in antique white and filled with equally pale soft furnishings. A portrait of Queen Elizabeth II hangs over the fireplace. In this heat it's hard to imagine they'd ever need to light a fire, but I suspect the early colonial settlers demanded some familiar architectural features, to make themselves feel more at home.

"Fancy," I whisper.

"Wait until you see the ballroom. Shall we?" He holds out his left arm and, tucking his right, champagne flute and all, behind his back like a courtier, he leads me through the double doors in the back of the room and into the ballroom beyond.

The dress code for this event was billed as 'Lounge Suit', so I've settled on a three-quarter length blood-red flared maternity dress with a tasteful scoop-neckline and cap sleeves. Slightly more pizazz than pure business dress, but not as glitzy as a full-on cocktail dress. I've finished my outfit with a nude pair of designer heels and matching clutch bag, and accessorised my outfit with my usual understated but classic jewellery. My grandfather's Masonic gold necklace, my diamond bracelet from the Cayman Islands, and in my ears are the diamond earrings Gav gave me after we escaped the clutches of Hurricane Ivan. And because it matches my dress, I've also added my granny's large ruby ring on the fourth finger of my left hand.

Stepping into the ballroom, my heels click-clacking on the parquet floor, my eyes don't know which way to look. Three huge chandeliers hang from ornate ceiling roses, although they're hardly needed: the room is bathed in early evening light from the four pairs of arched patio doors that run the full length of one side of the room. As Tim nods and smiles at a few people I assume he knows, I'm struck by the beauty of the women who swoosh elegantly past. Next to them I suddenly feel like a dowdy matron. Most are wearing full-length beaded ballgowns, or flimsy cocktail dresses with cut away sections that reveal bare flesh and open curves. More than one pair of male eyes follow these semi-naked Asian and British beauties around the room.

Thank God I don't ever have to put it out there like that anymore. The only person I want to show my body to is waiting for me back on the other side of the world.

Tim leads us to our table and holds out the back of my chair as I sit down. I'm seated between a fellow English entrepreneur and an Asian academic. Tim is seated between the academic and, on his other side, a venture capitalist. After everyone has introduced themselves, the conversation flows as seamlessly as the seven-course meal we're served. Despite being the only woman at the table, the men soon discover I'm not some tag-along-bimbo, here at the invitation of my rich financier friend, but that I'm actually well-versed in politics, economics, and all things business-related, and I have an informed and interesting opinion on the topics being debated.

On the other side of the academic I can hear Tim deep in conversation with the venture capitalist. By the sounds of it, Tim is about to invest in the growing infrastructure of Singapore.

"There's no doubt that the partly built Marina Bay Sands complex will have a huge impact on Singapore's gross domestic product when it opens in 2009," Tim says.

"Indeed." The academic picks up on the conversation adjacent to him. Turning back to myself and the entrepreneur, he adds, "At the moment it looks like three simple tower blocks. But you wait until it's completed. The whole top floor is going to be connected with one huge infinity pool."

"That'll take some engineering," I say.

"It will. Apparently it's going to be in the shape of a boat."

"A boat? On top of a skyscraper?" I exclaim. "That'll get people talking."

"The plan is to build something as iconic as Big Ben, or the Eiffel Tower. It will define the Singapore skyline," the venture capitalist says, as Tim gives me a *checking-in* wink. I give him a reassuring smile.

"Sounds amazing. I'll have to come back and see it when it's finished."

In the very short time I've been here I've gleaned a new appreciation for this tiny country. A thoroughly modern city which stands on the foundations of its colonial and trading past. A phoenix rising from its own ashes. Packed with a forward-thinking society, constantly looking to the future. Pushing the boundaries to find impossible solutions to old problems. Why else would they be in the process of damming the mouth of the Singapore River as one solution to their lack of water? In another few years what was once the original Port of Singapore, the trading lifeblood of the old colony, will become a life force of a different kind. Meanwhile a new purpose-built port, one that handles fifty percent of the world's crude oil and a third of the world's containers, has retained its prominence as a leading economy on the world stage.

I like ya style, Singapore.

My own sentiment is mirrored by the ambassador's rousing after-dinner speech, when after thanking us all for coming he reiterates the long history of combined Asian/British culture, economics, and education, and finishes by encouraging us to make the most of the networking opportunities, and to strengthen our trading ties.

Once the coffees are cleared away, Tim pushes his chair back and throws his napkin down on the table. "Gentlemen. It's been an absolute pleasure, but if you don't mind I'm going to steal my date away. Victoria would you care to take a turn of the gardens?" Leading me outside, he adds, "You never know when you may have another opportunity to see the magnificent back garden of Eden Hall."

Outside the sun has dropped and so has the temperature. The high humidity of earlier has been replaced by a cool fresh breeze that whistles through the Tembusu and Yellow Flame trees that line the pathway from the main house into the gardens.

"So, I'm your date am I?" I take a dig at his previous comment.

He ignores me and continues guiding me down the garden path. "Pregnancy suits you. You're positively glowing."

Another swoosh of wind carries with it the smell of bougainvillea and jasmine as he leads me past a hedgerow of multi-coloured bougainvillea and into the farthest corner of the garden, where flashes of shocking pink, lilac, orange, and white have been trained into an intertwined kaleidoscope of flora.

"Well that's very kind Tim, but I have to admit it's not been much fun in this heat."

He leads us towards a shaded seat in the farthest corner of the garden. "It's going well then? You and Gavin? I haven't seen you since your dramatic escapades in the Caribbean."

"Yes. Couldn't be happier. It's been a long road to get this far." I affectionately stroke my burgeoning bump. "And he's not long been made redundant, which isn't great. But generally things are really solid. Definitely a keeper."

"Oh, stop please. No one's ever that perfect. Everyone has flaws. Well everyone except me, obviously."

I roll my eyes at Tim's overt arrogance, but he's already laughing at me. It's hard to tell how much of his bravado is for my benefit, or to prop up his own ego.

"If Gav has any flaws, I've yet to find them. Other than he's a Liverpool supporter, but that just makes Saturday afternoons more interesting."

"He hasn't slipped a ring on your finger yet. There, that's his flaw."

I unconsciously rub my thumb and forefinger over the diamonds in my ears.

That's because he knows I don't want him to, I think to myself.

"And how are your marriage negotiations coming along between you and Lydia? You've been engaged forever." I purposefully steer the conversation away from me and back to Tim's relationship.

The mysterious Lydia, who no one's ever met. He's told me before that she prefers to remain based at the 'barn' out in the Cotswolds while he lives out in Hong Kong. They seem to be happy spending a few days together each month as they both fly back and forth at regular intervals, but it's not the kind of relationship set-up I would want.

There was a time when I wondered if Lydia might be a Leo or a Luis, but Mel—who used to rent a room in Tim's house, back in the days when we all lived in Wootton Basset and before she and I shared a house—assured me I was wrong.

"It's all you modern woman," he says. "Wanting to hold onto your independence. Why can't you let a man take care of you anymore?"

"You mean, keep us chained to the kitchen sink." I raise my eyebrow in his direction. "Careful Tim. You don't want to inflame the feminist in me. Don't forget I'm only two generations on from winning the vote, and it horrifies me that my mother wasn't allowed to open a bank account without her husband or her father's signature when she turned eighteen. Of course women want their men to love and support them… but *take care of her?* No thank you. It's not the 1950s."

"And you're a perfect example of that. A thoroughly modern woman breaking gender stereotypes. Good on you. It didn't escape my notice that you were the only businesswoman at our table this evening."

"That's kind of you to say…"

Although I do wonder if my ambition and desire to 'break barriers' is more a form of survival. Having been left emotionally and financially destitute at previous times in my life, and always after a breakup, I may love Gav with all my heart but I'm determined to be completely self-sufficient.

"I've sometimes wondered, if things turned sour with Lydia, whether I'd make a go of it with you."

I turn sharply and glare at him.

"Oh don't look so shocked. You can't tell me the thought hasn't crossed your mind at least once in the last twelve years."

"No, never."

My mind flits back to the beach barbecue when I first travelled to the Cayman Islands at Tim's invitation, when my marriage to Craig was in tatters. There was a particular moment when I had wondered whether Tim's feelings for me were more than friendship. Smoothing down my skirt, I brush away that notion, just as I did back then.

"Well there's no way it would ever happen now," Tim continues. "Not when you have that bastard child in your womb. You're soiled goods."

"Tim, with respect: Go. Fuck. Yourself." I tenderly stroke my belly.

Laughing, he pulls me into a hug. "Oh come here. You know I love you really and would do anything for you. I hope you know how special you are, and I hope you and Gav live a long and happy life together. And your yet-to-be-born bastard child." He lets out a long sigh, before standing and brushing non-existent crumbs off his trousers. Turning back to me he holds out his hand. "Shall we go back inside and find the bar? I, for one, could do with a stiff drink."

"Good idea," I reply, standing and taking the hand he's offered.

Kissing the side of my face, he wraps his arm around my waist and pauses, our gaze meeting. After a microsecond, as if he's wrestling an internal demon, he straightens up, his bravado façade firmly back in place, and steers me back in the direction of the main house.

Chapter 37

The following afternoon I step back from the podium and soak up the applause from the two thousand or so delegates who fill the main hall of the Suntec Convention Centre. Out of the corner of my eye I see Tim standing on the sidelines, adding his applause.

Placing my hand over my heart I bow graciously before exiting the stage and heading back into the Green Room, where the technician unhooks my microphone from the lapel of my suit jacket.

I turn round and Tim is there, grinning like a proud parent. He plants a kiss on the top of my head.

"Well done you. Aren't you the proper grownup entrepreneur?"

I look back at him with steely eyes. "Don't patronise me, Tim. This is my profession you're mocking."

"I'm not patronising you Victoria... for once. I know I take the piss out of you all of the time, but you should feel very proud of what you've accomplished here today. You were amazing. You had them hanging on your every word. You're very good at what you do."

"Thank you. That means a lot, especially coming from you."

"And to think I knew you when you were nothing more than a naïve and easily led astray travel agent."

ISABELLA WILES

"Mostly led astray by you, I might add. And I can remember when you were nothing more than an ambitious accountant, not the high-flying global financial leader you are now."

"We've both grown up," Tim says magnanimously.

"Ms Fenwick, Ms Fenwick!" One of the conference runners rushes into the Green Room. "The audience... they won't leave. They want more time to ask questions."

"Really?" I reply, my eyes stretched wide. "They want me back on stage?"

"Yes. We're not closing the conference until all their questions are answered."

"Better go back and re-find my seat. Get settled for the encore." Tim's eyes dance with amusement.

"They'll have to wait while I mic you up again," the sound engineer says.

"Do you have a spare handheld already set up?"

He nods and passes me a roaming mic.

"Perfect. See you on the other side." I bob my head in Tim's direction as the runner escorts me back out of the Green Room and towards the stage.

✦

Later that evening Tim checks his watch. "Thirty more minutes. Then I must head back to the airport. I've got a breakfast meeting at the Yacht Club first thing in the morning."

"One more Singapore Sling before you go?" I signal to the bartender, smartly turned out in his Raffles uniform. He acknowledges my request and prepares two more cocktails. Fully loaded for Tim and virgin for me.

Above us ceiling fans whirr incessantly, offering only marginal comfort from the hot air inside the famous Long Bar. Underfoot the sound of discarded peanut shells grind into the wooden floor.

"It's been lovely to see you again. Let's not wait so long before the next time," I say.

"I agree. And this time I haven't had to rescue you, or send the jet or anything," he teases.

"I know. It's been as close to normal as I've ever known an encounter with you."

"I am proud of you though, Victoria. You should be too. Your keynote today was exceptional. You deserve all the success in the world."

He throws his drink back in one, stands from his chair, retrieves his jacket which he throws over his shoulder, hooking it onto his index finger so it hangs loosely down his back like a cape.

"I really must go. Now you take care of that baba in there." He places his hand on my belly. "And I'll see you again sometime soon." He looks me in the eye and adds, "I really am pleased everything has worked out for you. You've always handled life's challenges with such grace; it's about time you had some joy."

I feel the brush of his lips against my cheek, and catch the lingering scent of his aftershave, then he is gone.

I motion to the waiter that I'll sign for our drinks. I hate drinking alone, even if I am in the most respectable and established bar in the whole of Singapore. Despite all the business trips I take and all the travelling I've done over the years, I've never gotten used to eating or drinking alone in a strange city. Especially as a woman. Unless I'm with clients, or happen to hook up with old friends like Tim, I usually end up ordering room service.

Back in my room, I turn sideways and admire my burgeoning bump in the bathroom mirror. A worried thought skitters through my mind.

I've not yet felt the baby move. I know it's too early for that, but other than my scan photo safely tucked away in my purse, or the obvious changes in my body, or the fact I haven't had a period since April, why do I not *feel* pregnant? At least not since I touched down in Singapore four days ago.

My morning sickness stopped the minute I stepped off the plane, but then I haven't had much of an appetite either. I put both down to the insufferable heat and high humidity. But my boobs, although two cup sizes bigger than normal, have also stopped aching.

Maybe this is all normal for the second trimester. I wouldn't know. I've never gotten this far in a pregnancy before.

Keep on cooking little Peanut. Only a few more weeks until I'll be complaining that you're kicking my bladder.

My thoughts are interrupted by the familiar *beep-beep* of a text arriving.

Walking back out of the bathroom, I retrieve my phone from my bedside table.

> How did it go? Were you splendiferous? Missing you. Gav x

My heart expands inside my chest as I read Gav's warm words. I text back:

> Knocked it out of the park, also made some great connections out here if I ever decide to expand into Asia. Topped the day off with a Singapore Sling with Tim.

> Just back in my room now. Pooped. Will text you when I leave tomorrow. Love you, V x

> Cool. Rest up my Angel.

> I've something BIG to discuss with you once you're home. While you've been away I've been putting together a business plan. And here's the really exciting bit... Anth wants to do it with me. There's lots of details to work through, and he won't be able to leave his job immediately, but I'm super excited. See you soon. Love you too, Gav x

My thumbs flying across my phone, I punch out:

> Oh Wow! That sounds amazing. Can't wait for you
> to tell me all about it. Love you more, V x

Not possible. Today, tomorrow, always, Gav xxx

Smiling, I flop onto the bed and pick up the TV remote. Flicking through the film channels I settle on a re-run of *Bridget Jones: The edge of Reason,* when my phone *beep-beeps* again.

Without looking I pick up my phone a second time, expecting to see a return message from Gav, except it's not his name at the top of the screen.

> Hey Goose, you popped into my mind yesterday.
> Is everything alright?

There's only one person in the entire world who calls me that. I suck in a deep breath.

Why oh why does Chris always seem to drop back into my life at the most random moments?

My mind flits back to the reception dinner at Eden Hall last night and the large spray of calla lilies on the reception table. The exact same flower and colour Chris always used to give me.

Was it my mind that unconsciously thought of him first? Are our vibrations so connected he can pick up whenever I think about him? No matter how fleetingly.

> Hey Chris, all good here. Trust all is good with you
> and yours.

Keep things light and breezy, I think as I press the Send button.

> Good. I do worry about you though and thought
> something might be wrong with your pregnancy.
> Congratulations BTW. So happy for you. Always
> here if you need me. Chris x

Something wrong with my pregnancy? *How does he even know I'm pregnant?* Mellie must have told him. She and I still write every few months. Even though in this day and age, texts are faster and easier, as we've always written to each other, we've continued the tradition. After she wrote to me on my birthday back in June, I replied not long after and told her my news. As a mum of two now, she wrote back immediately, saying how excited she was to hear my news and offering me lots of advice.

However, regardless of any telepathic chord keeping Chris and I tied together, I haven't forgotten he has family of his own now too. A son, according to Mike and Fiona, and as much as a part of me is warmed knowing he's still out there in the ether thinking about me, I sincerely hope his worries are not a negative premonition.

Chapter 38

I knew I was in trouble when I went to the toilet before boarding the connecting flight up to Bangkok and noticed a tiny spot of blood in my knickers. Now I'm in the Business Class lounge in Bangkok Airport and a panic the texture of cold hard steel is leeching through my body. I swallow down a scream and claw at my own neck. Frustration, anger and fear consuming me.

I shouldn't even be in bloody Bangkok, but the flight from Singapore to London was overbooked and they offered me two options. Stay another night in Singapore, checking in and out of an airport hotel, before flying back economy tomorrow, or fly an additional two hours up to Bangkok and catch the overnight flight home from Suvarnabhumi Airport. I want to get home in time to turn myself around before work on Monday, as well as sleep as much as possible in the air, so I chose the latter.

I head to the toilet for a second time since arriving forty minutes ago and discover the tiny spot has turned into a pool of bright red blood in the gusset of my knickers.

Nothing to worry about, I tell myself. I'm fifteen weeks pregnant. More than a few weeks out of the danger zone.

'A little bit of spotting is normal,' my midwife has told me before.

Except now it looks like I've just passed a small clot.

Shit!

I don't have any sanitary products with me, so I clean myself up as best I can, and place a wedge of toilet paper in my knickers.

Sitting back down on the closed toilet seat lid, I drop my head into my hands, my heart feeling eerily hollow and empty as if someone's taken a rusty old spoon and scooped out all my confidence.

I'm all alone and at a loss to know what to do.

Should I travel home as planned and hope that the bleeding stops by the time I get back to Newcastle. Gav can then take me to the RVI to be checked out.

Or I could talk to the airline here. Ask them to take me to a medical facility. I'm insured so the cost isn't an issue.

But I don't speak Thai, and what if they take me to hospital in the city. I don't know Bangkok or anyone here? But they could find the heartbeat. Put my fears at rest.

But what if they don't?

That thought terrifies me even more than the thought of being stranded, all alone in a strange city, and for how long?

And what if everything is alright? And I'll I've done is make a fuss over nothing and delay getting home; and I just want to be home. With Gav.

Oh God. My insides are gripped with fear, while externally I consciously attempt to control my breathing. Anything to cover the panic and rage that threatens to envelop me.

I can't lose this baby too. I just can't.

Either way, I need Gav by my side, I justify to myself, so when British Airways calls my flight, I board the plane and strap myself in.

"Hang in there, Peanut," I whisper, stroking my belly. "I'm gonna get us home to Daddy."

If I don't eat or drink anything, then I won't need to leave my seat, and the flat bed Club Class seat means I can keep my legs elevated the whole way back to London. Give us both the best chance of survival.

Once airborne, I slide on my eye mask and tune my iPod to my

Chakra guided meditation. Curling my thumb and forefinger into Gyan Mudra, I focus inwards. Using my breath to relax.

It's all I have left within my control as I will the hours to fly by.

⁕

Thirteen hours later, when I arrive at Heathrow, I head first to Boots the Chemist to buy some sanitary pads, then to the Business Class arrivals lounge to take a shower. Tipping my head back I allow the refreshing flow of water from the shower to run over my body and wash away the grime from the flight. A stabbing pain rips through my gut, forcing me to bend double and clutch my stomach, and when I look down at the water around my feet, it flows blood red.

No. No. No. I cup my hand between my legs and dry myself as best I can.

Hang in there, Peanut. We're almost home. Then Daddy can fix it.

Back in the arrivals lounge I realise I can't put off the inevitable any longer, and call Gav.

"Hey sweetheart. Are you back on terra firma? Only a few more hours until you're home."

"Oh Gav," I wail down the phone.

"Oh my goodness, Angel. What's up?" His voice suddenly changing from one of cheerful greeting to deep concern.

"I'm blcc d ing." My words hardly make it out through my heaving sobs.

"Is it bad?"

"Yes. No. Sort of. I don't know. I hardly dare look. I just want to get ho-ome," I sob, my staccato breaths short and ragged.

"Don't worry. It's only a few more hours and you'll be back in my arms."

"I know. That's all I'm focused on."

"How long… have you been bleeding?" he asks, solemnly.

"Fourteen hours. Maybe more. It was only a couple of spots when I left Singapore, but now…" I can't finish my sentence.

At the other end of the line I hear Gav suck in a deep breath. "Do you want me to bring your maternity notes with me to the airport?"

Although neither of us say it, both of us understand the implications of what this means.

I don't answer. I can't answer. Saying 'yes' means I have to acknowledge what is truly happening. I'm losing the baby.

If I can just make it home, then it will be alright. Somehow they'll be able to stop the bleeding. They can give me the same drug they gave Julie when she went into early labour. Our amazing NHS managed to save JP, I know they can do the same for my baby.

They *have* to.

Very quietly, my voice hardly a whisper, I reply, "Yes. I think you'd better had."

✦

I take my time changing to the domestic terminal at Heathrow before boarding my final flight back to Newcastle. Once airborne I know it will be less than an hour before I'm back in Gav's arms and he can take me straight to the maternity unit at Newcastle's Royal Victoria Infirmary. My knees bob incessantly as the minutes tick agonisingly by.

Hurry up, I think over and over.

I check my watch. Only twenty minutes to go.

Then it happens.

A vice-like cramp grips my stomach like an iron fist reaching inside my guts and squeezing the life out of me. The pain is so intense, it slams the air out of my lungs and I lurch forward in my seat, beads of sweat breaking across my brow as I clutch my stomach.

I need to vomit.

The man in the window seat next to me looks across, perturbed. "Are you alright?" He reaches up to press the call button when he sees me dry-wrenching into my closed fist.

"No don't," I stutter.

I still don't want anyone official to intervene. In my delirium I somehow believe their intervention will stop me getting back to Gav. And all I need to do is get back home to him.

Then everything will be alright.

Somehow he can make it alright.

As another cramp rips through me and I swallow down the bile that has risen up the back of my throat, I hastily unclasp my seat belt and rush up the aisle to the toilet at the front of the cabin.

Thankfully the cubicle is empty, and before I've even had a chance to pull down my jeans and knickers, an enormous gush of warm, metallic liquid spills from between my legs. Soaking my clothes and covering the tiny sticky airplane toilet floor.

Sitting down urgently on the open bowl, both hands between my legs, attempting to stop the torrent of blood, my fingers now covered in bright red liquid and deeper claret red clots, I mutter over and over, "No, no, no." My mind in survival mode, unable to truly comprehend what is actually happening.

I can't catch my breath; the pain is as bad as when I broke my leg as a teenager. On a school skiing trip. I caught an edge. Then the faulty binding in my other ski flew off and I lost control. A heartbeat later I was wrapped around a wooden fence with a spiral tibia fracture. A singular moment in life that would prevent me from accomplishing my dream of becoming a professional ballet dancer. Is this another one of those moments? A heartbeat in time that changes the course of your life irreversibly?

Another cramp rips through me. Someone has their claws inside me and is trying to turn my womb inside out.

Somewhere in the distance I hear the *bing* of the fasten seat belt sign being illuminated and the muffled sound of the purser. "Ladies and gentlemen the captain has switched the seat belt sign in preparation for our landing. Please now return to your seats and ensure your tray tables and seats are returned to the upright positions."

I tune out the sound as another vice-like cramp takes hold.

I can't move. The pain racking through my body, and the weakness caused by losing so much blood, anchors me to the plane toilet.

My other senses deadened, I'm only focused on the searing pain ripping through me.

I'm drowning in the pain, unable to catch my breath. I want to wail. Scream out at the top of my lungs but I hold it all in, as if not giving in to my primal needs can somehow alter my reality. Even though my thighs and hands are shaking uncontrollably.

"Excuse me?" Someone, presumably an air steward, raps lightly on the outside of the toilet door. "You must return to your seat. Ten minutes to landing."

"Aaaaah," I whimper.

Mustering all my strength as another visceral surge rips through me I attempt to stand, but as I engage my stomach muscles, yet another cramp tears me apart and something about the size of a small peach or kiwi fruit passes, and disappear into the aluminium toilet bowl.

"NOOOOOO!" I scream, standing just enough to see the blood twirling around the bowl and disappearing under the silver flap at the bottom.

The very action of standing activates the automatic flush and a blue disinfectant liquid releases into the bowl, cleaning it, before the vicious, loud suction hoovers away any last remnants in the pan.

"NOOOOOO!" I scream a second time.

"Madam," the air steward on the other side of the door shouts. Her voice more authoritarian this time.

"Peanut!" I cry, my blood-streaked hands frantically searching the toilet bowl for my baby.

Resting my bare bottom back on my heels, my shoulders heave with wretched sobs as I wrap my bloodied arms around my body and weep for the child I know I've just lost. Brutally sucked away before I'd even had the chance to say goodbye.

Not again. This can't be.

Life can't be this cruel.

Still on my knees, I bleed onto the floor and weep.

"Madam." The air steward bangs on the door again. "You must

return to your seat." When I don't answer, she says, "I'm coming in."

Using the emergency override lock, the door behind me opens and I hear her exclaim, "Oh my God. Lyndsey, come quick."

I turn around and look at her through tear-stained cheeks. I try and wipe them away before I realise I've simply smeared my face with my own blood.

The other air steward looks over her colleague's shoulder. She doesn't miss a beat. "I'll tell the captain. Find out what's wrong with her. Regardless, we need to get her into a seat."

The first air steward side-steps around the pool of blood that is still pouring out of me, and beginning to leak its way out of the tiny bathroom and onto the floor outside the cubicle. Lyndsey half-closes the toilet door and opens the security door into the cockpit.

"Come on, dear. Can you get yourself back onto the toilet?" The first stewardess helps lift me under my armpits, and I allow her to help reposition me over the metal pan.

There's no dignity in miscarriage, and with my lower half still exposed I'm only thankful that it's a woman who's helping me.

Now that I'm safely positioned over the toilet bowl, and no longer adding to the mess on the floor, she empties the canister of paper towels and throws them down, before crouching on bent knees.

Looking at me with sympathetic eyes she asks, "Can you tell me you name?"

"Victoria," I mewl, still unable to give her eye contact.

"And which seat were you in?"

"10D"

"Okay. Can you tell me what's happened, Victoria? Why you're bleeding?"

I don't want to answer her. Saying it out loud makes it real. My heart wants to believe the impossible—that my baby is still in there—even though my head knows the truth.

Peanut is gone.

… just like all the others.

Before I can say anything we're interrupted by the pilot making an announcement. "Ladies and gentlemen, this is your captain speaking. It appears we have a medical emergency on board, meaning we're going to have to abandon our final approach and circle Newcastle until we have the cabin safely secured. I'd kindly ask you to remain in your seats and cooperate with Lyndsey and her team as we manage this unexpected situation. On behalf of British Airways I apologise for this short delay, but assure you we'll have you on the ground as soon as is safely possible."

I hear a communal groan from all the other passengers as I drop my head into my shaking hands. I can't bear to look at the kindly face of the stewardess. I still haven't answered her question and I'm still bleeding, if not as heavily as ten minutes ago.

"Okay, Victoria," the stewardess says softly. "We need to get you back into a seat before we can land. Do you think you can let me help you?"

I nod, childlike, tears still spilling from the corners of my eyes.

Lyndsey appears over the first stewardess' shoulder. "What do you need?"

"Sanitary pads. Lots of them. Or whatever you can find to stem this bleeding. And some blankets to cover her with. She's in shock, but I suspect she's having a miscarriage. This is way more blood than a normal period. Either that or it's something more serious. Regardless, we can't land with her on the toilet."

Miscarriage.

The word slices into me, over and over, like a thousand paper cuts all over my skin. My face crumples as a fresh wave of emotion crashes over me; my shoulders shaking from uncontrollable sobs.

"On it," Lyndsey says, business-like, immune to my personal tragedy. "The captain's alerted the ground crew."

"Understood," the first crew member says, before turning her attention back to me.

Over the next fifteen minutes the two kindly stewardesses find me some cloth hand towels and sanitary products, and I attempt to sort myself out as best I can, although my clothes are soaked through.

They discreetly ask the Club Class passengers in the front two rows if they would mind relocating a few rows further back in the cabin, and with my stripped bottom half wrapped in a blanket they seat me in the front row, opposite them as they too strap themselves into their crew seats.

I have nothing left in me, and I allow them to guide me like a small child. I'm sure I'll look back on this episode and want to shrink with embarrassment at the indignity of it all, but right now I don't care. All I want is to suck in my last breath and never breathe out again.

I stare numbly out the aircraft window as the ground draws closer, and close my eyes anticipating the touchdown *bump*, but the plane lands so smoothly it's as if it has furry wheels.

Thank God, wheels on the ground, I think to myself, knowing that I'm finally back in the same city as Gav.

I'm offloaded first, into a waiting ambulance which rushes Gav and myself towards the RVI.

Gav grips my hand and repeats over and over, "I've got you. You're safe now. I've got you." I don't have the energy to respond.

But I'm not safe.

He couldn't save me and he can't stop the pain.

Still in shock, my teeth chatter and my body jerks with uncontrollable shivers as, with my eyes closed, I try and block out the wail of the siren. Try and block out this whole torrid nightmare.

We're taken straight from A&E up to the maternity unit, and Gav hands over my maternity notes to the waiting midwife.

Within minutes my worst fears are confirmed. The clock in the corner of the room ticks loudly as, attached to multiple monitors the team search for our baby, but Peanut is gone.

No heartbeat.

No pregnancy sac.

No baby.

It's as if he or she never existed. But I know they did. They were alive and now they're not.

"I'm so sorry," the consultant says empathically, and a little bit of me dies all over again.

"I shouldn't have done it," I whisper. "It's all my fault."

"Don't be silly," Gav replies, kissing my blood-stained knuckles. "You did nothing wrong."

Except he doesn't realise I'm not talking about my trip to Singapore; I'm talking about the decision I made over a decade ago.

Chapter 39

1 week later

I can't breathe.

My arms flail and my legs kick as I gasp for air. I'm being pushed down, and as hard as I try I'm unable to break free.

Thump. Thump. Thump. The sound of my own blood pumps in my ears as adrenaline surges through me.

I'm fighting, fighting.

No, no, no, I whimper.

Thrashing. Pushing back.

Against what? I do not know.

Under water, the last of the air in my lungs bubbles upwards towards the silvery surface. No matter how hard I try, it slips further and further away. The watery moonlight far above, at odds with the dark depths that swamp me.

I swim frantically upwards. Towards the silvery light. My arms aching, thighs burning. With every last ounce of strength, I try and drag myself upwards, trying to break free of the current that's pushing me further and further down.

Something is pulling me back. A thread connecting me to something dark and sinister. I look down into the abyss, but there's nothing. Only blackness.

I shrug out of my clothes, relinquishing everything I can. Vulnerable and naked I swim upwards with all my might.

I know my life depends on it.

Pushing, harder and harder; but it's useless. I'm being dragged down, until suddenly... I sit up in bed and gasp. Clutching my throat, I take a few long, deep breaths.

I've had similar nightmares every day since I came home from Singapore.

A feeling of being swallowed. Being chased, or drowning. The one common factor: being pulled back just as I'm about to break free. I always wake up before I find out if I survive. The terror of what's not seen more frightening than the running, or the fighting, or the drowning, and I wake up covered in sweat. My heart racing.

I glance across to the other side of the bed where Gav sleeps soundly.

I know he's hurting too. The pain of our most recent loss something we're both still processing. But he's being strong for me. Lightening the domestic load. Making dinner every night. Spoiling me with extra bunches of roses and long, scented baths.

I'd rather he didn't. His desire to make things *normal* is not natural. I want him to scream and shout. To pound a pillow in rage. I want us to share our pain. For him to stop telling me, *'It'll be alright'* when it won't. When it isn't. It's fucking shite is what it is and I wish he'd simply acknowledge that and stop being artificially cheery around me. Compensating for my melancholy with his uptight tidying.

I throw back the soaked bedsheets, pad downstairs and flick on the kettle.

Maybe a mint and liquorice tea will soothe my nerves? Liquorice is supposed to calm the adrenal glands, or so Julie tells me.

Taking my tea, I saunter through to the front room, beautifully furnished in hues of cream and light blue. It's stunning, and wouldn't be out of place in a lifestyle magazine; however I've seen the state of all my girlfriends' front rooms. Strewn with Ikea buckets filled to the brim with plastic toys, their carpets permanently stained with juice and spilt milk. Their plug sockets child-proofed, their coffee tables smeared with tiny fingerprints. Chaotic to some; homely to me. I'd already decided to change our colour scheme and swap out the sofa covers to a more practical colour once the baby was here.

Once the baby was here.

A sob swells in the back of my throat like a song. The feeling of loss is indescribable. Like falling with no bottom.

After everything Gav and I had been through, I'd allowed myself to believe that this child would be the one I'd get to hold in my arms.

But how dare I? What right do I have to assume I will ever have a child when I aborted one eleven years ago?

Holding my tea, I blink a few times in quick succession. As I said to Chris all those years ago, around the dying embers of the campfire during our New Year trip to the Coromandel Forrest, *'Maybe that was my one and only opportunity to have a child.'*

Well, I've got my just rewards.

Karma's a bitch.

I shake my head, knowing these negative thoughts are unjustified, but I'm consumed by them. My head filling with poison every waking moment.

Throwing open the curtains, I stare out at the full moon. Clouds crossing its surface momentarily shading it from view, before it beams bright once again.

I roll out my yoga mat and begin a moon salutation flow. Starting with an upright stretch before I sink into Goddess pose, I allow my breath to roll in the back of my throat as I engage my Ujjayi breath and feel immediately more centred and in control.

Closing my eyes, I work through the flow. My senses turning inwards as I disconnect from everything other than my own body. My sinews stretch. My muscles shake. And my heartbeat slows.

Ending in Tadassana or Mountain Pose, I softly blink my eyes open and stare out at the moon.

Calm tears roll down my cheeks as I silently ask, "Tell me what to do. I don't know what to do. But I know I can't keep doing this. Thinking like this."

While I stand in the stillness, behind me Leo meows his way into the room. He jumps up onto the bookcase and pads his way along the shelves; climbing to the top, he walks along the top of the books stacked there. Turning round and round, he tries to make a comfortable nest to settle in.

"You mad cat," I laugh, wiping away my tears with the heels of my hands.

He glares at me, plonks his arse down and sends a pile of books clattering to the floor.

"Oi ya dafty. Be careful with those."

I bend and pick them up. A couple of hardbound classics that I've started collecting, together with some notebooks and old Ordnance Survey maps. Replacing them gently on the shelf, I stop dead in my tracks when I realise what I'm holding in my hand.

I roll the pads of my fingers over the scratched leather journal, taking in the indentation of the '1994' emblazoned in gold letters across the moleskin. My first ever journal. The one Mel gave me all those years ago. The one that holds some of my most painful memories.

Nineteen ninety-four was the summer I met Chris, when he rocked up in my office, a rucksack thrown casually over his shoulder.

I begin to flick through the pages, scrawled with random dates and notes as my mind continues to serve up long-buried memories from that time.

The picnic at Tooting Bec Lido in the blistering heat of a London summer. Chris rolling in as casual as anything. I remember how pissed off I was. His lackadaisical communication a constant source of friction in our relationship. That was the night I told him I loved him.

It took him a further six months to tell me I meant the same to him, merely magnifying my own insecurities. Yet our mutual sexual attraction was the drug that pulled me back to him time and time again.

His words from when we reunited in the pool that day as fresh in my mind today as they were back then: "No matter how complicated our lives are, or whatever happens next, you know this thing is bigger than the both of us and we're powerless to resist it… you have to give in to me—you have no choice, just as I have no choice but to always come back to you."

No matter how many times he abandoned me, emotionally as well as literally—his own wanderlust a bottomless well that needed constantly topping up—I always ended up forgiving him and taking him back. Until the one time I didn't.

I'm not the same young, inexperienced and naïve woman I was when he bounded into my life twelve years ago, but my gut is telling me the answer to *'what I need to do'* lies within these pages. Why else would the universe have dropped it at my feet moments ago?

I know it's not going to be easy to reread some of these memories, but I also know that if I'm ever going to move on with life, I need to finally face my deepest of fears. The fear I can't ever be freed from the shame of the decision I made all those years ago.

Tucking my legs underneath myself, I curl up on the sofa. Leo jumps off the bookshelf and snuggles into me, purring like a tractor; his head pushing into my hand, demanding I stroke him as I settle in and begin reading.

I'm only a few pages in but already I don't recognise the person I was back then. How infatuated I was with this 'Greek Adonis' risen from the sea of mythology, as I'd described Chris after our first meeting, when he'd pulled me into him and I'd melted like an ice-cream left out in the sun. Or how much he frustrated me. Communication wasn't what it was now and I read how I'd spent days—not hours—staring at the landline willing it to ring, or rushed down the stairs the moment I'd heard the post land on the mat, hoping for a flimsy blue airmail letter. Any delicate tendril to reaffirm how much I meant to him.

It's clear as day how insecure I was. Constantly needing his validation to feel worthy of his love. I'm shocked rereading my own words; how chaotic I was. Essentially handing over all my emotional wellbeing to Chris.

Did I take no responsibility for how I responded or how I allowed myself to feel back then?

No wonder I felt so justified in feeling so low and abandoned whenever he left for long periods, or when he reneged on a promise.

I flick through the scribbles and crossed-out lines around the time of my encounters with RC. It was wholly wrong of me to have slept with Edwin, or Mr Red Carnation, as Mel and I had nicknamed him. A senior director from work, married no less, I knew he had a soft spot for me, but we both should have known better. However, rereading my desperation and sense of abandonment at that time, I can appreciate how my boundaries melted when he gave me the one thing I was desperately lacking at that time—validation, a sense of safety.

Yet of all the times Chris left me without any word, or didn't validate my feelings, his greatest betrayal has to be the night I needed him most. The night before I terminated our pregnancy.

I reread the prayer I wrote that night for my unborn child, while I waited and waited for Chris to come home. Lost, abandoned, angry, but most of all: petrified. The delicate pages brittle and crisp, the ink smudged from the tears I'd bled onto the page.

Please forgive me for what I'm about to do. Know that you are loved, you were created in love, but you're here too soon and I can't offer what I would want for you.

The secret I've kept all these years. Initially to protect Chris, who was concerned about any backlash from his staunchly Catholic mother, but now to hide my own shame.

My breath quickens as all the memories come flooding back. How humiliated I'd been buying a pregnancy test. Pregnant by accident after a contraceptive fail. How Chris had instantly checked out and dismissed any course of action other than abortion when I tried to talk through our options. And the hours and hours afterwards I'd spent alone, agonising over what to do.

I would have loved to talk to Mel or Michelle. Ask their advice and receive their comfort. But, scared of Chris's reaction if I'd betrayed his trust, I kept his confidence.

My mother, I'm sure, would have supported me if I'd asked for it, but likely on condition of my dumping Chris. Something I wasn't ready to do at that time. It seems inconceivable now that I felt I couldn't reach out to Nessa or Julie, but at that time, I'd hardly spoken to them since I'd moved away.

The only other person I'd considered talking to was Tim. But Chris hated the guy. The fear of losing Chris's love far outweighing the notion of standing up against the injustice of his demands.

Of course I'd considered carrying the baby to term, before putting it up for adoption. But how could I condemn another soul to the same living hell that had haunted me. The absence of only one of my parents at that time causing me so much pain. Always wondering who my other parent was, where they were, and whether or not they'd loved me. The sense of abandonment contributing to my own low self-esteem, and subsequent poor choices.

Thank God I've healed that wound, I think to myself, as I continue to flick through the pages of my journal.

I'd considered every possible option. Even keeping it and raising it myself, but I had no money. No job security. No home of my own. I had nothing and no-one.

It was a desperate situation, and I'd felt choosing an abortion was the only choice. The right choice. Confirmed by the mere fact I ended up going through the whole thing alone. I had no support from anyone. No emotional, physical or practical support: nothing.

Looking back, it's hard to comprehend where I found the strength to cope. I suppose it's the same inner strength that's kept me going despite my recent traumas.

Will the cycle ever end?

Looking at my scrawled handwriting with fresh eyes, I have to wonder why I've kept this secret all these years.

So much secrecy. So much shame; and like a bolt of lightning, I realise *this* is the shackle that keeps me enslaved. The weight that pulls me back in my nightmares. Not the decision I made—it was the right choice—it's the shame that surrounds my actions that's keeping me captive.

I jolt upright as I realise if I'm truly to be free of my past, I must own this.

I had an abortion.

It wasn't an easy decision.

It was heartbreaking and desperately sad.

But I made the right choice. The right choice for me *and* the baby.

And regardless of how I lost that child, it doesn't mean I don't grieve for that baby, or somehow relinquish my *right* to grieve for that child, but it was *my choice* to terminate that pregnancy.

Unwittingly, Chris turning away from me in my moment of greatest need inadvertently gave me the greatest gift. The appreciation now that this was *my decision and mine alone.* And in the same breath, I owe him nothing.

It was my body, my choice, and my decision.

Like an arrow of clarity hitting me between my eyes, I realise the shame I've harboured all these years was born from my coerced duty to protect him.

Why, therefore, am I still shouldering *his* shame? *His* secret?

"No more," I say quietly into the ether.

Flicking to the back of my 1994 journal, I find a blank page, scrawl today's date at the top, and write:

This ends here.

I will hide no more.

I own my past and all the decisions I made. Both good and bad.

I had an abortion and need give no justification for the reasons why. They are my reasons and mine alone.

Still, I grieve the loss of that child, as well as all my others.

I'm the mother of four unborn babies, and I love them all.

I may never have the privilege of holding any of them in my arms, but their stars will forever shine down from the heavens above and I hold their love in my heart.

I refuse to live with regret and gracefully accept whatever life has in store for me now.

I surrender to the future I have not yet lived and place no conditions on whether I shall ever mother a child of my own.

If my destiny is to mother someone else's child, or offer support as an honorary aunt, then I accept that role with gratitude and humility.

I willingly accept whatever my future holds, without condition, and shall continue to love unconditionally, regardless.

Exhaling, I slam the journal shut, my eyes dry. My body fizzes with a renewed energy and I feel instantly lighter.

I shall no longer deny the true circumstances of my past. The only challenge now, is deciding how to broach the subject with Gav. I don't have to tell him immediately, but I also don't want any more secrets between us.

Gently moving Leo off my lap, I crouch down in front of the hearth and light four tealights.

One for each of my babies. My unborn stars that are as much a part of me and my past as every other person I've ever loved.

I remain seated in front of the flickering flames until they slowly burn out.

"You're all my children," I whisper. "Today, tomorrow, and always."

Smiling, I return to bed and sleep soundly.

Chapter 40

GAVIN

1 month later, Friday 8th September 2006

*H*e's such a cute baby." Gav watches as Vicky leans over JP's crib and gives his damp curls a gentle stroke. JP is lying on his back, fast asleep, arms splayed, his mouth sucking hard on his dummy.

"Hardly a baby now," Gav says as they both peer lovingly into his crib.

"I know, he's growing up so fast," Vicky says. "He pulled his own socks off and threw them in the bath earlier." She chuckles at the memory.

Julie and Clarky are taking a well-earned night off while Vicky and Gavin babysit their godson.

'We'll stay over,' Gav had heard Vicky saying to Julie on the phone a few nights ago, when Julie had started fretting about what time to book a taxi home. *'It'll be our pleasure,"* Vicky had continued. *'Why don't you book into that new hotel on the Quayside? Make a proper night of it. Let Clarky spoil you."*

Gav and Vicky tiptoe quietly out of JP's room and close the door. Standing on the top of the landing, Gav pulls her into a hug, kissing the top of her brow before they tread their way back downstairs to the waiting bottle of wine Gav has chilling in the fridge. Since losing the last baby, the rigid eating plan and alcohol ban appear to have been temporarily relaxed in the Fenwick-Williams household.

"I'm sorry," Vicky says, as she watches Gav pull the cork.

"What for?" Gav looks up, confused.

"That this isn't in our future," Vicky says quietly, her eyes glancing around the arty black and white photographs of JP which adorn every surface and wall in Julie and Clarky's home.

Surely, Gav thinks to himself, she can't be ready to give up. I know how desperately she wants a child. We both do.

He doesn't respond immediately, instead focusing his attention on pouring two long glasses. Passing one to her, he locks eye contact and asks, "Is that it then? Are we done?"

She dips her head and wraps an arm around her torso. "For whatever reason, it seems my body won't carry a baby to term."

Gav sucks in a deep breath, his blood simmering.

Not yet. But that doesn't mean she can't.

"Plus age isn't on my side," she adds.

"Don't be ridiculous sweetheart. You're only thirty-six. Some women don't start their families until they're in their forties." Gav's tone is harsher than he'd intended.

"True. But a woman's fertility falls dramatically after thirty-five, while the likelihood of miscarriage increases threefold. And I've had three in a row now."

"Four, if you count the miscarriage you had with Chris's baby as well."

She jerks her head back slightly before visibly recomposing herself.

"Yes, four if you count the baby I lost back then as well. Either way, it doesn't look promising. I'm not sure I can keep going if… if I keep losing them. It's not just the physical loss…" She looks at him. "It's a lot, that's all."

He turns his back, not wanting her to see the hurt in his eyes.

"Why don't we wait until we've spoken to the specialist in a few months' time."

Having now suffered three miscarriages in quick succession, the latter being deemed a 'late miscarriage', Vicky's GP has referred them to a specialist miscarriage unit at Newcastle's Centre for Life.

"But there are other ways to have a family," she says tentatively, like a timid child approaching a grumpy parent, unsure if their request for a sugary treat before bedtime will be granted with the flick of a dismissive hand or whether they'll respond with a sharp word and an instruction to go to bed immediately.

Why is she even suggesting this? She knows my feelings on the matter.

"I've told you before, I don't want to adopt, if that's what you're insinuating," he replies, his tone bristling.

"I'm not insinuating anything. Only that if we're serious about having a baby, we may have to consider other options. Adoption? Surrogacy? We could consider a donated egg fertilised with your sperm."

He shakes his head. "That feels like cheating on you."

"Babes, that's ridiculous," she says softly.

Gav tenses his jaw. "I don't know what it is, sweetheart, but I just don't think I could love a child that isn't biologically mine, or yours for that matter."

"But you love JP?"

"Of course. But as his godfather. It would be different if he were ours."

"How so?" she pushes.

He screws his eyes closed. "I don't know, Victoria." His tone sharper than a moment ago, the tension between them mounting. "It just would be. I want to be a father to your child. A baby that is the product of you *and* me."

He hears her let out a long sigh. "Well that may not be possible."

"So what? We just give up?" Gav's frustration bubbles over.

She cannot seriously be about to give up on our dream. It's the one thing they both agreed they wanted after he lived through the hell of Hurricane Ivan two years ago.

Gav had followed her wishes by not insisting they get married, but the agreement to have a baby together was meant to solidify their commitment to each other. To show the world they are a real couple. A real family.

"Really?" He glares at her when she doesn't answer. "You've had me taking all those stupid supplements all this time while you chart your fertility with military precision, not to mention turning our sex life into a benign routine, only for us to give up now?"

Why the fuck did I say that? She must know that's not what I meant.

"That's hardly the point," she replies, her eyes glassing over.

Gav touches her upper arm. "Sorry, I didn't mean that."

"All I'm saying," she continues, "is if we find out it's not possible for me to carry a baby, which means I can't ever give birth, then I'm okay with that. I've made my peace with it. If a baby is in our future, however it happens, I'd welcome it with open arms." She glares at him, a steely strength emanating from her emerald green irises. "My capacity to love a child is not dependant on how it's made."

"But—" Gav goes to say something more, but she raises her hand, cutting him off.

"However, if having a baby is not in our future, for whatever reason, I'm fine with that too. Really, I am. I already feel like a mother, even if I've never had the privilege of holding any of my babies in my arms."

"Our babies," Gav interjects.

"Yes, our babies," she says, before quickly averting her eyes. "I have enough love for all the other children in my life, and I love being their crazy aunty Tor. I shall focus all my mothering energy on them, and that will be enough. For me, at least."

Gav's eyes soften and he touches the side of her cheek. "Oh, Angel."

"Maybe that's why I haven't been able to have a child of my own." She leans her head against his shoulder. "Because my purpose is to help raise other people's children. Perhaps that's my gift. It may be a different definition of family, but it's still family nonetheless."

"Come here." He pulls her in for a hug. Wrapping his arms around her torso and kissing the top of her head. "Let's wait and see what the specialist says."

꙳

The smell of disinfectant burns the inside of Gav's nostrils as, three weeks later, he and Victoria wait for their names to be called. All around them posters offering counselling, bereavement and adoption services do little to calm Vicky's shaking hands. Gav reaches across her lap and grabs one to hold. He grips it tight, interlacing his fingers with hers, and rolls his thumb back and forth across her smooth skin. He's hiding his own nerves for her benefit.

"Ms Fenwick," a nurse with a clipboard calls, and they follow her down the corridor and into a consulting room where a grey-haired gentleman wears a once white, now faded to a lack lustre grey, shirt. The white doctor's coat he wears over the top is marred with pen stains on his top pocket.

He reaches over the desk and offers them his hand.

"Ms Fenwick. Mr Williams," he says with a well-rehearsed sympathetic smile, before indicating for them to take the two seats on the opposite side of his desk.

Tilting his head so he can see beyond his reading glasses, he looks at his computer screen and then back to the brown A4 file in front of him.

Gav sees Vicky's NHS number printed on the white adhesive label in the top right-hand corner.

Is that what she's been reduced to? A mere series of letters and numbers. A statistic.

The doctor clears his throat. "I believe you're here today because you've suffered a number of concurrent pregnancy losses."

"That's correct." Vicky keeps her eyes focused on the floor, and Gav gives her hand a little squeeze.

"Well let's see if we can get to the bottom of it shall we?" He purses his lips, elongating his sympathetic smile.

Turning back to the screen he says, "So I see you've had four pregnancies. Three miscarriages and one—"

"Actually, before you go any further," Vicky interjects, turning to Gav and reaching for both his hands to hold, "sweetheart there's something I need to tell you."

"Oh?" Gav says perplexed.

"I should have told you long before now, but I was ashamed and worried how you might react, especially after you told me about what Samantha did."

"What has my ex-wife got to do with this?"

"Sorry," Vicky says to the consultant, "but I want Gav to hear this from me. Sweetheart, my first pregnancy, the one with Chris. I didn't have a miscarriage. I had a termination."

Gav feels like he's been hit by a truck. All the air is punched out of his lungs. Pulling his hands back from Vicky's, he pinches the bridge of his nose.

"Sorry, did I hear you right? You're telling me you had an abortion?"

"Yes, that's correct," Vicky says, her tone even, her eyes level.

"And, what? It merely slipped your mind? You never thought that that was something you should have shared with me? Especially after what we've been through these past few years."

The doctor coughs into his closed fist. "Would you like me to give you a moment's privacy?"

"No, it's fine," Vicky says. "You can continue. Yes, this is something we should have discussed before now, but it was such a long time ago I didn't think it was relevant to today. Then when you started to say it just now, I realised I wanted Gavin to hear it from me first."

How could she have not told me? Gav thinks, dumbfounded.

"I see, and yes, you're a G4, x1TOP x3Spot misc," the doctor says, consulting Vicky's notes again. "Four pregnancies in total, one termination of pregnancy in 1995, plus three spontaneous miscarriages between March 2005 and July this year," he adds for clarity. "And I can see the most recent one was a late miscarriage at fifteen weeks two days, is that right?"

"Yes. That's correct," Gav hears Vicky saying through the fog that's formed inside his head.

How could she have lied to him all this time? Let him believe she lost Chris's baby through natural causes, just like all of their unborn children. How could she have terminated a pregnancy, just like Samantha did with his first child.

Gavin sits mute.

She's not the woman I thought she was.

Vicky turns to look at him, reaching for his hand to hold, but he snatches it away.

"We can talk about it later," she whispers.

"Oh we will," he replies through gritted teeth.

Gav can't hear what the doctor is saying anymore. His voice has morphed into Charlie Brown's teacher: *A-whaa whaa whaa …* on he goes, Gav only catching the odd word.

Chromosomal problems. Incompetent cervix. The list goes on and on.

The sound of blood whooshes through Gav's ears as his heart pounds inside his chest, like he's being chased by a tiger. It's so loud it drowns out every other noise.

"Look at me, Gavin. Please," he hears, and slowly turns his head which feels ten times heavier than it did five minutes ago. "Did you hear the question?"

Shaking his head, he refocuses on the conversation taking place between Vicky and the consultant.

The doctor patiently asks, while Vicky reaches for his hand again, "Do you know your blood group Mr Williams? We will of course test you, but I wondered if you know it already."

"O, I believe."

"O-positive or O-negative?"

"I'm not sure, but I think I'm the same as my mum. O-positive."

"Ahh, well that's something else to add to the list," the doctor says knowingly.

"How so?" Vicky asks, leaning forward.

"Ms Fenwick—"

"Call me Victoria," she interjects, smiling.

"Victoria, I don't suppose you can remember if you were ever offered an Anti-D injection after your termination, or your subsequent miscarriages?"

"I have no idea? What's that?"

"Has anyone ever told you you have Rhesus negative blood?" The doctor ignores Victoria's question, and continues with his explanation. "B-negative, to be precise."

She draws her eyebrows together and purses her lips.

"Very rare. Less than two percent of the population have your specific blood type."

Gav watches as she reverses the muscles in her brow, stretching her eyes wide.

"It's nothing to be concerned about. In all blood groups you can be either Rhesus positive or Rhesus negative. About fifteen percent of the population are Rhesus negative, which simply means you don't carry the Rhesus antigens on the outside of your red blood cells, but it does mean that if your partner has Rhesus positive blood, and your unborn baby were also to have positive blood, if their blood were to come into contact with yours for any reason, usually through giving birth, or possibly an incomplete miscarriage, or a termination, your body will make antibodies against the Rhesus positive protein… to protect your own blood. It's a normal immune response. However, in any future pregnancies, if you then carry a further Rhesus positive baby, those antibodies can cross the placenta and cause some problems."

"And is that what's happened in my case?"

"We won't know for sure, as we weren't able to test any blood from your lost pregnancies, but we can test you and find out if your blood has been what we call *Rhesus sensitised.* Which would mean you've already developed antibodies. It's one of the many tests we'll be doing." He turns and checks his notes again. "I can see you had a D&C abortion under full anaesthetic, which is a more invasive treatment, so it's possible that could have happened. These days most women are offered a medical abortion."

"What's the difference?" Gav asks, perplexed.

"A medical abortion is a series of pills the woman takes twenty-four or forty-eight hours apart, which induce bleeding, whereas a surgical abortion is as it sounds. The pregnancy tissues are removed from the uterus under anaesthetic. It depends on the circumstances and the gestation, obviously, but it appears Victoria was given a surgical abortion which, assuming she wasn't offered an anti-D beforehand, may have slightly increased her chances of her blood becoming sensitised. Assuming that baby was Rhesus positive, of course."

"So what you're saying is her previous termination may have caused the loss of my babies."

Everyone freezes and the air inside the tiny office thickens.

Vicky pulls her hand away from his and places it between her knees as she looks stoically ahead.

Gavin turns away and looks out of the window, running a finger around his collar.

When did it get so hot?

He feels like he's inside a pressure cooker and someone is slowly turning up the heat.

"As I said," the doctor continues diplomatically, "that's just one of the many things we'll be investigating."

But Gav is no longer listening. The walls around him are closing in and he can't breathe.

"Today, we'll start with a standard set of tests. Look for any hidden chromosomal abnormalities, in either of you—"

"I'm sorry." Gav stands up, the legs of the plastic chair scraping across the floor. "I can't be here," he says, his voice sounding strangled, like a person in an ever-tightening noose.

Without a backward glance, he bolts from the room.

Chapter 41

"*D*o you want to go after him?" the consultant asks.

"No," I say, shuffling and sitting up straight, anger simmering through my veins. "Quite frankly... and pardon my French... he can go fuck himself."

Yes, this is something I should have found a way to tell Gav before now and not spring him on it in the doctor's office, but how could I when I knew he'd likely react like this.

The consultant jerks his head back, his eyebrows raised.

"Sorry, I don't mean to sound harsh. Clearly there's a conversation we need to have, but your time is valuable and if he's going to judge me for a decision I made a long time ago, without knowing any of the circumstances surrounding it, then I'd rather he wasn't in the room. Please. Continue."

"Right then," the doctor says, pushing his reading glasses further up his nose. "Victoria, you need to know that despite what I've said, Rhesus disease is not a confirmed cause of miscarriage. Testing you for this and a whole host of other chromosomal issues is merely investigative, to perhaps offer preventative treatment in future pregnancies rather than explain why you've suffered miscarriages in the past. You don't seem to have any issues conceiving, and there's a good chance you've merely been exceptionally unlucky. Generally speaking, you're in good health. You don't smoke, drink only in moderation. You're a healthy weight. Yes, you're approaching the latter years of childbearing age. But plenty of women go on to have healthy babies well into their forties. My guess is that if you were to become pregnant again you would be absolutely fine. Almost all early miscarriages are caused by problems with the foetus. It's nature's way of ensuring a healthy offspring." He gestures towards the nurse who's been quietly hovering in the corner of the room. "Right. Shall we get started?"

Back in the car, I turn and glare at Gavin's profile as he concentrates on the road ahead. If my eyes were lasers I'd have burnt a hole in the side of his cheek by now.

"Are you planning on giving me the silent treatment all the way home, or are we going to talk about this?"

"Not yet. The traffic's really heavy and this weather's atrocious," he says, flicking the windscreen wipers up to their highest level. "I need to concentrate."

Out of nowhere he pulls out and I hold my breath as he pulls off an aggressive overtaking move seconds before another car's headlights blind us, its horn blaring as it whizzes past in the opposite direction.

"Jesus Christ, Gav. Are you trying to get us killed?"

"What? Like you've killed all my babies?"

"What did you just say?" I reply, dumbfounded.

"You heard me," he says, gripping the steering wheel so tight his knuckles have turned deathly white.

"Is that what you really think? How fucking dare you!" I say slowly, enunciating every syllable.

"How dare I?" he hisses back. "How could you have done it, Vicky? How could you have had an abortion? You must have known how wrong it was. Why else keep it a secret all these years? I thought I knew everything about you, but somehow you forgot to share that tiny, rather important piece of information, despite it being the most likely cause of all the miscarriages. I don't know who you are anymore."

"Stop…The… Car," I say, my voice low and controlled, but laced with fury, my hand already on the door handle.

"No. Now you're being ridiculous."

"I said, STOP… THE… FUCKING… CAR!"

I open the door and, seeing I'm prepared to get out of a moving vehicle, he reluctantly pulls over.

"And where the fuck are you going to go?"

"Anywhere, away from YOU!" I spit, gathering my things and climbing out. "Have you any idea of the implications of what you've just said?" I add, leaning my head back inside the car, my mouth swilling with spittle. "You say you don't know me, well I sure as hell don't know who you are anymore."

"Don't be ridiculous, Victoria. Get back in the car."

"Like hell I will. We're done here."

"But it's lashing down. You'll catch your death of cold."

"Then I'll only join all the babies—your babies, apparently—that I've intentionally killed."

His jaw tenses as he closes then re-opens his eyes. "Fine. Have it your way."

I slam the car door with as much force as I can muster and watch, incredulous, as he spins the wheels, pulling away as fast as he can. It seems he, too, can't stand the sight of me any longer.

Pulling my collar up against the hard rain, I think through my immediate options.

Walk the ten or so miles home in the pouring rain. Wait for the next bus, which could be at least another hour, or call one of the girls to come and get me.

I'm already shivering as I pull out my mobile and punch out Julie's number.

★

"Of course you can stay at mine," Julie says thirty minutes later, wiping condensation from the inside of her windscreen.

She's turned the car heaters on full blast, and being wet through, I've inadvertently turned the inside of the car into a steam room.

"I'm sure this'll all blow over once you've both had a chance to cool down," Julie says.

"I'd love to believe that, but actually Jules this is a lot more serious."

"Oh?" Julie says, flicking on the car's indicator and pulling onto her drive.

Over the next few hours, whilst supping a full-bodied bottle of Chablis, I tell Julie and Clarky everything. Warranted, not all the circumstances surrounding the abortion and how Chris left me alone the night before, but they both empathically agree I had no choice.

I also tell them about Gavin's history. How his ex-wife, Samantha, terminated her own pregnancy in the lead-up to their wedding. And how he only found out years later, and how when I almost told him in San Diego he made it clear he can't forgive anyone *who takes a life before it has a chance to live,* so I always knew he had strong opinions on the subject.

"Wow," Julie says after I deliver that extra nugget.

"Yup. I say that that's the reason I haven't told him before now, but it's definitely contributed.

A strangled cry crackles through the baby monitor and breaks into our conversation.

"I'll go," Clarky says, standing and finishing off his wine.

"Give it a few minutes," Julie says. "He needs to learn to self-soothe." Turning back to me, she adds, "Gav's hurting right now. Just like that little fella upstairs, waking up in the dark and things not being how he wants them to be. I say, let the dust settle tonight, and I'm sure you'll both find a way through this."

"I'm not so sure. I can understand he's hurt that I never told him, and I owe him an apology for that, but he also needs to take some responsibility for why I didn't tell him sooner. Regardless, I'm not sure I can forgive him for the things he said to me tonight. He was despicable."

"What would he have to do to turn this around?"

I shrug. "A massive bunch of roses and an apology would be a start. If he doesn't show any remorse, or any inkling that he'll change his view, then I'm not hanging around. I'm not prepared to waste another moment of my life with a man who thinks I'm a monster."

✦

I wake in Julie and Clarky's spare room to the sound of laughter and the smell of sizzling bacon. Drifting downstairs in a pair of borrowed pyjamas, I find the little family dancing around their kitchen, singing and clapping their hands to the latest Teletubbies episode.

"Bacon sandwich?" Julie plates one up for me without waiting for an answer.

"Thanks." I take it gratefully. "Any chance of a lift home once I've got dressed? I need to face the music at some point, it might as well be this morning."

"No problemo," Clarky says. "I've got to shoot across to Mark's anyway. He wants my help shifting some flagstones in their back garden."

Neither Gav nor I have messaged each other since yesterday. The first time I've not communicated with him in a twenty-four-hour period since the five agonising days between losing communication with him during Hurricane Ivan and him texting me to say he'd been safely evacuated to Miami.

After I've showered and dressed in yesterday's clothes, now that they've had a tumble in Julie's dryer, I let myself back into my home.

"Gavin? Are you here?"

I make my way through to the kitchen and do what I've always done in these types of situations—flick on the kettle.

The house seems eerily quiet. Every sound magnified. The chink of the two cups clashing together as I lift them down from the shelf. The slamming of the kitchen cupboard after I've retrieved the tea bags. The water in the kettle as it boils and rolls at the bottom of the jug. I feel like a tiny mouse trespassing in someone else's world, and that somewhere upstairs is an angry ogre that at any moment could explode with rage.

Leo *meows* and wraps himself around my legs, demanding my attention. I pick him up and tickle him under his chin. He vibrates like a tractor as he *purrs* his delight.

At least someone is showing me some love.

I pour the boiling water over the two tea bags. Walking the two steps across the room to the fridge, my head jerks involuntarily backwards at the sight of Peanut's baby scan. Secured with a magnet, it has pride of place in the centre of the fridge, surrounded by other notices of local fundraisers, flyers for handymen and the bin-day rota from the council. Neither of us has had the heart to remove it and so it has remained where we'd placed it. A stark reminder of what's not to be.

Even though it has been there for months now, it catches me unawares. I remove it from the fridge and hold it gently in my hands as I've done so many times before. I rub my thumbs over the curling corners of the paper. I've framed the other scan we were given on my birthday, and it has pride of place in the living room. Staring at the grainy black and white image of the tiny baby, its oversized head and tiny limbs, a ball of melancholy sits heavy on my chest. How can I possibly love something so much when it never even existed?

Except that it did. A star unborn.

I hear footsteps in the hallway and quickly fix the scan back in its place before pulling open the fridge door, hiding myself from view.

"I see you're home," Gav says gruffly. He doesn't sound like he's had a good night's sleep.

"U-huh." I shut the fridge door. "I stayed at Julie and Paul's."

"Yeah. Clarky texted me to say Julie had gone to pick you up."

"Well that was nice of him. Voluntarily letting you know I was safe."

Not that you deserved to know, I don't add.

A deafening silence falls across the room as the air between us hangs heavy.

I pad across the tiles, avoiding Gav's glare, and finish making the drinks. The teaspoon chimes against the side of the ceramic mugs; the sound reverberating around the room as I stir the steaming liquid.

Silence again.

Neither of us wants to start this conversation, yet we're both in limbo until someone makes the first move. I pass Gav his mug and he takes a sip.

"Do you regret it?" he asks.

"Do you regret what you said to me?" I counter.

"You first."

"Do I regret not telling you I had an abortion? Of course, I do. You have no idea how many times I wanted to tell you. But do I regret terminating that pregnancy? No, I don't," I say, my head held high.

I watch as he visibly shudders.

"How. Dare. You," I stutter, watching his reaction.

"I can't help how I feel. I just never thought *you* of all people, the woman I love with all my heart, would turn out to be one of *those* people."

"Those people? Jesus Christ, Gavin. Can you hear yourself?"

I put down my tea and ball my fists.

Who is this man? How can he be saying these things?

"You have no right—absolutely no right—to judge me. It was over a decade ago. I was desperate. I had nothing to offer that child. There's no way I could have become a mother at that time. I was going through hell and it was, and remains, the hardest decision I've ever had to make in my entire life. If you love me, as you say you do, then surely you'd know I'd never make a decision like that lightly. How can you not appreciate how hard it was for me? And until recently, how ashamed I was. Can you at least appreciate the reasons why I felt I couldn't tell you?"

"And how can you not understand how hideous it was—is—for me? I can't believe history is repeating itself. This is my worst nightmare."

"I'm not Samantha. How can you compare this situation—compare me—to what she did? I didn't even know you then. It wasn't *your* child I aborted."

"Yes, but you've kept it from me all this time."

"Well perhaps if you hadn't described *anyone who takes a life before it has a chance to live* as *an unforgivable monster,* I might have thought differently about telling you."

"So it's my fault?"

"No. I completely own the decision to keep this from you, although a few weeks ago, I had decided I was going to tell. I was waiting for the right moment. If I'd known it was going to come out yesterday, I would have made sure I'd done it before we were sat in front of the consultant. I owe you an apology for that. I am truly sorry. But you need to own your part in this too."

He jerks his head back and crumples his brow.

"Seriously, some of this is on you as well. You've got such a fixed mindset; there's no reasoning with you. And unless you can not only say sorry for the things you've said to me, but change your opinion on this, I don't think we have a future anymore."

"You cannot be serious."

"I'm deadly serious Gavin. I'm not ashamed of my past, and if that contravenes your own beliefs, then there's no point prolonging the inevitable. We can try and get past this, but if we don't share the same opinion on something this fundamental, then it's always going to be a wedge between us and will eventually drive us apart."

"I see," he replies, dropping his head. "So I have to apologise *and* change my beliefs, or we're over."

"You owe me an apology. Only then can we try and find some

middle ground. I can't change my past, but you can change your opinion about it."

The air around us freezes as I wait for him to respond. When he does, he doesn't say what I was expecting, and instead mutters the fatal words, "I suppose I'd better go pack?"

I *humph* out an incredulous puff of air.

How can he be this pig-headed? He'd rather throw away everything we've got than apologise for insulting me, never mind trying to find some middle ground in our differing views. Well, if that's how he's going to act, I don't want to be with him anymore.

"If that's what you think, then I think that's for the best," I say, my shoulders back and my head held high.

He plonks his tea down and storms out.

I lean back against the kitchen bench and wrap my arms around myself.

Alone again.

Despite the realisation that Gav isn't the man I thought he once was, that his love for me was not without condition, even though I thought he was the best thing that had ever happened to me and I shall miss him dreadfully I haven't been hit with the sledgehammer of loss I experienced when all my previous relationships ended.

As I stand in my kitchen and listen to the sound of the Third Great Love of my life shuffling around the bedroom above me as he packs up his things and prepares to leave, sure, I'm sad, but broken? Hell no.

Later that evening as I walk through the hallway, preparing to go to bed, my sole companion, Leo, curling his black tail around my ankles, I glance into the jumble of keys in the bowl on my hall side table and notice that Gav has added his house key to the pile.

Wow! A clear statement he has no intention of coming back.

Chapter 42

5 weeks later, Friday 3rd November 2006

*O*ver the next five weeks I throw myself into my business. Other than Leo for company, I have no other distractions so I'm able to fill my days travelling up and down to London, taking Skype calls with my clients at all hours—including calls from those in Paris, Milan and the US—whilst also spending time with the team developing our portfolio of services and marketing our company.

Now that we have a bigger team, I offer both Angela and Clive directorships and issue them and Helen with share options. Having nailed them to the floor, so to speak, I feel more secure that they'll be with me for the long haul. If something ever happened to me, the business would survive under their leadership.

The increased workload also begins to yield additional financial benefit and I've finally matched my previous level of earnings. With Gavin now gone, I'm covering all of the household bills myself. We weren't married, we don't have kids, so he doesn't owe me any financial support, and we hadn't gotten around to changing the mortgage or any of the utilities into joint names. In reality, untangling our lives was remarkably easy. Other than a couple of pieces of furniture he brought with him, and a wardrobe full of his clothes which I've agreed to store (and promised I won't throw red wine or coffee granules over) until he finds somewhere more permanent to live, our decoupling was painless. Unlike the reason for our breakup.

Damn his stubborn, pig-headed views on the family construct, and his opinion on a woman's rights over her body.

Still, my decision a few years back to take control of my financial destiny and never be reliant on a man for my standard of living appears to have paid off.

'Are you sure we can't help you two work it out? Nessa had pleaded one night, not long after our breakup. 'He's holed up in our back bedroom, mopping about, permanently on his laptop, only coming downstairs to eat. Whatever it was that came between you two, are you sure it can't be overcome? You were so good together.'

'Were… being the operative word, Ness,' I'd replied. 'He's made his position clear. And if there's one thing I know about that man, he's as stubborn as a mule. I don't hate him, far from it, but I know he won't change his mind, so the best thing I can do is focus on myself and move forward with my life. No point dwelling on what's done.'

After a couple more attempts at interventions by our friends and family, everyone has finally accepted we're over, even if only Julie and Clarky know the real reasons why. Everyone else has assumed my last miscarriage proved to be the final breaking point for us.

★

At the end of a long week, I'm curled up on the sofa, a cool glass of wine in my hand and my laptop balanced on my knee while I look at this week's key metrics and update our cash flow. In the corner, the TV is showing a rerun of *Home Alone*. The Christmas telly schedule already in full swing, even though there are still seven weeks until the big guy arrives.

I'm not sure I can be bothered with decorations this year, I think to myself. But I know Nessa will have a fit if I try and dip out of it. She's the one who always goes full hog on all things Christmassy.

When I look down the street, a couple of bay windows twinkle with flashing fairy lights. Leftovers from Halloween. They're the same households who I know will have their Christmas trees up in the next few weeks. Always the first to spread the Christmas cheer.

My Blackberry rests on the arm of the chair. Instinctively I look at the screen moments before it buzzes, announcing the arrival of a text. I pick up the phone and then drop it again like a hot potato.

Can you talk?

Call me. It's urgent. Chris x

Other than that one time in San Diego when we talked and then Skyped, we've only ever communicated via text. It enables me to keep him at arm's length and maintain a safe, invisible boundary. I reread his messages and do the mental calculations. It must be 6:00 a.m. on Saturday there. What could have happened? This isn't a request, like a, *'Hey, it would be great to hear all your news. Give me a bell when it's convenient.'* No, this is a clear instruction. Something's wrong. I press the Call button against his name in my contacts, and he answers within two rings.

"Hey Goose."

A shiver runs down my spine and an unconscious smile spreads across my lips at the familiarity of both his deep raspy voice and his pet name for me. It originally started as a general Kiwi saying, *'Ya old Goose,'* which Chris would use for any of his friends, much the same as I would call any of my friends *'canny lasses'*, or *'canny lads'*. Like saying "Eeee, do you know so-and-so? She's a proper canny lass." But it wasn't long before *'Ya old Goose,'* or the shorter moniker, *'Goose'* became Chris's special name, just for me. Just as Gav ended up calling me *'Angel'* all these years.

Another pang in my gut catches me unawares. I may have adjusted to life without Gav, but it doesn't stop me missing him, or grieving for the love we once shared. I swallow down the lump at the back of my throat. I know it's over and I'm determined to remain focused on the present.

"How ya doing?" Chris asks.

"Good thanks. More to the point, how are you? What's so urgent you needed to speak to me? It must be super early over there."

"Are you sitting down? You're not gonna like what I have to tell ya."

He begins to share with me the reason for his call and my hand flies up to my mouth as I sit and listen.

No, this can't be true. If I'd thought life had served me some shit soup lately, my drama is nothing compared to what Chris is telling me.

"I don't know what to say, Chris. I can't believe it. It's too hideous."

"I knew you'd want to know."

"Thanks. I appreciate you telling me. I'll see what I can do."

We sign off and hang up.

If Chris's news tonight proves one thing, it's that life is for living and you must live each day to the fullest.

I think through my options, regardless of how hard or complicated it's going to be, I can't not act on what Chris has shared with me. There's no question what I need to do. And quickly.

Downing my wine in one, I put my plan into immediate motion, firing off a couple of quick emails, including a group notice to Clive, Angela, and Helen, before making a phone call to the one other person who I think needs to know what's going on.

I head upstairs to pack and not knowing how long I'll be gone, so I pack for every eventuality. A couple of suits in case I end up working, and lots of easy casuals, including comfy clothes for a long flight.

I don't have time to sort out all the finer details or let anyone here know what's going on, but I'll text Julie later, when I get to London. Hopefully by then I'll have more information, and if it's too late tonight, I'll message her in the morning.

I need someone to take care of Leo. She has a house key and I've filled up his 5-day feeder so he'll be fine in the short-term. Julie and Paul have taken him in when I've been away before; hopefully she'll be happy to do so again.

Thirty minutes later I'm waiting for my taxi to arrive, to take me to the train station, when the doorbell goes. Assuming it's the driver and I've not heard them pull up, I open it, except instead of a taxi driver on the doorstep it's a dishevelled and bleary-eyed Mark, an overnight bag in his hand.

"Mark? What on earth are you doing here?"

"Long story. But I wondered if I could stay tonight. I don't really have anywhere else to go."

"Of course, but what's happened?"

"Becca threw me out." He shrugs.

"Threw you out? *Temporarily* out, or *It's over* out?"

"Not quite sure. She's mad as hell. I made a run for it when she started hurling pans across the kitchen."

I stop myself from asking if they were clean or dirty and whether that was the reason for their bust-up.

"Actually, stay as long as you want. You've inadvertently solved a major problem for me."

I spy the taxi turning down into the end of my street.

"No time to explain. Here, take my keys. Make yourself at home. Finish off everything in the fridge. I could really do with someone to look after the place. I'm not exactly sure when I'll be back. Oh, and remember to fill up Leo's feeder. His food's in the cupboard under the stairs."

Looking more than a bit confused he asks, "Why? Where are you going?"

"London initially, then overseas."

"Eh?"

"Like I said, it's a long story and one I haven't got time to explain now. Someone I love is in dire need of my support, and I've got nothing holding me here. I can run my business from anywhere. So like I said, I'm not exactly sure how long I'll be gone."

349

The taxi driver opens the boot and lifts my case inside. It slams shut with a solid *clunk*.

"Oh, and Mark…"

"Yes?" He looks at me, still confused.

"Stop being a lazy arse. Pull your weight and make up with Becca. Your missus needs you to pick up some of the slack—that's all."

I wave out of the window as the taxi pulls away. My final view is of him standing on my front doorstep, still as confused as he was five minutes ago.

Part V

Chapter 43

ou okay?" Tim asks, noticing I've not said anything since boarding his plane. After we push back and are taxiing out to the runway, I grip the armrests so tight my nails are in danger of ripping the cream leather.

"Mmm-hmm," I reply, staring straight ahead.

After an imperceptible pause the engines roar to life, like a lion unleashed. The G-force pins me back in my seat, before I'm weightless. Instead of being pulled back, down into the dark depths of my past, with every inch of altitude gained, and despite my fear, my heart lifts.

Tim leans over and pats the back of my hand. "You'll be fine."

"I know." I look back at him and smile. "I *know* I will."

A beat passes.

"I can't tell you how grateful I am for the lift. I'm not sure I could have made this trip on a commercial aircraft. Not yet, anyhow."

"Understandable," Tim says magnanimously. "Plus, how could you turn down an opportunity to fly halfway around the world in a private jet. Just as well you have friends in high places." He smiles, before adding, "It's fine, honestly. Lucky I was in London last week and on my way to Hong Kong. After a night stop there, we'll carry on down the day after. I'm immensely grateful you gave me the

353

heads-up. I know it's a long way to go, but it's the right thing to do…" He trails off before finishing and I watch as he blinks a few times in quick succession.

Tim doesn't do emotion, so I know this trip is as important to him as it is to me. After I left him the message on Friday night, he called me back the next morning and after discovering he was in London, we made a plan.

"Tomorrow you can either hang out at mine, or do some shopping," he adds.

"Actually I need to work. Could I possibly steal an office? If you have one spare that is? I only need a flipchart and a stable internet connection, but I must catch up with the team. They'll be wondering what's going on after I cancelled our Monday morning huddle."

We both register the familiar *bing* of the seat belt signs going off, and the stewardess at the front of the cabin releases herself from her crew seat and heads into the galley.

Meanwhile Tim turns, looks at me, and gives me a knowing smile.

"What?" I ask.

"You never cease to surprise me, that's all, Victoria. *Can I steal an office? I need to catch up with the team,*" he chuckles.

"You should know by now: do not underestimate me, Tim. As you said in Singapore, I'm *a proper grown-up businesswoman.* Breaking barriers 'n all that. I'm CEO of my own perfectly formed but global business, and I feel personally responsible not only for my own mortgage, but for the mortgages of every one of my employees."

"I've never underestimated you, my dear. If anything I've always thought you underestimated yourself." He raises his empty whisky glass in the direction of the air stewardess. She nods her acknowledgment. "It's nice to see you're finally standing in your power."

The stewardess brings him a fresh drink in a crystal glass, served up on a silver tray. "Anything for you, madam?" she asks.

"Just orange juice, please."

She disappears again.

Tim's usual prickly persona suitably back in place, he continues, "I have to say Ms. Fenwick, you're looking super gorgeous, as ever. If only you were ten years younger."

"Oh give over. Are we still playing that game, Tim?" I turn and eyeball him. "It's never gonna happen. When are you going to get that into your thick noggin?"

"I know." He takes a slow, languorous sip of his drink. "But I still enjoy the game. And I meant what I said, Victoria. I know you've had the most horrific time of late, what with your breakup and … other things."

"Are you referring to my horrific miscarriage in an aeroplane toilet?" I say, dryly. "You know me, never do anything by halves." I make light of the trauma, but the sympathy in Tim's eyes gives away the empathy he feels.

It's four months since I was last on a plane, flying the final leg home from Singapore. On one hand that day seems years ago, and on the other–like it was only yesterday.

He raises his hand to silence me. "Spare me the details, my dear. But since I saw you last you seem different somehow. Stronger, but not in a macho kind of way. You seem to have found a quiet power. Like you've finally connected with your inner secret sauce. The kind of strong femininity that drives all us men mad."

"That's what happens when you finally accept yourself for who you truly are, and instead of looking outward for your inner peace you let all that shit go and accept that other people's stuff is not yours to own."

"Ah-ha? Someone's had a personal epiphany?" He smiles. "And how do you feel now you've seen the light?"

"At peace. So much of *me* makes sense now. The black hole I didn't realise I was carrying has gone. If I'm honest, despite all the crap I've had to handle lately, I feel…" I search for the right word, "…invincible."

"You look it. I'm assuming you've finally realised that *loving yourself first* should always be your top priority. Something I believe I've been trying to tell you for years."

I nod appreciatively as the air stewardess places my drink down in front of me. I take a sip.

Mmmm. Freshly squeezed.

"I'm no psychologist but do you think you tried to fill that hole through all your disastrous choices in men this past decade?"

"Ab-so-lute-ly. I thought after Chris, and then again after Craig, I'd broken the pattern. But although I understood it intellectually, I wasn't congruent. I was still living a lie; hiding parts of me from Gavin, worried that he wouldn't love me if I shared the whole of me. Turns out I was right. When I finally stepped into my power, and showed him all of me, he turned his back—quite literally."

"Hmm. I must say, I had thought Gav was different. He's the only one of your love-interests I've ever approved of."

"So did I. But if he can't accept me for who I am, and the choices and decisions I made long before I met him–all parts of me that make the whole me–then we're not right for each other and I'm not going to denounce any part of me to fit with who he wants me to be. I've played that game too many times, and lost. Anyone would be lucky to love me. Warts and all."

"Hear, hear." Tim chinks his glass against the side of mine. "But do you still love him?"

I suck in a deep breath. "Sure, a part of me is still grieving for the future I envisioned with him, and we both loved each other deeply —that doesn't go away instantly—but on this particular issue we're poles apart, and once it came to light we both knew deep down it wasn't something we could get past. Better to cut our losses now. And thankfully before we've had kids. Although, it was his choice to leave rather than try and work through it. He's not prepared to change his opinion, nevermind apologise for the things he said to me, and he hasn't made any attempts to reconcile with me since he left. Perhaps I didn't mean as much to him as I thought I did. Best we go our separate ways. Get on with our lives. With dignity and our heads held high."

I turn and look out of the airplane window, curling my fist under my chin to rest my head. "I'm not expecting him to make any attempts to reconcile. If he was going to, I think he would have do so by now. The balls in his court. I'm not chasing after him."

We're flying east at sunset so the sun is behind us. Illuminating the black horizon with a soft warm glow. I imprint the image onto the backs of my retinas before softly closing my eyes.

Like all the men before him, Gav has shown his true self through his actions, or lack of action. But rather than hold onto the past, I'm looking forward. Flying into a new chapter and whatever that may bring; I'm open to it.

"Have I ever told you I was adopted?" Tim announces out of nowhere.

"No? Really?!" I turn my head sharply.

"No not really, but I needed to say something to lighten the mood," he laughs.

"Oh Tim, behave." I slap his arm lightly. "You're the worst."

"Yeah. But what would you do without me. Now are you going to finish that orange juice and get a proper drink? We've got a long flight and a full bar to get through."

Chapter 44

The late afternoon sun glints off the water as the plane banks and turns. I look out of the oval window and recall the last time I cast my eyes over these shores. Ten years ago I was running away. Heading home. And now I'm returning... home. Or so a part of me feels.

I watch the sea below as it continues its gentle roll up and down the sandy beach at New Brighton, just as it has done every moment of every day since I last set foot in this land. The crests of the waves glistening like someone has sprinkled them with a million diamonds—just as I remember. The comforting reminder of the perpetual presence of Mother Nature.

When I last left these shores, I was leaving to get away from Chris. Now I am returning, not for him—for Mellie.

Tim squeezes my hand as we're jolted forward, the aircraft bouncing its way to the end of the runway at Christchurch International.

I inhale.

I'm back in Aotearoa. Back in my spiritual home.

All the upheaval and trauma of these past few months seems to evaporate when I exhale. Once again my soul in tune with the land.

Like some ancient Māori energy has begun re-thrumming inside me. Come back alive, as I bring it back to its source.

We taxi towards the terminal and my thoughts turn to Chris. If I'm honest I've hardly stopped thinking about him since his phone call last week.

I can't imagine him *not* wanting to see me. Not when he knows I'm coming all this way.

Am I tingling because I *want* to see him too, or is it because I'm nervous he'll pull me off my newfound centre? That he'll find a way to pull on those invisible heart strings and I'll find myself entangled back inside his web. All these years, my only defence against his attraction has been twelve thousand miles.

Tim and I clear customs and wheel our luggage into the arrivals hall.

"Taxi rank this way," Tim says, reading the airport signs.

"No need," a masculine voice replies.

I look up and it's him … except he's wearing long pants!

I can count on one hand the number of times I've seen Chris in long trousers. At a wedding, or Christmas dinner perhaps, but during our entire relationship he lived in shorts, or perhaps jeans, but only if there was snow on the ground. Today he's in smart slacks, a tailored shirt worn open at the neck. I notice the glint of cufflinks and a Breitling on his right wrist. He wears his watch on his right wrist as it's his *seeing* side. Whenever we were together, unconsciously I always came to his right side. Slept on the right. Sat on the right. It was easier for him.

He looks like he's just stepped off a Forex trading floor, not come from… wherever he's come from. The beach, the pool, some friend's barbecue, smoking weed in the back garden? That's what our lives consisted of before. Not a life that required formal pants.

"Chris! What a pleasant surprise!" Tim says, an edge to his voice.

Tim knows the ultimatum Chris once forced on me, and he's never forgiven him, even if he tolerates him when required to, like the last time the men overlapped—at Mellie and Karl's wedding in Spain.

"We weren't expecting to be chauffeured," Tim says. "How did you find out our arrival details?"

Chris taps the side of his nose with his index finger. "Now that would be telling." He holds out his hand and Tim shakes it. "It seemed the least I could do, both of you having made the long trip here. How could I not extend you some warm Kiwi hospitality?"

I shuffle from foot to foot, unsure of the appropriate way I should greet a once *Great Love* of my life whilst he's posturing with my male companion. In the end it's Chris who makes the decision for me, coming around behind my trolley and pulling me into a bear hug.

"C'mere Goose." He buries his nose in my hair and inhales deeply. "God, it's good to see you Vicky."

I'm knocked backwards by the boorishness of his embrace and the intoxicating masculinity of his scent. A heady mix of musky sweat and manliness, almost exactly as it was twelve years ago when he first walked, uninvited, behind my desk and introduced himself in much the same way; only this time his natural smell is overlaid with an expensive cologne. I inhale notes of sandalwood and patchouli.

Wrapped in his arms, my knees soften and, to my shock, a spark of desire ignites between my legs.

Get a grip, Victoria, you're not a teenager anymore! Still my heart skips a beat and a flush rises up my neck.

As I feared, it's all so familiar.

Comfortable.

Dangerous.

Pressed against him, my nipples tighten and I know I'm in danger of falling. Toppling over that dangerous cliff once more.

Locked in our embrace, time is suspended while the rest of the world moves around us. The sounds of other families and loved ones reuniting swirls through the arrivals hall. The *'over here's'* and shrieks of reunions fill the space with joy and happiness. Chris and I remain silent. Lost in each other's embrace, time bends, and no time has passed since our last embrace. It takes all my inner strength to stop myself from tilting my head and inviting his kiss. That's what I want to do. What my body wants to do.

I close and open my eyes slowly, as I inhale.

Tim coughs in the background. "Errr, shall we?"

Ignoring him, Chris pulls back and looks directly into my eyes. His hands gripping the outsides of my upper arms, he holds me still. Drinking me in.

His face is exactly how I remember it. Deeply tanned. Perhaps a slightly deeper hairline, but his hair is just as thick and wiry, if peppered with a few greys now. He has a three-day growth on his chin, fashionably trimmed and kept neat around his jawline. There's maybe a few more laughter lines around the corner of his eyes, although his face is not laughing now.

There is no pretence on his features. His truth so raw, it almost hurts. It's his eyes! Peeling back my layers and boring into my soul. I'm stripped naked as he *sees all of me.* But then this man is the *only* man who knows *all of me.*

I don't remember his eyes being so multicoloured. Flecks of green and gold nestled inside the soft hazel brown. They look kinder. Wiser than I remember.

He reaches forward and tucks a stray strand of hair behind my ear. A familiar unconscious movement that he has made so many times before, causing a decade to evaporate.

We may not have made love since New Year's Eve in 1995, on a camp bed in the Coromandel during our trip to the North Island (if you discount our shared night of intimacy three years later at Mellie's wedding in 1998, when we shared a bath and a passionate kiss), but anyone observing us now would be forgiven for mistaking us as lovers reuniting.

"It really is so very good to see you, Vicky. I've missed you," he says softly, his voice as smooth as melted chocolate that he has smeared all over my naked body and licked off with his eager tongue.

Within a few days we've gone from friendly banter on an occasional text, to the familiarity of hearing each other's voices again in our phone call last Friday, to the remembered smell of each other's bodies, to the powerful energy of one another's physical attraction. All of which anchors us back to our past and our once-shared passion. I feel magnetised. Paralysed. His sheer physicality rendering me mute, unable to control my own senses, as if the world has opened up and swallowed us both whole.

"Do you want to go to your hotel first and freshen up, or would you like me to take you straight to see Mellie?" Chris says, finally breaking his eye contact with me and turning to Tim.

"As you've kindly come for us, I think we'd like to go straight to see Melanie if that's possible. That is the reason why we're here, after all," he snaps. "Victoria and I were able to shower on the plane."

"Well I suppose that's the benefit of a private jet at your disposal," Chris quips over my shoulder.

"One of the many benefits," Tim replies, dryly.

"Right then. This way." Chris grabs the handles of my trolley and leads us out of the terminal, leaving Tim to catch up behind.

✦

"Hey Mel," I say, gently pushing open her bedroom door an hour later.

The sun is setting outside, casting dying sunbeams across the white walls.

Melanie and Karl's bedroom is on the north side of their two-storey family home in Cashmere, a middle-class suburb to the south of the city, nestled at the foot of the Port Hills. As is usual for many properties in this part of the world, the downstairs is open-plan and surrounded by a large deck that opens onto a north facing-garden and the pool beyond. The master suite benefits from a balcony that extends west over the top of their double garage, offering stunning views of the Port Hills behind, the Southern Alps to the west, and the city laid out below.

Watching through the window on the car journey here, it feels more and more as if I've come home. My body fizzing with energy for the city I once lived in. Of course some things have changed. New out-of-town shopping centres have sprung up along the main artery roads that connect the airport with the city centre, and new houses, clustered together in new estates, have appeared on the outskirts, as the city continues to expand.

Mel is dozing. Her face pale. Contorted with pain even in sleep.

"Mellie." Karl sits on the edge of the bed and pats her hand gently. "You've got some visitors. All the way from England."

Tim and I stand aimlessly in the doorway, waiting for her to open her eyes. When she does her face lights up with a smile.

"Tim. Vicky." She looks at each of us in turn, registering that we're not an apparition and that we are in fact standing in the doorway of her bedroom. "Chris said you were coming. You really didn't have to."

"Are you kidding?" I sit on the opposite side of the bed and stroke her face. "I don't know why the hell you didn't tell me."

"Because I knew if I did, you'd want to come and see me, and it's such a long way."

"Tough tits..." I crumple my mouth; she tries to laugh until the pain stops her. "Sorry, poor choice of words, but it's nice to see you smile."

Tim pulls up a wicker chair from the corner of the room. "So how've you been?"

"Honestly?" She coughs, her lungs rattling. "I've been better. Chemo's a bitch and I've only had the first round."

I glance at her flat chest under her nightgown. An aching reminder of where her breasts should be.

"I'm so sorry, Mel." I reach for her hand.

"Oh don't be, Vicky. When you discover your boobs are trying to kill you, you kinda have a different perspective when you're told they need to be whipped off."

"Still they were a very nice pair," Tim says, "from what I remember. We shall raise a glass tonight in their honour. May your breasts 'Rest in Peace'."

ISABELLA WILES

"A-hem." Karl coughs into his enclosed fist. "I'll go and sort your next round of meds. They're almost due." He heads downstairs where the muffled sound of him and Chris chatting provides a much needed background to the thick silence in Mel's bedroom.

I glance towards Tim, then Mel, then back to Tim again.

Oh my good God!

Watching the way the pair are staring at each other, I suddenly feel like a spare penis at a wedding. An uninvited extra in someone else's love story. They look like how I imagine Chris and I appeared to passers-by in the airport mere hours ago.

How the hell have I not noticed before? All this time. It was Mel. Tim never held a flame for me. It was Mel he was in love with. Holy moly with bananas on top. How the heck did I miss that?

My mind flits back to all the times I've seen them together. All the parties we shared. Even sharing beds... as platonic friends, or so I'd thought.

I blush pink when I remember how I climbed in with them both after his infamous Halloween party in London all those years ago. Believing we were simply a bunch of friends crashing for the night.

At the time he must have thought I was the biggest cock-block ever. But wasn't that around the time she met Karl? I remember her gushing over him when we chatted on the balcony the night before, whereas I remember I was pining for Chris who was stuck back here selling his shipment of cars.

Tim's been with Lydia the whole time Mel and I have known him. And sure Mel met, fell in love with and married Karl, but what the hell has passed between these two!

The pair of flippin' dark horses. Did he refuse to give her up? Or did Mel turn him down? My mind is racing with a myriad of unasked *and* unanswered questions that I shall be digging for over the next few days. Breast cancer or not, she's got some confessing to do.

"Where are you staying?" Mellie asks, directing her question to Tim.

"I've booked a place in town," Tim replies.

"And your mum has offered to put me up," I add.

"I can only stay until the weekend I'm afraid," Tim says, both of them continuing to hold each other's gaze. "I've had to move heaven and earth to fit this slight round-the-world detour into my already packed schedule," he continues, scooching his chair forward so that his knees touch the side of the bed.

"Whereas I'm here for as long as you need me." I throw my arms up in an exaggerated gesture. She turns her attention towards me and smiles. "I've handed over the reins of my business to my very capable team, and I'm staying for as long as it takes to get you better."

"What about Gav?" she asks.

"Ah. Now there's a story." Tim flicks his head in my direction.

"Sadly Gav and I are no more," I say.

"What?! Oh no, Vicky."

I raise my hand. "Don't. It's all fine. I'll tell you the nitty-gritty when you're feeling stronger. Like a lot of things, it was going great... until it wasn't. But his loss is your gain. It means I've got no ties pulling me back to the UK in the short-term. I can stay for at least three months... until immigration kick me out."

"What is it they say... some friends are in your life for a reason, some for a season, and some for a lifetime," she says.

"There was a time in my life, Mel, when you rescued me." I reach for her hand. "More than I think you will ever know. Without you, I'd probably be married to Steve the man-child."

"Oh God. I'd forgotten about him." She laughs and then closes her mouth just as quickly, clasping her hand over her jaw. "Mouth ulcers," she offers as way of explanation.

"Without you, my life would never have gotten started. You were the catalyst for every adventure I've had in the fourteen years since."

"Remember Istanbul?" She raises an eyebrow.

"Do I ever!" An involuntary puff of air snorts out my nose. "That is a weekend I shall never forget!"

"And probably the only one we wish we could. What the hell were we thinking?"

"I know. Complete idiots. But meeting you changed the course of my life. I can still remember you arriving arse first through the office door with a tray of teas in your hand. You were this refreshing effervescent bubble of energy. So full of life."

"Friends forever," she says patting my hand.

I swallow the hard lump in the back of my throat as I compare my memory of that young woman to the person lying in front of me now. The look she gives me tells me she knows what I'm thinking.

Straightening up and patting the back of her hand, I continue, "I'm here to help bring that Mel back. We need that crazy, wild, full of life Mellie back in our lives and I will offer my support in any way I can. Nursing you. Helping out with your kids. Supporting Karl, and your mum. Cleaning your house... even though I absolutely hate cleaning."

"Yes. You were rubbish at that when we lived together. I had to remind you where the washing machine was."

"Yeah. Scrub that. I'll hire someone to clean your house for you."

She goes to laugh but coughs instead. Her lungs making a horrid rattling sound as she loosens whatever is sitting on her chest. Her face contorts with pain.

"Now that sounds more like you," she says through her coughs.

Tim, who's been listening patiently to our exchange, leans forward and strokes a tendril of hair away from her face. I glance from him to her and back again.

"Okay, I think that's enough from me," I say. "Let me go and see if Karl needs any help. Leave you two to catch up. Tim's time is more limited than mine."

Neither of them are listening; both lost in each other's smiles.

I make my way out of the room, closing the door silently behind me.

Well, well, well. Just when you think you know the whole story, I think to myself, smiling and making my way down into the kitchen.

Chapter 45

*W*ithin a few days, my life slips into an easy routine. I settle into one of Mel's mum's guest bedrooms in her California style bungalow on River Road in Richmond, a sweet suburb about twenty minutes' walk from Christchurch city centre along the banks of the meandering River Avon.

'It'll be like old times,' Lynne had said, opening her arms in a welcome embrace when I turned up on her doorstep after that first visit to Mellie's.

'I thought I'd put you in here,' she'd said, opening the door to the guest suite which, along with her own master bedroom, opens directly out onto the deck through a sliding patio door. *'I use Chris's old bedroom as storage now.'*

She doesn't. I've checked. But she'd considerately thought putting me back in the room I once lived in with her youngest son would have been too weird on the already mildly weird scale of the situation I now find myself in. Sharing a house with my ex-almost-mother-in-law.

Just like I used to, I go for a swim or a long walk most mornings. Either walking east along the river to the Queen Elizabeth II Park, before knocking out fifty or so lengths in their pool, or taking a route west along the grassy banks of the gentle river into town, for a morning pot of tea and a croissant.

Lynne has kindly added me onto her car insurance, so once she arrives home I drive over to Mel's in the afternoon and resume my shift in the cycle of her care. Karl is a full-time partner in an accountancy firm downtown, and although his fellow partners have been extremely flexible given his wife's illness, the bulk of Mel's care has fallen to Lynne and me.

Between us, we're juggling the children: Hannah, the eldest, attends the local primary, whilst Sophie goes to kindergarten four days a week. I've gladly taken up the mantle of collecting the children each day from school, making them their tea and helping with homework and bathtime. My practise as an honorary aunt to all my friends' children back in the UK is paying off, and I already adore Mel's two little ankle biters.

Some days I've just sat by Mel's bedside whilst she's slept. Quietly reading a book. Other days I've ferried her to the hospital and waited with her whilst she receives her treatment. Although she's not lost her hair yet, I'm thankful I insisted she went and had her eyebrows tattooed before that moment comes.

'A girl can lose her boobs and her hair, but you'll feel like a new you if you have your eyebrows and your nails done,' we'd sniggered together in the nail bar.

I've been and bought a new PAYG mobile phone. It makes no sense to be racking up international calling charges using my UK mobile when the only people I'm calling are all here in Christchurch. I've slung my Blackberry into the back of the drawer with my passport.

Mel is living in the present, and so am I.

I've put as much distance between my old life and my current circumstances as possible. Helen stays in touch with a weekly update email, and I hold a weekly Skype call with Angela and Clive, where they update me on our client contract delivery and I can answer any questions and give some leadership and direction, but they're handling everything brilliantly in my absence.

I've called my mother, once. Telling her not to worry and that I'm taking some time off to travel and recharge. Always best to keep the details light. The less she knows, the less she has to worry about.

Seven days after I arrived and ten days since I left so abruptly, I know I can't put off the inevitable any longer. Gingerly opening my laptop I ignore the folder marked 'Gav' which is auto catching any emails he might have sent, and instead open a new message. Typing both Nessa and Julie's email addresses into the top, killing two birds with one stone, I type:

Hi Nessa and Julie,

Yes it's me. I am alive and I promise I haven't been abducted by aliens.

I apologise profusely for rushing out on everyone without saying why, but I needed to get away quickly and didn't have the energy for a whole host of tearful goodbyes.

I'm in New Zealand. My old friend Melanie is gravely ill and I've offered my support in helping her recover … that's if she does recover. It's Stage three breast cancer, which is why I haven't copied Becca into this.

Knowing what she went through with her mam, I didn't want her reading this firsthand, but I'm sure you'll find the right words to explain to her why I need to be here for the foreseeable future, and I know she—of all people—will understand.

Mel's had her double-mastectomy and I'm helping her through her chemo, which is pretty shite as I'm sure you can image. With a young family still to raise, it's a tough time for everyone here and I'm really pleased I came as soon as I heard.
However, I wanted to let you know I'm fine. Really good, actually. It seems a change of scene and some different air is good for the soul after all, and of course putting yourself into the service of someone you love.

Please don't worry about me. I promise you I haven't lost my marbles, and I'm not having a nervous breakdown. I'm actually feeling better than I have in a long while. Putting some space between me and everything that's happened this past eighteen months has given me lots of opportunity to reflect on what's truly important in life, and what makes me happy. And right now, despite the sadness of Mel's situation, being here makes me happy.

I don't know when I'll be back. The business seems to be coping well without me so I'll stay as long as I'm useful.
Right now, this feels like home.

To that end, can I ask you both for a massive favour? Can you keep an eye on the house? I've asked Helen to pop in every couple of weeks and pick up the post, and she'll let me know about any bills that need to be paid. But between you two, can you keep the plants watered (or adopt them) and make sure the place stays standing, and most importantly make sure Leo's okay. Mark's welcome to stay there as long as he likes, providing he keeps the place reasonably tidy assuming he hasn't made up with Becca yet. If he has, can either one of you take Leo in?

And can you give all my godchildren a massive hug from their mad aunty Tor. I miss them all terribly and can't wait to see them, and you, again. I will come back, I just don't know when.
Take care my friends. You've all been so good to me all these years and I'm forever grateful.

Much love,

Tor x

P.S I'd appreciate if you didn't share this with Gav.

Even though I've added the postscript, I have no doubt that the grapevine will leak some of this information to Gav. But he lost the right to know anything about me, my life, or my choices the day he walked out.

Sucking in a deep breath I click on the folder marked 'Gav', expecting it to be overflowing with emails begging me to take him back. Apologising for his pig-headedness, saying he's changed his point of view and can we at least *talk about it*. But there's only one lone email titled, 'Collecting my stuff.'

I huff out a puff of air. If anything, his lack of communication only confirms that it was right we went our separate ways. I have no interest in reading anything he's written, especially if it's merely a mundane request to come round so he can collect his suits and the bowl of rose petals his father once gave to his mother.

My own bowl of rose heads is on the opposite side of the chimney breast. A memento from every bunch of flowers or bouquet of roses he's ever given me. I had considered chucking them out, but anticipating he might want to return to the house at some point, and would definitely want to collect his mother's bowl of petals, I've left one conciliatory olive branch for him to find—that's if he looks for it. Our social group is so enmeshed, it would be nice for us to reach a place where we can be friendly towards each other, at least.

Still, it's better if I don't have to be involved in him arranging a time to come round and collect his stuff, so I click the 'Forward' button on the email and write a quick note to Nessa asking if she can take care of this. It makes sense. I assume he's still living at theirs, that's if he hasn't given his tenant notice and moved back into his old flat.

Flopping back in the chair I let out a long sigh. A sigh of both relief and regret.

I've know his opinions ever since he blurted out the reasons for his divorce during our holiday in San Diego, but discovering his unwillingness to listen or empathise with the opposing view, regardless of how painful or unique the circumstances, is a hard pill to swallow. There was a time I really thought Gav was *the one*. Clearly not.

I click 'Send' and press my lips into a thin line

Closing my eyes I lean my head back and long for the day when I can think of him without my gut clenching or my eyes springing with tears.

Still I don't regret my decision. Too many times I've bent my life to fit the whims of my lover. Believed the promises that were made, and the lies that were told.

No more. From now on I own every choice, every mistake, and every decision.

I have no regrets. But I also know I have no more to give.

I've loved and lost three times now, and I don't have it in me to open my heart again. I've enough love locked away to last me a lifetime.

Closing my laptop, I sniff loudly, throw my head back, and stand.

Right, what needs doing next? I think, checking my watch, making sure I'm not late for Mel.

Chapter 46

GAVIN

---

2 days later, Friday 17th November 2006

*W*hat do you mean *she's taking a sabbatical?"* Gav blurts down the phone, screwing his eyes tight shut and nipping the bridge of his nose.

"That's all I can really tell you, Gavin. I'm not even sure I should be sharing this much information with you." Helen pauses. "Now that you're no longer … you know … together."

"I appreciate your loyalty to Victoria, Helen, I really do. But I'm concerned, that's all."

I'm a fucking idiot, is what I am, Gavin thinks to himself. As soon as he heard via Paul, who heard it from Mark, that Vicky had taken off to fuck knows where, he's been beside himself with worry. He should never have stormed out. And he sure as hell should have swallowed his pride and made up with her before now. He was mad, so mad, but not mad enough to throw away the life they'd built together.

"All I can tell you is she sent a company-wide email last Monday saying she's taking some time off, and to forward any urgent emails on to me. She Skyped us all the next day, and again at the beginning of this week."

"And did she say when she's coming back?"

"She told us to be prepared to run without her for six weeks, maybe up to three months."

"Three months?" Gav repeats, dumbfounded.

Where the hell is she? And why the sudden urge to disappear?

"And did she say where she was?"

"Gav, I can't tell you that, she specifically asked us to remain tight-lipped about her whereabouts. But she looked well, if that's what you're worried about."

"Did she?' he asks, his voice softening.

"Yes. She seems really well. Very clear-headed. At least in managing all of us."

"Well at least that's something." Gav releases a long sigh. "One more thing. When you next speak to her it probably wouldn't do any good to let her know about this conversation. I don't want her thinking I'm checking up on her."

"Except that you are," Helen replies, a smile in her voice. "Take care, Gavin."

"And you, Helen."

He hangs up and stares at his phone, wishing the screen would miraculously reveal where she is.

I'm such an idiot, he thinks to himself again. Why the hell didn't I come to my senses sooner?

When Gav had packed his stuff that day, he hadn't intended for them to break up permanently, but he knew they both needed space from one another. To process each other's revelations and decide how they could reconcile their differing beliefs. He'd always believed, at some point, they'd be able to get past this. Now he may never have that chance.

The next day Gav goes with Anth to meet the rest of the lads in the Red Lion for their regular Saturday evening drinks. It's the one chance in the week the men escape the clutches of family life and remind each other what it was like before they had kids and domestic life trumped all else.

Gav is still not comfortable in loud public spaces, but over the years the familiarity of both the crowd and the atmosphere in the Red Lion have eased his social anxiety. Although today the atmosphere between the men is frosty.

"Any news of our Scarlet Pimpernel?" Gav asks after everyone's discussed this week's football scores.

Anth, Mark and Clarky all look down into their respective pints, avoiding Gav's penetrating stare.

"Clearly you all know something I don't... so who's gonna spill first?" Gav glares at each one of them in turn.

The other men shuffle from foot to foot and sup their beers. Anything to divert attention away from them as individuals.

"Come on Clarky, I'm godfather to your son. You owe me an explanation," Gav pushes.

"I'm not sure that's strictly true," Paul replies, a warning tone in his voice.

"But you do know something?"

"*A-hem*," Anth coughs into his closed fist.

"And you, Mark?" Gav turns his attention to the final member of the group. "Are you telling me Becca hasn't heard anything? Come on boys, help me out here."

"She's asked the girls not to say anything to you," Anth says.

"You mean, she's been in touch?"

"She sent an email to Nessa—"

"And Jules," Clarky interjects. "A couple of days ago."

"And then they called Becca," Mark adds.

"So what is it you can't tell me? Why all the secrecy? I only want to know where she's gone and why she felt the need to take a sabbatical, and at such short notice. It's so out of character. I'm worried about her."

"It's not so much a secret, more that she feels you don't have the right to know where she is," Anth says, looking down at his feet.

"But that's ridiculous. We have so much history, and… I still love her."

Clarky rolls his lips inwards, pressing them together. "I'm not sure she feels the same way anymore."

Gav falls silent. Shocked at Clarky's revelation.

She can't possibly have stopped loving me already. It's only been six weeks. A love like ours doesn't die that quickly.

Anth, Clarky and Mark look to one another. Telepathically deciding how much to share.

"I'm sorry, but I can't *not* say this," Clarky continues. "I know you're hurting mate, and we're here for you, but after what you said, what did you expect?"

Gav continues to look down at his feet.

"I can only give you my opinion, but as a man I don't believe we have any right to judge any woman for her decision to have or not have a child. And regardless of what she did or didn't do, I think you broke your relationship the moment you judged her."

"You don't know what you're talking about, Paul," Gav hisses.

"I don't know your side of the story, I only know what Vicky's told us, but she told me and Jules what happened at the fertility clinic, what happened to her a decade ago, what you said when you found out, and also what your ex-wife did to you."

Gav looks up and meets Clarky's gaze.

"I know she's had an abortion," Clarky continues, "and from what she's shared, I know you have very strong feelings on the subject; but surely you can't believe what you said?"

"I thought I did," Gav sighs. "But then I never thought the woman I love, who I wanted to spend the rest of my life with, who I wanted to become the mother of my children, would turn out to be one of those people."

"Jeez, *those people*," Mark says, shaking his head. "Mate, I gotta call you out on this. You're being an absolute dickhead. When my Becca fell pregnant, we were both in shock… and terrified. We were so young. Neither of us knew what was for the best. Eventually, she decided she wanted to keep it, and of course I supported that. But equally if she'd decided she wanted to terminate—for any reason—I would have supported her decision just as much. It's a woman's right to choose. End of."

"Mark's right," Anth says. "I appreciate what your ex did to you was despicable, Gav. But it doesn't change the fact a woman has the right to decide what happens to their body."

"What? You know as well?"

"We all know," Mark and Clarky say together.

"I don't think you know this," Anth says, "but Nessa's had an abortion as well. And it was awful. We were super young. In our first year at uni. She had an ectopic pregnancy and almost died."

"But that's different," Gav says. "She clearly wanted to keep the baby and couldn't. Vicky voluntarily got rid of a child. And I can't seem to understand how, regardless of the circumstances, that's okay."

"It's irrelevant," Anth adds with a shake of his head. "And you're wrong. Even if it hadn't been ectopic, she wasn't sure what she wanted to do. Just like Vicky, she knew she wasn't ready. And until science can find a way to grow babies in artificial wombs, like Mark and Clarky have both said: as much as it might hurt us we cannot and should not take the right to know what's best for woman away from them. This is two thousand and six, not the nineteen fifties. You're waaaay out of touch."

"And personally, I don't know how you feel justified to judge Tor," Mark says.

"Without having any compassion for the circumstances or reasons why, I might add," Clarky says, grabbing Gav's shoulder and giving it a supportive but firm squeeze. "I get that it was shock to find out Tor kept something as monumental as that from you... I'd be gutted if Jules had kept something like that from me. But you've got to ask yourself, *why* she didn't confide in you."

Gav looks to each of the men in turn. "You all share this sentiment?"

Mark shrugs. "Dude. I might be a short-arsed meathead at times but there's no other way to say this... you fucked up."

"Big style," Clarky agrees.

"If you want her back, before you even think about any grand gestures or anything, I think you need to re-examine some of your own beliefs," Anth says.

"Otherwise she'll only push you away," Clarky adds.

"Of course everyone's entitled to their own opinion," Mark says, "but on this one, mate, you're wrong. You're the one who needs to change, not her."

Gav looks at each of his mates in turn. They all return his gaze with compassionate but steely stares.

How could I have got it so wrong? he thinks to himself. I've always believed that abortion was wrong, or at least, taking that choice away from the father was wrong.

Anth checks his watch, then necks his pint. "If you want a lift back to ours, we need to go now. I promised Ness I'd be home for bathtime."

Still reeling from the opinions of his closest friends, Gav finishes his pint. "Coming," he says quietly. "I think it's time I called it a night. Clearly I've got some thinking to do."

Placing his empty glass back on the bar, giving the barmaid a cursory nod, he follows Anth outside into the car park, his head swirling with questions.

Was I wrong to judge her? I didn't realise I had, until Mark pointed it out.

And as if he's just been plugged into the mains, a thunderbolt of clarity surges through him.

Is it possible the pain Samantha caused me has clouded my judgement? I felt so helpless and inconsequential when I found out, is it possible I redirected my anger as a way of regaining a modicum of control over a situation I could, and should, never influence?

"Shit!" Gav mutters under his breath as they arrive back at Anth's and he realises how wrong he's been.

Chapter 47

VICTORIA

Saturday 18th November 2006

*T*oday is a good day. Mel is feeling slightly stronger, so I've brought her up to Victoria Park for some air. It's a balmy twenty degrees today and spring is transforming into summer. The scrubland all around is covered in a deep, rich green carpet, and the Karma shrubs are covered in their distinct bright orange berries.

She sits on a wooden bench and I take the seat next to her.

I suck in a deep breath. "It's so good to be outside. I don't know about you, but I'm tired of the smell of bleach, disinfectant … and death. No offence."

"None taken. You're right. Death has a very distinct smell."

"Mel, you are *not* dying. Well, actually we're all dying, we just don't know when… and I can tell you… it's not your time. You're going to beat this bastard disease and live a long and happy life."

"I wish I had your optimism. Everyone keeps telling me I've done nothing to deserve this. That I'm just unlucky, but I can't help wondering if there was something I could have done to prevent it … or even if I have done something to deserve it."

I go quiet, before reassuring her. "Stop that now and get those thoughts out of your head. You did nothing to deserve this, but I do know what you mean. We like to think the universe makes random choices ... but when you get to our age you can't help but wonder about the 'what ifs' of life, and trust me, I've got a canny few of those up my sleeve."

She looks out at the vista that falls away below us. Christchurch Central Business District laid out in the valley at our feet.

"It was hard saying goodbye to Tim." She dips her head.

Although neither of them have said so, they both know it might be the last time.

"Yeah, what was all that about? I've never felt more like a spare penis at a wedding than when I was standing in the corner of your bedroom when we first arrived."

She turns to me and *humphs* a small laugh. "It was never common knowledge, but, well... you know."

I turn to her, my mouth wide open. "No, you never! You dark horse. Okay... I *neeeeeed* details."

"Oh, it's far too long and complicated to worry about now. It was a long time ago. Before I met Karl. But you remember that farmer guy I dated?"

"Yeah, what was his name?"

"Tom," she reminds me.

"It was around that time that it happened. All very complicated. Tim and I have known each other forever, and although there's always been lots of flirtation—right from when I first lodged with him, but he wasn't long divorced back then and I didn't want to be his rebound—I made sure my knickers stayed well and truly on. Plus, I liked the game. Tim is the ultimate at cat and mouse."

"Is he?" I reply, knowing fine well he is. Tim is the biggest flirt I know, and there's been more than one occasion I've questioned his intentions. Sharing a hammock, or around the fire pit in The Cayman Islands, or dancing with him at Mel's wedding just some examples where if I'd allowed him, I'm sure he would have taken our flirtations to the next level. But emotionally, I've always viewed Tim as a big brother. A non-family family member who loves you deeply but delivers that affection with a side order of sarcasm.

"So what happened?" I ask.

"It tickled along for a while, but he was on-again, off-again with Lydia and I was on-again, off-again with Tom. In the end there were just too many barriers to make it work. Then Karl appeared on the scene and I broke it off. I think I broke his heart though, and he's never really gotten over it."

"A bit like Chris with me."

"Exactly like Chris with you." She glances sideways at me.

She's observed her brother's heartbreak at close range, so she would know.

"He says she's the one who won't commit, but do you think that's why Tim's never married Lydia? Because you're the Great Lost Love of his life?"

"Who knows?" She shrugs. "It's ancient history really. We agreed a long time ago that we would remain friends, and we've never crossed that line since. Still, it was really lovely of him to fly down here and see me."

"Thank goodness he did. I appreciated the lift!"

The smell of roasted vegetables and sizzling meat greets us when we arrive back at the house. Chris has come over and is helping Karl with the barbecue. The girls are bouncing on the trampoline, shrieking every time they successfully complete an airborne front roll.

"Something smells good. What's for tea?" Melanie asks.

"Steak for us, and chicken strips for the kids," Chris replies. "Figured we need to get as much iron into you as possible, sis." He steps forward and kisses his sister on the cheek.

"The chef's pinny suits you, Chris," I tease, his hairy legs protruding from under the picture of a bikini-clad sexy woman.

Chris twirls a tea towel around and around, before flicking it at me, catching me on the thigh like a whip. "We'll have less of that cheek out of you, Vicky," he says, his eyes dancing as I shriek and turn on the spot. "Now if I remember correctly, you like your steak medium-well done. Yes?"

I nod in reply.

"Some things you never forget," he replies knowingly.

"I think I'll go for a little lie-down," Mel announces. "I seem to have run out of puff."

"Do you want me to come with you?" I ask, the light-hearted mood of moments earlier replaced by a more sombre one as we all remember the disease that's ravaging her body.

"No. I'm fine. Give me a shout when dinner's ready," she replies.

"Girls," Karl shouts to his daughters, "help Aunty Vicky set the table please."

"Are we eating outside tonight?" I ask.

"Might as well. It's warm enough," Karl replies.

I busy myself with the children, setting the place mats and preparing the drinks.

Once we've polished off our delicious meal—I'd forgotten how healthily I eat when I'm in New Zealand, it's easier somehow—the children help me clear the plates away and I do the dishes.

"I'd better get them into the bath," Karl says as Chris and I prepare to leave.

"Okay, no worries. I'll see you tomorrow."

"That's okay, Vicky. Take the rest of the weekend off. You've been amazing, but I'm here. The same goes for next weekend. Take some time to yourself."

"I understand and I will," I say, hugging him.

I know it's as important for him to create as many memories with his wife and children as he can in the time they have left. I would be an unwelcome addition to their precious family time.

"Do you want me to give you a lift home?" Chris asks.

Lynne dropped me off earlier, and I was planning to call a taxi to take me home.

"No. I'll be fine. I'll call a cab. You'd have to go out of your way to drop me at your mum's before heading back out to Sumner."

Chris has settled in the coastal suburb of Sumner, south-east of the city, having purchased a stunning clifftop home, which Mel has told me has jaw-dropping views out over the Pacific.

"Don't be daft, ya old Goose. I'd have you home before a taxi gets here."

"Okay then. If you don't mind." Turning back towards the family, I hug each of the girls in turn. "See you all in a few days." I stroke their long blonde manes and plant big fat kisses on each of their cheeks.

"Bye Aunty Vicky," they chime in turn.

"Bye," Karl says, leaning against the front door frame. "And thanks for everything," he adds as Chris and I head to the car, waving our goodbyes.

Once inside Chris's black BMW M5, he turns to me and asks, "Do you really want to go home? Or do you fancy doing something else instead?"

"Why, what did you have in mind?"

Since arriving back in New Zealand two weeks ago, Chris and I have fallen into an easy friendship, the kind you only have with someone who knows you inside out. Our banter is playful, our body language in sync, but I'm conscious about maintaining safe boundaries. Holding firm to that fine line etched in the sand that stops us falling into dangerous territory. All it would take is one swoosh of a wave to wipe it away.

Despite this, being around him feels so familiar and easy. His energy as attractive and dangerous to me as it's always been.

"It's a surprise." He glances sideways at me.

This is the first time we've been alone since being back here. I've managed to ensure we're always around other people. Mel, Karl, the girls, or his mum. And for good reason. His physical presence is wrapping all around me in the confined space inside his car and the air feels charged with the crackle of electricity.

"Oh here we go!" I laugh nervously. "Another one of your famous wild goose chases."

"But haven't I always come up trumps?"

He leans over and squeezes my knee, sending a jolt of energy through my body. Heat pools in my stomach before sinking down to between my legs.

Fuck! Keep it together, I say to myself. Chris is a friend. Nothing more.

"It's your choice," he continues. "Say the word and I'll take you straight home and put you to bed." He raises one eyebrow in my direction. "Or we could live a little. Have an adventure. Even if only for an hour. If Mellie's disease has taught us all anything, it's that life is precious and you should grasp every opportunity that comes your way."

I stretch out in the passenger seat, throwing my arms over my head. "Chris. The way the world is at the moment, you couldn't be more right." I point my index finger in his direction. "No funny business mind."

"I promise. No funny business."

"Okay then. But the last time you said that… we ended up in a bath together."

"But wasn't it good?" He squeezes my knee a second time.

I turn and shake my head. "Chris, you're insufferable."

He turns the car away from the city and heads south into the hills. "Close your eyes. I'll tell you when to open them."

Feeling relaxed, I do as he says.

The car twists and turns as we wind our way up into the hills. Chris tunes the radio to a station playing smooth drive time, and the dulcet tones wrap around me like a warm hug. James Blunt singing

"You're Beautiful" combined with the motion of the car lulls me into a light sleep.

It's so luxurious to have no schedule, no one to answer to, no one pestering me on email or text. No one waiting for me at home. Right now I don't know where we're going and I don't care. Chris is chauffeuring me and I can't remember the last time I consciously relinquished even the tiniest bit of control. It's remarkably freeing.

My old life was so structured. So pressured. Everything on the clock. Everything minuted, figuratively and literally. When I think back to when I was trying to get pregnant, I was relentless. Wanting to force the stars to align. To control the uncontrollable. Obsessed with spreadsheets, charts, and forecasts.

I've learnt the harder I push for what I want—the storybook endings to all my loves, a happy marriage, a loving husband, a babe to hold in my arms—the more the universe has different ideas. Just when things seemed within my grasp, they were cruelly ripped away, time and time again.

I can't control the stars. They will line up in the way they're destined to and no matter how much I try, there's nothing I can do to change that. It's time for me to recognise that some things in life I have to *let be.*

I let out a long exhale.

Reclining in the car, listening to the music with no idea of our destination, or our timescale, for the first time in a long while I'm free of my self-imposed confines.

I've surrendered. And it's liberating.

"Now," Chris says as I feel the car turn a sharp bend. "Open your eyes, Vicky."

I do… and gasp.

Laid out before us is the expanse of Lyttelton Harbour, or to use its Māori name, Whakaraupō Harbour. Formed from a collapsed volcanic crater, one of two that form the Banks Peninsula to the south of Christchurch.

Chris pulls the car over and the tyres crunch on the side of the road. He's driven us over the summit of the Port Hills and has stopped in a lay-by on the side of Dryer's Pass Road. Below us the turquoise waters of Governors Bay, a smaller inlet of the huge expanse of water, sparkle and glisten in the hazy evening sun. My eyes follow the ripples out into the expanse of Lyttelton Harbour and then the Pacific beyond.

Instinctively I step out of the car, and Chris walks around the back and comes to stand beside me. His hands thrust deeply into the pockets of his cargo shorts.

"Oh, Chris. It's so beautiful."

"I know. I forget sometimes. But I remembered how much you loved this view the first time you saw it."

"I remember too. We were on our way back from Akaroa, across on the other side. Parked up somewhere over there I think." I point to the other side of the bay.

The sight of this view brings my past slamming into my present as violently as if someone has hit me square in the middle of my chest. I stumble a few steps back and Chris, a hand out of his pocket, reaches for mine to hold. Steadying me. Holding me still. His touch as familiar as it first was twelve years ago. And just as it did when he reached for my hand to hold in between the seats of the darkened cinema as we watched *Four Weddings and a Funeral* as part of his oldest sister Michelle's thirtieth birthday celebrations, the spark of electricity that shoots through me causes the air around us to crackle and fizz.

I don't pull away, and with a sense of ominous foreboding I watch the metaphorical line in the sand being slowly washed away. I'm no longer a grieving, battle-weary thirty-six-year-old woman; I'm once again a young, naive twenty-three-year-old, in danger of giving in to the magnetism and powerful pull the man standing next to me has always had. Yet the comfort and familiarity I feel through our intertwined fingers overrides any desire to withdraw.

His eyes gazing straight ahead, I sense he feels the same as he says quietly, "We were so in love back then."

"Were we? Or were we just in lust, Chris?"

"Lust fades. Love lasts." His voice cracks slightly and he tries to cover it over with a fake cough into his fisted hand.

"If we really did love each other, how come we kept hurting each other so badly?" I turn to look at him, my eyes pleading.

He sucks in a deep breath and comes to stand behind me, wrapping his arms around my waist and resting his chin on my shoulder.

"Not a day goes by when I don't go back over every mistake I made... or wish I could turn the clock back. Make it all right."

"It wasn't all you, Chris. We were young. *So young.* Immature. Inexperienced. We've both grown up since then. I made mistakes too."

"Perhaps. But some of mine were unforgivable. I don't blame you for leaving me. I just wish I'd got to you before you finally left the country."

He drops a light kiss onto my shoulder, and a ripple of desire dances across my skin.

"Even if you had, Chris, I still don't think things would have worked between us. Not long-term. We had too many other issues. Not least that your life was here, and as much as I love this country, I was completely reliant on you. I would have had to give up everything to stay here. The gap between us was simply too wide —literally."

He gives my waist a squeeze and I hear him suck in a deep breath.

"Maybe. Maybe not. But I suppose now we'll never know."

"Still, I'm happy that we're here now." I pat one of the hands he has wrapped around my waist. "I like having you as a friend."

Who the fuck am I kidding! Chris will always want more from me than I'm either willing or capable of giving him.

We stand in silence before he announces, "Come on. I'll take you home. We can go back via the tunnel. It'll be quicker."

"Okay." I turn and smile.

He holds my gaze and we stand staring into each other's eyes. Watching as a lifetime of regret and memories, some joyful but most painful, pass between us. I notice the slight rise in his complexion, the tips of his ears turning pink, his one seeing eye, its pupil dilating, and I feel his energy stilling.

Our faces only inches apart, we continue to gaze at each other. Both suspended in time. Like the moment before two lovers kiss. Each of us longing to find comfort in the lips of the other, but I know if I cross that boundary where it will lead… back to the past. Yet neither one of us wants to be the first to pull away.

Our bodies draw ever closer. Like magnets unable to resist the unconscious force that pulls them together. I hold my breath. Anticipating the soft, sensual touch of his soft yet firm lips on mine, but just when I think he'll lean his face towards mine and kiss me, he sucks in an urgent breath and pulls back.

Business-like, he steps back and stands by the car, holding the door open for me. My body feels the immediate loss. Wobbling and unsteady, like being thrust out into the cold and being slapped by a harsh wind. I let go of the air in my lungs, force a smile on my lips and climb back inside the car.

Indicating, he turns the car left, rejoining the I-74, and turns into the tunnel that cuts through the hillside from Lyttelton Port to Christchurch. I blink as my eyes adjust to the artificial strip lights inside the tunnel, but twenty minutes after leaving the viewpoint, we pull up outside his mother's house.

"What do you have planned next weekend, now that you're relieved of Mellie duties?" he asks.

Laughing, I reply, "I notice you didn't ask, *'Are you doing anything next weekend?'*"

"You know me so well, Vicky."

"So tell me, Chris. What *are* we doing next weekend?" I say, smirking. "I'm assuming, the fact you're even asking me means your son doesn't need you? You've not told me anything about him. Why all the secrecy?"

When I'd landed back in New Zealand, I'd assumed Chris was still with the mother of his child, and although Mel seems reluctant to share any of the details, she's told me they're not together anymore

"A conversation for another day," he says dodging the question. "I thought we could take a trip to Hanmer Springs. Have a soak in the hot pools. You know it's one of my favourite places."

"Shame. I was planning to stay in and wash my hair."

"Bollocks. Saturday morning. 8:00 a.m. Be ready… and Vicky?"

"Yes, Chris?"

"Remember your togs. Unless you'd rather skinny-dip," he adds, leaning over my lap to pull on the passenger door handle from the inside.

"A-hem," I fake cough before slapping his hand away and climbing out of the car. Turning around, I lean back in through the open window. "No chance."

"Aww shame," he replies, smiling.

A ripple of nervous anticipation rolls through me.

Jesus Victoria. Control yourself.

"Thanks for the lift, and the nice drive. Sleep well, Chris, and I'll see you next Saturday if not before," I say, before letting myself into the house.

Leaning back against the closed front door, I slide to the floor and hug my knees.

It'll be fine, I tell myself. I'm not some silly schoolgirl incapable of any self-control. I'm a grown woman who's learnt from her past, and whatever happens I won't let history repeat itself.

Chapter 48

GAVIN

Still Saturday 18th November 2006

North-East England

*G*av is more than grateful to Nessa and Anth for allowing him to stay while he waits for his tenant's lease to run out on his flat so he can move back in there. It's also given the two men the opportunity to refine their business plan, which they've submitted to the bank. They're now waiting for confirmation of their start-up loan, both of them having put their respective properties up for collateral.

"Can I do anything to help?" Gav asks as Nessa cooks them all tea.

"No you're fine," Nessa replies brightly, but Gav hears the unasked question: *'How many more weeks before you move back into your flat?'* He senses their open invitation is fast approaching its sell-by date. "But judging from the chaos upstairs, Anth might want some help with the twins," Nessa says.

Taking the hint, Gav follows the cacophony of laughter emanating from the bathroom. Pushing the door open, Anth is sitting cross-legged on the bath mat, while Ethan and Emily are in the tub, covered in bubbles.

"We're p'aying tennisth," Ethan lisps.

Each toddler has their chubby fingers wrapped around the neck of an empty shampoo bottle as they bat a rubber duck back and forth between them.

"Who's winning?" Gav asks.

"Me," Ethan replies.

"No. Meeeeeeee," Emily shrieks.

"NO. MEEEEEEEE!" Ethan shrieks even louder, and Emily starts to cry.

"Thanks for that," Anth says, rolling his eyes. He spends most of his life refereeing his competitive offspring.

"Well, as umpire I have the honourable pleasure of declaring you both winners," Gav says.

"What do we win?" Emily asks, flashing Gav a toothy grin.

"A cuddle and a bedtime story?"

"Perfect," Anth says, gathering towels ready to dry his children. "Who wants Uncle Gav to dry them off?"

"Meeeeeeeee," both children say in unison.

"Thanks for that," Gav laughs, repeating Anth's words from moments ago. "How about we do half and half then swap?" he suggests.

"Story of my life," Anth replies. "Splitting myself down the middle for these two." He lifts Emily out of the bath, her bright red hair slick down her back, and passes her to Gav who has a towel ready.

Later, once the children have been put to bed and the dinner plates cleared away, Anth pulls a couple of bottles of Bud from the fridge, looks towards Gav who nods his agreement, and passes him one. Nessa rejoins them around the kitchen table, her hands wrapped around a fresh cup of tea.

"You're so lucky," Gav says. "Your children are perfect."

"Sometimes," Nessa says, one eyebrow raised. "I can't deny there are days I will to be over, only so I can sit down with a cuppa without a constant chorus of *Mam, Mam, Mam,* in the background."

"I know they're hard work, but I can see how happy you all are. The older they get, the more they look like you."

"Like Nessa maybe," Anth says.

Gav cocks his head as Anth continues, "It would be remarkable if they grew up and looked like me, when they're not biologically mine."

"What?!" Gav turns his head sharply towards Anth.

"You know how hard it was for us to conceive," Nessa says.

"Not really. Vicky told me little bits but all I really know is you had them via IVF. I've always assumed they were yours. I mean, Emily's hair is the double of yours," Gav says, looking towards Nessa.

"True, and they are from Emily's eggs, just not my sperm," Anth says. "After Nessa had the ectopic pregnancy and lost one of her tubes, it became doubly hard to conceive."

"Then Anth's had a couple of varicoceles in the decade since, which have lowered his sperm production."

"Yup, my soldiers can't make it out of the barracks, or the few that do seem to be two-headed mutants."

"So after years of trying and failing to get pregnant they gave us two options. ICSI was the first."

"Intra-cytoplasmic sperm injection," Anth clarifies. "It's when they take one of my swimmers and inject it directly into one of Nessa's eggs, before re-implementing it back into Nessa's womb."

"But it only has between a fifty to eighty percent chance that the egg will even be fertilised. And as we'd only been able to harvest three viable eggs from me, the other option was to use a sperm donor. Which is what we decided to do."

Gav sits back in his chair. His mouth falling open. "I had no idea. You've never said."

"It's not something we've broadcast," Nessa continues. "Not because we're ashamed or anything, but because it's not a big deal.

To us at least. Anth's name is on their birth certificate, and as far as we're concerned, he's their father."

"We'll tell them one day, when it's appropriate," Anth says easily. "But it doesn't define my relationship with them. As far as I'm concerned, they're my kids."

"But…" Gav struggles to find the words. "I can't think of a politically correct way to say this without sounding like a twat."

"Just say it," Nessa says, offering him an encouraging smile. "No judgement here."

"Doesn't it affect how you feel about them?" Gav asks, looking directly at Anth.

Anth crumples his brow. "No?"

"Sorry, it seems all my beliefs around family and fertility are questionable. I'm just trying to understand."

"Love is not defined by genetics," Anth adds. "Ness and I wanted a family. This was the best way for us to bring children into the world. It didn't matter how our family was formed, what matters is the love we have for each other."

"I guess. And I have heard people who adopt, and like you guys, use sperm donors, or surrogates, or whatever, say they don't feel any different, even if they've got biological children as well. I've just always believed I wouldn't love a child as much if it wasn't biologically my own. That's what I've always wanted. A child that was half mine and half Vicky's."

"Sometimes, Gav, life doesn't give you what you want, it gives you what you need," Nessa says, her eyes soft with sympathy. "Maybe you need to be open to that possibility and you'll find you make a family in a way you weren't expecting."

"Which if I don't find out where Vicky's gone, and make a plan to win her back, is never likely to happen."

"Maybe Tor needed to boot you out—"

"To be fair, it was me who left. I'm sure if I hadn't stormed out, she would have sat me down and given me a right talking to."

"Perhaps, but maybe you needed to have this time apart for you both to reflect on what's truly important and what you really want out of life."

"I think you're right, Nessa. I've been a complete idiot. But if I don't know where she is, how the hell can I win her back?"

Nessa looks from Gav, to Anth, then back to Gav. Anth gives his wife a little nod and Nessa sucks in a long breath, pressing her lips into a thin line. "She's in New Zealand, Gavin."

Gav plonks his beer down on the hard table with such force the liquid inside foams and bubbles over the neck of the bottle. His anger as volatile as the oozing liquid inside.

"Tell me that's not true," Gav says, his gaze flicking between Nessa and Anth. When neither of them respond, Gav pushes his chair back, its legs scraping loudly, and paces around the room, his hand rubbing the back of his neck. "I'm such a fucking idiot. I always knew she'd go back to him eventually. I told you, didn't I?" He points his finger in Anth's direction. "That evening in Keswick, in the Dog and Gun, they'd been back in touch. I asked you your opinion and you said to *trust her.*"

"Whoa there, tiger. I think you're jumping to some massive conclusions," Nessa says, her tone more firm than a few moments earlier.

"I know he still loves her." Gav throws his hands up in exasperation. "And now I'm out of the picture, it's clear she feels the same way. Why else would she go scuttling back to New Zealand at the first opportunity?"

"To look after her dying friend," Nessa cuts in.

Gav stops dead in his tracks.

"Yes, Gav. She hasn't gone running back to Chris. Mel's really poorly. Stage three breast cancer. The minute she heard, she packed her bags and flew straight over there. If anything, her actions show her integrity and loyalty to those she loves."

Gav flops back down in his chair and runs his hands through his hair.

How could he have got it so wrong? Again?

This is all my fault, he thinks to himself. All of it. The reason she's over there without me has nothing to do with Chris, and everything to do with me.

Gav stares out of the kitchen window at the cold November rain. A tumble of revelations crumbling around him.

Everything he once thought was true and right appears to be all wrong.

Nessa leans forward and reaches for Gav's hand. "We all know you loved Tor. Clearly love her still, but maybe you should take some time to figure out why you've jumped to all these conclusions."

I don't need time, Gav thinks to himself. I know exactly what I need: I need her back.

"I've been a complete and utter idiot. I'm the one that's got it all wrong. She's not to blame for any of this."

"Except perhaps for not telling you about her past."

"But like Clarky said, I need to own a part of that as well. If I hadn't been such an arse before she flew to San Diego she wouldn't have felt the need to call Chris instead of me. I was grieving, wrapped up in my own little bubble. That first miscarriage brought it all back. How much it hurt when Samantha told me what she'd done. And all the while Vicky was reliving her own pain from her past and I didn't notice. If I wasn't there for her, of course she'd want to speak to someone who could relate to what she was going through, and Chris was the natural choice. Then, like the idiot I am, I flew off the handle when I found out. She'd done nothing to warrant my mistrust, but that was the first mistake I made. There's no way she'd want to tell me the full story when I'd inadvertently already labelled her."

"Well, you know the fastest way to break rapport," Nessa says, "is to judge someone."

"So I'm fast learning. I thought loving each other was enough. I didn't realise how hard it would be to accept the person she used to be, as well as the person she is now."

"But the people we all are now are merely the healed versions of the people we once were," Anth says.

ISABELLA WILES

"Assuming we heal, of course, and don't hold onto our pain," Nessa says.

"And I thought I knew everything she'd been through, but it appears not," Gav says.

"A woman's soul is a very deep vessel. You may never reach the bottom," Nessa adds.

Gav drops his head in his hands. "I wish I'd known about your family struggles sooner," he says, letting out a long sigh. "When it became clear she was struggling to carry a pregnancy to term, she tried to talk to me about adoption, or even surrogacy, and I placed impossible conditions on that as well."

"Let me guess. You told her you couldn't love a child if it hadn't come from your knackers," Anth says.

"I didn't put it quite like that. But yes, words to that effect." Gav snorts out a laugh. "God, I'm such an idiot."

"What are you going to do?" Nessa asks.

"I'm not sure. Even if I was to jump on a plane and rush over there, I'm not sure that's what she'd want. She might see it as another example of me not trusting her."

"Or she could see it as a grand romantic gesture," Nessa counters.

"Hmm, maybe. But if she's gone to support Mel, the last thing she needs is me rocking up on her doorstep, unloading all my regret and apology on her."

"If that's what you think," Anth says.

"I do need to pop back to the house, though. I have some paperwork in the office I need to get, and I could do with picking up some more shirts. I assume that's okay?" Gav asks Nessa, appreciating that both she and Julie have been appointed unofficial guardians of what remains of Vicky's life over here.

"Of course. She forwarded me your email. Go in the morning. Use my key."

The following morning, Gav unlocks the back door of the house he once called his home. It's the first time he's been back inside since he left in such a fury of misplaced anger and rage.

He glances around the kitchen; everything looks as it was. With the exception of Leo's missing bowls and litter tray. Mark and Becca have temporarily taken him in, now they've made up and Mark's moved back home.

Gav moves through the kitchen as if it were a crime scene. Not wanting to displace anything, or touch anything that is no longer his.

His eyes glance over the flyers and postcards pinned to the fridge, and that's when he notices.

Peanut's scan. It's gone.

He has to resist the urge to bend double, the sucker punch in his stomach as visceral as a physical blow. He checks in the living room, and the framed scan has also vanished. He knows she won't have destroyed it, and has taken them with her.

He's sure if he was to rummage through her dressing table he'd find the collection of positive pregnancy sticks would also be missing.

The only reminder of the other babies that never were.

Drifting from room to room, he looks at everything as if for the first time. He'd half expected her to destroy all evidence of him, but the house looks exactly as he remembers it. His books are still on the bookshelf. His DVDs of Liverpool's FA Cup wins and last year's Champions League win still tucked into the nook next to the TV.

He breathes a sigh of relief when he sees the crystal bowl of dried rose heads his tad gave to his mam over her lifetime. He knew she'd never throw them out, but his gut settles when he sees the reminder of his long-departed family still being respected.

Walking through the room, he plumps the cushions even though they don't need straightening. His fingers trailing across the light blue and cream damask silk.

I never noticed the texture or detail of them before, he thinks. That's the thing about true beauty, you often only appreciate it after it's gone.

It's the little things he misses the most. The vibrant emerald green of her eyes. The way she never sneezes only once, instead her sneezes come in quick succession, building into one enormous *Atchooooo*. Or the way she makes everyone else feel instantly at ease. Or the tiny details she remembers about everyone she meets. He's often said she has a memory like an elephant.

At night when he closes his eyes he can still smell the scent of fresh, clean strawberries in her hair. Or the rich oriental smell of Coco Channel on her skin. He yearns for the nights they would lie under the covers and hold hands as they fell asleep. A simple, intimate gesture: *I'm here for you.*

Except he wasn't, and now he's paying the price.

Gav tenderly touches a petal from his mother's rose bowl, its delicate and dry structure disintegrating between his thumb and forefinger.

His eyes gazing along the marble mantle above the fireplace, that connects the two sides of the chimney breast, he notices four white candles. Their glass encasements each engraved with swirling gold lettering. He leans in closer, deciphering the letters.

He catches his breath when he realises each candle is printed with the dates of conception and loss of each of her pregnancies.

Slowly he rolls his finger over the lettering of each of the candles in turn, before picking up and holding in his palm the candle set to the left. The one representing the baby she lost before he knew her. Yet, cradling it in his palms and looking down lovingly at the memorial she's created for that unborn soul, he feels no different than when he acknowledges the other mementos for the babies that were biologically his.

Anth was right. Your love for a child is not tied to their genetics.

Gently replacing the candle above the fireplace, his eyes travel over the rest of the pictures and ornaments, landing eventually on the crystal bowl on the other side of the chimney breast. It has some way to go to reach the same level as his mother's bowl, but it still contains a dried rose head from every bouquet of flowers he's ever given her. He'd half expected to find it empty and is secretly relieved when it isn't.

Next to the bowl is a brown leather journal that was never there before. Leaning in for a closer look, he wonders if it's Vicky's personal journal.

Over the years he's seen journals and notebooks around the place. Sometimes on her bedside table. Sometimes underneath a wooden ballerina-engraved keepsake box she keeps in the bottom of her wardrobe. He can't ever remember seeing her write in it.

Leaning in closer, he's reluctant to touch it, feeling as if picking it up would be an invasion of her privacy, but placed on top is a sealed envelope, and on top of that, the diamond earrings he gave her. His alternative to an engagement ring.

Either she's left them behind on purpose as she didn't want to take any part of him with her to New Zealand, or she left them as a clue for him to find.

He picks up the earrings, closing his hand to make a fist around them, and squeezes his eyes tight shut. He still remembers holding onto them, all through the hurricane, and knowing he wanted to give them to her the moment they were reunited as a sign of his commitment to her. It was in that moment they'd decided to try for a baby.

Underneath the earrings lies the letter, addressed to him. He recognises Vicky's looped handwriting immediately and his stomach twists into knots. With shaking fingers he opens it, not knowing what's inside. Is this her final letter to him, telling him she never wants to see him again, or could it be an olive branch?

Settling on the sofa, he reads:

Friday 3rd November,

Gav, if you're reading this then it means you've found the clue I left for you. I didn't know whether it would take you a few days or even months, but despite everything that's been said, I hoped and prayed that you would eventually find yourself reading this letter.

As I've said before I'm sorry I didn't tell you about the abortion. I can't really explain why I kept it from you all these years, other than I felt ashamed. But I don't anymore, which is why I wanted to be the one to tell you, and didn't want you to hear it from the doctor, even if I wish with all my heart I'd told you before then so it wasn't sprung on you like that.

I'm sorry it was such a shock and I'm sorry it triggered all your past pain and hurt from your previous relationship. But Gav, that's on you, not me. You need to make your peace with that, just as I have with my own demons.

That day, driving home from the fertility clinic, you said you don't know who I am anymore. Well there is still more you don't know, and I refuse to hide or feel ashamed about any parts of me anymore.

If you want to know everything, the real me... every inner thought, every mistake I've made and every wrong deed that has been done to me or I've done to others, and how I've tried to hide them all, then you'll find them all in here.

Gav pauses and picks up the journal. Briefly flicking through it, he can see it contains dates and doodles, interspersed with one-liners, sometimes paragraphs or pages of handwriting. It seems she used this journal not as a way of documenting her life but more as a dumping ground to untangle her thoughts. The first entry is dated 26th September 1994, just over twelve years ago.

He turns his attention back to the letter.

I'll warn you, it doesn't make for comfortable reading.

I've made plenty of mistakes, done some things I'm not proud of, as well as been treated appallingly by others.

Sharing these innermost thoughts has always been my greatest fear, but I'm revealing all of myself to you even though in the past this has only brought me more pain... no more perfectly demonstrated by your behaviour on the day you blew your stack and walked out.

But if we're ever to have any chance of reconciliation, I don't want there to be anymore secrets between us. No censorship. No more walls to hide behind. This is who I am and once you've read this journal you'll know everything.

And if after reading all of this, you can still find it in your heart to love me, then come find me. You'll know where to look. Otherwise I'll respect your decision and I'll never bother you again.

As my dearly departed Granny Fenwick once said to me, 'You have to fight. Fight for what you want.'

Am I worth fighting for Gav? I suppose time will tell.

Today, tomorrow, always,
V xxx

Clutching the letter to his lips, he squeezes away the tears in his eyes.

Pulling out his phone, he punches out the number for Julie and Clarky's landline. When Paul answers, he asks if Julie's there.

"Hi Gav. What's up?" she asks, taking the handset from her husband.

"You know when Vicky lived out in New Zealand, and you wrote to each other?"

"Yes."

"Do you still have that address?"

"Yes, why?"

"Because as soon as I can get my shit together this week, I'm off to New Zealand. I'm going to win her back."

"Yay. Go Gav. Go get her!" Julie shouts back down the phone.

Chapter 49

VICTORIA

1 week later, Saturday 25th November 2006

*C*hris arrives at 8:00 a.m. on the dot, and we waste no time hitting the road. Heading north, we follow the coast, turning inland at Waipara for the final leg of the journey up to Hanmer Forrest and the resort, famed for its thermal springs.

I'm already safely submerged in one of the hot pools when Chris steps out of the changing room, wearing only his board shorts and carrying a rolled-up towel under his arm.

I blink a few times in quick succession as I'm reminded of the magnificence of his body. Lucky bastard hasn't aged at all. His shoulders are as broad as I remember, his arms still roped with muscles, his rippling six-pack and perfect legs still deeply tanned. If anything he's gained more definition, lost some of his puppy fat and become even leaner in the last ten years. Other than a surgical scar on the side of his torso which wasn't there the last time I saw him stripped bare, he looks as sexy as he ever did.

Despite my self-restraint I can't help wondering if the areas inside his shorts are also how I remember.

Stop it. Get a control of yourself, woman.

My cheeks grow hot as all the delicious memories of our passionate love-making flood my brain. Hours and hours spent exploring each other's bodies. Licking, kissing and sucking every part of each other. There was not one inch we didn't explore. Chris was the lover who gave me my first orgasm, who taught me how to appreciate my body, and who opened me up to my own sexual desires. He lit my flames of desire and kept them well and truly stoked.

I hastily look the other way before he notices the flush that is fast creeping up my neck.

"Still surfing then," I say, lying back against the side of the pool and pulling my sunglasses down over my eyes as he slides into the water beside me.

"Not so much these days. I don't have the time anymore."

"How do you keep so trim then? You're even more Adonis-like than I remember."

"Is that a compliment?" He smirks.

"Like you need me to tell you you look good. Just look around. Every woman under the age of forty is eyeing you up."

"Actually I'd like to think *every* woman, regardless of their age, is eyeing me up."

"They probably are."

"Meanwhile I only have eyes for one." He gives me a cheeky wink.

"Oh pack it in." I playfully slap his arm, reminding him to temper his banter. Still, the flutter in my stomach appreciates his compliment.

"I have a trainer," he offers as way of explanation. "Four very intense workouts a week with Bruce keep me in shape. I'll give you his number if you want. Help tone up those thighs of yours."

I turn sharply to look at him, my mouth falling open, only for my lips to clamp shut when I realise he's teasing. His face breaking into a wide smile.

"Where did that come from?" I point at the scar on his right side.

"Grumbling appendix. Needed to come out. It was then I

realised I needed to prioritise my health if I was going to live every day to the max. Bruce helped me back into shape after my op last year."

I jerk my head backwards. "You never told me you'd been ill."

He shrugs. "It wasn't a big deal. I was only in hospital a few days, although I'd lost a lot of weight before they realised it needed to come out."

"Well Bruce has done a great job. You look the picture of health now."

"I call him 'Bruce the Brute.'"

"That vicious, eh?"

"Pure evil. But he gets results. He's changed my diet and got me on a tonne of supplements as well."

"So with The Brute as your secret weapon, how come you're still single? Mel's told me you're not with anyone at the moment."

He slides one arm across my shoulders and his thumb lazily strokes the nape of my neck. I shiver with a remembered desire.

Damn.

"Because there's only ever been one person for me, Vicky."

I turn to face him. Slightly aggrieved. I can take the banter, but I have to hold the boundary firm. The line in the sand is fast disappearing, but I have to stop that wave washing it away completely.

"Chris, will you stop this. It's not going to happen, okay?"

He pulls his hand back, raising them both in a defeated gesture.

"Okay, okay. I'll behave, I promise."

Tucking one leg underneath himself, he turns and faces me, more serious now. "Obviously I've not been celibate this past decade, but I am serious when I say that no one's ever measured up to you."

It's my turn to break the gaze, feeling a tad guilty for my outburst moments ago.

"What about the mother of your child? I know you're not together at the moment, Mel's told me that much, but when I saw Mike and Fiona in The Cayman Islands they told me you were happily shacked up with someone you knew before me. And that you'd had a baby together. A son, I believe. I was really pleased for you. Thought you'd finally settled down and found your happy ever after. Fiona said you'd all been on holiday together. Said they liked her."

He stretches out once more, placing his hands behind his head, and looks sideways at me. "Ah yes, the lovely Sharon. The second woman to ruin my life."

A bolt of adrenaline rushes through me. The woman he went back to after me... was Sharon. The evil bitch who'd tried to come between Chris and I. My jaw falls slack before I splutter, "Wait, what?!"

I know he's expecting me to playfully slap him again, but I don't. Beneath the banter I can see his pain. His pupils constrict and I spy a minuscule twitch at the corner of his mouth. She's hurt him, possibly more than I did when I left.

When I don't respond with a teasing retort, he continues, "We'd been on again, off again for a while, but it was after Mellie's wedding things got serious. I think after I saw you, and saw how committed you were to that wanker you ended up marrying ..."

"Yeah, and look how well that worked out for me. Ran away with a Thai bride months after we got hitched."

He turns and studies my face, waiting for me to laugh. When I don't and he realises I'm serious, he reaches for my hand and gives my fingers a tight squeeze. "I never knew that. I'm so sorry he hurt you."

"Thanks... but you were saying," I prompt. He still hasn't told me what happened between him and Sharon.

"Yeah. So when I came back from Spain, I realised I should go all in with Sharon, or call time on our friends-with-benefits gig. It wasn't fair to keep stringing her along. She was always more into me than I was her."

"From what I heard, I assume you decided to go all in."

"Not initially, but after I told her we should go our separate ways she announced she was pregnant. I don't think I've ever told you that she's older than me. You know how I've always been attracted to more mature women," he says, smirking at me again.

I'm eighteen months older than Chris, something that seems less important now, but when we were younger highlighted the chasm between our levels of maturity.

"How much older?"

"Eight years."

"Wow … you found yourself a cougar!"

He turns and looks at me, but says nothing. Instead shakes his head slowly, as if he can't believe how cheeky I'm being.

"Anyway we had the baby. A boy. Louis. And we all lived happily ever after … for three years. Until she upped and left."

"Wow. Why did she leave?"

"Went to live with the boy's true father."

My hand flies up to my mouth. "So she passed him off as your son for three years, before coming clean?"

"Yup. Something like that."

"Oh Chris. I'm so sorry. I can't imagine what that must have been like. To lose your son, twice. Once when he's taken away from you after three years, but then again when you find out he was never yours in the first place."

I thought losing babies before they were born was hard, but my heart bleeds for the pain that must have caused Chris.

He shrugs. "It's all immaterial, Vicky. As far as I'm concerned he's mine, regardless of what she, or the law, says. Always was. Always will be. She may not allow me to see him, but I still provide for him. And I notice she doesn't return the money I give her. Plus, I'm building up a nice little trust fund for him that he'll inherit one day."

"That's very magnanimous of you, Chris. Especially when you have no legal or parental responsibility towards him. Many men would simply walk away. I hope that one day he appreciates it and comes looking for you. If only to say thank you for what you have done for him."

My mind filters back to my own reconciliation with my father, mere months after I left Chris. The desire to heal that wound largely prompted by our breakup.

"Sometimes you've just got to do what's right," he says. "Make up for all the crap mistakes you've made over the years."

"Well for what it's worth, I'm proud of you."

"Thanks. That means a lot... especially from you."

I slide my hand back into the water and reach for his to hold again, where it remains. We sit in a comfortable silence, soaking up the morning rays that warm our faces as we tilt our heads towards the sun. I feel the tension in my lower back being leached away by the healing qualities of the minerals and warm water in the thermal pools. All around us steam evaporates into the crisp, clean air.

Surrounded by mountains and coniferous forests on all sides, it's as if the earth is cupping her hands. Protecting us. Protecting this moment.

If only we could live permanently in the moments like these. Where the rest of the world disappears and we're cupped purely in the safety of each other's souls. Where nothing and no-one can reach us, or harm us, and we're both free to bask in the hedonistic pleasures of the present. But that's always been the story of mine and Chris's relationship. A fantasy, incapable of sustaining the harshness of real life.

"It would have been nice to have had a child of my own," he says softly.

"Tell me about it," I reply dryly and he squeezes my hand again. "But there's still plenty of time for you. You don't have an expiry date on your fertility. I can imagine you as an ageing rocker. Siring a set of twins in your seventies."

"Hmm," he replies, quietly. "If only that were true, Goose."

I crumple my brow and press my lips together. I sense that comment had a deeper meaning and turn to look at him, but he offers no more explanation, keeping his chin tilted towards the sun, his eyes shaded by sunglasses.

After another few long moments in silence, he rises from the water, rivulets dripping over his sculpted body, accentuating every hard muscle and dinted curve. "Come on," he commands. "Let's get a coffee."

"Coffee? Hello … do you know me at all, Christopher Williams? Since when did I ever drink coffee? But I could murder a good cup of tea."

Smiling, he holds out his hand and helps me out of the pool. I stride confidently ahead, in the direction of the outdoor cafe, only to turn and catch Chris openly ogling me from behind.

"Oi. What are you doing?" I wag my finger at him. "No funny business, remember?"

"The rules don't say anything about admiring your lovely wobbly bits now, do they? I think I'd better give you Bruce's number after all."

I shake my head and place a challenging hand on my hip. His teasing is relentless.

He comes up and puts an arm around my waist and plants a friendly peck on my cheek. "Come on," he says again. "Time for some tea."

Chapter 50

*A*fter our tea break we while away the hours soaking in the pools, before enjoying a side-by-side massage in the outdoor cabana. After a light lunch of green-lipped mussels in white wine sauce served alongside warm crusty bread, we change out of our togs and he leads me up into the hills that surround the resort. We wind our way up through the forest hillside, our footsteps softened by a carpet of pine needles. At the top, we watch the sun fall behind the hills, throwing out its last rays of light that split the sky with a kaleidoscope of burnt orange, bright yellow and vibrant purples.

"Red sky at night, shepherd's delight," he whispers, his warm breath tickling my ear.

'Careful, Vicky,' my inner voice screams, even though I've enjoyed myself more in the last twenty-four hours than I can remember having done in a long time; I need to stay strong, before I'm sucked too far back into his clutches.

As we make our descent in the dusk, despite the steep, uneven terrain and Chris's steadying hand always on standby, I keep my hands firmly to myself.

· · ·

Later, as we pull onto his mother's drive and the car tyres crunch on the gravel, he switches off the engine and turns to look at me. I can tell by the look in his eye, just like the evening of his sister's wedding in Denia, he's not ready for this day to be over. The problem with Chris has always been that no matter where I set the boundary, he has this uncanny knack of pushing it ever so slightly, then ever so slightly again, and again, until you look back and realise you can't remember where the boundary was originally drawn.

However, I realise I'm not ready for our time together to be over either.

Relenting, I sigh. "I could invite you in for coffee, but coffee means just that—okay? Coffee. Or in my case ..."

"...tea." He finishes my sentence, his eyes dancing with mischief. "Come on," he says, unclipping his seat belt.

I have the house to myself this weekend, as Lynne has driven up to Nelson to visit Michelle and her brood.

We walk into the kitchen and I flick on the kettle. He leans back against the units, tucking one jandal-encased foot underneath his bum, resting the sole of his flip-flop back against the units underneath himself, while his eyes track my every move.

More for something to do than to stave off any hunger pangs I busy myself chopping carrots and peppers to make crudités to go with the hummus and cured ham I've pulled from the fridge. All under the watchful eye of his penetrating stare. I feel naked, despite my clothes.

This whole scenario is beyond weird. He may no longer live under this roof, preferring his sleek, black and chrome bachelor pad overlooking the sea in Sumner, but I'm hosting him in the house that I once shared with him; the home grew up in, which on some level means it's still technically his.

I reach up to retrieve something from the cupboard directly behind where he's standing. He makes no effort to move aside, instead smiling his usual mischievous grin, forcing me to press my torso into his. While I'm at full stretch he places one hand on my waist and the air inside my lungs freezes. His touch is red hot and my skin tingles with longing. His masculine scent, mixed with that distinctive cologne, shoots up my nostrils, and I wobble backwards. My mouth devoid of saliva, my tongue sticks to the roof of my mouth and the spark between my legs ignites and throbs for attention.

Suppressing my instinctive desire, I force myself to remain focused as I fumble around in the cupboard, eventually finding the crisps and peanuts I was searching for. Gingerly, I close the cupboard door as our eyes meet. We're nose to nose. Breathing in and out in sync.

My body aches for him, and at a base level I want nothing more than for him to take me in his arms and kiss the hell out of me, but my mind holds back.

What if I lose myself again? He's too powerful. I mustn't let myself go. I simply can't. If I do, I risk losing everything.

My independence.

My identity.

My soul.

A beat passes between us before I break the spell, taking a small step backwards and exhaling. Turning around, I grab two bowls from another cupboard and pour the crisps and peanuts into them. Overcompensating on the task in hand to detract from the palpable sexual tension in the air.

I force myself to focus on my breathing. In, two, three, four. Out, two, three, four.

Eventually I hand him the filled bowls, trying with every fibre in my body to deny what's just passed between us, but when I turn to him I find his eyes still locked onto me and he hasn't moved. He doesn't want to let the moment pass.

"Here. Take these outside," I instruct, forcing the energy between us to shift. "I'll bring the drinks out in a minute."

Once I've got myself back under control.

"Go, Chris," I point. "I'm right behind you."

Reluctantly he leaves and I fall back against the sink, gripping the worktop behind me.

His pull remains as powerful as the day we met.

I remember that first night so vividly, after he'd rocked up at our office in Swindon, wearing nothing more than a crumpled T-shirt and a pair of cargo shorts, a rucksack thrown nonchalantly over his shoulder. His attitude savoir-faire, his musky scent, a heady mix of manliness and travel sweat, I remember how he stuck out like a sore thumb in our suited and booted corporate environment. He was exciting. Different. Sexy.

That evening, overcome with jet lag, he'd crashed on our sofa and I remember tiptoeing past him to the kitchen for a glass of water, and that was the exact moment I first fell under his spell. And he wasn't even awake! I remember the overwhelming need to touch his sleeping face, like a magnet drawn helplessly towards its polar opposite. But even then, I sensed he was dangerous. That I could become trapped. Like being mesmerised by a beautiful tiger. Breathtaking to look at, deadly if allowed too close.

Just breathe, Victoria. Keep breathing.

Sucking in another lung-filling breath, I push my shoulders back and set my jaw before walking outside to join him, balancing the cafetière and the pot of tea on a tray.

Chapter 51

6 hours earlier, 2pm, Saturday 25th Nov 2006

"*D*amn you Air New Zealand," Gav mutters to himself as he turns and walks away from the customer service desk at Sydney airport.

After travelling for two and a half days, leaving the UK on Thursday morning—the earliest ticket he could buy that didn't cost more than three grand; despite their start-up loan being approved earlier in the week, he couldn't justify blowing more than three grand of his savings—he'd first taken the short hop down to Heathrow, before the thirteen-hour overnight flight to Singapore. A tight connection to the seven-hour flight down to Sydney Kingsford Smith had come next, where he should have had an easy connection onto Christchurch and arrived there by now. Little did he know when he set off from the UK that Air New Zealand pilots were being balloted about pay and conditions, and he'd arrived just as they were staging a twenty-four-hour strike.

"Idiot," he grumbles, remembering how he went against the travel agent's advice to delay a few more days and allow for an Australian visa, *'just in case'*. But as he was only planning to transfer through Sydney, not be stuck here for a full twenty-four hours, he hadn't bothered. Now he's trapped and can't leave the airport. He might have taken the opportunity to go sightseeing, or more likely find a hotel room, take a shower, and sleep. God, does he need sleep. Catnapping in an airline seat in twenty-minute stints was the equivalent of Chinese water torture.

Oh well, best find a row of airport chairs to bed down on and grab some much needed kip. But first… coffee, he thinks to himself.

Assuming no more hiccups, he should arrive at the address Julie has given him, Mel's mother's house, in a place called Richmond—which according to his A-Z of Christchurch is a suburb to the east of the city—just in time for Sunday brunch.

After mulling it over, he did call Vicky before he left, alluding to his plans to fight for her without giving any explicit details. As expected, the call went straight to voicemail. He suspects she's switched her phone off. Either that or she's screening her calls. But now he's on his way, he'd rather turn up on the doorstep unannounced and surprise her, so he's left strict instructions for the gang back home to keep schtum until he lets them know whether his grand gesture has worked or not.

'Go get her,' Mark had said when he'd told him and Becca of his plan.

'You're meant to be together,' Clarky had said when Gav had popped round to give JP a goodbye cuddle.

'Good luck.' Anth had slapped him on the back after dropping him at Newcastle International.

Wandering aimlessly around Sydney Airport, his eyelids heavy, he weighs up his options for food.

I can't even think about the 'what ifs' if she isn't there, he thinks to himself. I'll look like a right tit if I've come all this way only to find she's hot-footed it back to the UK.

Still, it's a risk he's willing to take. Even if she isn't at the exact address Julie's given him, he's sure whoever is will point him in the right direction.

He only hopes that when he does track her down she'll receive him, perhaps not quite with open arms, but with an open mind at least, and give him an opportunity to apologise and explain himself. It's three weeks since she wrote that note, but seven since their blow-up and a lot can happen in that time. There's a very real possibility she may have changed her mind. Or worse still... moved on.

It hasn't escaped his notice that she's back in the same city as her ex. Gav has no idea of Chris's current relationship status, but the text he sent to Vicky in San Diego, the one Gavin accidentally read, is still vividly imprinted in Gav's brain. He shudders at the memory.

> Hey Goose, how you feeling today? I'm around if you want to talk some more. I've not been able to stop thinking about you all week. No matter what you say, or who you're with, you'll always be my girl. Always in my heart. Love you, Chris x

Another example of a moment when Gav chased her halfway around the world, only to have their fairy-tale reunion marred by the presence of Chris.

The sooner Gav can get to her the better.

I'll show her we're meant to be together.

And regardless of what he finds when he finally gets to her, he's damn well going to fight. He's not giving up.

He looks around for a coffee shop. Ordering a double expresso and a cinnamon bun, he finds a seat and takes a sip of the steaming hot coffee. Biting into the pastry, his tongue zings from the cinnamon and spice. He's hoping the sugar and caffeine combo will keep him awake long enough to battle jet lag. Even though he realises he's in for yet another uncomfortable night, right now he could sleep on a washing line.

Whilst he'd been in the air, he'd had plenty of time to read and re-read Vicky's journal in its entirety. Despite the odd moment of joy and happiness, his heart bled over and over again as he waded through pages and pages of pain. He'd had no idea how much she'd endured, and he feels for the first time he fully understands who she truly is. It's testament to her character she's found the strength to rise above the trauma she's experienced and heal her wounds. If he ever needed a role model on how he should deal with his own past, she's it.

How could I have judged her so badly? he'd thought as he'd read of the true circumstances surrounding her termination, his eyes glued to the tear-stained pages, while he was somewhere high in the sky over Asia.

How the hell did she find the strength to go on after all of that? If only I could reach back in time and wrap my arms around her then, I would. I was wrong to judge her. Wrong to assume the whole issue is black and white, and as Mark said, wrong to assume I have any right to an opinion when it comes to agency over a woman's body.

As the early evening sun sets and he takes another sip of the bitter coffee, the caffeine hardly touching the sides of his jet lag, he fumbles in his rucksack for the precious journal. He flicks to the final entry, dated Saturday 5th August this year. One week after she'd miscarried on the flight home from Singapore. A city that he thankfully whizzed through. Never had he been more grateful for a one-hour-fifteen-minute connection. The less time he had to dwell on the association of that airport with one of the darkest moments of her life, the better. Thankfully, the rush to disembark the flight from London, then the run to his next gate, gave him no time to think.

Sipping his coffee again, the bitter flavour digging into his tongue he reads again:

This ends here.

I will hide no more.

I own my past and all the decisions I made. Both good and bad.

I had an abortion and need give no justification for the reasons why. They are my reasons and mine alone.

417

Still, I grieve the loss of that child, as well as all my others. I'm the mother of four unborn babies, and I love them all.

I may never have the privilege of holding any of them in my arms, but their stars will forever shine down from the heavens above and I hold their love in my heart.

I refuse to live with regret and gracefully accept whatever life has in store for me now.

I surrender to the future I have not yet lived and place no conditions on whether I shall ever mother a child of my own.

If my destiny is to mother someone else's child, or offer support as an honorary aunt, then I accept that role with gratitude and humility.

I willingly accept whatever my future holds, without condition, and shall continue to love unconditionally, regardless.

He blows out a long exhale.

Wow! Just wow!

No wonder she wanted to step into her power that day in the doctor's office. After living with her secret for over a decade, she'd only made this personal declaration a few weeks before their appointment at the fertility clinic. Knowing their appointment was coming up he suspects she must have been grappling with how to tell him, and as she said in her letter it was never her intention for it to come out in front of a medical professional, or maybe–unconsciously–it was.

Either way, in that moment, she'd decided she wasn't going to hide anymore. She wanted to be clear she wasn't ashamed and she wanted me to hear it from her.

Through her words even as she tries to make sense of all the pain she's endured, Gav is in awe at her humility and grace.

What a woman! There really is no one else like her.

Gav replaces the journal inside his carry-on pack. Next to the little black box he's also brought all the way with him.

Checking his watch and calculating how many hours it will be before she's back in his arms, he only hopes he hasn't left it too late.

Chapter 52

VICTORIA

8pm, Still Saturday 25th Nov 2006

The cooler air outside goes some way to temper my schoolgirl crush as Chris and I spend the next few hours reminiscing about old times. I drink my tea, he drinks his coffee. We both munch on the nibbles and laugh like old friends who haven't seen each other in years. I love watching him throw his head back and belly laugh.

There are no more obvious attempts at a pass, but the undercurrent of heat is never far away. A sideways look. A touch of an elbow or a squeeze of a knee. The licking of lips and combing of fingers through hair. The unconscious dance of seduction that neither of us are purposefully playing, but are unable to stop, continues.

He updates me on all the mutual people we used to know. He's still in touch with his car dealer friend, Mo, in North London, who's also settled down. An arranged marriage apparently, but one that seems to have worked out, judging by the three kids he and his wife now have.

"He's been over," he tells me. "Brought his mum. They had a great time."

"That's nice. I assume you're still in touch with Mike and Fiona in Manchester?"

"Skyped him last week. Apparently Fi's expecting again."

"Oh wow. I'll have to message her and send my congrats. I owe her a text. We're not as close as you are with Mike, but Fi and I went through a lot that week after the hurricane and we keep in touch randomly throughout the year. Although I'm always mindful they're your friends first. I never want them to feel like they have to divide their loyalty."

"You needn't worry about that, ya daft old Goose," he says, throwing a handful of peanuts into his mouth. "They're really happy you're back in touch. As is Michelle."

I feel an instant pang in my gut when he mentions his older sister Michelle. Although Mel, the younger of his two sisters, was always my original friend and the route into this family, when Chris and I lived in London we became much closer to Michelle and her partner David. Then when their daughter Jess was born, ironically the same day I had the abortion, I doted on the new baby. In one way baby Jess saved me, but in another, she tortured me. The constant reminder of the baby I was never going to have. Regardless, for the next few months little Jess was the only light in a very dark tunnel.

"It's hard to believe Jess is eleven now," he says brightly. "And once baby number two came along, Michelle and David… a bit like Mellie and Karl, decided New Zealand was the better option to raise their families."

"I know exactly how old Jess is…" I say quietly, looking off into the distance.

"I know you do," he replies, the corners of his eyes turning downwards.

With every passing year I know exactly how old *all* my babies would have been.

Not wanting to bring down the mood and open that wound, I say brightly, "I know Michelle and David are not married, but isn't it funny how both your sisters ended up snagging Pommy men. Dragging them back over here to live."

"True. But I think they both came willingly. Why wouldn't you want to live here? I nearly persuaded you." He leans over and squeezes my knee.

"Uh-huh," I say, making a point of lifting his hand off my leg and plonking it back on his own thigh.

We both know how close I came to making New Zealand my permanent home, and my reason for leaving had nothing to do with my love of his country.

A few seconds pass while neither of us speak, but the silence doesn't feel awkward. We're so comfortable around one another; if anything, the quiet is calming.

"You hungry?" he asks, changing the subject, cramming the last of the nibbles into his mouth and licking his lips.

"Starving."

"Chinese or Indian?"

"Chinese," I reply.

Once again, with practised ease we've found another reason to prolong our time together.

A short while later, the doorbell *ding-dongs,* and he goes and answers it while I set out the crockery on the outside table. The spring evening, although cooler than the heat of the day, remains warm enough to sit outside, provided you light the firepit and wrap up in a rug and we've done both as the temperature began to drop.

He returns with the food and a bottle of wine. Pulling the cork, he pours two glasses of the crisp white Marlborough. Passing one glass to me, he holds his aloft.

"What are we toasting?" I ask.

"To living for the moment and never again letting our fears or insecurities stop us going after what we want."

"Wow, that's heavy, but okay. To living in the moment," I repeat, chinking my glass against the side of his. Taking a sip, the cool fresh elixir zings on my pallet. "Oh I've missed this. Somehow New Zealand wine always tastes better when you drink it in New Zealand."

He looks at me over the top of his glass. Although neither of us say anything, we both know the popping of that cork means there is no way he can drive home tonight.

But he could call a cab. Leave his car here and collect it in the morning.

We eat our food and drink our wine, until he suggests, "It's starting to get proper chilly. Do you want to go back inside? I could light the fire in the living room."

It was dark before we came home, and other than the pool lights and glow from the firepit, we've been sitting in the dark for hours.

"Good idea," I reply.

We pick up our glasses and relocate to the living room. Chris lights the log burner, before joining me on the sofa. Picking up the remote he flicks through the channels, settling on a rerun of *Friends*. It's the one where Carol gives birth to Ross's baby.

Using a payphone, Monica phones her mother with an update. Although we're only privy to one side of the mother/daughter conversation, it's clear Monica's mother is saying something that suggests Monica may never have children and that this may be her only chance for her mother to have a grandchild.

Leaning into the payphone, Monica replies, "Mom, will you stop! I'm only twenty-six. I'm not even thinking about babies yet," before she crumples into tears as someone walks past with a newborn babe in their arms.

I take another sip of my wine. "This episode was on the day we had that barbecue with Dean, Lisa, and the kids. Do you remember?"

"No."

"It was the weekend they came down from Auckland, to meet me for the first time."

"Bloody hell Goose, you've got a memory like an elephant," he says, replacing his wine glass on the coffee table and throwing his arm nonchalantly along the back of the sofa, settling in to watch it.

To be fair, in the last decade *Friends* has become a global phenomenon and most people our age have seen every episode multiple times, but I distinctly remember this one. At the time it had stabbed me in the heart. My grief at having lost my first child, granted by my own choice, still catching me unawareness.

"Yeah, I remember you playing outside with Emma and Matthew and I had to switch the TV off as I walked through the lounge. It was still too raw. You know, after the…" I trail off.

He tenderly touches the back of my neck with his thumb.

He knows.

"Do you ever wonder, *what if?*" he asks, softly.

"Oh, Chris. Let's not do this again. We've had this conversation too many times. What's done is done, and can't be undone. But of course I wonder *what if?* Not a day goes by when I don't wonder if that was my true destiny and I made a wrong turn."

"Me too. I wonder how different our lives would have been if all the lights had been green that morning, instead of red, and I'd gotten home in time."

"Or not left at all," I reply, one eyebrow raised.

I have forgiven him for abandoning me in my hour of greatest need, but it's still hard remembering he decided to go out drinking with his business associates the night before my appointment at the clinic, rather than stay home and support me.

Wait… what did he just say?

I turn and glare at him, my gaze boring holes into the side of his skull. "What do you mean, *and you'd gotten home in time?*"

He breaks eye contact and looks down, removing his arm from the back of the settee and hunching over; rolling his hands over and over, as if trying to cleanse them and absolve himself of his sins.

"When you went out that night," I continue, "you'd promised you'd be home at ten o'clock. But we've already talked about that. How you let me down and I had to get the bus the next morning. So what did you mean just then? Other than being there to support me and hold my hand, what difference would it have made if you hadn't got pissed, and come home when you'd planned? Chris… look at me," I say, my tone insistent. "What are you not telling me?"

Slowly, he turns and meets my stare, his face etched with pain. Tears pool in the corner of his eyes and his bottom lip quivers. "I vowed I would never tell you this, because by the time I saw you the next day, when I came to collect you from the clinic, you were already in so much pain. The light had gone out of your eyes and I know a part of you died that day. But yes, I was racing back to you that morning. I wanted to stop you. I didn't want you to go through with it."

My hands fly up to my face and I shake my head from side to side.

NO! This can't be true. He can't be saying this to me. How could he have kept this from me all these years? It can't be true. It's too cruel.

He reaches for my hands. I try and pull them away, but he holds them firm. His thumbs rolling over the backs of my knuckles. "By the time I'd come to my senses it was too late. I woke up that morning with the worst hangover of my life, and the enormity of the situation hit me like a tonne of bricks. Feeling that sick was the physical jolt I needed to make me realise what an absolute twat I'd been. Not just that night, but for all the weeks leading up to it. I hadn't been there for you, and when I thought about what you were about to do, it broke my heart. I drove like a lunatic, trying to get back to you, but I was too late. Then when I didn't know where you were—my fault that I hadn't wanted to know the details—and I had to wait all day for you to call, it was without doubt the worst day of my life. Well, that and the day you left me."

A lump swells in the back of my throat and I can't catch my breath. My head hurts and the sound of my own blood swooshes inside my ears. I'm trying to focus on what he's telling me, but the room is spinning.

"When you first told me you were pregnant," he continues, "it was so unexpected. So overwhelming. I panicked. I didn't know what to do. We hardly had any time to process it all before you had to terminate it. Only a few weeks, and I was so scared, Vicky. I thought I was doing the right thing by you. Taking myself out of the equation and giving you the space I thought you needed. You know how irresistible I always found you and how hard it was to keep my hands off you. You remember me telling you, after all those of being called a leper, how important physical touch is to me, which is why I thought going away to Amsterdam and leaving you alone was the right thing to do. You've always been so much stronger than me, but I should have been by your side instead of shutting you out. When I woke up that morning it's as if I finally felt some of your pain and I realised I didn't want you to give up on us. On our future. On our baby. I wanted it all. I wanted you and the life growing inside you. My heart hurts when I think how scared you must have been. You *have* to know how sorry I am… for everything."

Chris holds my gaze but I pull my hands away, drop my head and weep. Big, wretched, heartbroken sobs.

This can't be happening. How could he do this to me? Just when I think nothing else can hurt me, another truth slams into me like a runaway train. Smashing my heart into a million pieces all over again.

"I realise now how petrified you were. Believing you were backed into a corner with no way out. Scared you'd end up raising it alone. Like your mother had had to raise you, and you wouldn't want the child growing up not knowing their father, or always wondering if their father ever loved them—just like you did with your dad."

I can't speak, but he's absolutely right.

I *was* scared. Too scared to bring that life into the world on my own. Yet, all this time, all these years, I've always believed *he* never wanted it. Right from the moment I told him I was pregnant. I know he's regretted his lack of support, he's told me that before. But I thought he'd only had a change of heart as the years had passed. As he'd gotten older and gained the benefit of hindsight. Not *before* I went through with it.

That changes everything.

Now I'm questioning every decision I made, all over again. Wondering how different my life might have been if only he'd made it home before I got on the bus.

That tortuous night was one of the hardest I've ever lived through. I was desperate for him to come home and make things right, but I couldn't reach him. Wondering if he'd been mugged, or in a car accident, or worse. And all the while I was having to come to terms with what I was preparing to do the next day. Despite falling pregnant by accident, together with all the other reasons why the timing was crap—I was too young, I had no money, I couldn't afford to buy a home and was only able to rent a crummy one-bedroom flat in a crappy part of town—the only way I'd envisioned it being possible to keep the child was if Chris had been on board. But when I told him I was pregnant, he made his feelings clear. His exact words at the time, *'keeping it's not an option. You'll have to get rid of it.'*

I never knew he'd had a change of heart. Everything I thought was once true has been flipped on its head.

"You never told me," I say, my voice hardly audible.

"What good would it have done? By the time I got to you, you'd already had the abortion. It would have only made it more painful."

My breath comes fast and shallow as I struggle to breathe. Just when I think I'm standing tall, Chris's latest revelation is like an avalanche crashing down on top of me. Suffocating me. Wanting to bury me alive.

All the emotion I've tried to bury all these years erupts like a volcano as an angry cry rises up in the back of my throat like a roar. Breaking through all the weight on top of me.

No more.

I will not be squashed.

I will not allow my emotions or needs to be made to feel less than someone else's.

I *will* be heard.

Angry now, my eyes burning with a mix of fury and repressed

pain, I spit, "Do you have *any* idea how much I've suffered all these years. The guilt I've felt. The shame I've carried. The torture I've put myself through on an almost daily basis. Always wondering *what if?* Wondering *why* it had to happen. *Why* it had to happen *to me!*" I throw my hands up in the air as my tone rises. "All these years, every time I've lost another baby, I've carried on believing the universe is punishing me for the decision *I* made, Chris. *My* decision. You made your feelings known from the get-go, leaving *me* to make the decision. *I* was the one who had to decide to go through with it. *Me,* Chris. *Me,* alone. You weren't there … for any of it! And *I'm* the one who's had to own the consequences of that day. *Me,* Chris. Not you!"

"I know you have, Vicky. But I've had to live with the consequences of my actions as well."

"Good," I say spitefully. "If that means you've felt a modicum of the pain I've had to live through. And now you're telling me if you'd only fucking come home like you'd originally planned, instead of getting pissed, my life… in fact the last eleven years of my life, might have been completely different. I wouldn't have had to live with all that shame and guilt and I would have, most likely, gone on to have our child."

He tries to place a consoling hand on my back, but I shrug it away.

Retracting his hand, he rubs the back of his neck. "I'm so very, *very* sorry, Vicky. God, if only I could turn the clock back…"

"Don't," I say, turning to eyeball him and pointing my finger in his face. "YOU don't get to say that. Ever. You don't get to make this about you. You have NO IDEA how hard it's been for me. Ever since that night I've spent my entire life making peace with *my choice.* It's been the hardest thing to accept, and I've only recently got to a place where I can own the decision I made without feeling shameful or guilty. And you don't get to rip that rug out from underneath me again. You made your choice and I made mine, but now you're telling me I went through all that self-doubt, self-pity, and self-loathing needlessly. No, you don't get to make this about you. And after it all, I *still* don't have a baby in my arms."

"I know and I'm sorry. You have to believe me when I tell you that *that*, and then losing you are the biggest regrets of my life."

"Yeah, well, what did you expect me to do?" I humph.

"Of course I understand why you left me, and I've never blamed you. I'm such a fucking idiot." He squeezes his eyes tight and his own tears roll down his cheeks. "I can't tell you how painful it was when I came home that morning and found the flat empty. Then when I listened to your voicemails, I wanted to curl up and die."

He pulls out his mobile, and scrolls through his phone. "I still have them. Transferred them onto MP4s a few years back." He presses play and the sound of my own tortured voice from over ten years ago rings out around the room.

'Chris, where are you?'

Bee-eep.

'Chris, I thought you'd be home by now?'

Bee-eep.

'Chris, this is not on. You said you'd be home by now. Call me.'

Bee-eep.

'Chris, I hope you're okay. I'm really worried now. Please call me.'

"Switch it off," I scream, standing and walking across to the fire-place, my hands at my throat. I can't breathe. "I don't want to hear it. Don't make me go through it again "

I don't need to hear those messages to remember how painful it was. I lived it and it's as raw today as it was the night he left me alone, crying into my journal, not knowing where he was, when he'd be home, or whether he was alive or dead.

He leaps off the settee and in two strides has enveloped me in his arms. Both our bodies racking with sobs. I try to push him away, but he's too strong for me.

His arms encircling me, he whispers over and over, "I'm sorry, Vicky. I'm so sorry."

My body still wracked with sobs he continues, "I know I can't change what I did. When you left me, I made a vow."

I tilt my head and look at him.

"I vowed I would spend the rest of my life doing good. Doing whatever I could to atone for hurting you."

He puts his finger underneath my chin, raising it so our lips are mere millimetres apart.

"I know I can't change what I did, but I vowed I would never allow myself to be happy until you're happy. I don't deserve to be."

This time I do push him off me.

"NO, Chris! You're not putting that on me as well. I'm not responsible for your happiness. You own your own choices and I own mine."

"I know, and I do. And you're right, my happiness is not your responsibility, but that's why I've kept your messages all these years. As a reminder of the pain I once caused. Whenever I need to keep my ego in check, I play them back. Hearing how desperate you were that night reminds me of what I did to you, and of the person I never want to be again."

"But why keep torturing yourself? It doesn't change anything."

"Are you happy?" he asks.

I shrug. "I'm not unhappy, and sure, my life has had moments that were happy."

"But are you really happy?" he asks again. "Deep down in your soul, content and happy?" His gaze meets mine. "When will you ever believe you're not being punished and you are *enough*?"

I look down at the ground. "I thought I did, but honestly... I don't know?"

He clasps the outsides of my arms, his stare piercing all my outer walls, and reaches into the centre of my soul, ripping it out of my body and laying it bare. "God, you're so beautiful and I love you so very much. I always have and I always will. And I need you to know, you *are* enough. It's my fault I didn't realise it until after I'd lost you. Which is why I decided if I couldn't have you, I would spend the rest of my life ploughing every ounce of my energy into doing right whenever possible."

I suck in a shaky breath as he takes my hand and, through the open buttons of his shirt, places my palm on his chest, over his heart. His skin feels warm to my touch, and the few chest hairs that weren't there when he was younger bristle underneath my fingers. I feel the vibration of his love beating in sync with mine.

"You're my reason for living, Vicky. Whether we're together or not. I love you as much today as I always have. If not more..."

"Don't, Chris," I say, cutting him off, a warning tone in my voice.

"I think, deep down, Vicky, you feel the same. People come and go, but true love never dies, no matter how hard you try and bury it."

"I can't go there again, Chris. Yes, I loved you once, more than I ever thought possible. You were everything to me. But loving you is just too painful."

"I know. And I hate myself for having made you suffer. I would do anything to take your pain away."

"But nothing will, Chris. It's hopeless. We're two fragile hearts that keep on smashing into each other and breaking all over again. I want so badly to get past this, and I thought I had, but every time I see you it brings it all back and I'm in the same pain all over again. I can't keep doing this, Chris. I can't keep reliving this same cycle."

He ducks down, so that our eyes are level.

"Sometimes pain is the price we pay for love. But we have to keep living. Turn that pain into something good and beautiful. At least that's what I'm determined to do." He tucks a stray strand of hair behind my ear. "And despite what I did to you, you've turned into the most beautiful, amazing person. I'm so proud of you and everything you've achieved."

"And I, you."

It's true. Everything he's said is true. As much as we've both hurt each other, we wouldn't be the people we are today if we hadn't lived through that pain.

We both suck a deep breath in and slowly exhale. My heart is no longer racing, the energy between us having deescalated.

The sound of the infamous *Friends* theme tune plays out in the background as one episode ends and another one starts. The Rembrandts reminding us that *'I'll be there for you.'*

"I know that life has to go on, Chris. I just wish it wasn't so damn hard all the time."

"I know, Vicky." He pulls me into a hug. "But then that's what makes the highs, when they do come along, so much sweeter, don't you think?"

"Maybe. But I'm tired, Chris. Tired of battling. Tired of fighting with life. Tired of fighting against my past. Against our history."

"So don't." He rolls the back of his fingers across my cheek, and I instinctively dip my head into the palm of his hand. "I don't know about you but today has been amazing. I've been the happiest I've been in a very long time."

"Me too," I reply, earnestly.

And with that final admission, we both know there are no more secrets between us. No more barriers. No more walls to hide behind.

He leans forward and rests his forehead against mine. I feel grounded by the weight of his head connecting with mine. Our souls are already intertwined, our spirits in sync as we breathe in and out as one. The only thing standing between our complete assimilation is a very fine line in the sand that is dissolving with every quivering breath.

As painful as it was to hear Chris's confession, on some level it was also cathartic. It doesn't change the outcome, nothing can turn the clock back, but realising, even if I didn't know it at the time, I wasn't actually going through it all alone, learning that Chris was suffering too, on some level makes may pain seem a little less.

Apparently the truth really does set you free.

"Thank you," he whispers.

"For what?"

"For giving me a second chance."

"This isn't a second chance, Chris."

"I know. But it could be a chance to create a different ending to our story."

"Are you sure that this is an ending and not another beginning?" I ask, knowing that he's about to kiss me and that I'm not going to stop him.

I want him to kiss me.

No, I *need* him to kiss me.

"I think we both know that," he replies, covering my mouth with his.

I don't push him away and instead invite him in. It's no longer my physical desire responding to his advances, it's my soul. Without realising it, all these years I've needed him to replace the part of me he took away that night.

I surrender to his kiss as my body already knows how he feels, how he tastes, and how he smells. His tongue explores my mouth and my body softens as his goes hard.

In one swift movement he scoops me up and carries me into his old bedroom. Laying me gently on the bed we once shared together. He peels my clothes from my body with practised ease.

For hours we kiss, suck, and lick every inch of each other's bodies, in the way only two intimate strangers can.

Everything feels so natural, so instinctive, so predestined, neither of us pause to consider using protection. When he eventually slides into me and calls out my name as our souls leave our bodies and dance in the ether above our heads, out of the corner of my eye I spot a shooting star blazing across the ink-black sky. Burning brightly before it fulfils its destiny, and dies.

Chapter 53

The next morning, the sun feels warm against my cheek as I clear the plates left on the table outside last night.

I sit quietly, sipping my tea, and soak up the moment. Bees hum in the lavender, and an olive-green bellbird perches on the edge of the garden fence, singing out its morning song.

Dressed only in my kimono and still naked underneath, I close my eyes, tilt my head towards the shinning orb in the cobalt blue sky, and take a moment to enjoy the solitude.

"Morning." Chris appears behind me, a towel wrapped around his loins whilst he uses another to rough dry his hair. He places both his hands on my shoulders and lands a peck on my cheek. "Sleep well?"

"Like a log. The best night's sleep I've had in a long while."

He takes the seat opposite me and smiles warmly. It seems last night was cathartic for him too.

"Coffee?" I lift up the cafetière and pour Chris a cup from the fresh pot I've made for him. He wraps both hands around the mug and lifts it to his lips.

"You okay?" he asks, locking his gaze with mine.

"Yes," I say earnestly. "Very much so."

Both of us know that last night will never be repeated. It was a moment of healing that has released us from the years of torment and guilt we've both held onto. But in that one beautiful moment, following our heartfelt honesty, we released the past with joy. The bonds that have kept us enslaved are gone and we're both at peace.

He reaches for my hands. Lifts them to his lips and kisses them. "Thank you, Vicky."

I pull our clasped hands back towards my own mouth, and press a kiss onto the back of his knuckles. "Thank you, Gav."

"GAV!" he exclaims, throwing his head back and belly laughing. "Well, if ever there was a sign that I'm not *the one,* then that was it, right there."

Horrified, I hide my mouth with my hands. "Oh my god, Chris. I'm so sorry."

Still laughing, he says, "Don't be. I'm part of your past. And it seems he should be part of your future." He looks directly at me and pauses. "I mean that, Vicky. There is nothing more for us other than our memories. Gav's your future. Not me."

"I know." I drop my eyes.

"So what's really going on between you two? You've been very evasive. I know you came here for Mellie. But I think you were also doing what you do best… running away. I should know." He raises his eyebrow, knowingly. "You can't run forever. At some point you're going to have to face him, and fix whatever's broken. Don't live another decade of regret."

I know he's right. At some point I'm going to have to fix my relationship with Gav. If only our beliefs weren't so far apart.

Tomorrow.

Tomorrow, I'll bite the bullet, recharge my Blackberry and check my messages. But not yet. Let me savour this one last morning with Chris before we part for good.

"So what went wrong?" Chris asks.

"There's not a lot to say, really. It was perfect. For a long time. Then when I told him about the abortion, he said some awful things, and left."

"So is it *over*, over? Or was he just pissed, and you've pushed him into the dog house ever since?"

"Honestly, I don't know. I suspect if I check, there'll be messages from him. But you know what, Chris?"

"What?"

"I'm tired of men filling me with hot air. And I can't be arsed listening to any more justifications. I like to think I judge people on their actions rather than their words, and so far his action was to leave in a fit of anger, and not look back."

"Just like you have." Chris smirks.

"It's not the same. He had five whole weeks to apologise before I got the call from you telling me Mel was ill. Five whole weeks and nothing. If I really meant something to him, he should have shown up."

"Like I should've when I had the chance."

"Exactly," I gesture. "What is it with you men? Does having a dingle-dangle between your legs make you blind to what's directly in front of you until it's too late?"

"Sadly… yes. Most of the time. It's the greatest flaw of my gender." He shrugs, then giggles under his breath. "Dingle-dangle."

"I would have resisted you if you had followed me, but I would have respected you more at the time if you'd shown up. If you love someone, you show up. I refuse to listen to any more useless waffle and empty guff. The same went for Craig. Even after everything he'd done, and even after I suspected he'd been unfaithful and spent the best part of six months having a mid-life crisis in Thailand, if he'd rocked up on the doorstep with a bunch of roses in his hand and said *'I'm sorry, will you give me another chance?'* I would have done it in a heartbeat."

"Stay there." Chris rises suddenly from his seat and disappears back through the patio doors and into the house.

He reappears a few minutes later, wearing yesterday's clothes and having combed his hair through. He looks like he's preparing to leave, but instead he sits back down. His face deadly serious, he looks me directly in the eye. "I did come after you, Vicky."

"What?"

"I tried to stop you leaving Auckland."

I jerk my head back, my eyes stretched wide. "What? No you didn't."

"Yes I did. When you left Christchurch, you made it seem like you'd left the country and gone straight back to the UK. I only figured out you were on the North Island the day you were due to leave. Michelle called and had a hunch you were with my brother. She'd figured out Mellie had flown into Auckland a few days early and not told anyone, we assumed to see you. Then Michelle called your mother back in the UK who more or less confirmed it. As soon as I put the pieces together I raced up there. Jumped on the next flight out of Christchurch, and as it turns out… missed you by a whisker."

"I never knew that," I say, tilting my head and looking down. "Our timing just seems to have been permanently off."

"No kidding. I watched your plane take off as mine was taxiing to the terminal, although I only found out for sure it was your plane afterwards. But at the time I knew instinctively you were on it, and that I'd lost you."

"Another bloody *what-if* moment in the long list of *what-ifs* of our entire relationship." I shake my head and look out across the garden. The flowers bob gently in the breeze.

"Obviously I was hoping you'd give me a second chance." He pulls out a small black box from the pocket of his shorts. "I'd planned to give you this."

I know instantly what it is and I shake my head, recoiling in my chair.

"I knew then I was ready to commit to you forever, and I was prepared to do whatever it took. I was ready to be the man you needed me to be, so that you'd never run away again. I was going to ask you to marry you."

He grabs my hand, steadying me. "Calm down, will ya. I'm not going to propose. That's not why I'm giving it to you now, but now feels like the right moment. I've kept it here, in my mother's safe at

River Road, all these years. Perhaps on some level, I always believed we'd find our way back here—together."

He opens the box and I gasp. Inside is a breathtaking yellow diamond ring. Pear-shaped and set in platinum. The main stone must be at least two or three carats. On either side of the main diamond, set into the shoulders, are two equally sparkly marquisette clear diamonds of at least a half a carat each.

I stare at the ring. Mesmerised by its beauty and dumbstruck that Chris had intended to give it to me as an engagement ring.

I had no idea. All through our relationship, I was waiting for him to step up and show me how much I meant to him. When all along he was committed, even if his actions said otherwise at the time.

"I've never seen anything like it, Chris. It's stunning." I pick the ring out of the box and turn it this way and that. Admiring the stones as they glint in the morning sunshine. "Such an unusual colour."

"I bought it when we were in Hong Kong. It reminds me of the colour of your hair."

"So they match the earrings you gave me on our last night there?"

"Yes, they're a set. Do you still have them?"

"Of course."

My mind jumps back to my ballerina box tucked away inside my wardrobe, where along with the yellow diamond earrings are Chris's letters and the blank postcard he sent me of a shooting star blazing through a night sky. Its tail illuminating the exotic beach and palm trees of a far-flung destination.

"There was a moment that night I thought you were going to propose," I say, remembering the night we *dined on top of the world.*

"Believe me, I'd thought about it. I thought about it a lot. But back then, I never thought I was good enough for you. Plus we'd had that massive bust-up just days before, and I didn't want to risk you turning me down." He dips his head before raising it to meet my gaze again, and smiles.

"Yup, making me choose between you and my friendship with

Tim was not your finest hour. Or the way you reacted when I tried to hold my boundary. You completely crossed a line."

"I know I did, and I've regretted that moment ever since. My stupid insecurities clouding my judgement again."

"You were barking up the wrong tree there, by the way."

He crumples his brow.

"Apparently, all these years it wasn't me Tim wanted; he was sweet on Mel."

"No way!" he laughs.

"Yup. Took me by surprise as well."

I place the ring back inside the little black box. "Chris. It's beautiful but I can't possibly accept it."

He reaches for my hand. "It's yours, Goose. It was always yours. Wear it as a dress ring. A memento of our time together, and the love we once shared."

I look inside the band and realise it's engraved.

My hands fly up to my mouth. "The inscription? I don't understand…"

How could he know those are the words I've always said to Gav?

Over the past three years I've signed off every birthday card, Christmas card, Valentine's Day card with those same three words.

Today, tomorrow, always.

"They came to me in a dream," Chris says. "At the time it seemed fitting. I believed we would be together today, tomorrow, and always, so I had them inscribed on the inside. Little did I know you would savagely dump me and walk out of my life without a backwards glance." He grins, but I'm still shaking my head. Incredulous.

"I realise now we were never destined to physically be together forever, but my love for you has been and will always be constant. Nothing's ever changing that. I made a vow to make things right, and I've fulfilled that promise," he says, his tone having changed from playful to sincere.

I know Chris and Gav are two very different men, and my relationships with each of them are totally different, but on some universal plane it seems my love for them is one and the same. As if I can only love one because I love the other.

He takes the ring from me and, holding my gaze, slides it over the knuckle of the third finger of my right hand. Lifting it to his lips, he kisses the diamond.

"There, sealed with a loving kiss."

I turn and admire the ring now that it's on my finger. "It's beautiful, Gav. SHIT! I've done it again."

I look at him and he's laughing. "No worries. You know my heart is yours, and I'm thankful for everything you've ever given me, Vicky." He pushes his chair back, which scrapes over the deck boards. "But I think it's time I left."

He rises and gathers up the empty cups, and I follow him through to the kitchen just as the doorbell *ding-dongs*.

We both look at each other.

"Are you expecting anyone?" he asks.

"Like who? The postman doesn't deliver on Sundays."

"I'll go," he says, while I deposit the empties in the sink.

"Errr Vicky," I hear him shout. "I think it's for you."

Wrapping my kimono tightly around me I head to the front door.

Filling the doorframe is a very tired, very dishevelled looking bloke with a crumpled bunch of multicoloured roses clutched in his hand and a suitcase by his feet.

We lock eye contact. Both of us, stunned.

Chapter 54

"GAV!" I exclaim. "Oh my God. What are you doing here?"

Chris whispers under his breath so only I can hear, *"Showing up... I would say."*

"I came here for you, Angel," Gav says. "It's taken me the best part of three and a half days, but I've travelled halfway around the world—literally, so that I could tell you to your face how sorry I am. What I said... I've had time to reflect and I realise I was wrong *and* out of order. I'd misplaced my anger, formed ridiculous opinions, and it wasn't right for me to take all that out on you. I've been an absolute knob-head of the highest order and would do anything to win you back. Can we please start over?"

He smiles feebly and lifts the bouquet, offering it to me.

I take a small step back. I'm still in shock. I can sense Chris next to me, a feeling of pride emanating from him, as if he wants to applaud.

"I'm not sure," I whisper. "It's such a shock. You turning up like this."

"I thought that's what you wanted," Gav says, his face crestfallen. "I found your letter and I've read your journal. I know all of it. Everything." Gav turns to Chris and gives him a hard stare. "And all I want is to take your pain away."

"*Ahem.*" Chris shuffles from foot to foot. "At least invite the poor bastard in and let him take a shower; offer him a coffee."

"Or tea," both Gav and I say in unison, dipping our heads and smiling.

Gav turns his attention to the other man. They've never met, but I know Gav knows who this is.

I hold my breath. Wondering if Gav is going to land a punch on the end of Chris's bonce. If he's read my diary he'll know all the ugly details of our past.

But he doesn't. Instead he steps forward and offers his hand. "It's Chris, isn't it?"

Chris shakes his hand, a wide smile on his face.

"Gav. I'm so pleased you showed up. She's a special one, *your* girl. Take care of her."

"I will." Gav smiles back at Chris, but his eyes are as hard as steel.

Both men hold onto their handshake, whilst gripping the outsides of each other's upper arms with their left hands.

Eventually breaking contact, Chris turns back to me. "Take care, ya daft old Goose. I'm sure we'll bump into each other, either at Mellie's or when I pop round here to see Mum."

"That would be nice." I stand on my tippy toes and plant a kiss on his cheek. "Thanks, Chris."

And with that, he's gone. The sound of his tyres crunching on the gravel fade into the distance as Gav crosses the threshold and closes the door behind him.

"What was all that about?" he asks.

"Oh, nothing. It's all in the past," I reply. "Come on through. I've just put the kettle on. Now, which would you prefer first? A fresh brew or a shower?" I ask, wheeling Gav's case out of the way.

"Oh, hard choice. I've not had a wash since Wednesday morning, and I dread to think what I smell like." He tentatively raises an armpit, sniffs, then recoils.

I don't tell him I think he smells lovely. Familiar. Musky. Manly. Dirty. Sexy.

"But I could murder a decent cuppa. All I've had is dishwater since I left London, and I'm parched."

"Tea it is. We can go outside, and you can sit downwind," I say, glancing sideways at him, my eyes dancing.

I make a fresh pot of tea, while Gav hovers awkwardly behind me still clutching his roses. "Vases are in there," I say pointing to a cupboard.

I purposefully haven't taken the flowers from him, even though I know they're for me, or suggested he take his case to my bedroom. I haven't decided if he'll be staying here tonight, or checking into a hotel.

As much as I appreciate he's followed my clues, flown halfway around the world and apologised on the doorstep, which in itself is a grand gesture and demonstrates his desire to make this work, it doesn't change our fundamental differences on some key issues. He's got some talking to do before my walls come back down.

I find a packet of Griffins Gingernuts at the back of the cupboard, and along with the tea things, carry everything outside. Gav hasn't unwrapped or arranged the bunch of roses, but has plonked them in a vase of water and left them on the kitchen bench before following me out into the mid-morning sunshine.

"This is gorgeous," he says, admiring Lynne's garden, his eyes travelling over the flowerbeds to the swimming pool beyond. "Is it south facing?" he asks, making the same mistake I made the first time I visited.

"No, but I know why you asked. We're in the Southern Hemisphere, remember. Their sun is to the north."

"Of course." He blinks a few times in quick succession. His brain clearly struggling to focus through lack of sleep. "Forgive me. I'm so weary I don't actually know what day of the week it is."

"I know. It's a horrifically long journey and the days and nights end up merging together. It'll take you a few days to get over it."

"You'd know," he says, before asking, "So how've you been?"

"Fine."

A silent beat passes between us.

"And Mel?"

"As good as can be expected. She has good days and bad days. She's in for a long fight."

"I'm sorry to hear that."

Another silent beat.

I cup both my hands around my mug and take a sip of the steaming liquid. Gav, meanwhile, opens the packet of biscuits and dunks a ginger nut in his tea.

I hug my knees up to my chest, and my kimono falls up my thighs before I remember I have nothing on underneath. I quickly return my feet to the floor and cross my legs, tucking the kimono tighter around my torso.

I watch as Gav registers my nakedness, but says nothing; instead he takes a calm, considered sip of his tea. I don't offer an explanation, but I suspect he knows the reason why I'm bare-skinned underneath.

His eyes travel around the garden, and when he does look at me again we both say at the same time, "So where do we go from here?"

Another awkward pause.

"You go first," he says, gesturing with an upturned palm.

"No, you go," I reply, and watch as he sucks in a deep breath and runs his fingers through his hair.

"I'm not sure what more to say, Vicky. I was wrong to say what I did and I'm sorry."

"And I appreciate the apology. But you said what you said with such venom, you clearly meant every word. You once said to me that you're one-hundred-percent sincere. And if you don't mean it, you don't say it. And what you do say, you mean. What's changed?"

"Everything's changed. God, has it changed. I was wrong to judge you."

"But it wasn't just me you were judging. You labelled every woman who's had a termination *an unforgivable monster*. I almost told you about my first loss when we were in Grand Cayman, but then the hurricane happened. Then I almost told you when we were in San Diego, but then you said what you said. How could I have possibly told you after that?"

"I know. I realise now I'd misplaced my anger. I suppose it was a coping mechanism. I had no one and nowhere to project my hurt, so rather than deal with it, I needed something to hang it on."

"There's no doubt what Samantha did to you was despicable. And if it's true she only did it to fit into her wedding dress, then it's hard not to be critical of someone who'd end a pregnancy simply because it would ruin her wedding photos."

"Or because it wasn't mine," Gav interjects.

"True. And I appreciate her not telling you would have made you feel powerless, but that still doesn't give you the right to tar all women with the same brush."

"Yeah. I know. Hindsight is a wonderful thing. All part of growing up." He smiles at me, repeating the words he first uttered in the early days of our relationship. "The lads didn't hold back either," he says, his head dipped while he looks up at me.

"So, they all know?"

"Yes, and they were all equally forthright in telling me how wrong I was."

"Good," I say, pressing my lips into a thin line and nodding my appreciation for the support I didn't know I had from my friends on the other side of the world.

He reaches for my hand. "I'm sorry, V. And I was wrong on so many levels. I promise you, I've changed. You did nothing wrong. It wasn't your fault you suffered all those miscarriages. And I'm sorry if I not only judged you for something in your past, but blamed you for the present."

I breathe out a long exhale.

"Give me a second chance and I'll prove it to you. All I want is you. And that is enough. Babies or no babies."

Tears spring into the corner of my eyes. All I want is him too.

"I have something to show you." He goes out into the hallway and grabs his carry-on bag. Rummaging through it, he pulls out my leather journal. He flicks to the back of the diary and pulls out a flimsy piece of tracing paper he's kept safe there. "I didn't have time to get this done before I left, but I'm planning on getting a tattoo."

"What? You? A tattoo? Don't tell me you're going to get the Liverpool crest on your arm, just so you can wind the rest of the lads up."

Most men in the North-East have their football club's emblem permanently inked on the outside of their shoulder. It was one of the first things I noticed about Clarky, the night I met him in the Quilted Camel. The same night I also met Craig. Clarky was a typical goth, all skinny black trousers, sleeveless AC/DC T-shirt and long ponytail, the Newcastle crest proudly inked on the top of his left arm. The skinny jeans and ponytail have long gone, but the ink remains.

"No. I planned to have this done." He passes me the piece of tracing paper. On it, in beautiful cursive script, are four lines of dates:

$$22^{nd} May - 21^{st} July 1995$$

$$22^{nd} Jan - 12^{th} Mar 2005$$

$$16^{th} Apr - 15^{th} May 2005$$

$$22^{nd} Apr - 29^{th} Jul 2006$$

I don't know what to say; the gravitas of his gesture rendering me mute.

"I was thinking of getting them here." He rolls the arm of his T-shirt up over his shoulder and holds the tracing paper against the inside of his left upper arm. "That way, I can see them when I lift my arm, but they stay close to my heart when it's down."

"But only three of them were yours," I splutter, my eyes brimming with tears.

"It doesn't matter. They're all yours, and I want all of you, Vicky. Now and always."

"Oh, Gav. I don't know what to say."

"Say yes, Angel."

"Yes," I reply, nodding vigorously, my arms stretching out for a hug.

Gav leaps up from his chair and pulls me into him. I stand as well and rest my head against his chest, listening to the solid sound of his heartbeat.

"There's something I need to tell you, and I know you're not going to like it, so I need you to hear me out before you react."

"Now you've got me worried. What is it, Angel?"

"Chris stayed with me last night."

We remain wrapped in a hug, but I feel his body stiffen.

"And?" he asks. "I assume you're telling me this because something happened?"

"Yes, Gav. It did. And if I'm honest, we both needed it to happen. *I* needed it to happen. It was the only way for us to heal all the hurt we've caused each other, and now I'm free. That was the final chapter in the story of me and him. We both knew when we woke up this morning, it will never happen again."

He hisses a long breath out through his teeth and I can feel him grappling with his emotions.

Eventually, he says, "I can't say I'm happy about it. I'm definitely *not* happy about it, but I can't be angry at you. I broke your trust and you didn't know how I still felt until I arrived here. After reading your diary, I can see how complicated your relationship with him was. I was quite shocked, actually. The person I know you to be would never stand for some of the crap you put up with from him. You certainly haven't with me."

"I suppose that's what happens when you get older."

"If you're telling me last night was a one-time thing and it won't ever happen again, then I have to believe you."

"I promise you, it won't ever happen again. Chris and I are done. Truly done. We've finally reached a good place. And when I think about him now, there's no emotional pull there. No sense of loss, or of things being left unsaid, or things feeling incomplete. I appreciate this is a really *really* tough pill for you to swallow, especially when you've just flown halfway around the world to find me, but if we're to make us work there can't be any more secrets between us. I need you to know even before you turned up just now, I chose you. I'd already decided I was going to call you and see if we could get over our differences. But then you surprised me."

"If bloody Air Zealand hadn't of been on strike I would have been here yesterday then maybe last night wouldn't of happened."

"Maybe you weren't meant to arrive until today," I say gently, knowing if he had arrived yesterday, Chris and I wouldn't have had the opportunity to heal in the way we have. "But regardless of what happened last night you must know, I choose you. Today, tomorrow, and always."

Very gently he hooks a finger under my chin and lifts my face. His soft grey eyes simultaneously dance, smoulder, and care. I'm lost in his gaze, but instead of feeling off-kilter, I feel safe. This time I'm falling into the abyss, knowing he's there to catch me.

"There's one more thing."

"What more could there possibility be?" he says, pulling back.

"He gave me this." I waggle my right hand in front of his nose, the yellow diamond ring catching the light. "But I don't want you to panic. It doesn't mean what you think. Apparently he's had it since we were together."

"So why give it to you now?"

"Because he's finally accepted we're over. Yes, when he bought it, he intended it to be an engagement ring, but he knows he's lost me, and he's made his peace with that. He wants me to keep it as a memento of the good times."

"Bloody expensive memento."

"Probably. It has something written inside that is strangely familiar, and exactly how I feel about you. He says the words came to him in a dream."

We both gaze at each other and utter our sacred words together, "Today, tomorrow, always."

Looking into my eyes, Gav's face breaks into a broad smile.

Bugger! Those damn dimples get me every time.

I hold my breath, as a million mini-fireworks explode inside my body. I want him, all of him, just as much as he wants me.

I'm expecting him to kiss me, but instead he pulls a small black box out of his jeans pocket. Opening it, I see my sparkling diamond earrings inside.

"You left in such a hurry, you seem to have forgotten these," he says, smirking.

Taking them out of the box, I slide them back into my ears, then he leans forward and plants a tender kiss on my mouth. The dryness of his lips making ours stick together. He tastes of ginger biscuits and seventy-two hours of airline food. The poor man is exhausted.

Licking my lips to re-moisten them, I whisper into his neck, "Let me put your case in my room, and find you a fresh towel. I'm sure you'll want to take that shower now."

"Point the way, my angel. I know how much I must stink."

Chapter 55

*W*ith Gav safely packed off to the shower, I load the dishwasher with all the plates from the past twenty-four hours.

Deep guttural groans emanate from the bathroom, I assume as the warm water washes away the layers of travel from Gav's skin. Padding slowly through the lounge and towards the bedroom end of the house, I hover outside the bathroom door.

Should I do this? Is it too soon? But what was it Chris said only yesterday? Live for the moment and never again let fears or insecurities stop us going after what we want.

Well my moment has just travelled halfway around the world to fight for me, and I'm damn well going to fight for him too.

Dropping my kimono to the floor, I tiptoe quietly into the bathroom and step into the shower behind him.

Gav sucks in a breath as soon as my hands touch his body. He doesn't turn around and instead presses his palms flat against the wall in front of him. I lather his back with body wash and take my time scrubbing every inch of his skin. Reacquainting myself with the bulk of his frame, the knots of muscles in his shoulders, his firm arms, the muscular 'V' of his back that leads down to two hunks of meat in his backside. I run my hands up and down his body, re-grounding him, just as his physical presence re-grounds me.

I lean forward and press an open-mouthed kiss onto his shoulder, which tastes of clean skin and warm water.

He breathes out through flared nostrils, his body shaking and shivering with need and pent-up emotion.

I slowly close my eyes at the same time I close my teeth, gently nipping and sucking his skin. Purposefully wanting to leave my mark. He is mine and I am his. There is no one else, only him.

Without warning he turns. His eyes hooded with desire. His body glistening with water. His pecs twitching involuntarily. I bite my bottom lip. The man has never looked more beautiful. A heady mix of strength, power, and vulnerability.

His eyes drink me in, as I fail to stop my own gaze travelling the length of his body, appreciating every rippling curve of muscle, settling on his erect cock which gives away his obvious need.

Saying nothing, he pours body wash onto his palms and cleans me. Beginning at my neck, his hands trail a feather-light path over my shoulders, down my torso. Cupping my breasts, gently feeling their weight, his thumbs rubbing over the tips of my throbbing dusky rosebuds which tighten at his touch. My head lolls back as my legs part slightly of their own accord, the spark between them pulsing with desire. The void within me aching for him.

The rising steam and heat of the water is no match for the burning flames that are licking their way through my body. My insides a white heat of desire.

Down, down, his hands continue in gentle circular motions, momentarily resting on my waist, before sliding down my backside and grasping handfuls of flesh. He pulls me towards him, closing the gap between us. Our bodies connecting as if for the first time.

His skin is on fire and I jump into the inferno with him. All the while our eyes remain glued to each other as the water beats on the back of his neck and waterfalls over the both of us.

He's washing away any remnants of Chris, and reclaiming me as his own.

"Oh Gav," I say breathlessly, my eyes glassy with tears. "I love you so much."

"I never doubted it," he says, sliding his hand between my legs, parting my folds and sliding two fingers inside my hot, wet core.

My knees give way as desire pulses through my veins.

"I need you in me," I say without hesitation.

"Be patient, my love. Let's not rush it," he says, his fingers stimulating the deepest part of me as his thumb simultaneously strokes my swollen nub.

"Jesus Christ, Gav, I'm on the edge already."

"Not yet, sweetheart. Be patient. It'll be worth the wait, I promise. I've had four flights and precisely eighty-six hours to imagine this moment."

Before I can protest further he covers my mouth with his. His tongue finding mine as he licks and sucks his way back into my heart.

"Sod it, we've got the rest of our lives to be patient," I mumble, jumping up onto him. He catches me easily, wrapping my legs around my waist as he pushes me back against the cold tiles. I suck in a sharp breath when my skin touches the freezing tiles behind me. The contrast between the heat of his chest pressing against my stomach and breasts, and the cold on my back is intoxicating, and I feel my body and soul detach. My physical form so connected yet disconnected all at once.

He kisses me more tenderly now, taking the lead and forcing me to slow down.

"I'm never letting you go again," I say into his mouth.

"I'm never leaving you again," he replies, holding my full weight with one hand while he smooths my hair back with his other.

"And I'm never running away again. I'm done with running."

"Pleased to hear it. Because I love you, Angel, with every fibre of my being. This is it. You and I are going to be together forever."

As his lips meet mine again, as if by its own accord his cock slides effortlessly into me. My warm wet folds welcoming him willingly as I stretch and spread to accommodate all of him.

We both release an appreciative groan as our bodies reunite.

We fit so well together, it's as if I were made for him, and he for me. I'm the perfect sheath to protect him. He's the perfect sabre to make me feel safe.

Still holding my weight, our hips unconsciously begin to rock back and forth. Each thrust then retraction an ebb and flow that brings us both closer to home.

I moan as he moves inside me, and he exhales small puffs of air against the side of my neck as he thrusts in and out.

"God you feel so good. So tight. I've missed you."

"I've missed you too," I say, searching out his gaze again, my own fingers running through his hair and cupping his face.

I allow my full weight to fall against him, wrapping myself around every part of him. Him, the solid tree trunk to my ditzy, dizzy blossom.

I feel myself fast approaching the edge, my insides quivering around him, ready to explode, but before I fall over the cliff, he whispers, "Not yet, my angel. Not yet."

Without warning he pulls out of me, and I give a little yelp of despair. He carries me, dripping wet, to the bed and lays me down on my back. Kneeling on the floor at the foot of the bed, he splays my legs wide.

For a long moment, he remains still. His eyes gaze over the whole of me. Every smooth surface, every fold, every crevice, every perfect imperfection on show for him to admire. I'm wide open and unashamed to show him all of me.

"Jesus, how is it possible you're even more beautiful than the last time I saw you," he says, his appreciation making me even more hot, wet, and swollen.

He reaches for my ankles and lifts my legs over his shoulders, burying his face between my legs. My eyes roll back in their sockets when he uses his tongue to part my folds and circle my clit.

"And you taste so damn good as well," he says lapping me up.

My arms collapse above my head, all my strength having escaped out of me. My damp hair spread out like a fan, my nipples tightening into hard pearls as I lie open and exposed.

Every nerve ending in my body is alive and zinging with electricity, and I'm not sure how much more I can take.

Gav's tongue is a masterclass in sensitivity. Adjusting to every quiver, every tremble, every pulse moving through me. Holding me on the precipice but not allowing me to fall over.

I feel free. Unbound. Connected. Authentic.

I know he has me, that I'm safe, and now we're back together again, no matter what ever life may throw our way, we will come through any challenge together. The strength of our love and trust in the other an unbreakable bond.

I release another deep guttural moan as he slides two fingers back inside me, pressing upwards, finding my G-spot.

"Holy shit," I moan, my back arching involuntarily.

It's almost too much, and just when I think I can't take any more, he reaches up with his free hand and rolls the tip of my nipple between his thumb and forefinger, sending a lightning strike of desire down to meet the warm expanding pool of desire in the pit of my stomach.

I want to tell him to stop. Not because I want him to, but because I'm convinced I will explode into a ball of flames if he doesn't, but instead I relinquish all control and continue to fall into the abyss.

I know he'll catch me when I need him to.

The feeling of his fingers inside me, pressing up into my core, combined with the licking and sucking of his tongue and the delicate dance of his fingertips on my nipple send a white heat spiralling higher and higher that transcends all physical pleasure.

I close my eyes, the rest of the world lost to me. All I'm aware of is the man before me, on his knees, worshipping me.

Just when I think I can't take any more he pulls his fingers out of me, places one hand on my stomach, one on my back, and flips me over.

Standing on the floor at the foot of the bed, he grabs my hips and pulls me back to meet him.

"You okay?" he asks softly, the tone of his voice in contrast to the urgency of his actions.

"I need you," I breathe. "Now."

He enters me, slowly at first, giving my tight muscles time to accommodate him, before he slides in fully. Filling me completely.

I grip the bed sheets, my hands scrunching into tight balls as the sweet feeling of him gliding into me over and over blocks out everything else.

I look over my shoulder at him and our eyes connect.

"God, I love you," he says.

"And I love you," I say, although those three words are not meaningful enough to convey the depths of feeling I have for this man.

He is it.

This is it.

Everything I've ever wanted—to love and be loved—is right here, right now in this moment.

He leans over me, his torso connecting with my back as he leaves a trail of kisses along my shoulder. All the while he fills me over and over. Each thrust deepening our trust in the other.

Wrapping his hand around my stomach he pulls me upright, my back flush against his strong hard chest. Our skin hot and wet, beads of sweat form at my temples and in between my breasts.

Still inside me, the intensity builds as his thrusts come deeper and faster. I really don't know how much longer I can hold on, but then he slides his hand over my stomach, down to between my legs and with one flick of his finger, I'm done.

The waves come crashing down around me, just as he freezes inside me. Restraining himself so he can feel every pulsating quiver as my walls crumble around him. I buck and writhe against him, but he holds me close, his mouth breathing against my cheek, his hands wrapped around me, our torsos connected, as I give all of myself to him.

Without expectation. Without condition. I give him all of me and he receives it willingly.

The waves roll on and on as I scream out and moan, my breath shallow and shaky in my body, yet he continues to hold onto me. Delaying his own gratification so he can keep me safe and delight in all that I'm giving him.

Just when I feel my orgasm ebbing away, he moves once more. And with one almighty thrust releases into me, triggering another cascade of pleasure to crash through me.

Bent over me, clamped together, he cries out as he empties himself of everything he has to give and I welcome his warmth into my very soul.

We are combined into one.

No more places to hide.

Nothing more to be ashamed of.

No more secrets to keep us apart.

Whatever happens now, we both know from this moment on, we're bound together forever.

Chapter 56

*S*atiated and spent, we spend the rest of the day in bed. Laughing, talking, eating (the poor man is starving; thank gawd for frozen pizzas) and we make love over and over again, but by late-afternoon jet lag finally claims him and he falls into a heavy sleep.

I leave him be, taking my yoga mat outside, and enjoy the sun on my skin and the feeling of authenticity in my gut, as all the pieces of my life finally slot into place.

The following evening, when Lynne arrives home from Nelson, she welcomes Gav in her usual mumsy manner, insisting that he stay at her house, with me.

However, having already discussed it, Gav and I both agree that that would be too weird on the already weird scale of domestic arrangements. We thank Lynne for her kind offer but ask if she knows of anyone with a short-term rental we could decamp to.

It turns out a friend of Lynne's is desperate for someone to look after their home for the next six weeks, as they've decided to fly to Australia to spend Christmas with their daughter and grand-children.

"I'd agreed to pop in and check on the house, but I know they'd prefer someone there all the time. You'll be doing them a massive favour," Lynne says. "And I'm sure they wouldn't mind putting you on their car insurance as well.

So forty-eight hours later, Gav and I are safely ensconced together in a lovely home, not far from Mel's, and while he sits at the kitchen table on a Skype call with Anth, discussing the ongoing launch plan of their new business, I'm humming to myself while I batch cook food for Mel's freezer.

When Saturday arrives, relieved once again of my caring duties for Mel, I take the opportunity to show Gav a bit more of what New Zealand has to offer and we drive up the coast to Kaikōura. A small coastal town a couple of hours north of Christchurch. I've booked us an overnight stay in a tiny bach and we spend the afternoon watching the waves roll in as we create more waves between the sheets.

The next morning we take a boat trip out into the bay, and although we're out of season for the famed migration of Blue, Humpback, and Minke whales, some of the resident Sperm whales grace us with their presence. Their enormous flat-nosed snouts breaking the surface, before they disappear back into the ocean, taking the sound of their constant sonar clicks with them. On our way back to shore, a pod of cute black and white Hector dolphins chase the bow wave at the front of the boat.

"I've never seen anything like them," Gav says, and I squeeze his hand tightly, thinking today couldn't be more different than the day I first saw Hector dolphins. Eleven years ago, almost to the day, when Chris and I visited Akaroa. I remember how much I was compromising myself back then. Denying my true self to try and make our relationship work, when everything was fundamentally broken. Seeing how free those tiny cheeky dolphins were, I'd wanted to jump in the sea and swim away with them. It wasn't long after that I left.

We head back to Christchurch in time for dinner, a warmed-up lasagne courtesy of my batch cooking earlier in the week.

Gav, his mouth full of pasta, béchamel sauce, and salad leaves, mumbles, "You know Angel, I've been looking at the numbers and I'm wondering whether to launch the business over here as well. Both Australia and New Zealand's adoption of UX and CX design best practises is about five years behind that of the UK, but I reckon it's about to explode. Their universities are already gearing up for it. They have a great talent pool of eager graduates coming into the workplace. If we took a punt, we could be at the forefront of that first market wave. Potentially clean up. I'm just saying it could be an option if we fancied staying on longer. Maybe for a year or so. I'm sure you could expand your business over here as well, if that was the case."

"But we'd need visas. At the moment we can only stay until mid-January. Finding a way to live here permanently is not easy. Neither of us have an employer to sponsor us. I don't qualify under their Skills Shortage List, and because you're self-taught you don't have the right degree. The only option would be to get an Entrepreneurs and Investor visa, and you need to have a big chunk of cash to do that. Trust me, I've looked into this before, and there's no easy way to gain residency here… other than marrying a Kiwi, of course."

"It was just a thought," he says, loading up his fork with another slab of lasagne.

The following week passes quickly as Gav and I settle into our new routine. Lynne continues to do the morning shift with the children, helping get them up and ready before taking them to school and nursery, then staying until lunchtime helping with household

ISABELLA WILES

chores. Meanwhile, I head to the pool, or take a morning yoga class, while Gav Skypes Anth, making the most of the few hours when their clocks overlap. It looks like the pair are close to closing their first major customer, meaning Anth can finally resign and things can kick-off properly.

I head over to Mel's at lunchtime, relieving Lynne, and we either head to the hospital if she has an appointment, or I take her out for some air if she's up to it, and if not, then I find another way to cheer her up. Watching reruns of *Friends* has become one of the many things we do together. I'm determined to spend those few precious hours in the afternoon being her mate, not her carer. What is it they say, *'laughter is the best medicine'*, and boy do we laugh.

Come school pick-up time, I swing back into action, picking up the ankle biters and giving them their tea. When Karl arrives home, I head back to Gav and our temporary abode, where he'll have prepared our dinner.

It's a simple life. Uncomplicated, but now that Gav's here as well, hugely gratifying.

On Friday Karl urges me to take a longer weekend off.

"You've been amazing, Vicky. But we can manage. Take the opportunity to venture further afield. Show Gavin around. Especially before the schools break up at the end of next week and God and his mother take their summer holidays."

The following day, at his suggestion Gav and I pack our bags and head down to Lake Wanaka, a holiday hotspot in the middle of the South Island.

Despite being further south, when we arrive the weather is still a balmy twenty-one degrees. We've rented another bach for four nights, in a prime position on the shore of the beautiful lake, and anyone spying on us would assume we're on honeymoon.

On Tuesday morning, after I've showered and changed into a light sundress I head outside, my stomach clenching into nervous knots.

Gav smiles as I join him out on the deck and climb into the hammock next to him. He lifts his arm, so I can nestle into the crock of his armpit, kissing the top of my head before returning his attention to the book he's reading. Something about a CEO's guide to tech start-ups.

The rising sun glistens on the surface of the water as it begins its upwards climb into the sky.

Another new day.

But this is a day that's about to change all others.

"Gav," I say.

"U-huh," he mumbles, his nose still buried in his book.

"I have something to tell you."

"U-huh," he says again, still not giving me his full attention.

I grab the book and toss it onto the ground. Now I have his attention.

"I'm pregnant."

His face explodes into a wide grin, and I want to reach up and kiss each of his gorgeous dimples in turn, but I hold back.

"Are you sure? Have you done a test?"

I shake my head.

"No, and I'm only a couple of days late, but I've been pregnant enough times to know."

"Angel, that's incredible. Who knew all we needed was a change of scene and an opportunity to connect on a whole new level, and our baby would come to us."

I sigh heavily, knowing what he hasn't understood.

"Listen to me. Getting ahead of myself," he says, his face beaming. "I know there's still a long way to go." His tone clouded with a sliver of worry.

He places a protective hand on my stomach. "Well, hello little one. This is your daddy here. Now, I need you to stay in there for the next nine months, but when you're big and strong and ready for the world, I'll be there to meet you."

I squeeze my eyes tight shut, suck in a breath and open them again. "The thing is…" I falter, trying to find the right words. "When I look back at the dates, it would have happened the weekend you arrived here. And there's a possibility it…it…"

…*might not be yours.* I can't actually say the words out loud. It's too cruel.

He freezes, looks at me, and I watch as a ticker tape of micro emotions race across his face:

Recognition.

Knowing.

Anger.

Understanding.

Sadness.

Resolve.

Forgiveness.

Love.

His hand still on my stomach, he says again, "Like I said little one, this is your daddy here, and when the time is right, I'm excited to meet you."

My eyes brim with tears and he pulls me into him. I collapse onto his chest, my tears leaving damp patches on his T-shirt.

"You know it only happened that one time."

"I know, and I wish it hadn't… God how I wish it hadn't." With one foot on the floor, he gently rocks us back and forth in the hammock. "But you shouldn't be crying, sweetheart, this is a happy moment. We're going to have a baby. And that's all I'm focused on."

"But what if it's not yours?" I whimper.

"I don't care. I'll love it regardless."

We both stay silent for another moment, allowing what we've both said to settle around us.

"We'll need to tell Chris. He has a right to know," he says, "and if it turns out to be his, he has a right to be involved. But regardless, I'm not going anywhere. I'm here for you… and this little one," he says, stroking my stomach again.

We fall into a comfortable silence again. A bird chirps directly

462

above us, and some early morning jet-skiers zoom past on the water down on the lake, leaving streaks of white crests on the otherwise perfectly still azure surface.

"But there's another problem," I say.

"Oh?"

"I can't fly home. Not until after the baby's born. I can't take that risk again. Even coming down here on Tim's private jet, as luxurious as that was, brought it all back. There's no way I'm flying until my baby's safely here. I don't care how small the risk is I may miscarry again, I won't do anything to increase that risk. I simply won't."

"Nor should you," he says, stroking the outside of my arm. "And I wouldn't want you to. The most important thing now is keeping you and the baby safe."

"So what do we do? You go back and try and raise over a hundred grand and we start the process of applying for an Entrepreneur visa? Even if we do that, it'll likely take months, and I'll have to stay in the country illegally until then. I'll be at risk of being deported and never being allowed back."

"There is an obvious answer." Gavin raises an eyebrow in my direction. "It's glaringly obvious, but I'm not sure you'll like it."

I cock my head, listening. "Go on. I'm all ears."

"I ask Chris to marry you."

I turn around so sharply, I lose my balance and almost fall out of the hammock. With one strong arm, Gav catches my flailing arms, and pulls me up onto his stomach.

We're nose to nose, and I can see he's deadly serious. "You wouldn't. I couldn't. I don't want to marry him. I want to marry you." My words tumble out of me at an alarming speed.

"Well that's interesting," he says, curling his lips into a smile. "I seem to remember a big long speech a few years back, something about *'you must never ask me to marry you'* and marriage being a *'sacrifice'* and that *'every day that we're choosing to be together, it's because we want to be, not because a piece of paper says so'.*"

"Yeah, well. A lot's happened since then. Maybe I've changed as well." I smirk. "I actually thought you were going to propose the day you stepped off the plane in New York. Instead you presented me with these."

I touch the diamond earrings that he gave me, now that they're safely clipped back into my ears.

"Hmmm." He crinkles the corner of his eyes in a mischievous smile. "Stay there one sec."

He heads off into the bach, returning a few moments later. When he doesn't climb back into the hammock, and remains standing, I swing my legs down over the side and face him.

He leans over, plants a light kiss on my lips, before sinking down onto one knee. My hands fly up to my mouth and more tears spring into the corner of my eyes.

"You were right, Vicky. I would have asked you to marry me that day, and every day since, if I hadn't believed it isn't what you wanted. I've been keeping these safe ever since our time in Grand Cayman. Why do you think I dashed off across the car park that day? I'd already bought these, but was getting them resized, and hurricane or no hurricane I was determined to pick them up. I figured you'd change your mind one day. I just never knew when that moment would be."

An involuntary shiver ripples through my body and I can't stop the smile that stretches all the way up to the corners of my eyes.

He flicks open the box and I inhale sharply. Inside is the exact same ring I was admiring the day Fiona and Mike were with us and we all stumbled into Gems International.

The engagement ring, a unique mix of white and yellow gold set with a stunning trio of diamonds, is as breathtaking as I remember. Also in the box is a matching eternity ring. Designed in a channel setting, the exact same style as my earrings and my precious bracelet that I've never taken off my right wrist. Ten small diamonds glisten around the circular band and together the two rings make a stunning set.

He lifts out the eternity ring, holding it between his thumb and forefinger. "I imagined giving this one to you on the birth of our first child, or our wedding day… whichever came first. So I think I'll hold onto that one for just a bit longer." He places the eternity ring back in the box and picks up the engagement ring. "But I always hoped that I'd get this on your finger one day."

Tears of joy roll down my face and my cheeks hurt from smiling, but I don't care. My heart swells inside my chest and I feel as if I will burst open with joy.

"Victoria, will you promise to continue choosing me, today, tomorrow, and always… but will you marry Chris—if it will keep our baby safe?"

Nodding my head and crying with joy, I lunge forward and wrap my arms around his neck.

"Yes, Gav. Of course I choose you, and yes I'll marry Chris… that's if he'll have me."

"Something tells me he'll do anything for you, even marrying you so that we can keep our family together."

Holding out my hand, Gav slides the ring onto the third finger of my left hand, where it fits perfectly.

I hold it up, admiring how it glints in the sunlight, which also bounces off the other diamond ring I now wear on the third finger of my right hand.

Chapter 57

"We have something to tell you," I say to Chris a few nights later. The three of us gathered in his sleek, black and chrome living room. The million-dollar view Mel has told me about, perfectly framed by the floor to ceiling windows.

"And something to ask you," Gav says, his eyes travelling around Chris's pristine bachelor pad. I reckon he's thinking the same thing as me.

There's no way you could have a baby in here. Not unless you wrapped them in cling film and stopped them touch anything.

"It's amazing news," Gav continues, "but potentially complicated." He squeezes my hand, offering me a supportive smile.

I slowly close then re-open my eyes, suck in a long breath, and force out the words, "Chris, I'm pregnant."

Chris's face instantly breaks into a wide smile.

"That's amazing news. Congratulations. You must be ecstatic, Goose. And you, Gav. What a result. And so soon after you've made up."

He leans forward and offers Gavin a strong handshake, and me a warm, friendly hug.

He hasn't figured it out, but he seems genuinely pleased... which is good.

"The thing is…" I falter.

I drop my gaze to the floor and the conversation comes to an abrupt halt.

"The thing is," Gav says, then pauses, before he picks up the thread again, "there's a chance it might be yours."

I watch as Chris's eyes meet Gav's, and Chris's smile falls away. A moment passes between them. Without either of them having to say the actual words, both of them acknowledge the truth.

Chris and I have slept together.

Chris looks initially shocked, then defensive, then confused.

"Vicky's told me everything," Gav continues. "And she tells me it's over between you two, and I trust her."

"And you're right to trust her," Chris says, his gaze drifting across to me. His feelings haven't changed one iota, I can tell. His eyes communicate everything he can't say out loud.

I'm happy for you, they say.

Thank you, mine reply.

I only want you to be happy.

I know.

And I'll never stop loving you. You're always in my heart.

I know.

"I'm glad we're on the same page then," Gav says, his tone brusque and businesslike, unaware of the unspoken conversation between Chris and I. "But that doesn't change the fact that this child may be yours."

"I know," he replies, looking down at his feet.

"You don't have to make any major decisions now," I say. "Regardless of its paternity, Gav and I are committed to raising it together, but obviously that won't take away from your rights, if you're its biological father. I know how painful it's been for you with Louis, and he's not even biologically yours."

"Irrelevant, he's mine," Chris says, with a brush of his hand.

"We want to be clear: we would never stop you having a relationship with it, if that's what you would want," Gav says.

Chris stands and walks towards the windows, looking out across the bay. It's overcast today and the clouds hang heavy and grey in the sky. The waves churning up foam along the shore edge. His hands thrust deep into his pockets, his shoulders rolled forward, he remains looking out over the sea.

"I'm not saying I don't want to be a part of this, but regardless of who the biological father is, I want you both to raise it. You're its family."

"But you might be its family too," I say. "And Mellie and Michelle, and your mum and dad, and Dean, and everyone else here. We can't forget that."

"And I'd never get in the way of them having a relationship with it, but I can't."

"What do you mean *you can't?*"

I know this can't be about money or his potential financial responsibilities. He's already shown how he's willing to support a child. One that turned out not to be his, and one he's not allowed to see.

Maybe that's it. He knows how painful it will be if he can't be its full-time dad, so he'd rather opt-out at the beginning.

"I just can't. But whatever you need, I'll support you," he says, turning back around, a small smile creeping across his lips. "And you, Gav. You have my full support."

Gav and I exchange a look.

This isn't how we were expecting this to go.

"Good," Gav says, "because we've one more thing to ask you. We need to find a way to keep Vicky in the country until the baby's born. It's too risky for her to fly."

"No problem. I can make that happen. I'd do anything for her, and your baby."

Chapter 58

*G*av and I spend a quiet Christmas and New Year together, adjusting to our news and, without getting too far ahead of ourselves, allowing a smidgeon of hope to creep into our hearts.

Could this finally be it?

I contact my GP in the UK and ask for my medical records to be sent over, so I can register with an LMC, or Lead Maternity Carer as they're known over here. Sadly, I don't qualify for free healthcare, as I'm not a resident, but Chris covers the cost.

He flies up to the North Island to spend Christmas with his brother, Dean, and his family, meanwhile Mel, Karl, and the kids all go to Lynne's for Christmas Day, but they invite us over to theirs for a Boxing Day barbecue.

From the one other time I've spent Christmas in the Southern Hemisphere, I remember it's a much more laid-back affair than the formal turkey with all the trimmings we have back in the UK.

Gav helps Karl grill meat patties on the barbecue for the kids, and tuna steaks for the rest of us, meanwhile I play with the children, and help prepare the salads.

"I'm bursting to tell Mel," I whisper to Gav, as I carry two large platters outside.

"I know you are, but let's wait a wee while longer. At least until you've met your midwife and we know everything's okay," he whispers back.

My LMC is a lovely jolly woman in her mid-fifties. Rotund in stature and matronly in every sense of the word. Now she's had the benefit of reading all my notes, including the additional tests the fertility consultant had ordered but had been unable to give me—I left the country before my follow-up appointment—she confirms, "No underlying conditions. Everything looks normal."

I visibly exhale, before another thought crosses my mind. "But what about the Rhesus gene? Have I been sensitised?"

She looks down at the notes and double checks. "Nope. No Rhesus antibodies in your blood." Looking up and meeting my gaze, a gentle smile spreading across her face, she adds, "Everything looks absolutely fine, Victoria. You've been incredibly unlucky but there's no indication that, despite your history, this pregnancy is at risk. Nevertheless, I'm going to keep a close eye on you. Just like all my other little Chookie Hens."

Over the next six months Gav splits his time between the UK and New Zealand, taking month-long stints in each country. His first job when he flew back home was to formally gift Leo to Mark, Becca, and their kids. It appears the cat, that was always a bit funny with men, struck up some kind of bromance when Mark stayed at mine and they've become inseparable ever since.

When back in the UK, with nothing to distract him, Gav spends every waking hour working on his fledgling business.

"I owe it to our future," he says, when I tell him I'm concerned about the long hours he's working, but then I did the same when I started my business. "It's fine V, I only have myself to look after, and we won't have the luxury of extra time for much longer."

I've also made Gav a director in my own company, so he can keep an eye on that while he's back in the UK as well. Although

Clive, Angela, and Helen are flying high without me. Thank goodness I had the foresight to give them all share options when I did.

Despite the forced absences, Gav and I never go more than five weeks between seeing each other, and now that connectivity has shrunk the planet, we text or Skype every day.

Compared to all my others, this pregnancy has been an absolute breeze. Warranted, I've never got further than fifteen weeks before, but my morning sickness subsides at twelve weeks on the dot, and during my second trimester I'm positively glowing. My skin has never been more radiant and even my hair and nails seem stronger. Both the lifestyle and the climate here in New Zealand seem to suit my pregnancy, especially as my third trimester coincides with the coolest months of the year. I'm not sure how I would have coped carrying around an inbuilt hot water bottle through the insufferable heat of an English summer.

In the end I didn't need to marry Chris to stay in the country, he created a fictious role in his company and has sponsored my so-called employment. Nevertheless, and more to keep myself occupied and not let my brain turn to complete mush, when I'm not helping care for Mel whose brutal battle with cancer continues, and I'm not keeping an eye on my business interests back home, I've used my spare time to overhaul Chris's company brand. Gav has also re-designed all his websites, upgrading the user experience, and together we've relaunched the marketing for Chris's latest property development. It seemed the least we could do after everything he's done to support us.

Gav and I moved out of Lynne's friend's house when her friend returned from Australia and we've rented a comfortable two-bed Californian style bungalow in the family-friendly suburb of Somerfield, not far from Mel up in Cashmere and only a short fifteen minute drive from the centre of town. It's not big or flash, but it's perfect for what we need. A large open-plan living space, that is the norm over here, opens onto a wide deck and sunny north-facing garden, complete with a sunken firepit.

The house came fully furnished and I haven't needed to buy a thing for the baby as Michelle, Mel and even Dean's wife, Lisa, have donated everything I could possibly need, and more.

As July gives way to August, everyone is increasingly excited about the baby coming, meanwhile I flip-flop between shaking like a bag of nerves and fizzing with excitement. After everything I've been through, I'm finally going to have a baby. Not a godchild (as lovely as they all are, and as much as I love them); I'm going to have a child of my very own. A new life that has chosen me to be its guide.

✯

After a week of Braxton Hicks, bang on schedule on my due date in late August, I feel the pang of a real contraction around 2:00 p.m. It catches me by surprise, and initially my veins flood with fear, until I consciously remind myself, that this cramp isn't the start of me losing a child, rather the opposite. In a matter of hours I should be holding my newborn son or daughter in my arms.

There's a chill in the air today, so I wrap myself in the duvet off our bed. I haven't slept well these past few nights, (my bladder seems to have shrunk to the size of a teaspoon); so I'm sneaking in additional naps wherever I can.

I pad through to the open-plan living space where Gav is working. Tapping away on his laptop on the dining room table.

"Babes," I say coyly, unable to wipe the grin off my face.

"U-huh." He doesn't look away from the screen.

"I think it might be starting."

He turns sharply and pulls the pen he had clamped between his teeth out of his mouth. "Are you sure?"

"I'll know in a few hours if they don't go away. Oh, hang on, here's another one coming." With one hand in the middle of my back, the other on the side of the kitchen counter, I close my eyes and breathe. Focusing my mind on relaxing into the contraction rather than tensing up and fighting against it. I exhale a long slow outbreath, the air leaving my body through pursed lips.

Gav rushes to my side. "Are you alright? What do you need? A glass of water? A lie-down? The yoga ball?"

"I need you to chill out," I laugh, the contraction having now passed. "This could go on for hours. Babies only come quickly in TV dramas."

Four hours of gentle bouncing on my pregnancy ball later, with Gav next to me the whole time, two stopwatches in his hand; one to time the length of my contractions, the other monitoring the gap between them, we pick up my maternity bag and make our way to hospital.

By now my contractions are five minutes apart and lasting a good two minutes, and when I'm examined my midwife announces, "Four centimetres already. Well done. You're well on your way."

Gav sneaks out to make all the necessary pre-announcement phone calls, meanwhile I slip into a nice warm birthing pool. I'm hoping to have a natural birth with as little intervention as possible, and for the last ten weeks Gav and I have been falling asleep to the sound of my guided hypno-birthing meditation CD. The gentle backing track music now playing quietly in the background as I settle into my labour.

I close my eyes and breathe deeply, visualising my cervix opening like the petals of a flower as a couple of stronger surges take hold of my body.

"Are you climbing in as well?" the midwife asks Gav when he returns to our birthing suite.

"Already got my togs on underneath." He twangs the elastic waistband of his tracky bottoms.

"I thought you Pommy's called them swimming trunks?" she says good naturedly.

"We do, but *togs* always sounds much more fun don't you think."

My eyes still closed; I feel him slide into the pool behind me.

Cradling me in his arms, we settle into a gentle rhythm, moaning and breathing in sync.

Although I'm aware of the pain, I'm on top of it and I trust my primal instincts implicitly. I know with every fibre of my being, *I am fulfilling my destiny.* I was always meant to be the mother of this child.

I've never felt more tuned in to my authentic self. Moving and shifting position whenever my body guides me to do so.

The hours drift smoothly by as in this dimly lit, calm space, Gav and I labour together.

A few hours later the midwife checks me again. "Eight centimetres. You're almost there, Victoria. Keep going. You're doing amazing."

"When will I know when to push?" I ask, my voice shaky, my focus having been totally inwards since I climbed into the pool, making the very effort of speaking feel alien to me right now.

"You'll know," she says, confidently. "Your body will tell you."

I open my eyes and Gav catches me look at the clock on the wall.

Two a.m.

Kissing my shoulder he murmurs, "Don't worry about the time, Angel. It'll take as long as it takes."

Meanwhile, in my own head I know with absolute certainty, *this baby will be born by 4.00 a.m.*

It's not long before my body feels the need to shift position again. On my knees and with my arms draped over the side of the pool I feel the energy shift. A reverse vortex spiralling down into me.

All the other times I've ever felt all my chakras lined up like this–as if I'd stepped onto some kind of invisible vortex–my energy always surged upwards and out of the top of my head. A sign I was connecting with my true inner power.

This feels the exact same, but in reverse.

The energy shooting down into me, entering the top of my head, spinning down through my core and into my base chakra. I know it's the spirit of my child connecting with its own physical form, and I know it's time for him or her to come into the world.

My eyes closed, I don't have to push that hard as I feel the life within me begin its first independent journey and leave behind the safety of my womb. The downward spiralling energy guiding it out into the world.

Come on Little One. Almost there, my inner voice whispers.

My midwife notices the shift in my behaviour and calmly instructs, "Looks like your baby's on its way, Victoria. If you put your hands between your legs, you can help guide Baby here."

I do as she says, and my fingertips connect with the soft downy hair and soft folds of my baby's crown as he or she pushes their way into the world.

It's the most magical sensation, and despite the discomfort of my sinews and muscles stretching, I relinquish all control and allow my body–and my baby–to do what it needs. The only thing within my control right now, is the visualisation in my mind and the timing and depth of my breath.

"That's it my angel," I hear Gav say somewhere behind me, his voice cracking with emotion as he witnesses the miracle of birth unfolding in front of him.

"Nobody move," the midwife says firmly. "Baby's cord is around its neck."

I feel Gav freeze behind me and I do the same. Holding my breath and battling every instinct in me to push.

No! No! No! my internal voice screams, I *CAN NOT* lose you now Little One. Hold still, just one more moment. Mammy's here. I've got you.

However, the midwife is unfazed by this unexpected complication and with delft fingers she reaches between my legs and untangles the umbilical cord from around my baby's neck.

"There. Done." Pulling her arm out of the water and shaking it dry, she announces, "Right then. I think Baby will be born with your next contraction."

But I know different. I know the time is now.

I suck in one enormous breath, and with every ounce of power and energy in my body I gently guide my baby into the world. Catching it between my legs and cradling it underwater in my palms.

Gav leans over my shoulder and cries, "Oh Angel you did it. It's a girl. We have a baby daughter."

But I'm not listening to him, my gaze is totally focused on the miracle in my hands. Knowing I'm still breathing for her through the umbilical cord, for one long moment I sway her gently underwater. Enjoying the final moment where we're still connected; two separate souls, but as one.

I'm instantly in love. Marvelling at how perfect she is. Her blonde hair wafting in the water like seaweed in a retreating a tide. Her eyes alert and focused on me. We already know each other. Our souls and our destiny long since laid out in the stars.

In one gentle move, I lean back into Gav's waiting lap and lift my daughter out of the water and into my arms; where she takes her first enormous breath and lets out a healthy cry.

"Congratulations," the midwife says brightly, as she methodically but discreetly begins her routine checks.

My newborn baby girl in my arms, I've never felt more calm, more centred, and more at peace.

"I love you so damn much." Gav kisses my shoulder, "You were amazing."

"I love you too," I glance over my shoulder and take in his beaming smile, his eyes glassy with unshed tears as he marvels at the new life in my arms.

"I can't believe it. We have a daughter. I'm a *tad*."

"Yes, you are." I kiss him lightly on the lips before turning my focus back to the baby in my arms, who having already rooted her way to my breast, is now nursing gently, her eyes closed.

Leaning forward, my heart full to overflowing, I plant a soft kiss on the brow of the daughter I've waited twelve years to meet.

Basking in my post-birth joy, with my newborn bairn in my arms and the greatest love of my life supporting me from behind, never could I have imagined that less than twenty-four hours later, my life would be ripped apart once again and I'd be plunged into the deepest grief I'd ever experienced.

Chapter 59

16 weeks later, Sunday 16th December 2007

Christchurch, New Zealand

*D*espite my fascination with graveyards, I never expected to be grieving at a graveside on the morning of my daughter's christening.

Beneath every grave lies a story. A life filled with joy, pain, hope, and despair, but most of all—hopefully—a life filled with love.

Marble headstones of dapple white and onyx black all standing ramrod straight, unlike the wilting flowers and gifts left at their bases by grieving loved ones. Each headstone with its swirly gold inscriptions, a physical reminder of the void now left on this earth. A chasm only partially filled by the memories and love their occupants leave behind.

I roll my hand over the indentations of the words chiselled into the smooth surface. Allowing the pads of my fingers to dip in and out of each rise and fall of every letter that spells out the name. I close my eyes to squeeze away the tears, and instead allow myself to soak up the love behind the inscription.

Today, tomorrow, always.

Life is so precious, and if the last sixteen weeks have taught me anything, it's that life can be given and taken away in a heartbeat. Therefore we must relish every breath. Eke out every moment of joy and live our lives authentically. Otherwise, we're only wasting whatever precious time we have left.

"Oh, how I wish we'd had more time together and you could have watched your daughter grow," I mutter, looking down at the headstone. "I promise I shall live every day of the rest of my life to the fullest. I promise to live without fear and to continue to love without reservation. And I shall do so, in your memory."

I lean forward and lay a single flower along the top of the headstone. Pressing my fingers to my lips and then against the marble, I leave a silent kiss for the spirit that lies here.

"Good night, my love. Fly free," I say quietly.

"It's a perfect outlook," Nessa adds, her red hair blowing about her face. She's flown here especially, along with all my other friends from the UK. A united show of support in light of such tragedy.

She's right, it is a perfect outlook. An uninterrupted view down towards Christchurch then out over the Pacific beyond.

"Come on Tor. It's time to go. Everyone's waiting," she says laying a comforting hand on my shoulder.

"Goodbye my love. Promise to watch over us. I shall do my best to make you a proud parent," I say quietly to the spirit beneath the grave.

I turn around and four pairs of sympathetic eyes stare back at me. Becca, Nessa, Julie, and Mel. We all smile feebly to one another, before Nessa passes me my sleeping child to hold.

Still reeling from the horrific loss that immediately followed the most joyous day of my life, I flew back to the UK six weeks after I gave birth, to introduce my newborn babe to all my UK family and friends.

The girls had gathered at Julie's and she greeted me with an enormous hug and a mug of welcome tea.

"Despite everything, I'm so happy for you Tor," she said, gazing dewy-eyed at the sleeping child cradled in my arms.

"Babies are so precious" Becca added. "And this one even more so." She'd leant over and tickled my daughter's chin. "You took your bloody time getting here missus; we've been waiting years for you, you know. But then you're lovely just the same."

"What's her full name again?" Nessa asked.

"A right gob-full," Becca interjected, making everyone laugh, despite the sadness that tinged the air.

"But also full of meaning," Julie said.

"Shhhh, you'll wake her," I replied, gazing down at her, my heart overflowing with love.

Regardless of how much everyone warned me, I could never have imagined the bottomless well of love I have for my child.

Looking back up, three pairs of eyes were waiting for me to respond.

"Seren Christiana Hine Fenwick-Williams," I said proudly.

"Well it's unique, I'll give you that," Becca had replied, before Nessa added, "A unique name, for a unique baby."

"It's perfect, as is she." Julie raised her mug in a toast. "To Seren, Christiana, Hine, Fenwick-Williams," she proposed, before everyone joined in and took a sip of tea.

My daughter needed a unique name, as the circumstances that led to her creation were also unique. Her very existence created from the culmination of all the love I've received and lost over the past thirteen years.

I named her *Seren*, as she is my little Celtic Star, and because this name perfectly reflects Gav's Welsh heritage.

Christiana is in homage to Chris, and the spirit of him she carries within her.

Hine is a Māori name and a reflection of the country of both her conception and birth. Its literal translation means 'girl', but it is also a derivative of Ōhinetahi, *'the place of one daughter'*. Named after the ancient valley to the south of Christchurch that I've always felt is my spiritual home.

She has a double-barrelled surname, *Fenwick-Williams. Fenwick,* the name of my ancestors as well as the name I shared through my marriage to Craig whom, at one time, I loved unreservedly—even if that love was unrequited.

And finally, *Williams,* after the two men–Christopher and Gavin Williams–who had a hand in her creation

"Are you planning on getting her christened?" Julie had asked.

"Yes, this Christmas… but I'm going to do it in New Zealand, and I'd love you all to come."

They'd all looked at me wide-eyed as I dipped my head. "I know it's a lot to ask, and it's a long way for you all to travel, but with what's happened… I simply couldn't do it here. It wouldn't seem right."

Nessa had come to sit next to me at that point, and squeezed the outside of my arms, while I continued to cradle my sleeping daughter, silent tears welling up in my eyes. "I really want you all there… in support, but I know it's a lot to ask. I'm not sure I can go through with it without you all there."

"We've all already talked about it," Nessa said looking around the room at Becca and Julie who both nodded in turn. "We had an inkling this might be your plan."

"Wild horses couldn't keep us away," Becca said, coming to kneel in front of me, placing her hands on my lap. "I mean who doesn't want an excuse for the trip of a lifetime."

When she'd said that I couldn't hold back my tears anymore. The outpouring of love, despite the horrific tragedy I've endured, left me feeling both disarmed and overwhelmed with gratitude.

Seren is bundled up tight against the crisp breeze. Summer may be on its way, the scrub of the hillsides turning from the light green of spring rebirth to the deeper greens and vibrant colours of summer, every hedgerow and tree bursting into a rainbow of colours, but this morning the air is crisp and sharp.

Underneath her handmade crochet shawl—a present from my mother—Seren is dressed in a bespoke christening gown of cream silk and delicate Welsh lace, topped off with a cute crochet bonnet (also made by my mother). With her huge eyes—that are already showing signs of turning emerald green like my own—currently closed while she sleeps, and her thick inch-long eyelashes, she is every inch an angel.

After my trip home, the girls began arranging their travel plans almost immediately.

Mark and Becca, along with their kids, stopped off in Sydney to catch up with a cousin of Becca's, who immigrated there fifteen years ago.

Paul, Julie, and a toddling JP organised a layover in Thailand where they spent some time with Craig. Julie has kept the details light. She knows I have no interest in knowing anything about Craig and his family, but it's easy to forget that Clarky and Craig were once best friends, and that Clarky was the best man at my wedding to Craig.

Nessa and Anth have taken the opportunity, before the twins start school, for a longer vacation. They've been tramping all over the North Island of New Zealand in a camper van, arriving here in Christchurch a few days ago. They're heading to Queenstown next. Retracing the route around some of the beauty spots of the South Island I myself took with Chris all those years ago.

Even my parents are here. My mam and stepdad waiting in their pews as I enter the church. My mother's spine rigid and my stepdad looking directly ahead. Both of them doing everything and anything to avoid any accidental or casual eye contact with my biological father and his second wife, who we've strategically seated on the other side of the front pew. My parents will never reconcile, but at least they've agreed to put their differences aside for the sake of me and their only grandchild.

Inside the church, the vicar calls all of the godparents forward and there's a momentary clomp of heels on the flag stone floor as they cluster around the Oamaru stone font.

I look around the group of friends I've chosen to support my daughter throughout her life.

From the UK, Julie and Clarky, Anth and Nessa, and Becca and Mark.

I mean, how could I have chosen between them?

I'm godmother to every single one of their offspring, so it seemed only right. And from New Zealand, Melanie and Karl, who have promised to remind Seren of her ties to Aotearoa as she grows.

Mel stands next to me and I slide my arm around her waist and give her a little squeeze.

I'm so proud of her. She's still frail, but has fought back against the disease that has ravaged her body over the past fifteen months. When she was first diagnosed she was given a fifty-fifty chance of living more than five years, and although the chemo and radiation were brutal, for now she is cancer free.

"Nice wig," I whisper in her ear.

She reaches behind me and pinches my bum.

"You okay?" she whispers back. She knows how hard the run-up and planning for this day has been on me. On all of us.

I turn and give her a wink. She nods back before turning her attention back to the vicar's sermon.

Using a conch shell as the baptism vessel, the vicar officially names my rainbow baby and we all begin to filter outside for photographs.

Seren is passed from pillar to post, but sleeps on. I nod. Shake hands and listen to umpteen, *'Such a lovely service, if tinged with a little sadness,'* from everyone in the congregation.

"I think we'd better get a move on," Mel whispers in my ear.

She is the only person who knows about our secret plan for the second part of this day. Everyone believes that we are heading to the gardens of Ōhinetahi, for a small celebration of Seren's christening; little do they know that my groom and I are about to spring surprise nuptials on them all.

When the guests arrive, instead of trays of canapés and flutes of sparkling champagne greeting them, they find the gardens laid out with rows of white-covered chairs and a flower-covered pergola. Strategically positioned to maximise the breathtaking view over the waters of Whakarupō Harbour.

I whizz upstairs and quickly get changed into my wedding dress while Karl, the only other person who knows of our impending nuptials, settles the guests in their seats.

Mel helps me into my frock and fastens the hundred or so buttons that run the entire length down the back of my gown.

"You look gorgeous," she says, standing behind me and looking over my shoulder into the full-length mirror in front of us.

My wedding dress is made of damask silk in an unusual blush oyster colour.

"Well I could hardly wear white, now could I?" I laugh. "Not when I'm about to carry a baby down the aisle."

My dress has a pretty sweetheart neckline, spaghetti straps and a nipped in bodice that pulls me in at the waist, helping to hold in my still soft postpartum tummy, before the material flares out from my hips down to the floor and collects in a delicate puddle train behind me. On one side, the silk is cut away to thigh-level, and is infilled with delicate folds of tulle, and the entire dress is covered in delicate silk appliqué detail.

Mel slides the fascinator into my hair and positions the 'Jackie O' veil over my right eye.

She holds my gaze through the mirror and squeezes the outsides of my arms. "He would be so proud of you today you know."

I drop my gaze. "I know."

"And I know he's looking down on you and would want you to be happy."

I feel tears sting at the corner of my eyes. I tilt my head back and sniff loudly, flapping my hands in front of face.

"Come on," she continues. "You don't want to smudge your mascara. Today is not a day for tears of sadness. Jesus we all cried enough of them these past few months. Only tears of joy allowed from now on. I think it's time we got you married. Don't you?"

I pick up Seren from the cot in the corner of the room, where she's been napping after her lunchtime bottle. She opens her eyes, recognises me and kicks her legs with glee.

"Are you excited to get downstairs and to watch your Mammy and Daddy get married?" I sing-song into her gurgling face.

Despite my engagement to Gav a year ago, and my almost-marriage to Chris–had I needed to get hitched in order to stay in the country–this past year the idea of marriage itself lost its appeal again: until Seren was born. With the events that immediately followed, I wanted Seren to grow up in a solidified family unit, with two parents raising her together; as one. So when I suggested it, of course he was over the moon. After all it's all he's ever wanted. To slide a wedding ring on my finger.

Wanting to make today as much about Seren's christening and the coming together of our little family, we chose to invite everyone to the memorial a few days ago, followed by Seren's christening today. They have no idea there's more to come.

Before we leave the room, Mel and I both hold each other's gaze.

She smiles and I take a deep breath in.

"Okay. Let's do this," I say as she follows me out of the room.

⭐

The string quartet strikes up and our baffled congregation turn their heads to see what's happening.

A solo sopranist sings out the lyrics of our chosen song, the Richard Rogers anthem from the musical Carousel, "You'll Never Walk Alone", and everyone stands, craning their necks to get their first glimpses of the bride.

I wait out of sight whilst I listen to the lyrics of the first verse, holding my head up high, determined to *not be afraid of the dark*.

I hear everyone shuffling from foot to foot, as their confused murmurs mumble through the crowd. The sopranist continues his serenade.

I sniff loudly, holding in my own tears for the second time in as many minutes. The lyrics hold such meaning. I have indeed walked through a storm, in fact more than one, but waiting for me at the end of this red carpet is my golden sky and I know, from this day forward—I shall never walk alone.

As the singer continues, I take my first few steps out of the house and into the garden, tiptoeing across the grass to stop my heels from sinking into it, until I reach the end of the rolled-out red carpet at the top of the outdoor aisle.

I look up, and there he is. Waiting for me. The first glimpse of my husband-to-be, standing at the other end of the red carpet. The man who stood by me through everything. The one who never stopped loving me, and the one who was always the man for me—in the end.

He's beaming. Love oozing out of every pore. Dressed in a sharp navy suit, his white shirt open at the neck. Since Seren's christening in the church he's pinned a white rose into his buttonhole, as has Karl who's acting as his best man and witness today. Mel is taking the role of Matron of Honour, everyone else having been kept in the dark, including all of my UK friends.

I glide towards him as if carried by angels. Perhaps on some level I am. There are enough in heaven looking down on me today. My other unborn stars. Maybe if we're lucky enough to have more children, perhaps they too will make it into my arms.

Savouring every moment, I walk in time to the beat of the music. Right, together. Left, together. On, and on.

On my right I spy Dean, Lisa and their children who've travelled down from the North Island, together with Michelle, David and their brood who've made the trip from their home in Nelson. Like my own parents, I've seated Lynne as far away as possible from her ex-husband John, who is seated next to his second wife, Susan.

I'm so chuffed when I spy Mike and Fiona out of the corner of my eye. It was a huge commitment for them to come all this way, especially now that Fiona is bouncing a chubby third child on her knee. They all smile warmly as I drift past.

The music continues to swell, as do the gasps and sharp intakes of breath as I glide down the aisle, everyone having now clocked what is about to happen.

On the other side of the aisle, the bride's side, I pass my crowd. Each couple sitting with their children between them.

Becca wags her finger at me and I hear her mutter, "You absolute minx, how could you keep this a secret."

"Radiant," Julie whispers, while the others all nod their heads in agreement and smile widely.

Tim gives me a slow shake of his head, and as I pass him I hear him *tut-tut*. "How could you do this without my permission," he whispers. He's teasing, as he's always done. His warm smile giving him away. Next to him is a woman with a hooked nose and beady eyes. Impeccably dressed, but judging by her ramrod spine and lack of smile, she's wishing she was anywhere but here.

So that's the illusive Lydia. She really does exist.

Both my parents dab their eyes with handkerchiefs as I near the front, while the strings build up to their final crescendo. Their harmonies reverberating with my own heartstrings and I feel as if my heart may fly out of my chest at any moment, I'm so overwhelmed with love. As the singer holds the final note of the aria, I reach the front and an expectant hush falls over the congregation.

I kiss my daughter on her forehead, and my groom does the same, before I pass her to Mel to cuddle during the ceremony. Turning back, I look directly into my groom's twinkling eyes. Everyone and everything around us falls away. It is just him and me.

"Hey," he says, smiling, reaching for both my hands to hold. Shaking them slightly, to knock out the nerves that he can tell are making my body tense.

"Hey," I reply.

"You look beautiful."

"So do you."

"You okay?" he asks.

I nervously nod my head.

"It's just us," he says. "You and me. No one else."

The celebrant coughs, and everyone comes to attention. My groom and I turn towards the officiator of the ceremony, who smiles, nods her head to each of us in turn, and begins the formal part of the proceedings.

"Gavin and Victoria have invited you along today, not only to celebrate the christening of their beautiful baby girl, but as you've just discovered, to also bear witness to their marriage."

A ripple of laughter flows through the crowd.

"Gavin." The stout female officiator turns to my groom and asks, "Do you take Victoria to be your lawful wedded wife?"

Tears building in the corner of his eyes, he looks deep into my soul and answers, "I do."

"Will you love her, cherish her and pledge to choose her every day from this day forward?"

"I will." He's so relaxed, meanwhile I'm quivering with a mix of nerves and jitters.

She turns to me and asks, "Victoria, do you take Gavin to be your lawful wedded husband?"

The knot in my stomach tightens and I open my mouth to speak but no words come out.

I've been here before. This is not the first time I've made this pledge, believing in a future that never came to fruition. All that transpired was a few months of marital bliss followed by years of pain.

A fleeting moment of doubt flashes through my brain.

Could I be about to step off that same cliff? Am I making a mistake? Everything is so good—finally—why risk it going wrong again?

I look over Gav's left shoulder and a beautiful butterfly flutters on the breeze behind him. It's a rich chocolate brown colour, with vibrant orange spots and stripes on its wings, like the markings of a tiger.

I inhale sharply.

I know instinctively it's him. The spirit from the grave.

Chris may not be here in person but I know this is his way of sending me his blessing. Telling me to get over myself and to stop overthinking and to *willingly accept whatever my future holds, without condition, and continue to love unconditionally, regardless.*

I exhale as a rush of love floods through my veins.

⁂

Chris had withheld his terminal diagnosis from everyone until almost the very end. By the time the doctors had detected the pancreatic cancer he was too far gone to be cured. His operation from eighteen months ago, despite what he told me, was never treatment for a grumbling appendix, but to remove a small tumour. The scans, however, confirmed the worst: the cancer had already metastasized. Any treatment thereafter was merely to prolong his life.

Watching first-hand the effect chemotherapy was having on his sister and her family, and knowing he had no chance of a cure, he refused to walk that path. Choosing instead less aggressive alternatives and with Bruce the Brute's help, as well as a team of nutritionalists and natural practitioners, focused on being as healthy as possible, for as long as possible. He astounded his doctors by living a further eighteen months as opposed to the three to six months they'd originally predicted.

Not wanting to burden his family, who were in the midst of supporting Mel through her own cancer journey, he decided it was best to keep his own diagnosis from everyone, including me.

When I turned up to support Mel, last December, he already knew he was going to die. It was just a matter of when.

There's a reason pancreatic cancer is known as a hidden killer. It's possible for someone to have the disease without anyone around them knowing. He certainly seemed the picture of health when we had our moment of reconciliation just over a year ago.

It was only when he finally shared with us all the reasons why he was losing so much weight, when I was around six months pregnant, that his reasoning for encouraging Gav to be the active father in Seren's life, regardless of her paternity, started to make sense.

Both men agreed amongst themselves that neither were interested in confirming the paternity of my child, instead agreeing Chris would be named on the birth certificate, allowing my then unborn daughter to take dual nationality, but always with the intention that Gav would formally adopt the child when Chris was gone, effectively giving both men paternity in Seren's life.

In the end Chris clung onto life until the day Seren was born. After giving birth, as soon as I was allowed–having had a short nap, a shower and some breakfast–Gav and I made our way across to his ward, where he was receiving end of life care. Holding her in his weakened arms, his body ravaged by disease, he looked down at her beautiful angelic face.

"She's perfect," he'd said. "She has your eyes, Vicky."

"And perhaps your nose," Gav had offered.

"But I think your chin," Chris had replied before handing the babe back to Gavin. "They're both precious. Promise me you'll take care of them."

"I will, Chris. I promise. For the rest of my life."

"Thank you," Chris had said, leaning wearily back against his pillows.

Reaching his hands behind his neck, he'd unclasped his greenstone Koru and passed it to Gav. "Will you keep this safe—for Seren. Give it to her when she's old enough."

Gav held the Koru in his hand. Looking down at it; speechless.

My eyes heavy with tears, I'd blurted, "Of course we will."

"And I'll make sure she knows who you are," Gav had added, his voice wobbling with emotion.

After Gav had left the hospital, I remained by Chris's side, holding his hand while Seren slept silently in a crib in the corner of the room.

"I told you she'd come to us," he'd croaked. His voice barely a whisper. "I told you on top of the mountain, in Spain, when we saw that shooting star. I told you when the time was right, the planets would collide, and she'd come to us."

"Yes, you did, Chris. And you were right. She's here. Safe and sound," I'd whispered. "And now you don't need to hold on anymore. I'll love her enough for both of us. Be at peace now, my love. I'm going to be okay." Crying floods of tears while I gripped his hand, I watched as he closed his eyes a final time. "You don't have to fight anymore. Everyone's okay. You can let go now. Let go of the pain and fly free my love."

"Always in my heart," he'd breathed, before slipping away surrounded by the two souls who meant the world to him.

Knowing he was gone; I still stroked his hair and left a soft kiss on his cracked lips.

"If I had to do it all again. I wouldn't change a thing," I'd whispered, tears dropping off the end of my chin. "Thank you for everything. And thank you for Seren. Always in my heart."

What neither Gav nor I had anticipated after Chris's death was his generosity in his final wishes. When his will was read, he'd asked for his estate to be split four ways. Twenty-five percent for Louis, twenty-five percent to Seren, (named in his will as my unborn child), twenty-five percent to myself, and the rest split amongst the other members of his family. In addition, he left his house to me. The multimillion dollar home overlooking the Pacific, on the cliffs of Sumner.

I remember frolicking on the beach below on Christmas Day back in 1995. How Chris and I had made love in the ocean. Never in my wildest dreams did I think I would own a house on those exact clifftops, where I could look down on those rolling waves every day.

When Gav and I had collected the keys from the solicitor, initially it had felt weird walking from room to room. All of Chris's personal items and the very essence of him all around.

"I know we'll only be here part of the year, but we'll make it our own." Gav had come up behind me and rested his head on my shoulder as we'd looked out at the view of the ocean, "But I think we should keep something of him here. Not erase him completely."

I'd turned and kissed him. "Do you know how amazing you are? How amazing you've been throughout all of this?"

Cupping my face with his hands, he'd continued, "I've never doubted your love for me, Angel. Or your love for him."

He's right.

Chris was my *first great love*. A love so powerful and all-consuming, at times it almost destroyed me, but at love as it turns out, that was predestined. At the beginning Chris's passion and visceral love for me opened me up to my own sexuality. He taught me how to access my connection with my most authentic self; that deep pool of still water, surrounded by burning hot flames of passion, and to own it. He met a girl and I left him a woman.

Then came Craig, the *second great love* of my life. The man who I loved unreservedly without realising neither of us were being fully vulnerable and honest with the other. It's not surprising then, we weren't destined to be together forever. However, my love for Craig was not without worth. When my own love was unrequited I found a depth of strength and resolve I didn't know I had. I am stronger because of him. I learnt my self-worth is not tied to how others perceive or accept me, I only need love and accept myself, and that sometimes the most powerful thing you can do when you love someone–is let them go.

Then finally Gav, the *third great love* of my life has taught me that when I show *all of myself* to him, and I'm brave enough to live as my most authentic self, even if that means risking losing his love, I will receive an unconditional love I never knew or realised was possible. Even if the road getting there was not without challenge, together we've shown each other that our love does not judge, it can forgive, it does harbour shame and it does not denounce or hide from the struggles of the past. Gav has shown me that despite the parts of me I may have wanted to keep hidden, no—because of the parts of me I wanted to keep hidden or felt ashamed of—he loves me even more. He knows I am the person I am today because of the choices I've made, the experiences I've had–and my other *great loves* who at one point of my life or another I've shared my heart–our relationship would not be what it is. The depth and strength of our love is only possible because I've also loved Chris and Craig before him.

I needed all of these *Three Great Loves* of my life to bring me to this exact moment. To a place and to a man in whose arms I truly belong, knowing he holds all the pieces of me in his heart, as I do the same for him.

Between Chris, Craig, and Gavin I've been known as Vicky, Goose, Tor, Tori, Angel, and even V, but all of these monikers are only individual parts of me. Pieces that when put together create the whole, authentic me. Short, affectionate nicknames that label the various steps of my own personal journey. The journey to *becoming Victoria.*

The butterfly rests momentarily on Gav's left shoulder, before it flaps its wings and flies off. My eyes follow it until it disappears into the ether, somewhere over the bay.

No, I'm not making a mistake. This is exactly where I'm meant to be, and exactly the man I'm meant to be with; today, tomorrow and always.

I turn back and connect with Gav's soft grey eyes. He's waiting patiently for my reply. Smiling. Trusting. Loving.

I suck in a deep breath and wait for my nerves to return. But instead I feel only calm and at peace. There is no more pain enslaving me. No more chains from my past holding me back. I double-check my soul, looking in every crevice for any sign of doubt, pain, or fear. But there is none and I know I am free.

I sense the congregation shifting about behind me, waiting nervously for me to respond, wondering if I'm having second-thoughts and about to do a runner. However, Gav's gaze never leaves my face. His confident smile, loving me unconditionally.

He's in no rush and he already knows in his heart my answer.

Thrusting out my chin, I smile back at him and reply, "I do."

As sad as it was standing at Chris's grave earlier today, laying a burnt orange calla lilly on his headstone, by contrast standing here, surrounded by love, living a life at one time I could only have dreamed of, I'm grateful for everything that has happened. Without it I wouldn't be here now, basking in the love of my husband with our baby daughter by our side. Our whole lives ahead of us.

Every loss I've experienced, every mistake or bad choice I've made, every traumatic event I've lived through and every bit of pain I've endured or caused others, all of it has led me right to this moment and I wouldn't change one bit of it.

It's made me who I am… and I am Victoria.

I know now—*I am love itself*, I am free and everything is as it should be.

The End

⭐

Want more?

Fancy finding out what happens three years later?

Join my Izzy's Reading Bees newsletter and receive **A Star Unborn** bonus Epilogue for FREE!

Click here to get your copy or go to
https://bit.ly/AStarUnborn-epilogue

Read on for a little snippet to whet your appetite. Enjoy! x

Bonus Epilogue

GAVIN

3 years later, New Year's Day 2011

England

avin gives Vicky a cheeky slap on the bum as he walks past her, her rubber gloved hands in the sink, hand washing the last of the wine glasses from last night's New Year's Eve gathering. All the gang, including their kids, came over to celebrate the turning of another new year. The children played silly boards games, or watched movies, while the adults drank, and the women discussed the latest winners of Strictly Come Dancing.

Josh is ten years old now–still an avid Stars Wars fan–and Livy, Ethan and Emily are all seven now at the same Primary School. Although the twins are almost a full year older than Livy, and they'll turn eight later this month.

JP is growing up into a contemplative five-year-old who, despite his challenging start in life, is showing signs of being a genius, just like his mother. He didn't speak–at all–for his first eighteen months, not even babbling sounds, initially worrying both his parents and the professionals alike. Instead he was taking it all in. Observing his world, like a little mini professor. His gaze following everyone and everything around the room, while he listened intently to everything being said. Figuring it all out. Deciding on when and how he would interact with the world. Then out of nowhere one day he announced, "I think I'd like to go to the play park please Mammy." A full complete sentence, that astounded Julie but confirmed Vicky's notion, that he's an old soul, and way wiser than his scrawny helpless newborn body would have had you believe.

Gav's own daughter, Seren, is growing into a beautiful, high-spirited, determined three-year-old. The blonde hair she was born with has been replaced by dark wiry waist-length thick curls, the exact same as Mel's two daughter's. Her ringlets bobbing and swishing behind her as she struts her way through life. A lion's mane to match her fiery star sign.

'*Some days,*' Gav had said to Vicky one evening...

Download the full Bonus Epilogue here
or go to
https://bit.ly/AStarUnborn-epilogue

✦

Dear Reader,
I want to say a massive thank you for firstly buying and then taking the time to read one (or all) of my books — it means a lot!

If you've enjoyed reading the final chapter of *The Three Great Loves of Victoria Turnbull* then I'm unashamedly asking for your help.

I don't have the weight of a massive publishing house behind me to help get my stories out there, and the best way for me to reach more readers is via your support.

One of the most powerful things you can do is leave a review on Amazon and/or Goodreads and Bookbub. It doesn't have to be long, just a single sentence will let others know what you thought. Do not underestimate the influence your review can have on a book's success.

- Leave a review on Amazon.com
- Leave a review on Amazon.co.uk
- Leave a review on Goodreads
- Leave a review on BookBub

… or head to your local Amazon or e-book store and follow the process from there.

If you're feeling super generous, I'd be over the moon if you'd recommend this story to all your friends, buy a copy for your friends or family, post about it on your social media, and suggest it to your book club (if you have one). Did you know you can invite me to Zoom into your Book Club meeting by emailing me on hello@isabellawiles.com

Feel free to tag me in any social media. I love interacting with my readers and replying to their comments.

Much love,
Isabella x

A word from the Author

It is recommended this section be read after reading the series, as it contains spoilers.

I remember distinctly lying in bed the night before I was due to have an abortion, and all of the overwhelming emotions I was feeling at that time. Desperation. Grief. Shame.

This was back in 1994, in England. A time when abortion was not openly talked about, yet thankfully was legal and safe, and I was able to access the care I needed.

I also remember the sense of injustice, anger and shame when I suffered not one, but three miscarriages a decade later. So, although Victoria's story is not my own, it's fair to say I was able to draw on my own personal experiences when crafting her character.

My intention when I had the idea for these stories was always to write a darn good yarn that had you turning pages long into the night, but also to shine a light on many of the topics I believe are not sufficiently talked about, mainly because they remain highly devise and often taboo subjects, yet are experienced first-hand by millions of women. Namely, coercive relationships, sexual and physical violence against women, divorce, miscarriage, and abortion.

So many women go through these experiences feeling desperately alone and ashamed, believing they have nowhere to go and no-one to turn to. I know that's how I felt. And…

Shame breeds silence.

Silence breeds isolation.

And isolation breeds repression.

Once repressed it's easier for those with power to take away our agency, which is why I wanted to write a story that represented women like me. I also wanted to write it for all the people who may not understand, or share the same opinions and beliefs as women like me, or understand why we've made the choices we have.

This was not an easy series to write, not least because of the trauma I put Vicky through, but because on more than one occasion I wanted to change the plot. I didn't want her to have an affair in the first book (and in the first edition, 'Belonging', actually wrote this as a rape scene, essentially taking away her consent) but by changing it to a consensual act, although I risked losing empathy for the character, I was able to show how desperately alone she felt. Enough to fall into the arms of another. Or, how in her attempts to atone for her guilt and deem herself worthy of Chris's love, she allowed herself to be coerced into an unhealthy relationship that on more than once occasion escalated into sexual violence.

In the second book, I would have loved for Craig to have had a change of heart and return to the UK and fight for Vicky. But then I wouldn't have had the opportunity to show her facing her deepest fears–the fear of being abandoned and left all alone, and the fear of being unlovable–and show her coming out the other side stronger.

And in the last book, it would have been so much easier to have given Vicky and Gav the child they so desperately wanted much earlier in the story, or only have them suffer one miscarriage before successfully giving them their rainbow baby. But by raising the stakes, I've not only represented a large swathe of women who suffer multiple pregnancy losses, but I've hopefully delivered a more gratifying finale. I should say, suffering three concurrent miscarriages is rare, (about 1% of women will suffer three concurrent miscarriages), however around 70% of those women will go on to have a successful pregnancy and birth afterwards, but miscarriage itself is very common. The NHS reports about one in eight pregnancies end in miscarriage and I know from personal experience how painful they are. It's impossible to *not* question yourself and ask what you might have done to cause it. The answer of course is – despite what your hormones would have you believe, it's not your fault.

However, the most challenging character to write, by a long way, was Chris. It would have been so much easier to depict him as an out and out abuser. Have Vicky leave him, and let their story end there, but I thought it would be much more interesting (and challenging for me as a writer) to show his own arc of redemption as the books progressed; and in doing so, elicit empathy for his character. You may not have liked his choices, especially in the first book *A Flame Unburned*, but as the books progressed hopefully you were able to understand them. And likewise, by having empathy for him, it made Vicky's choices even more frustrating, yet understandable.

It's very easy for society to judge women negatively for not leaving abusive relationships at the first sign of control or violence, or to tar their abusers with a single brush. Perhaps by reading Vicky and Chris's story you have a greater understanding of how complex these situations are.

However, my hope in all my creative choices is that I've successfully given a voice to woman everywhere who have lived through (or are living through) any of these experiences, and to collapse the shame surrounding them. In doing so, in my own small way, I trust I've taken back the power on our collective behalves.

And if that includes you, I hope I've successfully represented your voice along with my own, and as a result you feel more empowered to talk about your circumstances, and seek help if you need it.

Without shame and without judgement.

We cannot and should not stay silent. Share your experiences. Speak up and let your voice be heard. It's the only way we will build an inclusive and accepting society for all.

YOU ARE NOT ALONE!

And if you want to share your experiences with me personally, I'm all ears.

Much love,

Izzy

x

Book Club Questions

Below are some sample questions you may wish to use as starting points for a discussion about *A Star Unborn,* as well as some comparisons to other books in the series.

Warning: contains spoilers.

- At the beginning of *A Star Unborn*, Vicky seemingly has it all, a great career, financial stability, and independence; a belief shared by Becca. Yet, Nessa disagrees. How much pressure do you believe society puts on women to believe that their lives are not complete until they have a child?

- An underlying theme of the entire series is Vicky connecting with her authentic self, which initially she was only able to do through the conduit of male relationships, specifically through a sexual connection. At what point did you feel she reclaimed her own agency?

- What are your thoughts on Gav's initial view on his ex-wife's abortion? Was his opinion at all justified?

- Anth, Mark, and Clarky all had a very different opinion on abortion than Gav's initial view. Do you believe this is representative of the general male population? And if not, why not?

- *A Star Unborn* purposefully asks the question, 'What makes a family?' What are your opinions on the family construct and how might you answer that same question?

- One of the most emotional scenes is the resolution scene between Vicky and Chris, before they sleep together. If Vicky had been aware of Chris's change of heart at the time of her abortion, how might it have changed the course of their relationship, and more importantly, subsequent character arcs?

- In Gav and Vicky's passionate reconciliation in New Zealand, there's a moment when Gav is on his knees, worshipping her. Thinking back to the scene in *A Flame Unburned* where Chris is also on his knees worshipping her, what do you notice about the differences in Vicky's character and understanding of herself and her sexuality in both these scenes?

- Vicky clearly grows and changes across the course of all three books. What changes in her character and beliefs resonate the most with you?

Not part of a book club? Then hop online to Izzy's Reading Bees, our Facebook group, and start a discussion.

About Isabella Wiles

By day, Isabella Wiles is the CEO of her own Management Consultancy, something she loves but considers both a blessing and a curse. A curse because it takes her away from home, but a blessing because by night, whilst waiting for endless planes in faceless airports, or while stuck on trains with rubbish Wi-Fi, it allows her the opportunity to indulge her secret passion — writing compelling women's book club fiction.

She has written hundreds of business articles, reviews, and multiple bestselling works of non-fiction under the name Nicola Cook, which are published internationally and translated into multiple languages, however *The Three Great Loves of Victoria Turnbull* series is her first foray into writing fiction. She's currently writing her next romantic women's fiction series.

When she is not sitting on trains or stuck in airports, she lives in the north-east of England with her long-suffering husband, their two children, one looney Bassett Hound and two equally unhinged goldfish.

facebook.com/isabellawiles

instagram.com/isabellawiles_author

tiktok.com/@isabellawiles_author

bookbub.com/authors/isabella-wiles

goodreads.com/Isabella_Wiles

Acknowledgments

Wow, what a joy it's been to finally bring Victoria's journey to a suitably heart-busting satisfactory ending. I mean, let's be honest, I've put the poor lass through the wringer for the last 1200 pages.

As usual, I would not have got there without a small army of helpers propping me up and keeping me moving towards the finish line, however before I get to them, I want to thank YOU – my amazing reader.

I appreciate I've completely broken all the acceptable genre norms with the length of this book, so thank for sticking with me and reading to the end! I tried so many times to trim it to half its size, even considering splitting it into two books at one point, but that didn't seem fair to you, or the characters. And no matter how many times I tried to cut out sections, or subplots, the story fell over. Everything is so intrinsically linked to everything else in this epic saga, but I trust it was all worth it in the end, and I've left you feeling suitably satiated and satisfied.

Now back to the other lot.

Once again, I cannot express how grateful I am to my Storygrid developmental editor, Kim Kessler. I *love* working with you, Kim, and cannot wait to see what we come up with next.

Thank you also to Zoë Markham, from Markham Correct for your beady eye copyediting the final draft, and for all your hilarious comments in the margin. I'm also immensely grateful to you for jiggling your diary to accommodate me, meaning I could hit my ridiculously tight publishing schedule.

Thanks also to the amazing Stuart Bache of Books Covered for yet another outstanding cover.

To my expanding global network of fellow indie authors, thank you for keeping me accountable, sharing your knowledge on all things publishing, and for the many shared giggles, beers and WhatsApp messages that always seem to land at just the right moment: Bradley Charbonneau, Imogen Clark, Meg Cowley, Suzanne Fox, Anne F Hag, Debbie Ioanna, Daisy James, Sora James, Rachel Jones, Holly Lyne, Hilary McGrath, Poormina Manco, Janet Margot, Jan Moran, JR Pace, Rebecca Paulinyi, Elin Peer and her fabulous daughter Pearl Beck, Mia Sivan, Olivia Spring and last but by no means least, Alexandria Varian - aka The Winery Woman!

To all my amazing Advanced Readers thank you for getting behind this series and sharing your reviews, it really does mean so much, and to my wholly trusted BETA readers, Fiona Clark, Kate Freeman, Sarah Miller, Vicky Nunes and Bianca Robinson. Thank you for all your support and amazing feedback, (especially in helping catching those pesky typos that–quite frankly–should be given their own mention for making it past six rounds of editing!) Keep it coming folks. Every note, is sooooo useful.

Thanks also to my crazy but wonderful ex-trolley dolly sis-in-law Claire Love for answering all my 'what happens if' questions about medical emergencies mid-flight, and to my amazing friend Helen Patten and all her midwifery colleagues, who fact-checked all the pregnancy and maternity references.

Thank you to Craig Linkhorn and Katherine Walker for the advice and inspiration for the Māori name Hine.

Thank you also to the one and only 'Hubster' for double-checking all the Welsh references and correcting all the Welsh language spellings. I shall never be able to pronounce your mother tongue correctly, but will never tire of listening to you talk Welsh to the dog, who seems to understand you perfectly. Thank you also for your skills as my Chief Digital Wizard, creating my beautiful website and for taking on the uphill challenge of cracking ads.

To Vicky Nunes, my Chief Sorter Outer—yes that is her job title —you are an absolute godsend. Thank you for clearing the clutter, so I remain clearheaded. Our expanding reader community would not exist without you and your dedication.

To my mad bunch of girlfriends, Angela Blake, Rachel Farrell, Caroline Gallagher, Rachel Hicks and Michelle Sheini, thank you for plying me with alcohol and keeping my spirits buoyed whenever I needed pulling out of the editing cave; and for setting me the ridiculous *word challenge* to include a nonsensical phrase in this last book. I think you'll find I won the *furry wheels* challenge; warranted with a little extra help from Ange and Caz.

However, my biggest thanks of all has to go to my incredible husband, aka *'The Hubster'*, and my two amazing boys, for their unquestioning belief in me and unending support. These past twenty months have been some of the toughest of our collective lives, yet we've continued to navigate life's challenges with gratitude and grace. I'm so damn proud of our little family and how we're all empowering each other to live authentically. You three are my absolute world and I love you with all my heart.

Thank you everyone,
Much love,
Izzy
x

Resources

If you are dealing with an unplanned pregnancy, have suffered a miscarriage, terminated a pregnancy, or suffered a pregnancy or birthing trauma of any kind—or know someone who needs support —below is a list of organisations in the UK who can help:

Miscarriage Association UK
www.miscarriageassociation.org.uk
Tel: 01924 200799

Child Bereavement UK
www.childbereavementuk.org
Tel: 0800 02 888 40

National Unplanned Pregnancy Advisory Service
(NUPAS)
www.nupas.co.uk
Tel: 0333 004 6666

Samaritans
www.samaritans.org
Tel: 116 123

ISBN E-Book: 978-1-915137-05-0

ISBN Paperback: 978-1-915137-03-6

ISBN Large Print Paperback: 978-1-915137-04-3

Published by Aurora Independent Publishing.

A Star Unborn is written in British English.

Cover design: BooksCovered

Developmental Editor: Kim Kessler at Storygrid

Edited by: Markham Correct

Printed in Great Britain
by Amazon